Pat

Shadow Child

Best Wishes

Pamela Vass

Boundstone Books

First published in Great Britain in 2015 by
Boundstone Books, Little Boundstone, Littleham,
Bideford. EX39 5HW.

All characters, with the exception of Robert
Lenkiewicz, are fictitious and any resemblance to
real persons, living or dead, is purely coincidental.
Conversations with Robert Lenkiewicz are imagined
for the purpose of the narrative.

ISBN 978-0-9568709-4-0

Cover image: © Alon Othnay, Dreamstime.com

Printed and bound in Great Britain
by SRP Ltd, Exeter

www.boundstonebooks.co.uk

Also by Pamela Vass

Fiction
Seeds of Doubt

Non-Fiction
On Course for Recovery
The Power of 3

Edited works
In My Own Words

Reader Reviews for *Seeds of Doubt*

"I finished Seeds of Doubt last night. It was a great book... I loved the story, Ingrid's voyage and struggle, and the sense of Devon and history. The research struck me as particularly impressive... thanks once again for the entertainment of a great book."
> *Simon Hall - Home Affairs correspondent for BBC South West, author The Balance of Guilt www.thetvdetective.com*

"To build a conspiracy thriller on an event as well known as the Lynmouth flood disaster, and to make it both plausible and exciting, is no mean feat. The dialogue is well written and convincing and the plot is unpredictable with enough twists to keep any thriller reader happy."

"...thanks for a Great Book, can't stop reading it..."

"I've just finished Seeds of Doubt; WONDERFUL. I loved it; it has all the right ingredients - drama, tension, intrigue, love, secrets, danger and truth."

Author's Note

I worked with many children during my career as a social worker. They brought so much to our time together and I hope took something away that helped them forge a path as adults. My thanks to them all for providing the inspiration for *Shadow Child*.

There was one, I'll call him Sam, who made a deep impression on me. Years of neglect and abuse had left their mark. Three foster placements failed because of his behaviour and he was excluded from a special school for assaulting a teacher. Despite, or perhaps because of, this, he touched my heart.

We met regularly to work on his life story, a hard and painful process for Sam. After one emotionally challenging session, when his vocabulary for expletives ran riot, he said something that reminded me we must never give up on these children. As we drove back to the childrens' home, a track on the stereo repeated a mild swear word, nothing compared to his outpourings. To my amazement, Sam's face reddened. 'What's up?' I asked.

'You shouldn't listen to this,' he said. 'You're a lady.'

The children were my inspiration but my friends and colleagues have been invaluable in bringing this story to life. A heartfelt thank-you goes to Sheila Bees, Miranda Cox, Elaine Hennessey, Pip Jollands, Jeannette Kemlo, Catherine Lightfoot, Terence Sackett, Vicki Scott, Liz Shakespeare, Laurence Shelley, and the Hartland Writers Group for their contributions and feedback.

Here's to the kids who are different,
The kids they call crazy or dumb,
The ones that don't fit,
With the guts and the grit,
Who dance to a different drum.

Digby Wolfe

Prologue

Paul gazed at the identically dressed women filtering through the door. He stared at each face in turn, searching for the look, the mannerism, the feature that would unlock the past. He remembered deep brown eyes, tumbling hair, a raucous laugh and slender fingers... leaving their trace. He shivered. Sometimes his mind played tricks on him.

There were no physical characteristics to link him with any of them, not that he could see. Carol, the family liaison officer, gestured towards a slight figure with closely cropped hair, eyes cast down, walking towards them.

Carol nodded. 'Hi, Sonya. This is Paul.'

The woman lifted her head. 'You're taller than I thought.'

Paul removed his jacket and hung it over the back of the chair, tweaking the folds until it hung freely - anything to fill the space created by sixteen years of not knowing. Finally, he snatched a glance at the woman sitting opposite him - his mother.

'Can't believe it's you,' he said. 'I'd have come... years ago. But they didn't tell me. The bastards all knew but no-one told me!'

She shifted in her chair, her eyes flitting from one side of the room to the other. 'What good would it have done?'

'Good? I'd have told them it wasn't you, couldn't have been you...'

'I'm not having this conversation.' She half rose.

'Paul knows that.' Carol sent him a warning glance. 'You agreed to fill in the gaps. He agreed to stick to that. Paul?'

1

He shrugged. 'Questions have been in here so long…' he tapped his forehead.

Her face gave nothing away. 'So what do you want to know?'

The words welled up. 'What was it like? What was I like? I remember a caravan. Is that where we lived?'

'For a bit.'

'What did we do? What sort of a kid was I?'

'Christ, I don't know. It was years ago!'

'I don't think Paul's after anything specific, Sonya,' Carol mediated. 'Just something to help him fill in the gaps.'

She rubbed at an imaginary mark on the back of her hand. 'You used to go off round the site. You was always running off.'

'Why? I loved being with you. We were good, weren't we?'

Silence.

'I remember we used to go to town.'

Sonya picked at a chipped fingernail. He let the silence hang.

'Yea, we used to go to town,' she said.

'All of us?'

'Mostly.'

'But sometimes just you and me, yeah?'

'Maybe, when you needed something, like trainers. You was always getting through trainers.'

'What did we eat? What was my favourite?'

She pressed her fingers against her forehead. 'I don't know… fish and chips. Burger from the van.'

He'd tried, really tried. But he had to know. 'Why? Why did you say it was you?'

She looked at him now, for a fraction of a second, before pushing her chair back. 'Just a minute.'

'You're innocent… I'll prove it,' Paul called, fighting the impulse to run after her, to wait by the door, to make sure this minute didn't last another lifetime.

Chapter One

Spring 1989, Westward Ho! Devon.

The boy wrenched the door open and hurled himself into the caravan. He landed on the damp seat and clasped his legs tight against his chest.

A small hand reached up from under the table and tugged at his trousers. 'Minute now, Paul?' his sister whispered, her matted hair falling over her eyes.

'She's not there,' he snapped, his dirt-engrained fingers tugging the cheap fabric from her grasp. 'She's not anywhere.'

The grip on his leg tightened. 'Paul okay, all okay.'

'Shut it. You don't know. You don't know nothin'.' He wrenched his leg away. The toddler fell back, hitting her head against the table. He knew the howl would come. He pulled her up beside him. Anything to stop the noise.

'Hungry, Paul,' she sobbed. He shrugged her away but she clutched at his shoulder, reaching out her other hand to turn his face to meet her eyes. 'Hungry, Paul, hungry now.'

'Get away, Amy. You stink.' He bent to prise off his saturated trainers. 'Bloody, sodding, bloody things.' He tugged at the matted laces until the plastic uppers gave way, widened the slit with his finger, scooped out a stone and flung it through the open door.

'Mum'll be back, you'll see. She didn't mean a minute like you count, stupid. Just not a long time.' He stood on the seat and reached up to an overhead cupboard. His frayed sleeve slid up his arm as he moved tins aside to grab a bag of crisps. He tipped a pile on the table in front of his sister and stuffed the rest into his mouth.

Amy shuffled to the edge of the seat and clutched some in her chubby fist, spilling many more onto the floor. Paul pointed. 'Look at that mess. Pick it up. Pick... it... up!' he said, mimicking their mother's piercing gaze.

'What the hell's going on?' The voice at the door made him jump.

'Don't then. See if I care,' Paul hissed at his sister before dodging under his grandmother's hand and escaping out into the rain.

'Come back here or I'll do for you.' Her voice boomed after him across the caravan site until a passing car blotted it out. Mrs Harris grunted and watched him go. She was no match for Paul. An over-long waiting list for a hip replacement had seen to that.

Paul ducked into the bus shelter. His mum couldn't drive so she'd have to come back by bus. He'd wait for her...

...she'd be looking for him from the bus, her nose pressed against the window making it go all smudgy. And she'd have the widest smile you've ever seen as soon as she saw him at the bus stop. She'd leap off before it stopped, drop all the bags full of Coco-Pops and crisps in a pile and scoop him up.

'Paul,' she'd say, 'I've missed you.' And she'd hold him close and say, 'what do you think I've got for you today?'

And he'd say, 'Tickets. You got tickets to Alton Towers.' They were going in a taxi - the big black one that came to the posh caravans at the front where you could see the sea. And it would stop right outside the station and the driver would come round and open the door so everyone would look to see who was getting out 'cause they must be important. And they'd have so many cases a man would bring a trolley and load it up high so it wobbled and he'd have to shout to the people to clear the way.

On the train he'd have the biggest seat all to himself. And when they got to Alton Towers he'd ride Nemesis. It'd fling him through the air, crush him with a G force stronger than take-off in the space shuttle, scrape his skin back over his bones as he was thrown into outer space at over eighty Ks an hour. But he'd wrestle the controls from the evil warlord, haul with all his strength, and ever so slowly pull it round and save them from being blasted into millions of bloody pieces in space, where no one can hear you scream. (That's what they told him at school and they knew.) He'd save his mum. Not Amy. She was too small to come anyway.

They'd go on it again and again till it was dark - stopping to eat a mountain of burgers. And when they were too tired to do any more they'd go to the new hotel (he'd seen a picture in the paper) and have the best room with a chocolate fountain. For a month at least.

Nobody else would come. It would just be them, together, all the time. No strangers. They'd eat all the chocolate and giggle - his mum had a wicked giggle. They'd cuddle up on the bed and she'd tell him all about everything. Especially how much she loved him.

They were all dead jealous at school. He hadn't talked about it this week 'cause he'd been off. But he would when he went back. He'd tell them how he survived Oblivion, climbed right out of the atmosphere then plummeted to earth. Only his parachute opened just in time and he'd floated to the ground…

The smell of diesel filled his nose as the bus pulled away. Paul jumped up. Had she got off at the front? He ran round the shelter. There was only a stray dog peeing against the post.

She'd been in a hurry to get back to him. She'd disappeared between the posh holidaymakers caravans, that was it. He ran through the puddles, kicking mud up the backs of his jeans covering up yesterday's dirt. Their van was at the back of the site. Tucker, the manager, towed it there last week, said that'd do till they'd gone. Paul didn't know where they were going.

His grandmother was twisting the aerial on top of the TV. 'For Christ's sake shut that door,' she said as he stepped inside. 'It's worse in here than in my outhouse.'

His mother must be in the bedroom. Paul opened the door.

'What were you doing going off and leaving your sister like that?' his grandmother said.

'She was going on,' Paul called over his shoulder, staring at the empty space.

'Just like your mother. Always leaving some other poor

bugger to clear up the mess.'

'She ain't left nothin',' Paul shouted, rushing at his grandmother, arms flailing. She grabbed his wrists and held him at arm's length.

'Pack it up. That's your father's temper, that is. We don't want none of that. Sit.' Paul stood his ground. 'Now - if you want this.' She held a bag in front of him.

'What is it?' There was a faint whiff of something good.

'Sit and you'll find out.'

The pasty was almost cold but that didn't stop him wolfing it down. His grandmother turned back to the TV. 'Tuning's up the spout. Time your mother sorted herself out, made a proper home for the three of you. Not leaving me to pick up the pieces. It's not on. In fact...' She picked up her coat.

'Where you going?' Paul asked between bites.

'Where d'you think? Back to my place. I've got a dinner to get and Clem to feed.'

'What about her?' Paul pointed at Amy lying on the seat.

'Keep an eye on her till your mum gets back.'

He wiped his mouth with the back of his hand and swallowed. 'You take her.'

'Who d'you think I am? Mary bloody Poppins?'

'Please, Gran.'

That stopped her. She didn't often get a "please". 'What are you up to?'

'Nothin'.'

'Your mum'll be back soon won't she?'

He stared at her, then Amy. 'Yeah.'

'Well then.'

Paul watched his grandmother lurch across the site. She'd meet his mum on the way back from the bus. He'd just got the time wrong. That was all...

...or maybe she'd come in their new car, a red sports car, with spotlights all along the front and a roof that opened so he could stick his head out and shout at his mates on the corner. He'd make sure she

parked right in front of the skateboard park, then they'd pile in and play
tapes and stuff.

They'd go to the fair, on the dodgems. Win everything, even a fluffy toy
for Amy - to bring back 'cause she wouldn't be there. He'd go on the
rifles, shoot every duck, and laugh at the man with the money. Make him
get the long hook out and lift down the biggest prize right up high…

He shifted from leg to leg and rubbed his knees. The seat was
hard, it made his legs ache, but if he didn't kneel he couldn't
see through the window, couldn't keep watch. Even in the
dark he could watch. He rested his chin on his hands and
pressed his nose against the window. It misted over. He
rubbed a circle for each eye then huffed against the cold glass
some more, creating an outline of a pirate's hat. He added a
skull and crossbones. He was a master pirate on the high seas,
captain of his ship, feared across the land…

He woke with a start. Someone was tapping at the door.
'She's back, Amy, mum's back.' He rubbed his numbed leg
into life, ran to the door and reached for the catch.

'Can you open the door, Paul? There's nothing to worry
about, we just want to make sure you and Amy are okay.'

He froze. They didn't open the door to strangers. 'Mum's
gone for my dinner.'

'That's great. What are you having?' the woman called from
outside.

Paul could smell it, the leftovers his mum stuffed in the bin
when she brought take-away back late at night. 'Fish and chips.
Only I don't like fish so I'm having sausages.'

'Sounds good.'

'An' burgers an' beans an' egg.'

'And what does Amy have?'

He looked at Amy, asleep on the bench. What would she
have? 'Jam sandwich.'

'Would you like something, Paul? I'll ask my friend to nip
down the burger bar. Do you like onions?'

'No way!'

'Okay, no onions.'

Paul tried to peer through the door. 'My mum'll be back soon so I won't need it.'

'That's okay, more for me. And if mum isn't back we can eat it together. Won't be long.'

Paul ran to the window at the end of the caravan and pushed his head through the frayed orange curtain. A woman in a green coat was talking to a man. They turned. He ducked, counted to ten then looked again. The man had gone.

The woman called through the door. 'He'll be back in a minute, Paul.'

His stomach tugged at him. A minute! He was hungry now. His mum had only gone for a minute. His mum! She'd told him to watch and he'd forgotten. That woman, the stranger, had made him forget.

'Go away. My mum's coming and she don't like strangers.'

'Can you see her, Paul?'

He hesitated. 'Yeah.'

'That's great. I'll come round the front and you can point her out to me.' The woman appeared outside the big window. 'Where is she?'

Her face was close to his on the other side of the glass. She was young, like his mum, only with short, dark hair, like a cap. His mum's went right down her back. Sometimes, when she was on her own, she let him in bed with her and he'd wind his fingers round and round in her curls.

'Can you show me, Paul?'

'Over there.' He pointed across the empty park.

But the woman wasn't following his finger. She was screwing up her eyes and peering into his van. He pulled the curtains together.

'I'll go back to the door, Paul.' He heard footsteps scrunch round the caravan. Then voices. 'Okay, your burger's here now. Come and get it before it gets cold.'

No way. She just wanted to get into their caravan. To take things. Like all the rest. Like his mum said.

But it smelt good.

The catch was stiff. He gripped it tight and threw his

weight against the door. It burst open, catching the woman's face. Blood began to seep from her cheek.

Paul leapt from the stool into the bedroom, slammed the door and leant against it, shaking.

Nothing.

'It's okay, Paul, no damage done. Come and get your burger.' The caravan rocked as the woman stepped inside.

He peered through the crack by the hinge. She was sitting at the table eating a massive cheeseburger. There was another one right by her. He sauntered out of the bedroom, picked up the burger and slid on to the seat furthest away.

'How long has Amy been asleep, Paul?' the woman said.

'Dunno.'

'I don't think she's very well. She needs a doctor.'

The woman put her arms around his sister and lifted her, one hand under her floppy head. What had she done to Amy? They were stealing her. That's why they'd waited till his mum was out. They'd been watching. They knew she'd be back soon so they were doing it now.

He flung himself at the woman. 'Put her down, you can't take her!'

Suddenly a man was inside the caravan dragging him away, holding him down while the woman took Amy outside.

'Get off. Bring her back,' he shouted, lashing out.

'Paul... Paul... listen.' The woman had come back, without Amy. She wrapped her arms around him. 'Amy's poorly. We have to take her to hospital. We can't wait for mum.'

'Let her go!' He kicked harder, blindly.

The woman shifted her position to wedge his legs with her own. 'Amy needs help, Paul.'

His fist found her face, opened up the scratch. He was a super hero. With his special powers, the evil invader would have no chance. 'Give Amy back!'

The woman held him closer, trapping his arms. 'Where do you think mum is, Paul? We'll go and find her, tell her Amy is at the hospital.'

'She's comin' back,' he shouted. He pushed at her arm,

wedged his feet to shove her away. He'd get her off him, easy. No-one got the better of the champion kick-boxer - every bit of him was a lethal weapon. Hands chopping into her neck, feet lashing at her tits, that'd make her scream. And then her face. His head was close to hers now, close enough to bite, to tear her ears off.

Then he'd run... run away to their new house where his mum was waiting. Why hadn't she told him where it was? She could have told him directions; he was old enough to remember. Then he wouldn't have been alone for so long. He didn't like the dark.

'You know, Paul, being alone can be really scary,' the woman said.

How did she know? Know that he'd tried and tried to watch for his mum, but he couldn't, not when it got dark. He'd hidden under the table and wrapped his arms tight around him, like the woman's were now. And sometimes, and Amy mustn't ever know, he'd cried; wet, noisy, cries.

'It's okay, Paul, we'll sort things out. Here,' she handed him a tissue. He screwed it up in his fist and wiped his nose on her sleeve. With his head buried in her shoulder and feeling her arms holding him, the words finally fell out.

'Where's my mum?'

Chapter Two

'Good night was it?' Bill Stevens, senior social worker and Angie's team leader, scrutinised her bruised cheek. Angie dropped her briefcase and headed for the coffee machine.

'You should have seen them, Bill. Two kids on their own in a dingy old caravan at Warren Ridge in Westward Ho! Been alone for the best part of the day by the look of it.'

'How did you pick it up?'

'Mother and boyfriend turned up at the hospital with a young baby who'd died during the night. The boyfriend kept saying it had to be a cot death but the consultant wasn't convinced, started asking questions. Then he was called to an emergency and the parents disappeared. Nurse got the address, thank God. Police called us when they found the kids fending for themselves.' She sank into a chair and grimaced. 'Pass me Sarah's cushion, Bill. The boy's only nine but he had a hell of a kick.'

'How old was the other one, a girl was it?' He pulled a chair up to her desk.

'Yes, Amy. About three. According to the park manager, their mother hadn't been around since early morning. The boy was hungry but it was Amy that worried me.'

'Why?' He rubbed his hand round the back of his neck as if trying to delete a tide mark.

'Well...' Angie recalled the pitiful bundle on the seat. 'She stank - still in nappies and hadn't been changed - and then I realised she wasn't sleeping, she was unconscious. The boy said she'd hit her head on the table but given the circumstances...'

11

'And the mother?'

'It looks as though the baby didn't die naturally so my guess is she's done a runner.' Although it was never that clear cut. A few years with her finger in the dyke of human experience had taught Angie that. The mother would be going through her own nightmare, grabbing at anything to stop the chaos inside her head.

'How's the girl?'

'Conscious but unresponsive. The hospital will ring if there's any change. I'll get back there later.'

'And the boy?'

'With the Wilkinsons in Old Street.'

'The Wilkinsons?' He looked at her with surprise. 'I thought we agreed they had their hands full.'

'No other beds.'

He shook his head. 'At the last team meeting we specifically nominated Ellison Road for emergencies.'

'There was a fire at a foster home in Barnstaple. Everyone's been moved to Ellison Road. The place is overflowing. I rang round but there was nothing.' Having to justify her actions after the night she'd had rankled a little. 'The Wilkinsons were my only option.'

'Okay, I'd forgotten about the fire.'

Angie cleared a space for her coffee, pulled out a sheaf of files and placed the dictaphone on top.

Bill took the hint and stood. 'But move him soon as you can. It's volatile there with the eldest boy as he is. He might decide this Paul's fair game.' He picked up yesterday's paper from her desk. 'This Lech Walesa guy's got some guts.'

'Who?'

'The Polish ship worker.' He scanned the article. 'Rather him than me taking on that lot.'

'Was that all, Bill? Only I need to get this recorded.'

'Are you done with this?' He nodded at the paper.

'Take it.'

Bill paused. 'Has the boy got any other family?'

'There's a grandmother but I don't know where she lives.

No sign of the father, Fred Wells. Police have got a trace on him. He turns up like a bad penny from time to time but hasn't been living there for about six months. No-one seems to know about the boyfriend.'

'Okay. Keep me posted.' He moved on to another colleague, a young recruit, fresh out of college.

Angie re-filled her coffee mug and returned to her desk. Scraps of paper littered her diary, reminders of everything she hadn't got through yesterday. One by one she moved them on another day. Five visits scheduled. Mr Foster was at the cottage hospital waiting for her to take him round some residential homes. Postponed twice already. She'd have to get there tomorrow or it would blow up into a crisis - non-urgent cases always did when pushed to the bottom of the pile once too often.

Then a supervised visit between a mother and daughter at the children's home in Ellison Road. That was non-negotiable. The committee were meeting at the end of the week to decide whether the girl could go home. It was down to Angie to make her recommendation: long term fostering or back with her family? It was a responsibility she'd dearly love to give the tabloid editors, splashing 'family torn apart' headlines one day and 'social workers left child to suffer' the next.

A couple of hours later Angie put the tape on Paul in her tray for typing.

'Hi, Angie.' Sarah, the team's occupational therapist, poked her head round the door. 'Are you on for a run tonight?'

Angie smiled. 'I'm on call again but straight after work's okay.' The phone rang. 'Angie Turner.' It was Rosemary, their receptionist. There was no-one better at fielding troublesome callers. Before they knew it, they'd been listened to, sympathised with and ushered out without having launched into the complaint they'd been rehearsing all morning. 'The police?' Angie's face crumpled in mock despair. 'Please tell me it's not Walter.' She caught sight of Sarah smiling broadly. 'Could you tell the Sergeant I'll be there in a bit. And if they've space tonight... you know him well! Thanks, Rosemary.'

'Walter, eh?' Sarah was still grinning. 'Which window has he smashed this time?'

'Woolworths.'

'Oops. That'll cost him.'

'I should have expected it. They're forecasting a cold snap. He'll be looking for a nice warm cell to spend the night in. Sorry about the run.'

A light flashed across the top of the black bin bags heaped in the shop doorway. Paul shrank into the shadows and waited for the police to move on. He wanted to stand, shake his leg, get rid of the cramp. But he couldn't, not if he was to get back to his mum. She'd be so mad - waiting for him. He shivered. He'd say he'd gone to get something to eat, for him and Amy. Only it had rained so he'd waited in the shop doorway. Then he'd fallen asleep 'cause it was so late and he'd woken up and run all the way home. It wasn't his fault he hadn't kept watch. He had to feed Amy didn't he?

Amy. What would he say about Amy?

The street was clear now but Paul didn't move. He screwed his eyes up tight. He had to think...

'...Who's Amy?' The voice was soft, like a baby's blanket.

'Who wants to know?'

'Just a friend. Wrap this around you, it'll keep you warm.'

A sheet of bubble wrap spilled out of the cardboard boxes at the back of the doorway. It couldn't do any harm, taking it... could it?

'Run away have you? Why's that then?' the voice said, as the bubble wrap tucked itself closer around him. 'You can tell your friend.'

The voice was reading his thoughts!

'We all do it. Run away. Sometimes with our legs, sometimes in our heads. We take ourselves off to the places in our dreams.'

'Like Alton Towers.'

'Or where mums look after us.'

'And don't go.'

'I know how to make hurts go away,' the voice whispered.

'I ain't hurt.'

'You give them to your friend here, and they get sorted.'

'No they don't, not if they're this big,' he stretched his arms wide.

'Bigger the better. Just bundle them up and send them to me, every day if you want. Then you'll feel something warm round you, just like bubble wrap.'

'How do I send them?' he whispered as the voice drifted away.

'In your head. Just like you send yourself to Alton Towers…'

Gran! That was it. Gran would have Amy. She wouldn't have left him to look after her, would she? That's where his mum would find her.

Paul threw off the bubble wrap and stood, falling against the plate glass window as his numbed leg gave way beneath him. He pummelled his calf with his fists. 'Bloody leg. Stupid, bloody leg.' Then he was off, catapulting himself from one doorway to the next, heading for familiar territory.

Back at her flat, Angie opened the patio door and leant on the balcony rail. The evening air was chilly, softened only by a mist hanging over the estuary. One look at this view and she'd cancelled all her other appointments and signed the rental agreement on the spot. It was one of a block of thirty or so flats that sat back from the quay in the waterfront village of Instow. So many places had been overrun by cheap hotels and amusement arcades, but not here. Day visitors still came, but in the evening Angie could leave her flat and, in less than five minutes, be strolling along a virtually empty beach backed by rolling sand dunes.

She still couldn't believe the ever-changing landscape of the estuary outside her window. After years hemmed in by London's tower blocks it was too good to be true; a perfect antidote to days that were more of a reality check than she was comfortable with. And not only the days. It was her second night on call this week.

She drew the curtains, curled up on the sofa and picked up her book, a P.D. James, usually so addictive she'd stay up way too late reading just one more chapter. Not tonight though. She considered reading the page a third time then tossed the book aside and picked up the paper. *A Warsaw court legalised Solidarity today. Wild applause broke out in the packed courtroom as Judge Danuta Widawska read out the historic decision. Two hundred Solidarity supporters rose to their feet chanting "Solidarity, Solidarity" and "Lech Walesa, Lech Walesa" before singing the Polish national anthem....*

'Incredible,' she said to Garfield the ginger cat making his way to her end of the sofa. 'Literally incredible. Who could ever have believed it? Communism losing its grip...'

The phone interrupted her. She picked up the receiver, her hand trembling slightly. At least when it rang she knew what she'd have to deal with: maybe a suicide attempt or a child left to fend for itself... or worse. She shuddered at the memory of a little girl tied to her cot and left in her own excrement for days. The whole house had colluded in a sense of threat, from the abusive parents resisting arrest downstairs to the single light bulb swinging above the cot. She'd stood on the threshold of that room feeling so angry, so inadequate.

Seconds later she was contacting the police again. 'Angie Turner here, duty social worker. A child has absconded from a foster home. You were involved when he was taken into care last night, to 86 Old Road... yes, Mr and Mrs Wilkinson... I'm leaving now for Warren Ridge caravan-park over at Westward Ho! No photograph but he's eight or nine, slight, has dark hair, probably wearing muddy jeans, a black t-shirt and a brown jacket slightly too small for him.'

Angie pulled into the caravan site. Pristine mobile homes with names proudly displayed - Phoenix, Galaxy, Dalesman - were lined up like dominoes, picture windows all angled for the best view of the sea. The salt-laden air greeted her as she opened the car door. For a moment she was hypnotised by the seemingly endless rollers breaking across the two mile long beach in the moonlight.

She could just make out the silhouette of Lundy Island. Its sheer sides gave it an inhospitable air at first glance, and the featureless plateau that ran its length could be bitterly unwelcoming in gale force winds. But Angie could forgive all that for the days when Lundy was bathed in sunshine, and for the freedom this 'other-worldly' outpost offered. As soon as she set foot inside the Lookout, the most remote accommodation on the island, the world slipped away. Here she could indulge her love of photography, creating images full of beauty, colour, light.

Angie sighed, climbed back into her car and drove between the de-luxe caravans to an area at the foot of the cliff. She pulled up beside Paul's caravan. It reeked of abandonment. The two-tone green and beige paint was covered in algae, as if a camouflage net had been dropped over it. The site manager would have been only too glad to see it disappear. Yet it was Paul's only real home. He'd be back.

Curtains twitched in the neighbouring caravan but there was no response when she knocked. The door on another slammed shut in her face. The woman hadn't seen him and she wasn't sorry either. 'Bloody kid, always hanging around, peering through the window when we're eating. Good riddance.' On her third attempt, a shift worker sounded off at her for getting him out of bed, all because of 'those brats'.

She sought the refuge of her car, shelter from the freezing rain and the abuse that was a depressingly familiar part of her day. Huddled here, cold and wet, responsible for the safety of a child who'd suddenly lost the only family he'd ever known - however dysfunctional - was a sobering reality check. Paul would soon be in trouble if he was still on the streets. She reached for a rag and wiped the inside of the windscreen. Not long until her holiday on Lundy now. She pulled her coat tighter and allowed her eyes to close.

Paul pressed against the cold metal of the site manager's caravan and peered through the window. He watched Tucker's calloused hands throw one, two, three slices of bacon into the pan alongside a mound of mushrooms and sausages. He could hear the bacon spluttering. Was Tucker pressing the fat against the bottom to get it all crisp and tasty like his Gran did?

Paul knew that it would taste better than… than anything. Think. THINK.

He watched as Tucker turned, peered into the small worktop fridge, cursed and flung the caravan door open inches from Paul's nose. He threw himself under the van, stifling a cry as his head hit a rusted iron support.

Tucker strode across to a neighbouring caravan and knocked on the door. The top half swung open. 'Got any eggs Charlie?' Tucker boomed into the smoky interior before stepping in.

Now! It had to be now. Paul scrambled out and ran up the steps. The smell! There were two pieces of toast lying ready on a plate. Paul picked the bacon out of the pan with his fingers and sandwiched it together.

'Well, a fry up's not the same without an egg is it?' Tucker said, already on his way back.

Where to go? Paul ran to the bedroom at the end. The caravan rocked as Tucker climbed inside, his enormous presence filling the space. Paul opened the window as far as it would go and squeezed through, falling to the ground with a thud. He rolled away towards the ditch with his prize.

A mongrel suddenly appeared, dodging this way and that, its eyes fixed on the disappearing sandwich. 'Get off.' Paul pushed the dog away and began to weave through the site towards his caravan, his new companion following a sniff away.

Minutes later, Paul was watching and waiting again, the satisfaction of the bacon long forgotten. The car was back, the car that had taken him to the house where the boy had taunted him, said he must be a right loser if even his mum didn't want him. But it wasn't true. His mum did, and she'd be waiting for him. She'd be inside, right now. She wouldn't let the woman in so he'd have to get in round the back, through the window.

The figure inside the car didn't see him slithering across the grass. But the mongrel didn't know how to slither. It ran after him, tail up, barking its new-found loyalty. 'Get away.' Paul twisted and turned, trying to prise the mongrel's jaws from his jeans. 'Shut up you stupid dog. Let go. LET GO.'

The fraying jeans suddenly gave way and he fell back onto the wet grass, winded. Warm air pulsed across his face. He lifted his head and looked into the deep brown eyes of the mongrel. He smiled. The dog had stayed. It hadn't run away or bitten him because he was making a fuss. It stayed. He reached out to stroke the dog. It burst into life, spinning round and round after its tail. Then stopped dead - waited for Paul's smile to get bigger, for him to laugh - then began again, round and round and round.

But he'd forgotten his mum! Paul scuttled under the van and emerged with a pointed stick. Forcing the seal around the window, he was soon in. 'I'm back, mum. I just went to get...' He dropped into a cold, empty space. Why? Why hadn't she come back for him? He crashed his fists against the wall. Pain ricocheted up his arms. He shook his head, had to think. What did bubble wrap lady said he had to do? He screwed his eyes up tight and tried hard to see all the horrible hurt in front of him, to get it into a pile so he could wrap it all up...

...and that's when he saw the bubble wrap on the ground, and a roll of string to keep it tied up tight so nothing could get out.

The postman had a real job to pick it up because it was ever so heavy and he had to tell him the address - bubble wrap lady, the doorway in town. He could write brilliant 'cause every night his mum sat and helped him at their new home. It was massive, their new home. He had a room all of his own painted blue and white with a Spurs cover on his bed, a bed with two levels. He slept up the top and underneath was a table with a brand new Play Station on it. And the games were piled so high he had steps to get to the ones at the very top.

He spent all day playing games, apart from when his mum called him for food, a massive tray of burgers, chips and beans that he ate in front of their cinema sized TV. It was so big it took up nearly all of a wall and there was masses of room for all his mates.

And he'd get so expert at game playing that all the men from Sony would ask him to test out their new games. They'd queue downstairs waiting to find out what he thought and give him loads more. And he'd tell them about his superhero, Time Bubble Man, who had loads of superpowers like a magic cloak that caught bullets as he span round and round then PING, PING, PING, PING he'd fire them back and kill the evil invaders. And he had Radar Ears that found out lies and Searchlight Eyes that saw right through people and found out all their secret thoughts.

And the best was his Truth Tongue. When he switched his Truth Tongue on, everyone had to believe what he said. He'd play games, telling people it was raining frogs and watch them run. Or that they had a tarantula creeping down their neck. Only he was a superhero and it was his job to save people… not frighten them more.

But sometimes his mum would say 'Paul's not around today. He's coming to town with me. We're spending the whole day together. So he won't have time for you…'

'We're doing everything we can to find your mum, Paul.'

Paul opened his eyes. The bitch was inside his van.

'The police are looking. I'm sure she's okay, probably just sorting something out for herself. But until we find her you can't stay here on your own.'

Paul moved back. 'Get away. I ain't going back.'

'Why's that, Paul?'

He made a fist. 'Stay away.'

'What the bloody hell's going on here?' The voice came from a figure filling the doorway. 'Leave him be. Who are you and what you doing in 'ere?'

'She's tryin' to get me, Gran. She took Amy an' me, only I got away but she's gonna take me back and I ain't going.'

The grandmother pushed past Angie and wedged herself in front of Paul. 'Stop talking rubbish. Where's Amy and the baby? Where's your mother?'

'I told you. She took her.' Paul pointed at Angie.

'I'm from Social Services, Mrs…?' There was no response. 'It appears your grandchildren have been here on their own since yesterday morning. Last night we took Paul to a foster home for his own safety.'

The woman looked at Angie. 'What do you mean, on their own? Their mother looks after them. And I was here yesterday morning. They were okay then.'

'Was Amy all right?'

'Of course she was.'

Angie studied the woman's face. It was the job of the police to establish the facts but she'd have to make a decision very soon. Could she leave Paul with someone who'd left two young children fending for themselves, however briefly? 'We had to admit Amy to hospital last night, Mrs...' Still nothing. 'She was unconscious. You didn't notice anything unusual about her?'

'I told you didn't I? She was fine.' The woman turned back to Paul. 'What's all this about a foster home?' she said.

'They put me with this boy, gran. He slagged mum off. I wan't staying there.'

'Where's your mum?'

'Dunno,' Paul mumbled.

'Stop lying or I'll let her take you.' The woman jabbed a thumb in Angie's direction.

'I ain't lying,' he snapped at her. 'I dunno.'

'He's telling the truth, Mrs... What is your name?' Angie waited.

'Harris.' She eased herself onto a seat.

'Thank you, Mrs Harris. When did you last see your daughter?'

'Saturday night. I sat the kids.'

'She went out?' Silence. 'Where did she go?'

Mrs Harris shrugged. 'Out with some fancy man.'

'But you saw her when she got back? What time was that?'

'How should I know? Late.'

'And you must have thought she was here yesterday, or nearby anyway, when you left?'

'Suppose so.'

Angie sighed. What options did she have? 'Until we know

what's happened, can Paul come with you, Mrs Harris?'

'With me?' She looked at Paul, slouching on the opposite seat. 'I guess he can come over mine for dinner. But I can't cope with Amy or the baby.'

'Amy… and the baby are at the hospital.' Angie paused. Given the circumstances, some information would have to be dealt with by the police. 'Amy may have to stay in for a day or two. I can take you there now if you like.'

'Now? No, I've Clem's meal to get. Come on if you're coming.' Mrs Harris hauled Paul out of the seat.

'I'll need to know where you are, Mrs Harris.'

'Number 34, across the Park.'

Angie turned to Paul. 'Do you want to get some things together?'

'Things?' Mrs Harris said. 'I don't want him cluttering up my place with his stuff.'

'Just some clothes to last him a few days.'

'I can't have him long. Clem wouldn't put up with it.'

'I don't need no stuff. Mum'll be back.' Paul leapt out of the caravan and was ambushed by the tangled ball of hair waiting under the steps. He bundled the dog up into his arms.

'Where are you going with that filthy mongrel?' Mrs Harris said.

'He'll be okay, Gran. He can come, can't he?' Paul pleaded.

'What'll Clem say to that?' she said. 'Put it down… now.'

'But, Gran…'

Mrs Harris pointed at Angie. 'Put it down or go with her.'

Chapter Three

Angie gritted her teeth, stamped on the accelerator and crossed the lights on amber. Cancelling Mr Foster hadn't been enough. She peered at the clock on the dashboard - less than ten minutes to get to Ellison Road for the supervised contact. The mother, edgy at the best of times, would jump at the chance to blame a late social worker for the failure of this visit. No, Angie sighed, that wasn't fair. The mum had become much more reliable with her daughter lately. Just how reliable was something Angie now had to decide.

An hour later she was in the car again. The visit had taken longer than she'd hoped, but nowhere near as long as she needed. Mum was definitely making progress, she even sat on the floor and played with Shelley, but it was like she existed in a bubble, sealed off from her daughter's pleas for love. Whether she ever would, or could, respond was now Angie's call. She'd spend all day writing her report and probably all night tossing and turning, hoping she'd got it right.

It was late morning when Angie reached the hospital. The staff nurse pointed out Amy's cot. Angie could just make out a motionless form through the bars.

'How is she?'

'Far as we can tell the blow to her head hasn't caused any lasting problems. Difficult to be sure though.'

'Why's that?'

'You'll see.'

Angie leant on the cot. Amy stared right at her - or through her. 'Hello, Amy. I'm Angie. I've just seen Paul and your

Gran.' The eyes continued to stare. Angie dropped her hand on to Amy's bare arm. 'How are you, darling? Is your head poorly?' Angie rarely saw such stillness in a child of this age. It had to be the medication. 'I've brought a book. Shall we look at the pictures?' Angie slid the cot side down and sat alongside her. 'Here's a dog. Do you have a dog, Amy? Or a cat?' Amy gazed ahead, unaware of the dalmatian bounding across the page or the cat rolling round and round the ball of bright red knitting wool. Angie picked up another book. As she turned the pages strains of Incy-Wincy Spider reached the next bed where a pair of chubby hands waved in time to the music. She took Amy's hand in her own and made a spidery movement. Her limp arm slowly stiffened then withdrew until it was free of Angie's touch.

'What medication is Amy on?' Angie asked at the nurse's station on her way out.

'She's not on anything.'

'Nothing at all? Only she's so unresponsive. How long are you keeping her in?'

'No more than a few days. Unless anything else shows up. The only thing we're actively treating her for is nappy rash. Poor kid must have been in agony.'

'But she hasn't made a sound?'

'Nothing.'

'Who's the consultant?'

'Mr Andrews.'

'Okay. I'll fix up a foster home. Mother's disappeared but if she does turn up alert the police immediately. Under no circumstances is she to leave with Amy.'

'Cheers!' Sarah raised her glass. 'It's only taken six weeks to prise you out of that office for lunch.'

Angie grimaced. 'I know. Sorry.'

'Well, you're here now. So how's things?'

'Okay. Mostly. I've just picked up this case, a boy abandoned by…'

'Oh no!' Sarah interrupted. 'This is a work-free zone. What else have you been up to?'

Angie looked at Sarah. She was a breath of fresh air, always so upbeat. It was impossible to imagine her spending the evening slumped on the sofa watching whatever happened to be on the box. 'Honestly? Not a lot. But you're right. It's time I did something about it. Maybe I'll start jogging. I've got the Tarka Trail outside my window and the beach down the road, what am I waiting for?'

'Didn't you used to be in a drama group?'

'Yes, but off stage. Set design.' Angie paused as the waitress placed overflowing plates of fish and chips in front of them.

'God, that smells good.' Sarah picked at her chips with her fingers. 'Did I tell you I've signed up for a fish cookery class? I'm desperate for a change from lasagne and chilli. But tell me about the set design. Sounds impressive.'

'Not really. It was only at college. I loved the challenge of creating something, I don't know, unexpected I guess. The reaction when the curtain went up gave me a real buzz. Haven't done anything since though.'

'Why not?'

Angie paused. 'Good question.' She lived alone so her evenings were her own, other than when she was on call of course. Her social life was hardly packed. In fact, what social life? 'I really don't know. I was out all the time in London.'

'So what's changed?'

'Work I guess. It's such a...' she paused. 'I don't know how to put it. When you're dealing with real crises in people's lives day in, day out everything else feels so... superficial.'

'Hey,' Sarah squeezed Angie's arm, 'that's exactly why you need to get out. Get a bit of perspective.'

'You know what, you're absolutely right.' Angie grinned and raised her glass.

A couple of hours later, she shuffled the pages into some sort of order and leant back in her chair. Her report on the supervised contact was as complete as she could make it without a crystal ball. She was recommending Shelley return home to her mother. Her professional experience and gut instincts told her it would be okay, but there were no guarantees. Not that it was her responsibility alone. The committee had the final say.

'Police called while you were out,' Bill paused by her desk. 'About that boy, Paul. Still nothing on the mother. The father's no fixed abode, they come across him from time to time. Grandmother's no angel, but nothing to be unduly concerned about. The boy's best off there for a day or two.'

'Anything from the fostering team? I want to keep Paul and Amy together.'

'Nothing. This fire's clogged the system. And you'll need an experienced couple if the boy keeps legging it.'

'Anything just out of the area?'

'You can try. But I doubt it.' He paused. 'When do you go on leave?'

'Couple of weeks.'

'Anything I need to be aware of?'

'Well,' Angie smiled. 'There's Walter. If it gets too cold he'll send his calling card. It was a brick through Woolworth's window last time. Assistants still can't work out why he didn't run.' Angie picked up her report. 'And this might need your attention. I'm recommending Shelley goes home.'

'When's she going?'

'End of the week, if the committee agrees.'

'And she's been with the Clarkes?'

'Yes.'

'There's your answer.'

'You've lost me.'

'Kate and Steve Clarke. Experienced, reliable, registered for two, and with no-one there from the end of the week.'

Angie grabbed her coat. 'Bill, I could kiss you. Thanks. I'll be in late tomorrow. Case conference at Ellison Road. Don't let anyone pinch the Clarke's. No matter what.'

It was always a pleasure driving out to Kate and Steve's. A new housing development was encroaching on the fields separating Bideford from Abbotsham village but for now the countryside still began as the last house faded in her rear view mirror. Weaving through the narrow lanes towards the coast, Angie passed homes where parents were doing their best to love and care for their children with instincts that were a legacy of their own childhoods. But in others it went so, so wrong. Why?

The lane led to a gravelled parking area, protected on one side by trees slowly losing the battle to stay upright against the strong westerly's that swept this coastline. She was only half a mile from the sea. One day, Angie promised herself, she'd climb the stile and follow the path across the fields to the cliffs; maybe walk to where it dipped to meet the pebbled beach. She could borrow a friend's young son and go on a crab hunt in the rock pools.

She followed the path around the cottage to the back door, waving as she saw the outline of Kate in the kitchen window.

'Angie.' Kate opened the back door. 'Come in.'

'Hi, Kate.'

'Coffee?'

'Please.' Angie hung her coat over the pine kitchen chair and sat down. 'How's things?'

'Oh, you know.'

Angie did know - or at least she could tell from Kate's red-rimmed eyes. 'Doesn't get any easier does it?'

'No.'

'Especially when they come to you so young.' Kate had taken Shelley in at just eighteen months. Letting her go back to an uncertain future after nearly a year was tearing her apart.

'She's been doing so well. After all the tantrums we've finally got her to trust us. And now... you try explaining why she has to leave the only home she knows to go back to someone who's always letting her down. And even when she's there, ignores her most of the time.' Kate grabbed the kettle and filled a couple of mugs.

'Better recently though. Mum's been regular as clockwork

for the last three months. And Shelley's play therapy has been really positive,' Angie said.

'You think she'll be okay, do you? You think Shelley won't be locked in her room while mum 'entertains'. She won't have to find her own food or get left outside the pub? You're sure of all that are you?' Angie's coffee spilt as Kate pushed it across the table.

'No, I'm not sure. But the committee felt it was the only decision they could make.' Angie hesitated. 'I know Shelley won't get anything like the care you've given her, but we can't deny parents their children…'

'Sorry,' Kate interrupted. 'I know, of course I do. You made it plain enough when we registered. Only the theory doesn't help when it actually happens. You get to love them as your own, especially when they're so young.'

'And even more difficult without having your own around.' Angie was treading on sensitive ground, but she had to know if Kate's investment in the children was going too deep.

'I'll get over it.'

'Will you?'

Kate relaxed. 'Yes. Especially when these other two arrive.'

Angie studied her. 'Are you sure you want to consider another placement so soon?'

'Steve's home just now so it's a good time to take on two. He fell off the ladder on the last shout, sprained a ligament. It's not serious but he's off for a few weeks.' Kate's eyes drifted to a picture of Steve with herself and Shelley, her arms wrapped around the little girl, protective, fulfilled. She looked back at Angie. 'So tell me about them.'

'There's Amy, who's just three and Paul, nine. Mother turned up at the hospital with a dead baby claiming it was a cot death. But she took off when she got wind of the police coming. She left Paul and Amy fending for themselves in a caravan on the Warren Ridge Caravan Park at Westward Ho!'

'Where's she now?'

'No idea.'

Kate stirred her coffee. 'How long are we talking about?'

'Hard to say. Whatever the cause of death, mum needs help. And if she was responsible… well, Paul and Amy will be with us for good.'

'Oh my God!' Kate's hand shook. 'To think any mother could… could do that.' She stared out the window.

Angie sank back in her chair. Having to give up Shelley had left Kate's emotions painfully exposed. It would be a risk, going ahead with another placement so soon.

'Do you know anything about her, the mother?' Kate said, focusing on Angie again.

'No, the family's slipped under the radar.'

'How have the children reacted?'

'Chalk and cheese. Amy's withdrawn completely. Hasn't said a word to anyone. My guess is she'll regress and need a lot of mothering. Paul's protective, rebelling, defending his mum to the death. Oh, and he's a runner.'

'You said he'd be a challenge.'

'But not one you have to take on. The care you offer would be ideal for these two, especially Amy. But it's your decision.'

Kate stared at her. 'Do you have anywhere else for them?'

'No. But that's not your problem.'

'Steve'll be home soon. Give us the full picture and we'll let you know tomorrow.'

'Don't slouch, you'll get gut ache.' Mrs Harris handed Paul his sausage and chips.

Paul grudgingly shifted an inch, slumped back into the same hollow in the sofa, and picked up a chip with his fingers.

'About time your mother was back,' Mrs Harris said. 'Can't have you turning the place upside down every whip and trip. What did she say?'

'Nothin'.'

'She must have said something.'

Paul thought. 'Just a minute.'

'Don't be cheeky or you'll feel the back of my hand.' She raised her arm.

'I ain't. That's what she said, I'll just be a minute.'

'What did she mean, I'll just be a minute?'

'Dunno.'

'Where was she was going?'

'Dunno.'

'And she took the baby?'

Paul thought for a moment. 'Must have.'

'Well did she or didn't she?' His grandmother planted her feet in front of him, wiping her hands on her skirt.

Paul crammed more chips into his mouth.

'She's made you swear not to tell, hasn't she?'

'No.'

'She's told you something and made it a secret. Thick as thieves you two are. What is it?' She leant over him.

'Nothin'. Ain't no secret.'

'I wasn't born yesterday. You tell me right now or I'll get the police back and they'll take you away permanent.'

'No.'

'Don't you answer me back, my lad. You'll come to no good, just like your dad.'

'Won't. I'm good. Mum said so.'

'Is that right? And when did she say that?'

'When she got up. I told her…' Paul stopped.

'What? What did you tell her?' Mrs Harris grasped his wrist.

'Nothin'.'

'Secrets, always secrets.' She let go of him. 'Well she ain't here no more, so you'd better start doing as you're told if you know what's good for you. Just think about that.'

He was Time Bubble Man blasting a beam of radar vision through the evil woman's mind, criss-crossing all her secret thoughts. He'd catch them in his time cloak and spin them round and send them back all mixed up so she wouldn't know what she was doing.

With his Searchlight Eyes, he knew his mum was missing him. He could smell her perfume, the sort she splashed all over on special nights. She'd had lots of it on to go to the pictures. Only she wasn't going on her own. She had a date, she said, but not like the others. This was proper. He had a van and was going to be his dad.

He didn't want a dad. He was her man.

She'd made him promise, about van man. Their secret. Gran wasn't to know. So he'd thrown his time cloak to catch his thoughts and send them back to his mind-safe where the evil one couldn't get at them 'cause he was the only one who knew the combination.

He remembered her perfume. It was still there in the morning. Only just though 'cause Justin's nappy was smelly and his mum was holding Justin tight. But it was him she'd meant to take with her, not Justin.

Chapter Four

Angie knew she was rushing the family mediation but she had to fit in a visit to the Clarkes before she could get home, pack for her break on Lundy and fall into bed. She saw the couple to the door, though 'couple' was hardly the word; they left the building without a single shared glance. She cleared her desk, checked the answer-phone and locked her confidential notes in the filing cabinet.

Thirty minutes later she was at the Clarkes. Through the open kitchen door she could hear Kate's voice upstairs, warm, gentle vibrations that paused every now and then waiting for a response from Amy. It would come one day but not yet.

Angie heard another voice. She eased the door of the family room open. Paul was lying on his front on the carpet, his legs kicking up behind. Each outstretched hand held a different fantasy character, oozing green slime and malevolence.

'Take that, you evil kidnapper.' The figure in Paul's right hand crashed down on the assailant clutched in his carpet-bound hand. 'And that, and that. See, you can't escape the mighty warrior.'

The now armour-less figure raised its head. 'You'll never defeat me. Never know what I know.'

'Will,' the warrior screamed. 'Your head'll shrink and shrink till it's this small and everything spills out. Then I'll take what I want. All of it.'

'The forces of Thar'll get you before you find her.'

'Won't. Once she knows it's me she'll fight and slay her

guards and we'll get miles and miles and miles away.' The apprentice warrior rolled from side to side as the two figures locked in combat.

'You can run but you can't hide from the mighty Thar…aaaaaaah.'

'That's what you think.' The figure sailed across the room, disappearing behind the sofa. Paul was suddenly still.

Angie held her breath.

'Is that you, Paul?' a fragile woman's voice came from Paul's lips.

'Yes. I'm here to rescue you from the evil Thar. Quick, let's get the hell out of here,' her knight in shining armour responded.

'How did you find me?'

'I'll always find you, mum.'

The fragile voice whispered something secret for Paul's ears only. His head sank to the ground, his eyes seeing far beyond this reality to his real mother, the one who missed him, the one who was coming back for him.

'Hello, Angie.' Kate swung down the stairs with Amy on her hip. 'Sorry, didn't hear you come in.'

'No problem. I could tell you were busy.' Angie reached for Amy's limp hand. 'Hello, Amy.' The toddler stared straight ahead.

'Sorry,' Kate said. 'It's not you. She hasn't said a word to anyone.' She stroked Amy's cheek. 'But it will come, darling, won't it,' she said, kissing her. She looked at Angie. 'Coffee?'

'I won't, thanks. On a tight schedule.'

'Of course, you're off on holiday. Somewhere warm?'

'Warm might be a bit optimistic. I'm going to Lundy, for some photography.'

'Bit wild and remote isn't it?'

'Not everyone's idea of fun I know, but it suits me. Just wanted to be sure you know the arrangements while I'm away.'

'Sit down for a second.' Kate placed Amy in the high chair. 'Mind yourself. I'll clear up these bits.' She swept some broken china from the table.

'What's he been up to?' Angie said.

'What makes you think it was Paul?'

'If it was Amy you'd be delighted.'

'True.' She smiled.

'I ain't done nothing, and even if I 'ave it's none of your business.' Paul was out of the back door before either of them could respond.

'Paul, come back,' Kate called after him. 'It's time for tea.' She hesitated. 'I'll keep it warm. It'll be here when you want it.' She turned to Angie. 'Sorry again. He's cast you as the evil witch keeping him from his mum.'

'Does he take off a lot?'

'Every-time we say something he doesn't want to hear. Like every other sentence!'

'Where does he go?'

'Bolt hole in the woods.' Anxiety flashed across Angie's face. 'It's okay, we can see it from upstairs. If he stays there too long, Steve can usually talk him out. Although we had to call the duty team last night.'

'I read the report. They found him back at the caravan?'

'He's convinced his mum'll turn up and be mad when she finds him gone.'

Angie thought. 'Can I make a suggestion? Tucker will be emptying the caravan soon. Before he does, take Paul there, so he can see for himself whether his mum has been back.'

'Could help.'

'What would?' Steve Clarke came through the door, a walking stick in one hand.

'Hi, Steve,' Angie said, shaking the hand he offered. 'I was just wondering if a return visit to the caravan would help Paul.'

'Maybe,' he replied. 'Need to release his pressure valve somehow. He had a go at Amy the other day. Screaming abuse. I was only in the next room so I put a stop to it but he was out the door the instant I opened my mouth.'

'Giving you a rocky ride?'

'A bit, but don't worry,' he smiled reassuringly, 'we're not going to fall by the wayside. The school have been good, letting us know when he kicks off, how they handle it, that sort of thing. More background would help though.'

'I don't have much to offer,' Angie said. 'The police still haven't come up with anything on his mother. Any joy with the grandmother?'

'Came once but hasn't been near since.'

'Not at all?'

'Nope.'

'Sorry to hear that. She's a bit rough and ready but I thought she genuinely cared for the kids. Wasn't her husband any help?'

'Husband?'

'Clem, whatever that stands for. Mind you, it was obvious he wasn't keen on having Paul around.'

Kate and Steve Clarke looked at each other.

'What? Have I put my foot in it?' Angie said.

'No,' Steve wheezed, his breath short all of a sudden, 'It's just that... Clem doesn't like having his routine interrupted. Meals, grooming, naps in his basket in front of the fire.'

'Stop it, Steve!' Kate turned to Angie, trying to suppress a smile. 'I think there's been a bit of a misunderstanding. Clem's the cat.'

The gate cracked as Paul slammed it against its hinges. 'Take that you bloody bastard.' He crashed it shut, then took off down a track towards the wood. He pushed through a tunnel of brambles. 'Get off me you shitty, bloody...' His arm chopped through the thorns, becoming more and more entangled. 'Get off!' He wrenched his arm free and fell into a clearing. Dropping on to his hands and knees, he disappeared beneath a jagged sheet of corrugated iron smothered in ferns.

Inside, he turned to face the opening, pulling his knees tight against his body. 'Get away.'

Silence.

'You ain't taking me.' Silence. Where was she? It didn't matter anyway, not here...

...here he was King. With his army all round the walls. No-one got in without him saying so. His castle was the strongest in the land. Nothing happened he didn't want. Everyone listened and bowed to him and did exactly as he said. If he said, 'I want ice cream,' they got it. If he said, 'kill him,' they did. One word and his army marched on his enemies, tied them up and made them cough up what he wanted to know.

He had the biggest weapons all along the walls. Inside were loads of scientists working on a new, scarier weapon he'd use to take over the world. He'd go on TV with his face blotched out like Batman's arch enemy, and warn everyone if they didn't do like he said, terrible things would happen to them all - well not all of them. He'd save his mum... and Amy... maybe.

But how could he save his mum if he didn't know where she was? He'd have to say something only she'd understand. Like a code. Only how would she know it was him, with his face all blotched out? She'd know his voice. That was it. And she'd be so happy 'cause she'd been looking for him for weeks and weeks.

'It wan't my fault, mum,' he'd say. 'They took me away.'

'I know, Paul,' she'd say, putting her arm around him, 'I know you wouldn't run away from me. Not when I love you so much.'

And he'd curl up beside her and run his hands through her hair and she'd say, 'You've been so good, I'm going to take you somewhere really special - even better than Alton Towers.'

'Where, mum? Where are we going?' he'd say.

'You'll never guess,' she'd say, starting one of her giggles.

'The Dungeon,' he'd say. He'd seen it on TV. A place where they did torturing - and you heard people scream.

'Even better,' she'd say. 'And you fly there, and it takes ages.'

'On an enormous plane!'

'Yes. And when we get there...'

'Where?'

'Guess. Somewhere you can go on even bigger and better rides.'

'Disneyland. We're going to...'

Something snapped outside. 'Get away. I done traps.'

Silence, then more noises; they were invading his camp. Paul grabbed a branch and shrank back against the corrugated iron. 'I ain't coming.'

Then something else - a sniffing and a yelp. Flinging aside the branch, Paul scrambled out through the hole. 'Spider! Here boy. Spider!' He crouched down, holding his arms open, his eyes alight. The mongrel pounced, tumbling him over and over, his tongue washing Paul's face each time it passed. 'You found me,' Paul cried. He pulled the dog closer and buried his face in its coat. 'You found me.'

Chapter Five

Backtracking to the office to update the case file was a bad move. Angie had been sorely tempted to ignore the phone, but she wouldn't be back for a week. Tucker, the site manager, hadn't minced his words. 'Caravan's being cleared Friday. I can't have it standing empty so get here before then if you want anything.'

Angie pulled up beside Paul's caravan. The key bit into her finger as she struggled to turn it, but eventually it caught and the door opened. Inside, there were a few more cobwebs but little else had changed. She sat on the bench seat, listening as the wind prised at each creaking panel.

What happened here that night? Angie closed her eyes, imagined Sonya waiting for her mother, checking her watch, pressing her face to the window, lighting a cigarette, checking her make-up, again. Then suddenly opening the door and disappearing into the night. Angie screwed up her eyes. Did she leave the door open? Or if not open, at least unlocked. Yes, she'd left in a hurry. No time to pick up her keys, fiddle with the lock as Angie had done. Did someone get in? But who and why? Or was it just Sonya who returned, alone, to be greeted by the piercing sound of Justin's crying?

Who was the woman that stepped back into the caravan that night? A loving mother who wanted nothing more than to comfort her son? Or a single mother exhausted with caring for a sickly child, desperate to be with the man who was waiting for her, offering her a future, escape? Maybe nothing, absolutely nothing was going to ruin her evening. Was that when she snapped? When years of frustration drove her to pick up a pillow? According to the police Sonya said nothing when she was questioned. Why? She was suspected of killing her child - why didn't she protest? Because she was guilty? What other explanation was there?

Angie stared around the empty space as if the fabric of the caravan might hold the answers. She opened the door to the children's bedroom; two narrow beds with a cot slotted in between. Did Sonya stand here staring at Justin? She was dressed up, excited, couldn't wait to see her new man. Mystery man. Labelled Mr Wells at the hospital but that was just a trainee nurse making assumptions. She'd been disciplined, poor kid. What kind of luck was that, to have to deal with a suspected infanticide on her second day?

Angie closed the bedroom door. By all accounts, mystery man wasn't there at the beginning of the evening. Just the kids and Sonya. Waiting. Until she left them alone. 'Be there in five minutes', Mrs Harris had said to Sonya. Claimed she was true to her word, but who knows. Angie reached into her briefcase and pulled out a notebook. She flicked through it for the policeman's statement confirming that Mrs Harris had got there, friend in tow, sometime in the next half hour. So the children could have been alone from 7.45pm to 8.15pm. The pathologist put the time of death between 7.30pm and 9.00pm.

Could it have been the grandmother? She was no saint. Had Justin's crying got to her so she turned him into the pillow to muffle the sound? Or worse? It was possible, but cold blooded killing of a baby was hard to believe. If he'd been shaken to death, maybe, but not smothered. That took time, pressure, determination. Unless the baby was held so tight to a mother's body that it became impossible to breath. Angie rubbed her forehead. Nothing made sense. But Sonya had run. She must have felt guilty, believed herself to be guilty, was guilty. 'Take your pick', Angie muttered.

She walked into the second bedroom, filled by a small double bed and a built in wardrobe. She opened the doors. Neatly pressed clothes hung on ordered hangers. And beneath, polished shoes in matching pairs arranged over a rail. Angie shook her head. It didn't fit. She hesitated. What didn't fit? What assumptions had she made? That the grandmother's a rough diamond so the mother has to be? That she lives in a caravan so is less than adequate? That she's a single mother to three children so is promiscuous? This woman cared - about her appearance, about her clothes. About her kids? That was the big question.

Angie opened a drawer beside the wardrobe. Underwear, tights… the usual. The next drawer contained neatly folded all-in-one suits, jumpers, trousers, Justin's by the size of them. Next drawer - bigger stuff, maybe Paul's. Angie lifted out some jeans. They'd been taken up with neat, careful stitches, a tear in the leg repaired with a patch. She added them to the black bin bag she'd brought from the office. There wasn't much here worth saving but there was something about the care that had gone into those jeans.

She searched the bedside drawers. Some loose change, supermarket vouchers and several sheets of folded paper. Angie smoothed them out on the bed and was instantly drawn into a crazy, upside down world of comic strip characters spilling out of the boxes, filling page after page. Was the mother an artist? But the superhero holding back the chaos of smoky cities reminded her of something… of Paul lying on Kate's carpet, of the voices. Could these be his? If they were, he had an exceptional talent. She re-folded the sheets and put them in her bag. Perfect for Paul's life story work, time spent together disentangling fact from fantasy, making sense of what had happened and why - as far as anyone could tell.

The sun was setting by the time she drew up outside her flat.

'Angie?' The call came from behind. 'Long time no see.' A slender, auburn haired woman slid out of a silver convertible and walked towards Angie with her arms open.

'I'm sorry…?'

'I haven't changed that much have I?'

'Christine?' Angie was rooted to the spot.

'Hope you don't mind me ambushing you like this.' The woman kissed Angie on both cheeks, an easy, familiar gesture that belied the three years it had been since their last embrace.

Angie accepted the hug, allowed it to linger while her mind raced. 'What are you doing here?'

'Last minute job in Exeter. I was about to leap into the car and hit the motorway when I thought, why not? Why not come and see my old buddy.' She paused. 'Sorry,' she smiled sheepishly. 'I mean... just turning up like this... if it's not convenient I can...' she waved in the direction of her car.

Angie smiled. 'No. Of course it's fine, it's more than fine, it's great to see you. But why didn't you call? You might have missed me.'

'Plan ahead you mean?' She smiled. 'Still not too good at that I'm afraid.'

Angie searched her bag for the house keys. Her fingers had lost all contact with her brain and surfaced with a torch, paper clip, pen. 'They're here somewhere,' she said, aware of Christine beside her, poised as ever. Was it really three years since they'd gone their separate ways? Angie still remembered the day they'd met. She'd been browsing the club stands at the University fresher's event, trying to decide between badminton and the choir. Then she'd heard this voice, so distinctive, enticing enquirers to the drama group. Angie was mesmerised. Acting was her worst nightmare but there was something about Christine's smile, the way she focused on you, the way you felt when you were the centre of her attention. Suddenly Angie knew this was the only club she'd be joining - behind the scenes of course.

Christine, on the other hand, was made for the stage. She had no compunction about taking the leading roles and stripping off just that bit further than the part required. All done with a wicked sense of fun. Everyone wanted to be around her. Christine was a mature student, eight, maybe ten years older, but, amazingly, it was Angie she'd invited to share her flat. They were an unlikely pairing, the shrinking violet with the drama queen, but perhaps it worked because of their differences.

Christine put a hand on Angie's arm. 'Any danger of actually getting inside?'

Angie started. 'Sorry.' She tried her pocket. 'Found it!' She led the way through to the sitting room.

'Wow!' Christine exclaimed. The floor to ceiling windows framed the setting sun throwing a crimson shawl across the sky. 'That's stunning.'

Angie slid the patio door open and stepped on to the balcony. It was almost high tide and the sound of the waves lapping against the shore echoed between the flats. 'Bit different from our view in Camden,' she said. 'So do you still think I've buried myself in the back of beyond?'

'Definitely. But I can see why. Where's that?' Christine pointed at the village opposite, a cluster of tiny cottages facing each other across the narrow streets leading away from the estuary.

'Appledore. Lovely village, full of character. There's a new Bistro, though, so you wouldn't be a total fish out of water.'

Christine smiled. 'I'm not a complete Sloane. I do venture into the provinces occasionally.' She leant on the balcony rail and scanned the river. 'When you said your flat was by the sea I thought… I don't know, Brighton I guess. But this is really something.' She looked over her shoulder. 'It's obviously inspired you. I'm guessing these are yours.' She nodded at a series of framed photographs covering the sitting room walls. 'This one's stunning.' She stood in front of a mirror image of the sunset outside the window. 'Always admired your style. All this,' she swung her arm round the room, 'oozes creativity. You should have gone into interior design. Your stage sets were a masterpiece… What?'

Angie realised she'd been staring. It was Christine's voice. Her distinctive burr was just as captivating as it had always been. It drew you in like an open fire on a winter's night. The BBC agreed. She was a regular on Radio Two's *Late Show*. 'Nothing, it's just, you turning up here, like this. Feels a bit surreal. Sit down, I'll get a drink.' She disappeared into the kitchen. 'I've only got wine,' she called. 'Red okay?'

Angie gripped the edge of the worktop. She'd started binning Christine's occasional postcards from exotic locations and brief Christmas greetings a while back. No point in hanging on to something that wasn't there anymore. Definitely the best plan. And it had worked. But there was no contingency plan for spontaneous visits.

'So how is life in deepest Devon?' Christine called.

'Good. Who wouldn't want to be here? Five minute drive to work along the river - bit different to fighting for a place on the tube and walking along a road wheezing with exhaust fumes.' Angie found space for their glasses on the coffee table. 'Ever think of leaving London?'

'Not found anything, or anyone, worth moving out for yet. Besides just got a fantastic new flat on the river.'

'Oh? Where?'

'Docklands.'

'The East End!'

'When was the last time you got up to town, girl? Whole area is brand spanking new, well, most of it. My apartment's open plan, up into the rafters, two beds. Fantastic views.' Christine smiled. 'Very self indulgent I know.' She raised her glass towards the window. 'Can't compete with that though.'

Angie slipped on to the sofa next to Christine. 'It's my sanctuary at the end of the day. Unless I'm on call. I hate it when work intrudes here.' Hate it? Did she? Well, yes. But she'd never allowed herself to say as much before.

'So where's the fun? Any colleagues you hit the night-life with?' Christine eased her heels off and tucked her feet up beneath her.

'Just Sarah. We've started jogging now and then. Bill, my boss, is okay but must be in his fifties. Reliable, experienced but the public services equivalent of a company man, always on my back telling me what I can and can't do. Can't mostly.'

'So a boring old fart then?'

'Well… yes, actually.' Angie giggled. 'There's a couple of

43

older, sorry, more mature women in the team, dedicated, experienced but we don't have a lot in common, and a social work assistant fresh out of college. She's young, vivacious and usually plugged into her Walkman.' Angie leant forward and topped up their glasses.

'Sounds like I haven't come a moment too soon to rescue you from the sinking sands of social services. The Angie I knew had a wicked sense of humour and passion for... well, everything. Where's it gone? It's not good. Not good at all. I might have to stick around to thaw you out.' She squeezed Angie's hand.

'I don't know. Maybe it was right to change. You can't go on being like we were at Uni. When you're dealing with the stuff my clients are up against, real life crises, everything else seems so superficial. Especially with the kids. There's this boy, Paul...'

'You can't tell me you actually enjoy it?'

Enjoyment wasn't the first word that came to mind. 'It can be satisfying, fulfilling even, when you know you've made a difference.' Angie hugged her knees.

'But?'

'Social services are under-resourced, under-staffed and we get thrown to the dogs every time there's a tragedy.'

'So why the hell are you still there, girl?'

'I sometimes wonder,' Angie said. 'It's the kids I guess. If we all jumped ship what would they do?'

'Hey, come on. Reality check. You don't think you can salvage these kids single-handedly do you? I mean that was okay, admirable even, for an idealistic college graduate but not after three years in the real world.'

Angie watched as Christine sipped her wine. Everything about her was so... smooth. No awkward or hurried movements that spoke of stress or anxiety. It was catching. 'I know. But it doesn't stop you trying.'

'Well, you said this place was your sanctuary so you're going to forget all about them tonight. Don't take this the wrong way, girl, but it's taking its toll. You need this knight in crimson armour to pull you back from the brink.'

'Oh, Chrissy, I have missed you,' Angie met her eyes and smiled. 'But I haven't asked. How are you doing?'

'Oh, I get by. Just signed a two year contract with the BBC, got my new flat and booked a three week break in the Caribbean. It's tough but I guess I'll manage…'

'You poor thing, such terrible hardship.'

Christine scooped up Angie's hand. 'That's more like it. You've spent too long plodding along being super-responsible and forgetting how to live. What you need is a delicious diversion and I'm your girl. Let's go out. Where's the night life round here?'

'Christine, this is North Devon. If you're over twenty, night life is a quiet drink down the pub.'

'Okay. I'll get a take-away and we'll have a girl's night in. Where's the nearest Indian?'

They were sitting side by side on the sofa, empty foil containers swept away into the kitchen and a second bottle of wine open on the coffee table 'Did you get up to see your mother in the spring? I waited for your call but…' Christine shrugged and spread her hands.

'Sorry. Finally dredged up the strength for a visit at Christmas but couldn't face anyone afterwards.'

'Things no better then.'

'Oh, you know. All over me one minute then couldn't give a damn the next. When I was young she used to forget about me. Seriously forget. Left me in a café once, went off with her friends. Does great things for your self-esteem!'

'Just as well I decided to come and see what my neglectful friend has been up to then. Any drama groups?'

'A couple but I haven't got round to joining yet. Was fun though wasn't it? You were amazing in *The Threepenny Opera*. I used to sit in the stalls when you were rehearsing.'

'No kidding.'

'Well it was warmer than backstage, and I could see how

my set was holding up to the rough treatment you thespians dished out.' It was much more than that of course. She'd been mesmerised by Christine's performances, drawn in by her charisma, or something else she hadn't the words for.

Christine stretched out on the sofa, resting her feet in Angie's lap. She was so easy to be with, the impulse to relax into their old ways, sharing confidences, traumas and triumphs was almost irresistible. But too much had happened for her to trust so completely ever again, hadn't it? Angie eased away. 'Got to pack.'

'What for?'

'Going away tomorrow,' Angie called from the bedroom. 'A day later and you'd have missed me.'

'Somewhere fabulously exotic I hope.'

'Not quite how I'd describe Lundy.'

'Where's that? Mediterranean?'

'Bit nearer. Look out the window. Down-river.'

'You're kidding!'

Angie appeared at the bedroom door. 'You can just see the end of the island. Takes a couple of hours from Bideford.'

'What's wrong with you? Sun, sea and sand is what you need, girl. They've got an airport at Exeter haven't they?'

'Lundy suits me fine. You should try it. In fact, why don't you come?' It was Angie's turn to scoop up Christine's hand. 'They do day trips. We could go over together. I'm joining a photography course but I can bunk off. You'd be back by seven. Can stop over here before you head back if you like.' The words were out; Angie couldn't take them back even if she'd wanted to. But she didn't… want to.

'Love to spend the day with you,' Christine looked at her designer heels, 'but I'm not sure I'm equipped for island life. Got to get back too. You know how it is.'

Angie nodded. She did know, very well. But after three years it could have been different couldn't it? 'Well, if you change your mind I'm leaving at eight.'

'Then we'd better turn in,' Christine said, uncoiling herself from the sofa.

Chapter Six

'Amy asleep yet?' Steve said.

Kate looked up from her book. 'No. Just lying there, staring at the ceiling.'

'We should call Angie.'

'Give her time.'

'It's been three weeks. Maybe there's more to it. She had a head injury didn't she?'

'This isn't to do with that.'

'How can you be so sure?'

'I just am,' Kate said, turning a page.

'Well, I think we need to cover our backs.'

'Angie's on holiday.'

'So ring the duty number.'

Kate stared at him. 'And have someone come who doesn't know the first thing about Amy? Another stranger gawping at her is the last thing she needs.' Kate looked out the window. 'It's getting dark.'

'I'll give him until five.' He paused. 'So have you thought any more about it?'

'About what?'

'You know what. Giving up fostering.'

Kate put her book down, a smile on her lips. 'As a matter of fact, I have.'

'What? What is it?' Steve moved to the edge of his seat.

Kate hesitated. 'It's too early really, but I did a test this morning.'

'And?'

'It wasn't clear, only a smudge, but there was something, I'm sure of it.'

Steve wrapped his arms around her. 'Oh, Kate...' His voice wavered. 'I can't believe it. After all this time.'

She gave him a cautionary look. 'Don't get too excited. I shouldn't have said anything. Not until it's confirmed.'

'When?' His eyes lit up with anticipation.

'I'll get a proper test done after Easter.'

'We'll have to let Angie know as soon as she gets back. She'll understand. You need to put yourself first now.' The next few months had been planned in an instant.

'We can cope while you're still off. Did I tell you Amy snuggled up to me yesterday?'

'No.'

'I was rocking her on my lap while we watched Postman Pat. Usually she flops back but this time she half turned and actually cuddled up. And she stroked my cheek with her hand.' She looked at him. 'I know it doesn't sound much, but it's a real breakthrough. The first time I've felt any connection.'

Steve leant over and kissed her. 'I'm not surprised she's responding - with all the love you give.'

She snuggled in to his shoulder. 'Wish I could say the same for Paul.'

'Don't worry about Paul. He's a survivor.'

'But the last thing he needs is the slightest hint of another move.'

He turned her to face him. 'So he won't get one. Not until we know for sure and Angie has found somewhere else. Who knows, the mother might be back on the scene by then.' He smiled. 'And then it will be just you and me,' he placed his hand on her stomach. 'And our baby.'

It was pistols at dawn at the play-park. Two toddlers were having a stand-off at the bottom of the ramp to the pirate ship. They really shouldn't be there, it was meant for older children. Kate scanned the park. A young couple picnicking on the grass, two men meeting on a bench, a boy skateboarding past and, yes, two women gossiping on the far side with their backs to her, to their children.

She looked back to the pirate ship. The blonde-haired angel had planted her red-wellied feet firmly on the bottom of the ramp. Dungaree-boy wobbled to one side and tried to nudge past, his face set with determination. Then nudge turned to push, push to shove, and suddenly both children were tumbling to the ground in a tangle of flailing limbs.

Kate turned back to the women. They were still talking! How could they when she had to clutch at the fence to stop herself rushing in?

Dungaree-boy emerged first, pushing his padded bum aloft and grabbing at the edges of the gangplank. The blonde angel scrambled to her feet and launched a counter-attack, hauling herself up by his trousers; pushing past him with a hand against his ear, a foot on his shoulder. Her final thrust pitched him into the bark-chipping sea.

Kate waited for the inevitable wail. Where were their mothers? She turned in time to see the women shaking hands, striding off down opposite pathways. So who...? But there was no wail. Just burbling chatter coming from an enormous bright yellow pipe and the two men walking across to reclaim the now bosom buddies. Kate turned away. It had to be the hormones flooding her system. Everywhere she went all she could see were children... needing her.

Amy stirred in the pushchair. Kate leant down. 'Hello darling. Would you like to come out?' Amy raised her arms. It was nothing, a simple gesture most mothers wouldn't think twice about. But Kate felt the tears pricking her eyes as she bent to unclip the safety harness and lift Amy into her arms. 'Careful of the baby, darling,' she whispered as Amy swivelled round to tuck herself even closer. Kate automatically placed a protective hand over her stomach. Careful of the baby. Could it be true? And if it was, what then? As if reading her mind, Amy reached a hand up to her cheek and turned her face until their eyes met. Kate couldn't ignore the question they held.

'Angie will find you a wonderful new mummy and daddy, Amy. A family all of your own.' Kate stopped as the picture of herself handing Amy to another woman, another mother, washed over her. 'But it will be different this time,' she reminded herself. 'I'll have my baby to hold as I wave goodbye.'

So why didn't it feel any easier?

'Good break, Angie?' Bill asked, dropping a cluster of manila folders on her desk.

'Brilliant thanks. Took far too many reels of film though. Couldn't help myself, the scenery's so spectacular. I should probably...' The phone rang. 'Yes, Mrs Harris, I know these things are difficult to find but the police... not even when she was younger...? Well if you happen to come across a photo of her at any age... And I'm sure Paul and Amy would like to see you... I know you can't get there on the bus but I'd be more than happy to... well that's your decision of course but... well let me know if you change your mind.' She replaced the phone.

'No joy with the grandmother then?' Bill said.

'You could say that.'

'Or the mother?'

'Completely disappeared. Nothing since they left the hospital.'

'Didn't they have someone watching them? I mean, under the circumstances.'

'Everyone was needed at a cardiac arrest on the next ward. They must have grabbed the opportunity.'

'What about the father?' Bill flicked through the file.

'Can't find anyone with a good word to say about him. Never worked. Well known to the police. Petty thief, not a very good one. Left Sonya to cope with the three kids when the baby was diagnosed with cystic fibrosis. Self sacrifice not his strong point apparently. The nurse at the hospital...' A shout from outside distracted her.

Bill glanced through the door, then closed it. 'Charlie

making his weekly protest about his benefits. Go on,' he said.

'She told me she almost had to get security to throw him out of intensive care a few months back. Came in drunk and started shouting his mouth off.'

'Where is he now?'

'Around but no-one knows exactly where. He's not in the frame for Justin though. He was in custody charged with a break-in at the Off-licence in Mill Street.'

'Paul and Amy have been with us for almost a month so we need to be looking at full care proceedings. What's the news from the Clarke's?' Bill asked.

'Good. Amy's responding, clinging to Kate and howling whenever she goes out of the room.'

'And the paediatric assessment?'

Angie flipped through the increasingly bulky file. 'No sign of any residual damage from the head injury. Dr Martin thinks her problems are emotional. The full report's here.'

'And Paul?'

'I don't know,' she hesitated. In one way the Clarke's are doing a great job. Paul's tantrums and aggression don't worry Steve - he just rides out the storm and carries on. Which is great...' Angie paused.

'But?'

'It's more difficult for Kate. Paul's so defensive about his mother he rejects any attempt to take her place. He's hitting out at Kate.'

'Verbally or physically?'

'Both.' It was the moment conversations like these became serious.

Bill pulled a chair over and sat down. 'She's handled some serious acting-out before hasn't she?'

'Yes. That's where she's always shined, pouring love into these kids until they get the message she'll be there for them whatever.' She searched for the right words. 'But it's different this time. Paul's older and he's got Amy for competition.'

'Meaning?'

'You remember we had the review when they notified us

they were going for IVF.'

'Couple of years back, wasn't it?'

'Yes. And we reviewed things after their first failure but decided they were coping well enough to keep fostering.'

'Too good a resource to lose - what's your point?'

Angie hesitated. She didn't want to rock the boat for Kate and Steve. 'They're still desperate for a baby and Amy fits the bill. She's three but behaving more like three months. So when Kate has a rough time with Paul it's human nature to pour everything into Amy, her baby who needs her and isn't going to reject her.'

'You said Steve was handling Paul, so does it really matter?'

'Maybe not, up to now. Steve's been off work, but Kate rang earlier to say he's back from Monday.'

Bill stood. 'You've got all this recorded?'

'It will be later today - hopefully.'

'Okay.' He looked at his watch. 'We need to make a recommendation for these two. What's your view?'

'How hard would you resist losing the Clarke's?' The solution was staring them in the face but Angie knew what his response would be.

Bill shook his head. 'Not an option. We've precious few foster parents that'll take children in an emergency.'

'But if they can get over the hump with Paul, they could offer them so much. We're forever moving children around - how damaging is that?' Angie was surprised at the passion in her voice.

It floated over Bill. 'How long does it take to recruit foster parents of their calibre? No, we refer Paul and Amy for a long-term placement.'

Kate leant over the cot to check on Amy. 'You've worn yourself out haven't you, darling?' She stroked her cheek, gently brushing strands of tousled hair away from Amy's eyes. 'How could anyone leave you, my beautiful baby?' She paused. In a few months she could be leaning over this cot stroking the cheek of her own beautiful baby…

…*cheeks with a dimple in each one like Steve's. And when she woke (their baby was a girl, Kate was sure of that) she would look at Kate with the most enormous brown eyes and smile because the most important person in the world was there, her mother. Her baby would never have to shut herself away from pain and disappointment behind a lifeless face.*

Kate would watch as the children played in the garden (there would be others, and soon) small bodies rolling around in a tangle of excited shrieks. She would push their beautiful girl backwards and forwards on the swing, touching noses until she squealed with delight. When she was older she would sweep higher and higher, her long dark hair wafting in soft arcs beneath her as she threw her head back.

A rope would hang down from the top of the frame for the boy who was balancing on the rungs of the ladder shouting, 'look at me, look at me'. A real boy, always coming in with scratches and scrapes that needed a plaster and a hug before the next adventure on the high seas.

And no harm would ever come to their beautiful family. She would always be there to look out for them, to keep them safe. She'd insisted that their garden was enclosed and without a pond - definitely no pond. Angie had been impressed she was taking such care but it had always been for the children. Her children…

A car drew up outside. Kate tucked Amy's wayward arm back under the cover and went downstairs.

'Hi, Kate. Thanks for making time for me today.' Angie sat at the kitchen table and pulled some sheets from her briefcase.

'Not a problem - great timing in fact, Amy has worn herself out playing in the sand pit and gone off like a baby.' She picked up the kettle and filled it at the sink.

'Playing - that sounds good.'

'Yes, she really came out of herself over Easter. How was your break by the way?' she said over her shoulder.

'Blissful, thanks.'

'Did you go on your own?'

'Yes and no. I went with a photography group. I go every year for my dose of nature in the raw.' Angie paused. 'But you haven't been far from my thoughts. It sounds as though you're working wonders with Amy. But how's it going with Paul?'

Kate pulled out a chair. 'I... it's difficult to tell.'

'We knew Paul came with his own challenges. It's no reflection on you if his behaviour's getting you down.' Angie waited for Kate to fill the silence.

'It's not his fault, I know that... he tries, in his way, but it's like he's built this barrier and I can't get through to him. Anything I try he hits out at me.'

'In what way?' Angie kept her voice even, her body gently leaning towards Kate.

'Mostly a string of abuse, but if I try to touch him he... he lashes out.' Her voice shook.

Angie rested a hand on Kate's arm. 'You know it's not personal don't you. He's convinced he has to repel all comers to survive.'

'I know that... in theory.'

'But it's tough when you're on the receiving end.' Foster parents were trained, Angie had led the courses, but nothing fully prepared them for the constant rejection. The sense of failure could be overwhelming.

'Yes,' Kate said, her voice flat.'

'For what it's worth, he's just the same at school.'

'I know. They call whenever he's been in trouble so I know what to expect, suggesting ways of handling him, but...'

'It's not enough.' Angie hesitated. 'I've referred Paul for a psychological assessment.'

'How long will that take?'

'Waiting list is about three months.'

'Three months!' Kate's face said it all.

'I'll do what I can to speed it up,' Angie said.

'Thanks,' Kate said, but the word was empty. A window of hope had opened and closed within seconds.

'Looks like someone's appreciating your efforts.' Angie nodded at an enormous bunch of roses on the table.

'Steve,' Kate said, a smile returning to her face.

'Special occasion?'

Kate blushed and laid a hand on her stomach. 'Kind of.'

Chapter Seven

Steve watched as Kate listened, his second cup of coffee halfway to his mouth. After three days of waiting the call had come, as promised, at exactly 8.30am. Her face betrayed nothing. Seconds later she replaced the receiver.

'Tell me,' he said as the silence lengthened. 'Kate... tell me.'

'We... we can try again,' she whispered.

He turned and leant against the sink, staring across the garden to Paul's sanctuary in the woods. 'No... we agreed. This was the last time.'

'I know,' she moved across and placed her hands on his shoulders. 'But I could face just one more try.'

'Well, I can't.' He pulled himself free. 'I'm going to work.'

'Steve, please, at least let's...' the door slammed behind him, '...talk.'

Amy was having her afternoon nap when the phone rang.

'Have you heard?' It was Tilly, Kate's sister.

'Yes. And it's no,' Kate just about managed before her throat closed up.

'I'm coming round.'

'No,' Kate swallowed. 'Thanks, but no. Not yet anyway.'

'You need someone.'

'Don't you think I know that? But not you.'

'But I know how awful you must be feeling,' Tilly said.

'You've two beautiful children. How can you possibly know?' Kate spat the words down the phone. 'Just now I saw a pregnant woman walking along the street. I wanted to scream at her, 'Why you? Why not me?'

'I'm sorry, Kate, it was a crass thing to say.' Tilly left space for Kate's reassuring murmur. It didn't come. 'How's Steve?'

'We haven't talked but,' the misery closed in again, 'I don't think he'll try again.'

'I'm so sorry, Kate.' The silence lengthened. 'Listen, you need some time out. Why don't you go somewhere nice? Forget all about it, even if it's only for an evening.'

'Forget! Forget that some sadist has pointed the finger and said that's the one, the one that's not fit to be a parent!' Kate slammed the phone down.

Tilly felt sick. 'Kate...? Kate...are you there?' Of course she wasn't there. The phone was buzzing like a demented bee. Tilly blinked quickly, suppressing the inevitable tears. A stray cat was making an illegal entry through the cat flap. Her son's water pistol was just within reach. This time she'd get the ginger bastard.

'Tilly, where have the curtain brackets gone?' Jeff, Tilly's husband, stuck his head round the kitchen door. The cat froze with one paw lightly touching the terracotta tiled floor.

'I don't know. I haven't seen them. That was Kate. She's in a terrible state.'

'They were in the storage chest last time I saw them but they've been moved.'

The cat stealthily retracted its paw and slid back out. She'd get him next time. 'Maybe you put them in the shed,' Tilly said.

'Why would I do that when I need them in here?'

'I'll have a look round.' She was already on her feet.

'Don't bother, I'll find them myself.' He disappeared.

Tilly slumped into her chair. She shouldn't let Kate get to her. It wasn't her fault she got pregnant so easily, that real life had turned out so different from the games they used to play. Kate was always the one pushing her along in their old pram, taking her to the shops, sitting her down to go through her homework. Kate the mother, Tilly the child. Always.

The kitchen door swung open. 'No joy with the IVF then?' Jeff asked as he put the brackets on the worktop and reached for the kettle.

Till shook her head. 'I knew she was investing far too much in that clinic. She's been round all the nurseries in the area, even reserved a place at Tennyson Road.'

'That was jumping the gun a bit wasn't it?'

'She's in a terrible state. Do you think I should go?' Tilly absent-mindedly flicked the water pistol, spraying water over the kitchen.

'Did she ask you to?'

'Not exactly. Perhaps I should call her back. Do you think I should call her back?' An answer wasn't required. 'She's beside herself. She shouldn't be left alone like that. I think maybe I should go. Steve thinks she needs help.'

'When did he say that?'

'He called in.' She stared at her husband's back as he busied himself making a pot of tea. There was a trail of water running down his jumper from the water pistol. 'Didn't I tell you? Poor guy needed a sympathetic ear. Kate can't see past herself at the minute. I know she's my sister but I feel sorry for him.' Tilly paused to catch her breath. 'I don't think it's even occurred to her that he might need to talk. He's in a bad way, Jeff. You should call him.'

Jeff leant against the kitchen worktop, blowing his mug of tea. 'What can I do?'

Tilly pulled a half-upholstered chair towards her and began to tug the fabric tighter across the seat. 'Take him down the pub or something, give him a chance to let off steam. I've told him it's open house here anyway.' She grunted as she released the temporary tacks and gained another half inch. Tension was everything for a good finish. 'I told her they should get away for a weekend, have some fun, but she bit my head off.'

'Well, I'll put the kids to bed if you want to go.' He checked his watch. 'Are you getting George?'

'George!' she pushed the chair away. 'Oh, God. Where are my keys?'

The hand clutching the edge of the table was shaking. Kate supposed it was hers but it looked strange, remote. She glanced around the room, vaguely aware of the need to find somewhere safe to land as she sank to the floor. Everything was in slow motion replay. Frame after frame of the last few hours filled her mind until any illusion of completeness finally collapsed into the void that had been growing within her ever since the clinic condemned her with one word; negative.

She looked at Steve's flowers, remembering their overwhelming scent, the vibrant colours. But now, their colour had bleached away. Was everything like that? She looked past the vase to the garden - their safe, child-friendly garden. Suddenly she was on her feet, stumbling through the back door and across the paving to the shed. The tools were stacked against the wall. She picked a spade at random and walked to the centre of the lawn. The blade hovered in the air for a second then thudded down again and again shredding the turf. The loamy top soil shifted easily as she dug into it, accumulating in untidy piles around the growing hole. Messages from her strained muscles were blocked as she drove herself on, heaving the sub-soil up and out, dismantling her dreams shovelful by shovelful. There was even a downpour to fill the hole, a sadistic, satisfied, seal of approval on her vandalism. She fell back onto the grass, gasping.

'What you doing?' Paul stopped in his tracks as he rounded the corner of the house.

'Take your school things off,' she said without turning.

'It's wet.'

'Don't you think I know that!' she snapped.

'So what you doing?'

'It's none of your business. Go inside.'

Paul flung his school bag down and ran out to stand beside her. He stared at the muddy hole. 'Cool, a pond. You got fish? I always wanted fish but I wan't allowed…'

…his fish were all colours, like the ones you see at the pet shop. And there were Piranhas all round the edge. Everyone came to see but he was the only one they'd let close, and his mum. They'd grab the others, tear bits

58

off and eat them. And they'd all know his pond was the biggest, most dangerous of all. Only it wasn't a pond, it was bigger than a swimming pool, deeper than the bit where your feet don't touch. And down there, deep down, there was a secret entrance to an underwater world. You said a special password and this metal grill opened up and let you through. And on the other side was a world where you only had to think a thing and it came true.

There were bags of sweets that never got empty and transformers that never got broke and...'

'...*children,*' Kate whispered. '*Children playing make-believe games and laughing so loud they can be heard all the way upstairs where their mother's rocking the baby to sleep, feeling her soft warmth, all snuggled up, so peaceful, so contented. Knowing that all's well with the world because ...'*

'...*mum's there,*' Paul said, kneeling close to her. '*Getting the most enormous tea. And everyone's eating and eating and never getting full. And it's never time for bed 'cause no-one ever gets tired. They're all super human, so strong nothing ever hurts. And if they get scratches and cuts and burns and breakings they say the magic word and...'*

'...*mum says the magic word, that's what mum's do. Make it better.'*

'...*mum says the magic word and cranky arms and legs go all straight again so you can climb trees and get wings and take off and go up and up...*' Paul rested his head on Kate's shoulder.

'...until you get to this magic faraway land only it's different each time you go. What land is there today, Paul?'

'Dunno.'

'What land would you like it to be?' Kate said, putting her arm around him.

'Transformer land.'

'What does transformer land look like?'

'It's like... the caravan gets all creaky and bendy like this,' he made a wavy motion with his hands, 'and gets bigger and shinier, like a pop stars. And the toast on my plate shivers and oozes and the honey runs and runs. And Amy's hair goes short and her dresses change to trousers and she's a boy, my brother, and he plays football with me. And my dad's the referee 'cause he plays for Spurs.'

'I dream of the people who should be here too,' Kate said. 'In my transformer land the rocks in this garden start to soften and move and play and giggle and shout because they're all my children. And I'm their mum.'

Paul pushed her away. 'That ain't right. You got to make transformer land different. You got your land. You got me and Amy.' He leapt to his feet, ran towards the house then turned. 'No. No, you ain't, 'cause you're not our mum.'

Kate watched as Steve reached for the remote and sealed himself off in a virtual world. She gathered up the empty coffee cups, walked towards the kitchen then paused. 'We can't go on like this,' she said over her shoulder.

'Like what?' he said, still staring at the screen.

'Not talking.'

He threw the remote down and turned towards her. 'So what do you suggest, Kate? We can't be together for more than five minutes without getting stuck in the same miserable loop. I'm sick of it.'

'And I'm not?'

Their needs collided in the silence. 'What's that all about?' Steve pointed at the mud-bath on the lawn.

'I'd have thought it was obvious.' It was blindingly obvious to her. Couldn't he see her desperation? Why couldn't he just hold her, comfort her? Why couldn't they share the pain instead of sniping at each other?

Steve pushed himself out of the chair and grasped her by each arm.

'This has to stop, Kate. It stops now or we're...'

'We're what?'

He tightened his grip. 'You don't have a monopoly on pain. It's time you got out of your head and opened your eyes to how I might be feeling. I'm sick to death of being sidelined. I'm going out.' He grabbed his jacket and slammed the door behind him.

'That's right, run away why don't you. I wish I could.' The

tears welled up again. She got on her hands and knees to retrieve the tissue box from under the coffee table. The door opened behind her.

'I'm sorry, Steve I shouldn't have said…'

'Sorry if I startled you, Kate. Steve let me in. Is this a bad time?' Tilly hovered in the doorway clutching her son's hand. 'Only you sounded so unhappy on the phone I had to come over. I had to pick George up anyway…' Her voice tailed off. One look at Kate's face was enough. She simply hadn't thought. George needed collecting; Kate's was on her way. It never occurred to her that bringing George wouldn't be such a good idea.

'George,' Tilly steered her son in the direction of the kitchen. 'Go and get yourself a drink and watch TV for a bit. Aunt Kate and I are going to have a chat.'

Kate stared at her. 'Well done, Tilly. Full marks for sensitivity.' Her voice was harsh.

'I'm sorry, I didn't think.' Tilly hovered in the middle of the room, stranded between her good intentions and her sister's sarcasm.

'Why doesn't that surprise me?' Kate pointed at a chair. 'Well don't just stand there. Now you're here you may as well sit down. Where's Jeff?'

Tilly clutched at the olive branch. 'I've finally managed to get him doing some DIY. The upstairs has been in a state for ages. It's taken some serious nagging to get him working on it. Other than that, we've just been doing family stuff really.' Tilly saw Kate flinch. Both feet straight in… again. 'I'm sure it'd help, to talk. Did the clinic suggest anything? A counsellor or someone?'

Kate stared out the window. 'What good will talking do?'

'Might stop you tearing each other apart for a start.' Tilly blushed. She didn't usually find the courage to speak so directly. She stared at the carpet, bracing herself for the inevitable backlash. When it didn't come, she looked up to find tears silently streaming down her sister's face.

'I think I've already done it,' Kate whispered.

'Oh, Kate.' Tilly crouched by her sister. 'I'm sure you haven't. Steve loves you. He's feeling as bad about this as you are. Can't you see that?'

'Apparently not,' Kate snapped. 'Apparently I'm completely insensitive to how anyone else might be feeling. The fact that I haven't been able to get him to talk to me is completely irrelevant. The fact he refuses to see how desperate all this is making me doesn't matter.'

'So how does he feel?'

'He wants to give up. Not try any more. That's how little it means to him.'

Tilly put a tentative hand on Kate's arm. 'Are you sure about that?'

'He's seen me crying my heart out and hasn't shed a single tear. Hasn't once put his arms round me and comforted me. Not once.'

'Have you tried putting your arms round him?'

Kate pulled away. 'He's not the one falling apart, is he?'

'Is that what you think?' Steve was standing in the doorway. 'Just because I don't shout and scream or vandalise the lawn doesn't mean all this isn't tearing me apart.'

'How long have you been there?' Kate said.

'Long enough to know that you should listen to your sister once in a while instead of giving her such a hard time.'

Kate stood up. 'Thanks very much. Just what I need. All the family I do have queuing up to tell me what a lousy human being I am.'

'Stop it, Kate. Just stop,' Steve snapped.

'Maybe I should be going,' Tilly levered herself up from the floor, rubbing her cramped calf.

'Yes,' Kate said, holding out her sister's coat. 'Must be time for you to be getting back. Family things to sort and all that.'

'Ring me anytime. Anytime. I'll see myself out.'

'I'm here now,' Steve said. 'So let's talk.'

Kate slumped into a chair. 'So how are you?' she asked.

'Worn out. And you?'

What could she say? That she felt murderous? That she wanted to ban every pregnant woman and new mother from the streets? That she felt a lesser human being? That she hated herself far more than he ever could? 'I.... I... You said you wouldn't try IVF again. Did you mean it?'

'Can you go through this again, Kate? Honestly?' The words were soft but detached; defeated? 'All the hope, the planning, only to be devastated. I know I can't.' He sighed. 'I love kids, wanted them more than anything, but this is no life.'

Kate stared at the rain creating jagged rivulets down the window. 'Why us? It's so unfair.'

'I don't know.' He put his head in his hands, sighed, then looked up. 'But the sooner we accept it, the sooner we can get out of this pit and start living again. It won't be the life we planned... but who knows what's round the corner.'

'I can't let it go, Steve. It means too much,' she sobbed, wanting so much to reach across the space that separated them, to seek comfort in his arms.

He shook his head. 'Then I think Tilly was right. We get help. Because you need it, Kate, believe me. The clinic offered counselling. I say we do it.'

'What's the point?' she snapped. 'I don't want to be brainwashed into being satisfied with being childless.'

'We don't have to be.'

'What?'

'Childless.'

Kate looked at him, her face contorted by a cocktail of anger and grief. 'So what miracle do you have in mind? I've spent seven years miserably failing to get pregnant.'

'For Christ's sake, Kate!' He paced back and forth in front of the window. 'I know you're angry, but I'm tired of being the one to hold things together.' He turned to face her. 'Make your choice. You give the vitriol a rest and we find a way forward or you get help. Your depression is draining me dry. I can't take anymore.'

If he'd walked away she could have justified her usual

retort, allowed the familiar, almost comforting, despair to sweep over her. But he didn't. He just stood in front of her, his eyes brimming with tears, pleading with her to see it his way.

'I'm sorry. I'm so, so sorry.' She reached out and pulled him towards her, feeling his tears on her neck, his arms holding on to her - his need not hers. Deep inside she knew; knew she had to let go of the bitterness, of the anger, of everything that was destroying her, destroying them. 'What did you mean?' she sniffed. 'About not having to be without children.'

He took her face in his hands. 'I love you, Kate. And I would have loved our children. It's the biggest sadness of my life it hasn't happened, that it isn't going to happen. But it doesn't have to be the end of everything. We can still be parents, to Amy and Paul.'

Chapter Eight

'Okay, listen. If you're coming you got to be dead quiet. No stupid barking or any of that stuff. Right?' Paul wagged his finger at the mongrel. 'And this is top secret so no blabbing to the dalmatian next door. Get it?' The dog spun in a circle, planted his paws on Paul's chest and licked his face. 'Okay, okay,' Paul giggled, 'that's enough.' He pulled some string from his pocket and threaded it through the dog's collar. 'Wait,' he commanded, and crawled to the door of the camp. 'All clear.'

Boy and dog burst through the jagged opening and ran through the undergrowth. Hoarded coins jangled in his pockets as Paul dodged brambles and leapt over fallen branches. They broke cover at the edge of the wood and sprinted along the grass swathe fringing the field, safer than the roads where the enemy could catch him. He had to join the lane at the edge of the village though. Slow down. Act ordinary. Just getting stuff from the shop. That's the story.

Then he was there, at the bus stop. Bideford would be easy. He'd been with Kate. And the woman in the shop told him the time.

No-one waited with him. That was good. No-one to see him. No, not good. Where were the people? Had the bus gone? He shifted from foot to foot, looked up the hill. What side did it come on? Should he stand by the church? Or stay outside the shop? Who could he ask?

When the double-decker finally arrived Paul rushed forward in relief. Seconds later he'd claimed a seat at the front upstairs, where he could see everything, just like the driver...

...everyone would look at him driving his silver Aston Martin, just like James Bond. It was so powerful all the other cars looked like they were going backwards. And he used it whenever he wanted to go and see his mum and she would come with him, sitting next to him with a scarf over her long hair so it didn't fly up and get stuck in her eyes. And she'd say, 'let's go to London today... no, Australia'. So they'd drive to Australia and see the kangaroos. They were cool. Real karate kick-boxers. He'd seen it on TV. Kangaroos kicking each other and all the people running away, only they couldn't run as fast as the kangaroos could bound so they got caught and splattered face down on the ground. Only they wouldn't catch him in his Aston Martin 'cause that was faster than a space shuttle. No-one would ever catch him again.

Getting off was easy. It was when the bus reached the river, that's how he knew. And he had to wait on the same side for the next bus, the really long one the lady in the shop had said. It was okay asking her. He'd said Kate wanted to know only she couldn't come 'cause Amy was crying. Amy was always crying now. That's 'cause she was missing their mum too. So he had to find her, so Amy would stop crying.

He watched the buses come and go. They all looked just as long as each other to him. But the clue was on the front, on the bit that said the town they were going to. That's all he had to do, read the towns, until he saw the right one. And that was okay. He was a good reader. Mostly. Even though his teacher said he thought in pictures. Didn't everybody?

A girl in a red cardigan and cut-off jeans and an old woman with a shopping trolley were waiting at the bus stop. Paul moved a few yards away and leant against the wall separating the road from the quayside. He could just see a massive crane lifting stuff from a lorry onto a ship. It had giant doors all folded up on themselves sticking up above the deck. He wanted to watch, but it was too far away, he wouldn't be able to read the towns on the bus.

'Come here, boy,' Paul called to Spider. The mongrel had wandered over to the girl in the red cardigan, his eyes fixed on the biscuit in her hand

'Would you like this?' The girl's voice was weird, all high and sing-songy. Spider barked and jogged her hand with his paw. 'There you go then.' She held it out to him then looked at Paul. 'Waiting for a bus?'

'Yea.'

'Which one?'

Paul stared at her. She didn't look like someone who'd blab. 'Plymouth. The Barbie Can.'

The girl smiled. 'That's long way for a youngster.'

'I ain't young. I'm... I'm twelve.'

'You meeting someone?'

'My mum. At our new house.'

'Well twelve or not, you're too young to be fending for yourself. I'm going to Plymouth. You stick with...' Her voice was drowned out by the arrival of a single-decker bus.

Paul rushed to the front. This was it!

'Where to?' the driver asked.

'The Barbie Can,' Paul said.

The driver stared at the girl. 'He with you?' She nodded. 'Does he mean Plymouth?' She nodded again.

'The Barbie Can in Plymouth,' Paul hissed, piling coins into the tray. The machine whirred.

'Take it then.' The driver pointed at the ticket, 'and keep that dog under control or you'll be off at the next stop.'

Paul hauled Spider to the back of the bus and pushed him under his legs. 'Stay. You gotta be good.'

His mum had always talked about the Barbie Can in Plymouth. It was a stupid girlie name but she said their perfect house was right next to the best fish and chip shop in the world so that was all right. And it was by the water with loads of boats and it was her second home.

The bus headed inland away from the sea. Paul knelt up on his seat. 'This ain't right.' He ran to the front of the bus. 'I gotta go to the Barbie Can by the sea.'

'Get back on that seat,' the driver shouted. 'Or the only place you'll be going is the hospital.'

'I gotta go to the Barbie Can,' Paul insisted.

'That's where I'm taking you so sit down,' he said.

Paul staggered up the aisle, back to his seat next to the girl.

'Here,' she held out another biscuit. 'This one's for you.'

'Wake up. Hey, wake up.' The sing-songy voice was close to Paul's ear and the girl was shaking his arm. 'Time to get off.'

Paul sat up. The driver was leaning round the screen looking at him. 'Are you getting off or not?'

'Come on, boy.' Paul pulled Spider between the seats.

'Hang on a minute. What's your name?' The girl asked.

'Paul.'

'Paul what?'

Silence.

'Tell your mum… tell her to look out for you. And the Barbican's that way.' She pointed down a road opposite the stop. 'You take care.'

It was cold. Paul pulled his jacket closer; the denim was tight and torn under the arms but it was his favourite. His mum bought it.

He followed the rough pavement in the direction the girl had pointed. People pushed past him, walking so fast they had to know where they were going. Paul wound a little more string round his hand and crouched down to hug Spider. 'It's okay, we're going down this road and the house'll be right there. It will. And mum'll be waiting for us, and when she sees us she'll come running out of the shiny red front door. Only I'll have to tell her you're with me 'cause she won't know will she? Come on boy.'

'Look Spider - the sea,' Paul exclaimed. He ran to the edge of the quay. Away to his left the narrow channel opened out, exposing a wider stretch of water with boats moored either side. Paul scanned the houses for a fish and chip shop and the red door. He knelt down and released the string. 'Can you smell it boy? Go on, find it.' Spider bounded away, stopped, changed direction and burst through a gang of boys playing football in the open space at the head of the quay. He scooped up their ball with his nose and tossed it towards Paul.

'Hey, give that back.' The boy who shouted was older, like the bully at school who'd taken his football cards. Paul kicked the ball back towards the group - or would have done if Spider hadn't leapt in, forced it to the ground and dribbled it past three of the gang before being pounced on.

'Did you see that? Give it back to him,' the boy shouted. 'See if he can score.'

Spider was enjoying his celebrity, pausing every now and then to scan the growing crowd before weaving though the boys' legs to return the ball to Paul.

'Is he yours?' the older boy asked.

'Yeah,' Paul said.

'Cool. Wanna play?' The boy handed Paul the ball.

He threw himself into the game. From time to time the action would suddenly stop, when Spider discovered a new trick or someone kicked the ball into the water and they had to find a way to retrieve it, but otherwise it was fast and furious - until they hit an elderly woman sitting on the bench.

The gang scattered.

'Here, you, what do you think you're playing at?' The voice came from behind. Paul turned to see a policeman bearing down on him. 'See what you lot have done.' He pointed at the woman. 'Miracle she's not hurt. What's your name?'

'Pa... Paul,' he stuttered.

'Paul what?'

'Paul Wells.'

'Address?'

This wasn't right; they mustn't know. He yanked Spider away and ran, and ran. Round corners, down alleys, over roads, until he fell against a wall, his chest heaving. It was so painful he could hardly breathe. But he was alone. The policeman had given up. 'It's okay, boy,' he said, holding Spider close. 'Don't be scared. It'll be okay, honest.' He wiped his nose on his sleeve. 'Blimey!' He definitely wasn't alone. Figures, hundreds of them, slowly came into focus. 'Blimey!' He looked up until his head was thrown back so far it made him dizzy. 'Look, Spider, look at it.' A mural filled the entire end wall of the building opposite. Paul scanned the massive picture from side to side. 'It's... it's cool. All those people. Look, look here.... That's gotta be a tramp.' He pointed at another lifelike face. 'And that's Tucker.' He moved up close. 'He don't make no sense like this, but back here,' he walked back to Spider, 'you see the people. That's real cool.'

Paul sat, his arm draped over the dog. 'Who do you know, boy? Eh? How about that old woman up there... no, no, look down here,' he pointed to the bottom corner where a mongrel was looking between someone's legs. 'See, your mates are here!' He traced a line of strange dark figures, his eyes following them as they lunged towards the centre of the picture until.... 'It's her, Spider,' he whispered. 'It's my mum.'

'Fuckin' DHSS. What do they fuckin' well think I want the money for? Fuckin' caviar?' A bearded man leant against the wall and took a swig from a bottle partially obscured by a plastic supermarket carrier.

Paul pulled Spider back into a doorway.

A gate opened. 'Hello, Sally darling,' the man said, 'room for one more tonight?'

'Sober up, Archie. He's not too good today. Don't give him a hard time.' The woman pushed the gate open to let the tramp through, leant against the archway and lit a cigarette. She had long auburn hair parted to one side, falling over her face, just like his mum.

'I'm gonna ask her,' Paul whispered. 'Stay.' He sidled up to the woman. 'Is there a fish and chip shop here?' he asked.

The woman pointed to the end of the alley. 'Sure, up there on your right.'

Paul didn't move.

'You all right?' she said.

'Is my mum here?' He could see it, the red door, just behind the woman. This had to be the place.

'I don't think so. What does she look like?'

'Like that.' Paul ran back up the alley and pointed at the centre of the mural. 'That's my mum.'

The woman followed him. 'She's very pretty.'

'And she's waiting for me, only I don't know where, but she said it was by the fish and chip shop and a red door, and you got a red door and that's her.'

'What's your name?'

'Paul.'

She stared at him. 'On your own are you?'

'No.' He turned. 'Here, boy.' Spider obliged. 'I got my dog.'

'Are you hungry?' Paul nodded. 'And cold I should think. Listen, I don't know where your mum is but you can come in for a bit and we'll try and find out.'

He picked up the string and dragged Spider through the red door into a gloomy space. As his eyes adjusted, huge figures reared up out of the darkness. A group of people, just like his teachers, all looking over each others' shoulders and pointing at something - at him. It was like they were standing there - only they weren't. They were a picture - a massive picture. Paul stared at the faces. Voices filled his head. He shivered.

'Do you want this?' Sally asked, holding out a sandwich.

Paul took it.

'You can come through but be quiet, Robert's painting.'

Paul followed Sally into a cavern of a room with even more faces staring at him from the walls. And people sitting at the other end and…. she was there! Sat on a chair in front of an enormous mirror, with her back to him, wearing this gorgeous red dress with her hair hanging down the back in one of those plait things she'd tried to teach him to do. 'Mum,' he called, running across the wooden floor.

'Not so fast,' Sally caught him. 'Do you call that quiet?'

'It's my mum.'

'No, it's not. That's Justine. And you'll be out of here so fast you won't know what's hit you if you don't shut up. Now sit.' Sally took Spider's string and pointed Paul at a chair.

It was his mum. It had to be. But why hadn't she turned?

Why wasn't she rushing over saying, 'Paul, Hey - missed you.' Why was she just sitting there, all still, like she hadn't heard him? He slid off the chair and walked closer to the painter, a man with silvery-brown hair hanging down his back, leaving bits on his black jacket. Then closer still. If he stood in the right place his mum would be able to see him in the mirror. Then she'd smile at him. Let him know it was all right and that they'd be going home soon.

The woman didn't smile. 'You've got an audience,' she said to the man.

Paul had felt this horrible nothingness before. It was like everything had been taken away leaving a hole big enough to swallow him up. He turned away.

'No, don't move. What's your name?' the man asked, looking at Paul through the mirror.

'Paul.'

'Hi, Paul. I'm Robert, Robert Lenkiewicz.'

'That's a weird name.'

Lenkiewicz smiled. 'Suits me then.' He paused. 'I'd like to put you in my picture, Paul. Okay?'

Paul shrugged his shoulders.

'It means you'll have to stay still and quiet. Most boys I know can't do that.'

'I can. I'm good at being quiet.'

'Okay.' The man pressed some colour out of a tube and turned back to the canvas.

It wasn't a problem, standing still. Paul followed every brush stroke, looking from the woman sitting there, to the woman in the picture. They were both alive. He was sure of it. Her eyes did the same thing to him whichever ones he looked at. How did the man do it? How did he make her so real just with blobs of paint? And messy ones too. The paint was all mixed up on the wooden thing he held - all the colours running into each other. Lots of red and orange and pink making a bow on the back of her dress he could've reached out and untied.

'Did you do them people?' Paul pointed to the entrance.

Lenkiewicz turned briefly. 'Yes.'

'Don't like them.'

'Why's that?'

Paul thought. 'Cause they're like robots.'

Lenkiewicz laughed. 'Ha! You've got eyes. They're the goodly people at County Hall who decide what you'll learn and the people who try to teach it to you.'

'They don't.'

'Don't what?'

'Teach me. They don't see me right.' He pointed at himself.

'How should they see you?'

'Like I'm different.'

'How different?'

Paul stretched his arms wide. 'This different.'

'And what makes you different?'

'Nothin'. I just am.'

Lenkiewicz pointed his paint brush at Paul. 'Do you think that's a good answer?'

Paul fidgeted in his seat. 'Dunno.'

'Try again. You think you're this...' Lenkiewicz stretched his arms wide, 'different. I want to know what makes you different. And I'm listening. I bet your teachers don't.'

Paul screwed up his forehead. 'It's like they tell me stuff and I can see it. Like we was talking about Romans and I could see all these footprints making this wall. Only he told me I was stupid, the wall was made of stone and they laughed.'

'So will you tell them what you see another time?'

'Nah.'

'We have to keep some things hidden, Paul.' He paused. 'Who does understand what you see? Your English teacher?'

'She puts red lines through my writing.'

Lenkiewicz smiled. 'You remember you're different, special. What do you like to do, at your house?'

Paul dropped off the stool and hugged Spider. 'I ain't got a house.'

'Oh? What do you have?'

'Me and mum've got a caravan. Only they took me away so

73

now mum won't find me so I got to tell her.'

'You think your mum is here?'

'I saw her, on the wall.'

'Maybe she is, but that doesn't mean she's here now. You should go home.' He half turned. 'But come again and we'll do some more.' He pointed at Paul's outline on the canvas.

'It ain't my home. I ain't staying with them,' Paul said. But the man was painting again.

Sally beckoned him.

Paul pushed Spider under the seat and sat down. There were hundreds of pictures fighting for space on the walls. Mostly of people; tramps, ladies with no clothes on - he stared at those for ages. There were kids too. None like him though. He was different. And that was okay.

'Did he do all of them?' Paul whispered to Sally.

She nodded.

'And he's doing me,' he said pointing at the canvas.

'Yes.'

'I mean, really doing me.' He paused, watching the artist's movements. 'I want to. How can I do it?'

'Not many people *can* do it. Robert's special.'

Paul smiled. 'I'm special too. He said so.'

Chapter Nine

Angie waited until Garfield had curled up on her lap then flicked through the TV channels. Columbo should be on. She checked the Radio Times again. Saturday June 3rd, BBC One, 20.15, Columbo. But the screen said otherwise. Blurred images of crowds, soldiers and tanks were being played and replayed. She turned the volume up. *Several hundred civilians have been shot dead by the Chinese army during a bloody military operation to crush a democratic protest in Beijing's Tiananmen Square.*

'No!' Angie exclaimed.

Tanks rumbled through the capital's streets late this afternoon as the army moved into the square from several directions, randomly firing on unarmed protesters. The injured were rushed to hospital on bicycle rickshaws by frantic residents shocked by the army's sudden and extreme response to the peaceful mass protest.

How could she have missed it? Seven weeks they'd been protesting. The coverage switched to earlier in the day, to an ominous line of tanks entering the square. Then suddenly the cameras focused on a lone figure on the tarmac. He was simply dressed in a white shirt and black trousers and holding a bag in each hand; he could have been on a shopping trip. Only this was anything but. The tanks moved from side to side, attempting to pass, but each time he stepped in front, waving them back. Angie realised she was holding her breath.

The phone rang. Garfield arched his back and jumped down. 'Duty social worker,' she said automatically.

'I'm curled up with a full glass and an empty sofa. When are you coming to see me?'

'Christine,' Angie exclaimed. 'It's great to hear from you. How's things?'

'Oh, in a bit of a lull just now but good... yep mostly good. How about you?'

'Seems irrelevant now. Have you heard about China?'

'Caught something lunchtime. Awful, absolutely awful.' She paused. 'But what's your news?'

'Well,' Angie muted the TV. 'You got me thinking about joining something again. A local drama group are doing Bennett's *Habeas Corpus*. Do you remember when we did it? You were hysterical as Felicity Rumpers.'

'Remember? My finest hour, darling!'

Angie laughed. 'The guy playing the doctor certainly enjoyed himself, all that breast fondling.'

'Oh God, don't remind me... Seriously, don't remind me.' There was a brief silence while the image was banished. 'What else is happening?'

'Nothing madly exciting.' Angie thought. 'I'm still jogging. Do you remember the old railway track that runs past the flat, the Tarka Trail?'

'Between you and the river?'

'That's it. Since the weather's got better I've been doing a mile or so after work, as long as I'm not too knackered.'

'How is the sweat factory?'

'Christine!' Angie exclaimed. 'My professional life is fine.'

'Really?'

'Yes... apart from the usual frustrations. Two new referrals needed immediate visits, a mental health case blew up at lunchtime then I got hauled over the coals because my records weren't up to date. But apart from that...'

'All that stress isn't good. You must be due sick leave.'

'It's not that kind of job, Chrissy. People hang on to their crises. Take a few days off and it's all there waiting for you when you get back. Could manage a long weekend though. Fit in a visit to mum.'

'How is the Gorgon?'

Angie smiled. 'Sharp as ever. Not so mobile though. Her

heart's causing problems.'

'That sorts it. Plan a dutiful daughter visit then spend the weekend here. We could take in a show. Seen *Miss Saigon*?'

'No, haven't been to anything for a while.'

'Not good, Angie. All work and no play…'

'I know. Takes you to… God, I've got to go. Just remembered I'm on call. They might be trying to get through.'

'Who?'

'Police usually. Listen, I'll call. Soon.'

The phone rang almost instantly. 'Yes, I'm aware of him… when? No sign of him since?… He's a runner… predictable… have you tried the caravan site?… The grandmother…?'

The Sergeant didn't waste words. Paul had been reported missing at 7.45pm after not arriving home from a planned visit to a friend's. Turned out he hadn't been at school either.

'Okay. Keep me informed.' She replaced the receiver.

Duty Log

20.15pm	Call from foster mother. Child still missing.
21.05pm	Call from foster mother. Child still missing.
21.10pm	Call to Desk Sergeant. No reports of child.
21.30pm	Call from foster mother. Very anxious.

'He's got to have found shelter, Kate,' Angie said. 'The police would have picked him up otherwise.'

'But where? He's never been gone this long. Steve's been through the woods, back to the caravan site, everywhere we can think of, but he's vanished.'

Angie had never heard Kate so on edge. 'Try not to worry…'

'Not worry! He's nine years old. How can he possibly fend for himself?'

Angie kept her voice steady. 'You'd be surprised. He's very self-sufficient in his own way - you know that.'

Kate paused. 'Maybe. It's just that… it's a bit much on top of everything.'

'Oh?'

'We've had a … disappointment.'

'Anything you want to talk about?'

'I… we… there was a possibility I was pregnant - only it turned out, well, I'm not.'

'I'm so sorry, Kate, you must be feeling terrible.' Angie knew how much of an understatement it was. 'So all this worry over Paul, it's the last thing you need.'

'That sounds selfish, when he's out there, on his own.'

'We both know that's not how it is. When Paul's back we'll talk some more, but you need to get some sleep now. I'm on duty tonight. The police will ring as soon as there's anything.'

'And you'll call, straight away?'

'Of course. He's a survivor, Kate. He's been out all night before. He'll be fine.'

Angie replaced the receiver, stretched out on the sofa and pulled the rug over her. Of course he'd be okay. And when Paul was back she'd book another holiday on Lundy, a couple of weeks this time. Who knows, maybe one day it could be more. A barn might come up that she could convert into a studio. She pictured herself wandering the island bringing her artist's eye to the landscape, then developing the best shots to sell. Large panoramas would grab the holidaymakers attention, but smaller copies would be easier to carry home.

The phone rang. Angie sighed, threw the rug aside and reached for the receiver. 'Yes?'

'Is that the duty social worker?'

'Yes.'

'Desk Sergeant at Plymouth here. We've picked up a runaway - one of yours apparently. A woman from Lenkiewicz's place rang in.'

'Where?'

'Local so-called artist. Works in a warehouse down on the Barbican. Paints the local tramps, kids, women - particularly the women.'

Angie was too tired for this. 'Paul, is he okay?'

'Better than the officer who brought him in. If this lad was a couple of years older you'd be adding ABH to your file. We'll be seeing a lot more of this one. Shall I hand him over to social services down here?'

'No. No, I'll come and get him.' Angie paused. 'But don't tell him. Best not to tell him anything if you can avoid it. I'll be there in a couple of hours.'

The policeman opened the door to the interview room and dismissed the WPC with a nod. He turned to Angie. 'Wait till I've had a word. Might be young but he's a nasty piece of work this one.'

Paul was hunched on a seat with his back to them. 'He's just angry,' Angie said. 'Same as you'd be if you'd been abandoned and caught up in a whole load of stuff you couldn't make sense of.'

He shook his head. 'All the same you social services lot.'

'Excuse me?'

'No namby-pamby approach is going to work. He'll play you for suckers while he's out on the streets mugging soft targets like little old ladies.'

There wasn't any point in arguing. He might even be right, but it made no difference to what Paul needed. The question was - who could give it?

It took a promise to scour the Barbican for his mum and Spider before Paul finally calmed down. They eventually found the dog sleeping in the yard at the artist's warehouse, but there was no sign of Sonya, not that Angie could tell; Mrs Harris had yet to produce a photo. Sitting beside her on the way back to Bideford, Paul looked more defeated than defiant but it was only when he fell asleep that Angie finally relaxed.

He woke as they drew up at the house. Kate rushed towards the car. 'Thank goodness. We were so worried. Never do that to us again.' She bent to hold Paul.

He pushed her away. 'Get off me. I didn't do nothing. I didn't want to come back - that bitch made me,' he pointed at

Angie, 'but I ain't staying.'

'Go to your room. I'll not have you speaking to Miss Turner like that,' Kate said.

'It ain't my room.' Paul looked at Kate. 'And you ain't my mum. You can't make me do nothing.' He bundled Spider up in his arms, ran down the path and out the gate at the end of the garden.

'Come back here…' Kate began.

Angie placed a hand on her arm. 'Might be best to give him some space. He'll come in when he gets cold.'

'And if he doesn't?'

'Then call me.'

'But even if he does give in tonight, you heard him,' she hesitated. 'I don't think he's ever going to stop fighting me.'

Angie locked the car and turned back to Kate. 'I could do with a cuppa. Let's go in.'

It was dark in the woods. Paul pulled Spider close and buried his head in the dog's coat. 'It's just you and me boy,' a sob shook him, 'till we find mum. She's there, I know it.' He pulled the thin denim closer. 'The man knew. He painted me so he could show her.' He swallowed. 'It was so cool. P'raps he'll teach me, then people'll come to watch…

…he'd do loads of pictures, massive ones, so big everyone had to stretch their necks to see the tops. And they'd say, 'did you do these?' And he'd say 'yeah' and they'd give him pots of money to take some away. And he'd do the coolest cartoon you'd ever seen about Time Bubble Man and people from Spiderman comic would come and ask how much he wanted to do stuff like that every week. His strip would be on the front page. Everyone would see it. His mum would see it. And she'd know it was his 'cause he'd shown her once. And they'd give him his own studio and tell him they wanted his cartoon to be a proper film. He'd make loads of clay people and animals - like Spider - get them moving like he'd seen. Then he'd go to America and make pots of money. And he'd build a massive house right by the sea so his mum could go straight out the door onto the beach and play games with him.

Paul shivered. 'We gotta go back, Spider. Tell mum she don't need to hide no more. And I'll paint pictures of a super hero and each week he'll get this close,' Paul held up his hands an inch apart, 'to getting his head cut off or his insides poisoned or… loads of different stuff. But his super powers save him and he gets them, the ones who try to do bad stuff to him.'

'I do that.'

The bitch had been listening, outside his camp. Paul pressed back against the corrugated wall. 'Get away.'

'I tell stories with pictures,' Angie said.

'I ain't listenin'.' Paul stuffed his fists over his ears.

'We get a big book and the boy draws his mum.'

'Don't talk about my mum.'

'Then we find all the places the boy has lived with his mum and take pictures to put in the book.'

'You don't know nothin' about pictures. I'm gonna do pictures. Big ones.'

'…and they start to tell a story, a story of his life. And I ask the boy, what else do we need? And he puts his pictures in the book in the right places. Then I show the book to the people who want to help the boy so they can see his story.'

The words kept coming at him, forcing their way through his fists. He could see his story. He'd seen it loads of times in his head. 'And… and this boy gets to do pictures of his mum?'

'Yes - most important of all.'

'And gets to talk to the people what know her?'

'Yes.'

'And does his own pictures?'

'Definitely.'

Paul took a breath. 'And he don't have to stay anywhere he don't want to do?'

Silence.

'He don't, do he?'

Chapter Ten

Angie drew up outside Ellison Road, two semi-detached 1970's houses converted by the local authority into a children's home. Home: an uncomfortable word for this functional building. What was home? A place to be yourself, a sanctuary, a place for learning about love, for sinking into soft, squishy sofas. The staff did their best but the concreted front garden reflected reality for the children. Grey, hard, uncompromising - maybe that was why so many of them fitted in. They knew the rules of this dysfunctional life.

Angie walked through the space in the wall left by the gate, now lying on the concrete, its hinges twisted out of shape. She pressed the security buzzer and waited.

'Yes?' the speaker fizzed.

'Hi, it's Angie Turner. Here to see Paul.'

'Hi, Angie, come on in.'

The front door led into a large space: two rooms knocked into one. It was definitely a space not a room. A room had an identity, a role that it played in people's lives. But this space was just there - to be used and abused at will. Faded sofas lined two of the walls, the seats pitted where the springs had gone, and shelves of board games, toys and a few books lined another, looking like a jumble sale offering.

Adrian, the care worker on duty, came through the door.

'Hi, Adrian. How's the new arrival fitting in?' Angie asked.

'Too well.'

'Meaning?'

'Let's just say I can see why it didn't work with the foster parents. Institutional life suits Paul. He's determined to prove he doesn't need anyone. Spends most of the time in permanent fight mode, well able to hold his own - even with the older boys.' Adrian opened a door and ushered Angie into a smaller sitting room. This one felt more homely with a couple of comfy chairs, pictures on the walls and a box of toys that looked surprisingly complete.

'I haven't given up yet,' Angie said, sitting down. 'Maybe the life story work will help.'

'All he wants is contact with his mum. Still no sign of her?'

'No. Post mortem indicates the baby was smothered so my guess is she'll keep her head down as long as possible - that's if she's still with us.'

'Suicide?' Adrian raised an eyebrow.

'Has to be a possibility.'

'But the police would've picked it up.'

'Unless she changed her identity. She had a man with her at the hospital.'

'The father?'

'No. He abandoned the family weeks after the baby was born - no great loss apparently. No-one knows who this man was. The nurse took down name, address etc from Sonya and just assumed he was Mr Sonya. All we know is that his first name is Stuart.'

'But the police are treating it as murder?' Adrian said.

'Looks that way. And either of them could have been responsible.'

'So whether she's alive or not, looks like Paul's on his own.'

It was a cold statement of fact. The kind of thing said in numerous case conferences. But the reaction for Angie was visceral. 'Not if I can help it. I want him referred for adoption.'

'Adoption!' Adrian almost laughed out loud. 'You have to be kidding. He can't cope with fostering let alone your cosy two parent, two-point-four kids nuclear family.'

'I haven't given up on the foster parents. They're adopting his sister, Amy.' She could sense a losing battle but this was too important. Paul needed someone fighting his corner.

'But the notes made it clear the placement had broken down,' Adrian said, enunciating his words as if she was hard of hearing. 'The foster mother couldn't hack Paul's rejection of her. And from what I've seen, that isn't going to change any time soon.'

'Maybe not, but we can't abandon him.'

'Thanks a bundle.' Adrian stood and opened the door. 'You lot seem to think this is some sort of black hole. We do what we can for these kids. I'll get Paul.' He disappeared.

A radio was blaring out from a bedroom upstairs, a girl in the corridor was arguing over her curfew time and outside, a teenager was playing a solitary game of basketball. She watched as he took aim, threw, missed, picked up the ball, took aim, threw, missed... again and again. Always missing, always trying.

The door opened behind her. Paul was leaning against the opposite wall.

'Fifteen minutes or you're grounded,' Adrian said, pointing into the room.

'Hi, Paul,' Angie said.

'I ain't staying,' Paul slouched in and climbed onto the back of one of the chairs.

'And get your feet off the furniture.' Adrian waited for a response. 'Now.' Paul pivoted, swinging his feet away from the cushions and onto the window sill. 'All yours,' Adrian said to Angie, closing the door.

Angie stared at Paul's back. 'So how's it going?'

Silence.

'We had a deal. You came here, we did your story.'

Silence.

'So what ideas have you got?'

Silence.

'Okay, I'll tell you what I thought. I've got something...'

Paul laughed and shouted at the window. 'Give up, Jackson, you ain't never gonna do it.'

Angie continued. '...something here you'll want to see.'

Silence.

'It's your birth certificate. Tells us when and where you were born, your parents…'

Paul knelt on the windowsill, opened the small window at the top and shouted through it. 'Loser! Loser! Loser!'

'Fuck off…' The boy threw the ball at the window, catching the latch. It slammed shut.

'Did I tell you that we visit the places you've lived, meet people you've known?'

Silence.

'And take pictures to put in your book. I've brought two. For you to choose one.' Angie lifted two scrapbooks from her bag. One was covered with footballs, the other with splashes of colour, like a painter's palette.

'How long?' Paul snapped.

'Pardon?'

'How long have I been here?'

Angie looked at her watch. 'About five minutes.'

He glanced at the scrapbooks and turned back to the window.

Angie settled herself in the chair and waited. The noise of the ball bouncing against the tarmac outside was suddenly interrupted by a clang as it caught the basketball ring. The boy appeared at the window. 'Loser, eh!'

Paul pulled a face and slid off the back of the chair. He walked over to the toy box and kicked it. It rocked. He kicked again, harder. The top layer of toys spilled onto the floor revealing a house made of Lego. Large green and yellow blocks framed an oblong space. Inside, two large figures and two smaller ones sat around a table of bricks. Paul picked it up.

The silence that Angie now held was very different. Like blotting paper, it was absorbing years of confusion, anger, frustration - until it reached saturation point. Paul threw the model to the ground, grabbed the few pieces that remained intact and tore them apart.

'Where is he?' he shouted.

'Who?' Angie asked.

'Spider. What've they done with him?' He was almost

spitting in her face.

'He's at Steve and Kate's.'

'I want him.'

'I'm sorry, Paul, that's not possible.'

Paul raised his arms and beat at her chest. 'I want him. Give him back.'

Angie caught his hands and held him away. 'It's okay, Paul. We'll work it out. I'll help you. I promise.' The word was out before she could stop it. To a child like Paul, a promise meant one thing. Lies. Pain. Disappointment. If he were older he'd have called it betrayal.

'Okay, how about we go back to our deal?' she said.

Silence.

'You and me, together, telling your story. Do you want to start with Spider?'

Silence.

'Okay we'll start with Spider. I'll fix it up.'

'How long?'

Angie checked the clock. 'Fifteen minutes.'

Paul ran to the door. Paused, then turned and picked up the scrapbook that looked like a painter's palette.

Sarah was backing out of the office clutching a large box that was in danger of spilling its contents over the path.

'Here,' Angie rushed forward. 'I'll get the door for you.'

'Thanks. Always overfill it.'

'What's this?' Angie held up a long cylindrical item that looked suspiciously erotic.

'Not what you're thinking! It's a dressing aid. You try unravelling tights with arthritic hands.' Sarah rested the box on a low wall beside the path. 'Glad I've seen you.' She pulled a crumpled flyer out of her pocket. 'Fun run in the park next weekend. For breast cancer. Fancy it?'

Angie studied the paper. 'Why not?' She pointed at the small print. 'Not sure I've got a pink T-shirt though.'

Sarah smiled. 'In that case it's time you bought one.' She rebalanced the box under her arm. 'Go to go.'

Angie signed in at reception and climbed the stairs to her office. A group of colleagues were clustered around a portable radio. *The Iron Curtain has just opened wide. Some have waited all their lives for this moment. Leaving just about everything behind, East Germans have been making their way down through Czechoslovakia to Hungary, where, at midnight they began to tear down the fences that separate it from Austria and the west.*

'What's going on?' Angie asked.

'They've opened the border,' Bill almost shouted. 'People are streaming over.'

'What?'

'Sshhh…'

As a fellow communist-bloc nation, Hungary has long been an approved destination for East German travellers but in this extraordinary break in communist ranks they have made it possible for thousands to flee to the West. A family cheered and embraced as they touched Austrian soil. The mother told me, "we have no money, no home, but we are free," before she had to turn away in tears.

First Poland, now this. What was going on? Angie checked her watch. Only ten minutes before her next appointment; she'd have to catch up later. Did she write up her notes from Paul or prepare for the interview with Joan, a client she'd sectioned under the Mental Health Act? Angie smiled. Not that the poor woman's condition was any laughing matter. She was delusional, a danger to herself and others. But the final straw had come when she'd threatened all kinds of violence if her hamster wasn't taken care of. Driving to the hospital had been a challenge with the creature completing a circuit of the car every few seconds.

Even when she'd acquired a cage, Arnold the hamster had other ideas. This time Angie laughed out loud. She'd come home one evening to find the cage empty. She searched everywhere but he'd vanished. It was chilly so she lit the gas fire and settled on the sofa with the yellow pages to find Arnold number two. Seconds later there was a squeal and a distinctive smell as Arnold tumbled out the bottom of the fire, dazed but unharmed, apart from a punk make-over - a singed streak down his back.

Angie looked at her watch and extracted the psychiatrist's report from Joan's file.

'Angie,' Bill had followed her. 'Got a minute?'

'No.'

'You took the Atkins case didn't you?' It was a rhetorical question. He knew perfectly well that she'd been manoeuvred into taking two new referrals at the last team meeting. 'Only I've just come back from the housing review and their eviction has been brought forward.'

'To when?'

'Friday.'

'Friday!'

The phone on her desk rang. 'Yes... interview room one. Okay. Any chance you could get her a cup of something, Rosemary?... Thanks. I won't be long.'

'Can you get there?' Bill said.

'Not till five at the earliest.'

'Okay. Let me know what you've fixed up tomorrow.'

The sun was low in the sky by the time Angie reached the sanctuary of her flat. She dropped her briefcase by the door and sank onto the bottom stair. Ten minutes later she was still there, her coat untouched, her head resting against the newel post. Some days she felt fifty-five not twenty-five. Even the impulse to eat had deserted her.

The phone was just within reach. She lifted the receiver and dialled. 'Chrissy?'

'Hi, Ange. How's tricks?'

'Let's just say you were right about all work and no play. Had a pig of a day.'

'Spill.'

'Thanks, but it'd take too long. Is that invite still open?'

'You bet. When?'

'In a couple of weeks?'

'Two weeks! Come this weekend.'

'Can't. I'm on call.'

'Hang on a minute, Ange…' Angie heard steps and then voices. Raucous laughter pealed out. 'Got to go, Ange. There's a party brewing here.' She paused. 'Why don't you come?'

'What?'

'To the party. Leap on a train.'

'It's not that simple, Chrissy. It'd take hours.'

'No problem. We'll be here all night.'

Oh, God, she so wanted to say sod it and go. But what about the family facing eviction? Five kids she'd have to place if that went through. But she was always picking up colleagues' cases when they went off sick. Maybe it was her turn. And she could finish the mental health paperwork on Monday. Why not? It was crazy to think of travelling all the way to London at this time of night but…

'You still there?' Christine asked, her voice raised above the noise.

It was so, so tempting… but crazy. She was tired, it was late and she had a full diary. 'I can't.'

'Don't be such a stick in the mud.'

'Sorry, Chrissy, but I really can't. I'll come in a couple of weeks. Are you free?'

'Bound to be. You know me. Never planned that far ahead in my life. Got to go.'

Angie spotted her camera lying on the shelf. Moments later she was walking along the beach to the sand hills. From here she could watch the sun sink behind Appledore. It was surprisingly mild. Where had the last three months gone?

She removed the lens cap and checked the light. Sunsets were tricky - and she wanted this one to be perfect. The sky was already awash with colour. It was beautiful. So beautiful.

How easy it was to forget.

Chapter Eleven

'Okay, so you can close those three and put the mental health on hold while she's being assessed.' Bill created a separate pile on his desk with the four case files. 'Who's next?'

'Paul.' Angie produced the increasingly bulky file.

'Anything from the police?'

'No. There are warrants out on the mother and the boyfriend but they've disappeared.'

'Weren't they questioning the grandmother?'

'Briefly. Friend that babysat with her says they were together the whole time though, so Mrs Harris is in the clear.'

'Okay.' He rubbed his hand round his neck. 'How's your work with Paul going?'

'Sticky at first. Session one he hardly engaged at all. The last three have been tough but he's starting to open up.'

'Where are you meeting?'

'Ellison Road. The back sitting room. I'm sick to death of the sight of Lego but it works for Paul. That and drawing. He's got a real talent for storytelling - or truth telling - on paper. Here,' she flicked through the file. 'Take a look at these.'

Bill glanced at the drawings. 'Impressive. But it's taking a lot of your time. We're not resourced to do intensive work.'

'I thought it was our job to put the needs of the child first.'

'Maybe, but I'm concerned you're getting too involved. It creates too much pressure.'

'Are you saying I'm not up to the job?' Angie said, the muscles tightening around her jaw.

Bill shook his head. 'Nope. The opposite. But going the

extra mile piles on clients' expectations. Gets harder to pull back from in-depth work to leave capacity for your whole caseload.'

'So we have to do everything superficially, is that it?'

Bill sighed. 'I'm not the enemy, Angie. You're close to burn out if you don't ease up a bit. I want you to take leave and get some perspective. You're good - but you need to think about whether this job is right for you.'

Paul clutched his knees to his chest and rocked back and forth on the bed.

'You... you bloody bastard... I'll get you.' Swinging back violently, he dislodged a piece of bubble wrap from the wall behind him. He stuffed it in his pocket.

'And you can stop that.' The care worker stood over him, still flushed from manhandling Paul up the stairs. 'You're grounded for the rest of the day.'

'No I ain't,' Paul retorted.

'If I say you are, you are. You know the rules. Fighting...'

'He started it.'

'I don't care. You kicked him and that isn't acceptable.'

'Anyway, my social worker's coming. We're going out.'

'We'll see about that.' She turned and walked to the door, pushing it back against the wall. 'And this stays open.'

'Stupid, bloody cow,' Paul hissed.

'I heard that,' she called from half way down the stairs.

'Good,' Paul whispered. He wasn't frightened of stupid Jason Evans or any of the rest of them, he'd show them...

...lashing out with supercharged karate kicks from his bionic leg, he'd cut through their flesh like a knife and blood would gush all over the stupid, bloody care woman. She'd be first to fall flat on her face and he'd jump on her and tie her hands behind her so she'd be his slave and he'd make her eat porridge and do homework. He'd make them all do it... not Adrian though, he was okay.

And he'd kick Jason and Mark and stupid Ian out of the bedroom so they couldn't steal his money anymore and give him burns where no-one

91

saw and make it look like he'd wet his bed.

Sometimes he'd take the rope from under his bed and climb down to the supercharged turbo twin-carb sports car in the street. The car would say 'where to?' and he'd say, 'to the Barbie Can' and the car would put on its auto-pilot and take him there, to the alley, to the picture of his mum and the door in the wall. And he'd go in and say sorry he hadn't been back but he'd been a prisoner. But now he was in charge he'd be there all the time. And the man would paint him some more and talk about him, the real him.

And his mum would be there and she'd hold his hand like she was never going to let go and she'd say 'go on, see what I got for you.' And he'd push the door open and inside there'd be the most massive TV ever. Like the pictures. Only this was all for him. His mum had gone away to make the surprise. She'd just forgotten to tell him. Only she couldn't tell him could she! It wouldn't be a surprise then...

Paul stopped rocking and swung his legs to the floor. She couldn't tell him where she was going because it was a surprise. And the last time he'd gone to the Barbie Can the surprise wasn't ready. He smiled. But it'd be okay now. All he had to do was go back, this Saturday and the next, and the next till the man had finished the picture and the surprise was ready.

The care worker puffed her way up the stairs. 'Okay, Paul, this is the deal. You say sorry to Jason and you can go out with your social worker today. Then you're grounded till Saturday.'

Paul looked at her. 'I get to go out Saturday?'

'We'll see. Depends what happens before then.'

'Nothin' won't happen.'

'Like I said. We'll see. Now, what about that apology?' She walked towards the door and waited.

'Did you bring your book?' Angie negotiated a roundabout then glanced at Paul. He nodded. 'Done any more?' It had taken five weeks of painstaking work to engage Paul in the process but the pages of his palette scrapbook were finally beginning to tell a story - mainly of lies and broken promises.

With that kind of legacy it was no surprise he gave Kate and Steve such a rough ride. It would be years before Paul would trust an adult again.

'Bit.'

'Great. Writing or drawing?'

'Drawing.'

'What of?'

Paul shrugged.

'I'll take a look when we get there. Remember what I said we're doing today?'

Silence.

'Well, we got hold of your birth certificate, and we went back to the hospital where you were born - that's all at the beginning of your book. Then we went to the house you lived in till your dad left.' She paused. That had been a long session, convincing Paul that it was safe to remember, safe to be angry, safe to cry, safe to be comforted. They'd come a long way since. Paul had come a long way. 'Then we remembered how you spent some time living with Gran and...'

'We took a picture of Clem,' Paul interrupted.

'That's right. And of you with Gran outside the caravan.'

'But you didn't do it right.'

'No.' Angie caught a trace of a smile on Paul's face. 'Took a while to get one she was happy with didn't it?'

'But we couldn't get in my caravan,' Paul said, his face dropping.

'I'm sorry but Mr Tucker couldn't keep it for you.'

Silence.

'I know you're worried about your mum finding you. But Mr Tucker has my number. He'll give it to her.'

'He won't. He hates us.'

'He promised. Like I promised I'd be here at four today and I was. Okay?'

Paul relaxed into the seat.

'Anything you want to ask before we get there?'

'Will I see Spider?'

Angie smiled. 'Yes, you'll see Spider.'

Angie sensed Paul's growing tension as they reached the edge of town. 'Not far now.'

He swung his feet onto the dashboard.

'Not a good idea, Paul. You'll hurt yourself if I stop in a hurry. Put them down.'

He paused just long enough to make a point before pulling his left foot back. A few seconds later the other foot followed until, finally, both were back on the floor.

'That's it!' Paul exclaimed, pointing to the house at the end of the lane

Kate was leaning on the gate. She waved at Paul as he leapt out of the car. 'Hi, Paul.' She swung the gate open for him.

The words tumbled out. 'Hi, where's Spider?'

'Back garden, waiting for you.' Paul sprinted down the path and disappeared.

'Hi, Kate,' Angie said. 'How's things?'

'Come and see for yourself. Amy's biscuit making.'

'Did I hear right?'

'You did! She's responding in all sorts of ways.' Kate paused and looked at Angie. 'Some a bit challenging.'

'Like?'

'Doesn't like it when I leave.' As if on cue a wail escaped the house. They followed the sound into the kitchen. Amy was sitting on a waterproof sheet covered in flour, a couple of streaks meandering their way down her cheeks. 'I'm here, darling.' Kate handed her a shape. 'Can you make me a star?'

Angie watched. The transformation in Amy was amazing. She'd gone from passive bystander to active participant, calling the shots in this relationship. She looked at Kate. 'Have you and Steve decided?'

'Yes. We'd like you to set up a meeting with Mr Stevens.'

'You'll need to be a bit... well, adamant I guess, about adoption being the only option. You're registered as short term foster parents. Good ones. It will cause him all sorts of headaches to lose you.'

'I thought you supported us?'

'I do,' Angie said quickly. 'Don't get me wrong. Moving

94

Amy now is unthinkable. We just have to convince Bill.'

Kate looked at Amy, playing happily in a haze of flour. 'It would mean so much, to be a family.' She lingered over the word.

'And you got a greeting, of sorts, out of Paul.'

'I know.' Kate smiled. 'That was weirdly normal. Can't tell you how nervous I've been about today. You know how it was when he left. Felt like I was walking on eggshells, like he was primed to fight before I even said anything. But he seems less, well, angry, I guess.'

'That's exactly what he was doing. Classic fight or flight. Only with Paul it's fight *and* flight!'

'Maybe the children's home was the best place for him.'

'For a while. He needed time to work a few things out.'

'What kind of things?'

'Oh, how come all the people who should love and look after him have rejected him. It's a tough one to make sense of. The only answer he's come up with is that it's his fault, that something's wrong with him.'

Kate watched the noisy reunion in the back garden. 'I guess it makes sense… all his anger… it's about being frightened but it's hard to see it that way when you're with him.' Kate hesitated. 'It's like he presses this button inside me and suddenly I'm the one who's angry.'

'We all react. Most of the time it's no big deal but when the patterns are as destructive as Paul's, life gets difficult.'

Kate looked at Angie. 'Are you saying a nine year old boy is manipulating me?'

'Just good at triggering certain feelings.'

'How do I stop it?'

'Be aware of it. And there's lots of other…' A burst of laughter erupted from the back garden as boy and dog rolled over each other on the lawn.

'He's never done that before,' Kate said.

'What?'

'Laughed out loud.'

Angie shut the gate behind her. Kate was right; Paul hadn't

laughed out loud before. Such a simple thing, yet it had sparked something - a lightness she could only describe as hope. There was a now or never quality to these visits. Angie shook herself. Then again, this weekend might signal yet another night trawling the streets of North Devon looking for a runaway.

Something made her pause. Maybe it was the soft air on her face, or the sunlight broken into a kaleidoscope by the trees and scattered across the lane. Something inside was fighting for air. She looked at her watch. Three-fifteen. There were case notes to write up, a visit to Shelley to plan, new referrals to slot in somewhere... but maybe Bill was right; maybe she should pull back. Her trainers were in the car, right next to her camera. And it wasn't far to the coast.

Angie climbed the stile and crossed the fields to the sea. She passed a school group abseiling down the cliffs but otherwise the path was clear. It was easy jogging on the hard surface that followed the line of the old railway. What a spectacular ride it must have been. She could picture city-hardened children leaning out of carriage windows, brushing the smuts from their eyes, eager to catch their first sight of the sea. How must it have felt, to see those massive rollers building then breaking on the seemingly endless beach? To fling off their shoes and feel the sand between their toes; to gaze at such an immense horizon. A landscape populated with buildings all jostling for space couldn't offer this kind of freedom. And there was the icing on the cake - an island within touching distance that just had to be a pirate's hideaway.

'Please,' Angie whispered, 'give it a chance.' It was a heart-felt, gut-felt plea. If only Paul could let go of his ferocious defence of his mother. If he could only let Kate love him. What a life he could have.

She stopped by the haunted house, the first building as she neared Westward Ho! It was only gossip that it was haunted, but the crumbling exterior colluded with the rumours. She ran on past a row of beach huts and a jumble of buildings fringing the sea front before reaching the sand. The tide was high, and the impulse irresistible. She shook off her trainers and headed for the water. 'Aahh...' The first touch made her feet tingle.

Wavelets sparkled like strings of pearls as they crisscrossed around her. Almost unconsciously she began hopping over them. The space, the sea, the sun, it was a heady cocktail that prised the day just far enough away for a chink of something else to creep in. She felt positively light-headed. She spread her arms wide and spun round. How long had it been since she'd let her hair down, been irresponsible, carefree? When was the last time she'd laughed out loud?

Only two weeks to go and she'd be knocking on Christine's door. God only knows what would happen but one thing she did know - there'd be nothing responsible about it! And that was fine. It wouldn't matter if she stayed up all night, drank herself to oblivion, and was utterly and completely herself. She'd taken Bill at his word and booked not just a long weekend but ten days. Delicious!

Chapter Twelve

Paul rested the scrapbook on the table in the small sitting room at Ellison Road and flicked through the photographs. She'd be here soon. Four o'clock on Tuesday like always. And they were going to see Spider again, and Amy... and Steve.

Not that he cared. Not really.

He picked up a pencil and looked at the writing Angie had left for him to finish.

My favourite food is...   chips
My favourite place is...   alton towars
My favourite time was...   being with my mum
My favourite person is...   my mum

The door opened. 'Paul, Angie just called,' Adrian said. 'She's really sorry but she can't come. She's got to see someone else. It's an emergency.'

Paul threw down the pencil. 'No she ain't! She's coming here. She promised.'

'Not today. She can't.'

'She promised!' he shouted.

'Nothing she can do, Paul. They need a social worker urgently. She has to go.'

'It ain't fair! We was going...'

'Where?'

'Nowhere. It don't matter.'

'It looks as though it matters.'

'I told you it don't. I don't care.' Paul grabbed the scrapbook and pushed past Adrian up the stairs to his bedroom, slamming the door. He threw the book onto the floor. It fell open at a fresh page headed 'My Home'.

Paul stared at it, then grabbed a pencil and drew a box, filled in a square for a window and a lopsided door; then a triangle for the roof, criss-crossed with lines. He frowned. It wasn't right. He grasped the pencil in his fist and pulled it back and forwards, gouging out a jagged hole. Then he slashed at the chimney until smoke poured from all sides.

The pencil broke as he pressed harder and harder. He grabbed another and drew a tree beside the collapsing house and filled the trunk with a figure - jammed tight. A harsh black line across the mouth silenced him but in a bubble to one side the word escaped. 'Help!!!!!'

Angie put the phone down. Six sessions it had taken to get Paul to half-way trust her. And now one call...

'Are you ready?' Bill was at the door. 'We'll go in my car. The police are already there.'

'Why both of us?' she said, grabbing her coat. 'I had an important appointment.'

'The woman's threatening her child. I need a female there.'

'Do we know the woman?'

'No, but she's got a psychiatric history. Postpartum Psychosis. In-patient for three months, discharged last week. G.P's meeting us there.' They reached the bottom of the stairs and the waiting car. Bill pulled out into the traffic.

'I know it's not down to you,' Angie caught her breath, 'but I was finally getting somewhere with Paul.'

'Yeah, well, until the powers that be put some realistic funding into social services that's the way it is.'

Angie glanced at her team leader. He looked strained. Being responsible for the decisions most people were only too happy to ignore, and having newspaper headlines baying for your blood when it all went wrong, did that to you.

He pulled in behind the police car, ambulance and fire engine. Angie looked up to the fourth floor. A woman was wedged on a balcony clutching a small child dressed in a flimsy dress, offering sparse protection from the north wind blowing across the face of the flats.

'Angie,' Bill called back to her. 'We need to get up there.'

She shivered - but not with the cold.

'Thanks for holding the fort, Adrian,' Angie said, following him into his office. 'Sorry to take so long to get here.'

'Only doing my job.'

'It was a mental health emergency. A baby at risk.'

'So you said.'

'Coping with the fall-out took longer than I'd hoped.'

'Like the trouble I've had with Paul since your call.' There was no escaping his frustration. 'Sorry. I know it's not your fault.' He picked up a kettle from a tray on the filing cabinet. 'But it's hard when you see how these kids get knocked back. Tea?'

'Gets worse I'm afraid. I've got ten days leave booked.'

'Great.'

'Paul knows. I've been preparing him. He was okay.'

'Might find that's changed,' Adrian said.

Angie picked up her tea. 'I'll take this through.'

'Wouldn't if I were you. He's been off the wall ever since you called. I wouldn't want either of you to get scalded.'

She put the mug down. 'Where is he?'

'Out the back.'

Angie walked along the vinyl-covered hallway. A regular thud, thud, thud was coming from outside. As she opened the door a basketball smacked into the wall a few inches from her head. The cry was out before she could stifle it. Paul's face registered satisfaction.

She walked over to a bench. Paul turned and ran at the basketball ring. He threw, missed, caught the ball, returned to his spot, threw, missed... locked into the sequence, until the ball rebounded off the backboard and landed behind the bench. Angie reached for it, her hands scooping it up a fraction before Paul's.

'Give it back,' Paul demanded, leaning over to force it from her hands.

Angie moved the ball across her body. 'In a minute.'

'No!' he shouted into her face.

'After I've said something.'

'I ain't listenin'.'

'Well I'm still going to say it.' Paul walked to the other side of the yard and sat on the concrete, digging at the soil in the narrow border with a stone. 'I'm late. I promised I'd be here at four and it's almost eight. I want to say sorry.'

Silence.

'It's not good to break a promise but there was a little girl, like Amy, who needed my help. I decided to go. Like I decided to come to your caravan when you needed my help.' Angie put the ball on the bench beside her.

Silence.

'I asked Adrian to tell you I'd be late.'

Paul leapt to his feet, crossed the yard and grabbed the ball. 'I don't care you didn't decide for me.' He disappeared indoors and came back with his scrapbook. 'And you can keep your stupid book.' He threw it at Angie, ran back into the house and slammed the door.

She picked up the book. Paul's drawing was smeared in mud, but one word still cried out from the page. HELP!!!!!

Angie spread Paul's drawing on her kitchen table. It had all been going so well. The sessions when he opened up, the weekend with Kate and Steve when he didn't do a runner. But now - two steps forward, six back. Was she in too deep? Perhaps she should have gone home after the call out but she'd felt an almost visceral need to patch things up with Paul. And what had she got? Another twelve hour day. 'Yep, I hear you, Chrissy. It's not good. Not good at all.' Angie scooped up the drawing and put it back in her case. She was on leave and she was going to do just that, leave it all behind. She picked up

101

the phone. It rang until the answer-machine kicked in.

'Hi, Christine here. Well, not here as you'll know by now. Try again soon though won't you. Byeeee.'

'Hi, Chrissy, it's Angie. Be with you late afternoon tomorrow. Got to see mum first but I'll get away soon as I can. Can't tell you how much I'm looking forward to…' Beeeeep. The single tone cut her off. Ridiculous, but she felt rejected. 'Get a hold of yourself. It's just a machine with a short tape!' That was then. This is now. No reason at all for history to repeat itself. None at all.

The answer-phone clicked in again the following day. 'Hi, it's me. Hope you got my message. Just to say I'm leaving mum's now. It's,' Angie checked her watch, 'just gone four. Be with you very soon. Can't wait…' Beeeeep.

It was a Jekyll and Hyde landscape. Gleaming, glass-fronted edifices side by side with decrepit industrial warehouses waiting to be reinvented as fashionable apartments, some still in transition, swathed in scaffolding. Angie stood in front of the double height glass entrance to Christine's block and checked the address on the scrap of paper in her hand. A notice on a polished steel panel to her right invited her to press the button for the resident she required. Angie knew exactly where to look. At the top. Penthouse territory.

Angie pressed.

She pressed again, just as a young couple arrived. They held a key fob against a panel in the brickwork and the door swung open. She followed them to the lift. There were four doors leading off the hallway on the fifth floor. She recognised the number, but even if she'd forgotten there was no doubt she was in the right place. A stark white envelope was stuck to the door with *Ange* scrawled across it. Angie hated the way Christine shortened her name, so abrupt, uncompromising even. But not when it rolled off her tongue, caught up in her distinctive burr. Angie pulled out a thin piece of cream paper.

Hi Ange. Great excitement. Been offered a contract to cover Cannes for the Beeb. Right out of the blue. Can't believe it. Know you'll be dead chuffed for me. Tried to let you know but didn't have your mum's number and you'd already left home. Can't leave you a key, too risky round here. Sorry. Got to rush. Come again. Soon. Love Christine xxx

She wasn't here. Christine wasn't here. The answer-phone wasn't a temporary blip, on while she was out getting an outrageously expensive bottle of wine for their dinner. It was there to field calls while Christine sipped shorts somewhere over France. Angie slid down the rough brick wall onto the polished marble floor. Why didn't she give Christine her mother's number? But it hadn't crossed her mind... nothing had. Other than being with Christine again.

'Can I help?' A middle aged woman was looking at her from an open door across the hallway.

'No, no thanks.'

'You'll be going then.' There was no mistaking her apprehension at having a young woman slumped on the floor of her respectable pied-à-terre. Angie pulled herself up and walked towards the stairs.

'There's a lift you know.' The woman called after her.

She did know but she wasn't ready to leave in such a hurry. Wasn't ready to leave at all. She walked down, floor by floor, pausing by each plate glass window to scan the surrounding pavements. Irrational she knew, but part of her was hoping to see Christine's auburn hair, signalling a hasty return to tear the note from the door.

The modern office blocks that made up central docklands were courted by cafés on all sides. Bijou bistros, Italians, whole-food outlets; whatever your taste, it was here. Angie had no taste for anything, but the round steel table on the pristine marble forecourt was somewhere to sit. She ordered a coffee.

'Mind if I join you?' The office worker was already pulling out the chair.' Only got a fifteen minute break and everywhere's heaving.'

Angie shrugged. 'Break from what?' Merely a politeness.

'BT conference. Just got out of a presentation from Vodaphone. My God that guy has some vision. Predicting every adult across the western world will have a mobile within ten years. Be able to get hold of anyone, anytime.' He downed his coffee and wrapped a muffin in his serviette. 'Session on video-conferencing next.'

Angie would have given anything to sit at this table and dial Christine's number, knowing that wherever she was it would be her voice that answered, not a beeeeep.

She watched as her companion joined a stream of dark-suited men, yes, they were all men, hurrying back to their conference like crows gathering. Noisy, eager, purposeful. What a contrast. She had her case by her side, ten days leave ahead of her and nowhere to go. Should she find a cheap hotel and wait for Christine? Her heart sank. But where else? Back to her mother's? Definitely not. Back home? She wasn't ready for that. Not yet. No, she suddenly realised. There was only one place she wanted to be right now.

Chapter Thirteen

Angie joined the familiar bustle of travellers clustered on Bideford quay by the Lundy office. Another time she'd have been full of smiles and eager anticipation too, but today the scene was playing through the lens of an old fashioned movie camera, bleached of all colour and somehow distant.

She focused on the river. Familiar enough from her daily crossing to work, a broad expanse that both united and divided Bideford. The town centre was clustered behind her, on the hills fringing the western bank, with East-the-Water opposite. The Torridge was wider still outside her flat. From her sitting room, Angie could see a series of sandbanks called the Bar, churning the water before it reached the open sea. She'd be crossing it very soon.

She was distracted by a teenager walking perilously close to the edge of the quay, twisting his feet this way and that to avoid the cracks in the paving. His concentration was intense yet erratic, as though each moment held no connection to the next. As she watched, his attention swung from his feet to the Oldenburg. He ran to the front of the queue and leapt up the gangplank.

'Steady on, Tom,' the boatman said. The boy pushed past him and disappeared inside. The boatman caught Angie's eye and smiled. 'Might as well be talking to me'self.'

Angie showed her ticket and walked up the gangplank, her feet rolling over the ridges. Near the top she stumbled. She felt her arm being grasped as she was helped onto the deck.

'Are you okay?' the boatman asked.

'I think so, thanks.'

'Lundy isn't the place to be stuck with a sprained ankle. Enjoy your trip. So to speak!'

She smiled and turned quickly, anxious to hide the tears that were threatening to fall. What was wrong with her! It was only a turned ankle. But it was more than that. It was the catalyst for the warmth of a stranger's touch, filling the void left by a stark piece of paper stuck to a closed door.

She found her usual seat on the top deck. There was an inside cabin but for this trip there was only one place to be - up here with a clear view of the horizon. She watched as the boatman welcomed everyone aboard. He was comfortingly cheerful with a word here, a touch there. And eyes that really connected. She always noticed the eyes. Very few of the kids she worked with could bear direct eye contact. It was way too scary to let people see right into them.

The boatman had a clicker in his hand. Count them on, count them off. He'd repeat the process on the way back. Couldn't take the chance of stranding someone with nowhere to stay. Not now that she'd got the last place anyway. Angie wasn't religious, but when the Lundy agent responded to her call with news of a cancellation at the Lookout, she'd breathed a heartfelt, 'thank God'.

Thirty minutes later, with the hundred or so passengers safely aboard, the Oldenburg pushed off. The river fascinated her, particularly when the boatyard at Appledore came into view. A massive shadow filled the aircraft-hanger sized covered dock, the shipyard's latest contract from the Ministry of Defence. But today it was painfully familiar. On the other side of the estuary was her flat where her carefully chosen London wardrobe of shimmering tops and high heels had been disgorged onto the bed. So much anticipation and now... meaningless, a fantasy. The case loaded onto the Oldenburg was filled with waterproofs, jumpers and sensible trousers.

Angie gripped her seat as they closed in on the waves breaking over the Bar, creating a few moments of turbulence before the boat steadied into a gentle rise and fall. Angie sighed with relief and looked ahead to Lundy. Its steep sides seemed almost within reach but it was an hour and a half before the Oldenburg rounded the south-eastern tip. She leant on the rail and watched as a couple of smaller boats tied up alongside, ready to board the first tranche of passengers. Plans for a pier still hadn't come to anything so impatient visitors had to wait on the congested middle deck for their turn to be shuttled ashore.

As the crowds eased, Angie made her way down.

'How's the ankle holding up?' The boatman who'd helped her aboard was beside her.

'Fine now. Thanks for your help.' She looked away, assuming the pleasantries were over.

'My pleasure. Day trip or are you staying?' he said.

She turned back. His voice had such a genuine ring to it. 'Staying - at the Lookout.'

'Not for the faint-hearted. Been there before?'

'Yes. I love it.'

He caught and secured the rope as the empty tender came alongside. 'There you go.' He nodded at the boat and held out a hand. 'Do you eat down the Marisco?'

Angie concentrated on making the transfer. 'Sometimes,' she called back.

'Maybe I'll catch you there. Name's Michael. Mike mostly. There you go.' He released her hand.

Angie found a seat. Was it her imagination or had his hand supported her that little bit longer than the other passengers? The urge to look back was irresistible. But the gap in the Oldenburg's hull was empty.

She found herself close to the boy from the quay, restless as ever. As the Lundy warden caught and secured the rope at the beach he pushed forward and leapt the gap. Angie followed along the narrow plank. 'Want a ride, Tom?' the man called. But the boy was already out of earshot.

The warden took her case and led the way to an ancient tractor and trailer. Angie paused. 'I think I'll walk too, thanks.'

'Okay. Enjoy your stay.'

She'd just take a quick look before she tackled the track up the island. Angie picked her way through a gap in the rocks to the left of the slipway, eager for a glimpse. It took a while but then they were there; two, three... no, four grey seals - their unblinking eyes scanning the beach before they disappeared beneath the waves, often a second before she clicked the shutter. But they'd be back, and then she'd be ready for them.

Angie checked the clock. Twenty past five. The rain lashing the heavy mullioned windows had woken her more than once, that and a weird collage of Paul's haunting images overlying the facia of Christine's apartment. She pulled the covers over her head.

Hunger eventually persuaded her out of bed. The galley kitchen offered half a dozen tea bags, butter and a granary loaf. That, and the banana she'd rejected yesterday, would do. Hugging her dressing gown closer, Angie sat at the pitched pine table in the sitting room, folded her hands around a mug of black tea and stared out the window.

She shouldn't have come. Shouldn't have polluted paradise with her dismantled dreams. 'Shit, shit, shit!' She took a sip of tea. 'Aargh!' She poured the rest away and went back to bed.

...she was rushing to get somewhere. Where was it? London? No, closer to home. Just needed to see more clearly. Barnstaple. That was it. Was it Tuesday already? She had to be get there, be there for four. But the traffic wasn't moving. It was blocking her way. 'Move, damn you, move!' She couldn't be late. Wouldn't be late. She'd show them. The door at Ellison Road was open. No, it should be shut, keeping him there for her. But the clock was chiming. She was too late.

Angie woke with a start. The panelled walls of the Lookout's small bedroom washed in and out of focus, moving like ship's timbers. She gripped the sides of the narrow bunk, counting her breaths until her heart slowed. She was on Lundy. On leave. This was her time.

But it wasn't that simple, was it? Would Paul be okay?

Would he do any more without her there to encourage and support him? His drawings were good. Disturbing, brutal even, but he had a flair for… what? It wasn't anything technical, like perspective. It was more than that. His pictures told a story. It only took one look for the whole plot to unfold in your head. You knew the people, what they were thinking and what they were going to do next. But what was next for Paul? All she ever seemed to do was buy time, fending off one miserable sequence of events after another for a week, a month maybe. Angie shook her head and swung her legs out of the bunk. She'd so looked forward to some time out but sitting here with thoughts of Paul ricocheting round her mind, she'd hardly succeeded.

'Okay, Angie. Here's the score. You can stay here maudlin for the rest of the day, or you can shift your backside up the shop to buy an obscene amount of chocolate. What's it to be?'

'Hmmm. Tough choice. But if you're pressing me…'

'I am.'

'Has to be the chocolate.'

'Congratulations. Correct answer and you win…'

'…an extra four pounds that I'll have to lose later.'

'But that's later. So indulge yourself. You deserve it.'

'If you say so.'

'You don't sound convinced.'

'It'll have to do.'

The air was surprisingly balmy, almost caressing her as she jogged along the rough track that followed the spine of the island to the one and only shop. To the south, across the deceptively benign stretch of water, she could see the plunging cliffs that marked the contours of Bideford Bay from Westward Ho! to Hartland Point. She knew every challenging inch of the coastal path. It wasn't that far, but distances were deceptive walked vertically. One minute she'd be wheezing her way up a cliff face, the next plunging down the other side, her calves protesting at every jarring step.

Angie gratefully accepted the offer to deliver her bags overflowing with blatant comfort food. It left her free to wander. It felt good, just walking - nothing to work out or resolve. Just put one foot in front of the other. She passed 'The Lookout' away to her right, and walked on until she recognised a track leading to the western side of the island. Seconds later she was striding across the soft turf towards the brow of the slope. The last time she'd stood here she'd been stunned by the soaring cliffs and a view that went on forever; nothing between here and America. She'd found paradise, her own personal island paradise.

Angie hurried down the path to a grassy spot overlooking the sea. Such a pristine landscape, she had the sense no footprints preceded hers to the cliff edge. And one look reminded her why. It was a sheer drop of at least four hundred feet to the sea pounding against the jagged rocks below. She instinctively grasped a reassuring handhold, edged back up the slope and settled herself into a dip in the grass.

She scanned an outcrop of rock - a customer in the shop had seen puffins here within the last few days - adjusted the focus on her camera and waited. Above the cliffs a phalanx of gulls planed back and forth on the wind. Apart from their cries and the regular thud of the waves below, all was peace, perfect peace. Not just the absence of noise, but a full, rounded peace. She lay back and closed her eyes.

'Yeaaaaaaaaa….' The long cry echoed Tarzan-like across the cliffs. Angie woke, her body rigid with tension. She followed the sound to a figure running along the headland. She picked up her camera and zoomed in. It was the boy on the quay. What had the boatman called him? John? No, Tom.

Without pausing, he began to play chicken with the cliff edge, running back and forth, challenging the grass tussocks to give at the very moment he turned. It was too dangerous. Wasn't anyone there? She was on her feet and moving towards him without thinking. But slowly, carefully. She'd covered half the distance when he suddenly stopped, like a wild creature, intent on diverting all its attention into one sense. She knew he was acutely aware of her yet, at the same time, wouldn't acknowledge her. She mirrored his stillness, creating an instant frozen in time like a tableau from a sepia photograph. Then, without warning, he sat. A few moments later he began rocking back and forth, his lips forming some kind of mantra in time with the movement.

Angie released her breath and returned to the hollow. She was shaking. It was always the same with these kids. They pressed a button, stimulating an almost irresistible desire to help. Maybe she should resist. After all, by trying to connect with Paul she'd only reinforced the hurt. One missed appointment and weeks of relationship building had been sabotaged. No. No, that wasn't right. His very hurt meant that deep down he wanted that connection. But who could withstand the buffeting? Steve maybe, but not Kate, not now.

She was on her way up the slope when something made her turn. The boy was standing where she'd been sitting, staring at the puffin's rocky outcrop. He'd shown no sign of acknowledging her, yet there he was... exactly where she'd been... looking in exactly the same direction.

Chapter Fourteen

Paul bit his bottom lip. Just a few more minutes and his cartoon would be finished. He didn't care, it was all stupid stuff anyway but he could finish it, if he wanted. And if the pig-ignorant kids, that kept taunting him, saying his drawings were crap, shut up.

'Baby's drawing bubble wrap. What a loser!' the boy to his left hissed.

'Loser, loser.' Three others took up the chant.

'Quiet!' Jim Brooker, art teacher and Paul's year tutor, swung round. 'I've had enough of the four of you. This is your final warning. Any more disruption and you'll be down the corridor.'

'But I ain't...' Paul began.

'What bit of final warning don't you understand, Paul Wells.' He waited. 'Well?'

'Nothing.' Paul selected another pen. Time Bubble Man had rescued the family, all of them - the mum, the boy, the girl and the baby from the burning caravan. He'd known where they were 'cause he had radar vision. And he'd used his Time Cloak to catch all the flames and spin them round and shoot them outside so they were all safe.

Suddenly red paint oozed across the page, blotting out his drawings. 'You bastard. You bloody bastard,' Paul yelled at the boy next to him, pulling him to the floor. His fist connected with the boy's eye socket with satisfying force. Seconds later he was being hauled outside, but not before he'd seen blood start to ooze from the wound. The wound he'd done.

'Well?' It took Adrian just fifteen minutes to reach the school. He sat on the opposite side of the head teacher's desk.

Silence.

'It's now or never, Paul. Coming right on top of the incident at Ellison Road…'

'That wan't my fault. She shouldn't have took it.'

'You kicked, spat and swore at Alison. That's unacceptable behaviour. All she did was remove some tatty bubble wrap that was accumulating dirt and God knows what else.'

'It was mine!'

'I'm not going there again. You need to remember that actions have consequences. Lost privileges. No pocket money. No outings…'

'Like bloody prison.'

'We can do without the language. This is serious, Paul. The boy you hit is at the hospital having his eye stitched.' Paul half smiled. 'This isn't a game. The consequences this time…'

'I don't need no stupid, bloody pocket money.'

'If you don't need money, why did you steal the petty cash?'

'I didn't steal nothing!'

…Time Bubble's Man's truth tongue was so strong he only had to switch it on for everyone, everyone, to believe what he said. Anyway, it was true. It was his money. They were the ones stealing - not giving it to him. He'd counted it proper, even down to the pennies. Two weeks pocket money, his money, in his coat. Enough for the bus to Plymouth. Lenky thingy was going to show him how to make Bubble Wrap Man work. He said his pictures were good and he'd looked at them, really looked.

'This is good, Paul,' he'd said in his gravelly voice. 'Really good. Want to see how it could be even better?'

Hours and hours Lenky had spent showing him stuff. Not all in one day. No. He'd been two, no, three times now. Bunking off. Told them he'd hung round the shops. It's what all the kids did. Hang round in gangs. Stupid carers believed him! Not him though. He knew the bus now. Knew where to go at the Barbie-can. Knew all the times.

Only thing he didn't know was where his mum was. He asked. Every time he asked.

The door opened behind him. He spun out of the chair, heading for the gap. But his way was blocked by the head teacher.

'Paul Wells, I might have known. Get back in that room. We deal with this right now.'

'You ain't doing nothin' to me.'

'Sit down, Paul.' Adrian caught Paul's arm before he could make contact. 'Now!' Paul slouched against the office wall. 'You're in serious trouble. Sit.'

The head teacher picked up a file from his desk. 'According to Mr Brooker you've been in detention twice in the last week.'

Silence.

'Both for aggressive incidents towards other pupils. Why?'

Silence. Paul slouched in the chair, kicking the desk.

'You know the procedure. Where incidents are considered outside the school code you get one opportunity to make the right choice. Seems to me we've stretched our side of the agreement way too far already.' He looked at Paul, waiting for a response. Then sighed. 'You're suspended from school for one week pending a decision on your future.' He turned to Adrian. 'Will you call the case worker?'

'She's away. I'll get hold of Bill, the team leader.'

'I need a conference within a week.'

'Do what I can.'

Bill Stevens turned down the lane to the Clarke's. He checked his watch. Covering Angie's duty had set him back. The time taken by the two adults, six children, two dogs and a budgerigar he'd finally managed to usher out of the building had been particularly frustrating. He'd stopped being surprised long ago that some people completely missed the concept of actions having consequences, but it still aggravated him. What the hell did they expect *him* to do now they'd been thrown out of the in-laws because of their constant bickering? Go round and ask nicely for them to be taken back? Offer a nice detached four bedroom house at a nominal rent? Changing their unreasonable behaviour to keep a roof over their children's heads hadn't even crossed their radar.

'Come in, Mr Stevens.' Steve opened the door. 'Didn't expect to see you again quite so soon. No problem with the decision is there? About the adoption?'

'No. I know I didn't make it easy for you but that decision's done and dusted. We'll support your application. No, I've come about Paul.'

'Kate's putting Amy to bed, she won't be a minute. Come through.' He led the way into the sitting room, clearing a path through the Lego.

'How's it going?' Bill asked.

'Good, mostly. Mind you, I sometimes dream of the quiet little girl who came to us.'

'Angie mentioned she's become a bit clingy.'

'Howls whenever Kate leaves her. Inconsolable at times. I'm told that's progress! Anyway, what's this about Paul?' he asked, a frown shadowing his face.

'Can you tell me about his last visit?' Bill asked.

'Wasn't too bad really. Paul was his usual impossible self to start with but then I took him sailing. Just me and him. Seemed to… I don't know, release the pressure a bit. He threw himself into it. No back talk - what a relief that was. We actually had some fun.' He paused. 'Good grief. Can't believe I said that about Paul!'

Bill leafed through his notes then looked up. 'Can't put my finger on the date. How long ago was that?'

'About three weeks. He was due again this week but we put if off until Angie gets back. Kate wanted to talk to her. We know Amy's the only family he has, and we'd like to keep them in touch if we can, but with the application… it's difficult.' He looked towards the stairs.

'What would your decision be?' Bill asked, senses alert for the unsaid.

Steve hesitated. 'If it was down to me I'd carry on. He's a good lad at heart. Who knows? If we could be the one family that doesn't desert him maybe it would get easier, over time.'

'And if I told you that in the last three weeks he's been in trouble at Ellison Road for stealing money and beating up his room-mate? And that he's been suspended from school for giving a pupil a black eye?'

'What!' Kate joined Steve on the sofa. 'What happened?'

'I had a call from Adrian at Ellison Road. Apparently Paul's losing the plot. You know Angie managed to get him in to Whiddon School? Well, for a few weeks it's been relatively quiet. Art teacher even rang to thank him for sending some talent at last.'

'But calm before the storm by the sounds of it,' Steve said.

'Yep. Just had incident piling on top of incident until he was suspended yesterday.'

'So what happens now?' Kate asked.

'Case conference, as soon as Angie gets back. I'd like you to come - if you can.'

'I'm sure we can. Can't we?' Steve looked at Kate. She shuffled on the seat, tucked her legs up beneath her and crossed her arms.

'What's up?' he said.

'Nothing.'

'Like hell it is. Spit it out.'

Kate looked from Steve to Bill. 'If we come... does it mean... are we committing to anything?'

'No. But it would be useful to have a picture of Paul from your point of view.'

'Who else will be there?' Steve asked.

'Angie of course, Adrian from Ellison road, someone from the school, the police...'

'Police!' Kate interrupted. Why? He's only nine years old!'

'They were called over the money.'

Kate leant forward to place a coaster underneath her mug. She rubbed at an imaginary mark on the coffee table.

'So? Are we going?' Steve asked.

'I can't leave Amy, not now,' she said.

'You know she'll be fine with Tilly. And your sister is desperate to make it up with you. Why not let her?'

'It's not that simple.'

'Kate, what's this really about?' Steve clasped her hand in both of his, protective but inescapable too.

'I sorry, Steve, but I can't do it.' Her voice was unsteady. 'I've tried, I really have, but he just keeps on and on at me. I'm worried that…' Her voiced tailed off.

'Your concerns are important to us, Kate.' Bill said. 'What's bothering you?'

'That him coming will affect Amy,' she said suddenly. 'All the tension, it's not good for her.'

Bill leant forward. 'It's our duty to place the child's interests first and foremost. To do that, everyone will want to thoroughly explore all the possibilities. But I have to tell you, Kate, it's my opinion that the children's home is the best long-term placement for him. Sustaining emotional relationships is always going to be a challenge after the start he's had. The home might be the best compromise.'

Relief swept across her face. 'Do you really think so?'

'Yes.'

She half smiled. 'Only I wouldn't want him to think he's being rejected. I mean, maybe, when Amy's adoption has gone through, maybe he could come, sometimes.'

Bill had heard enough. 'Possibly. It's not down to me to decide a care plan in advance of the meeting, but I'll suggest we pause contact while he gets specialist help.'

'What kind of specialist help?' Steve asked.

'From a psychologist initially. Then we'll take it from there.' He paused. 'So can you both come - to share your experiences and help us put a care plan together?'

Steve looked at Kate.

'We'll be there,' she said.

Chapter Fifteen

Dawn broke at around five. For a few glorious seconds the sun pealed through the narrow aperture between horizon and cloud but then it was gone. Maybe a duvet day was called for. No plan, no schedule. Just chocolate-fuelled, fiction-filled oblivion.

But the pressure to move on, a sense of things left undone, was embedded so deep it forced Angie prematurely into the day. She was soon crossing the plateau of the island. But something was different. 'No wind,' she whispered. That was it. The morning was completely still, rare on this exposed outcrop stranded in the middle of the Bristol Channel, but perfect for exploring the Atlantic facing side of the island. She'd go further north, to the end. It was only a mile or so.

It must have been the noise that made her change course. The professional inside her was drawn to it like an addict to drugs; unwanted but at some level incomplete without it. The boy was on the same headland. She walked forward, a reluctant guardian. They engaged in a curious dance as Angie moved to stay within his eye-line while he constantly shifted his view to exclude her. At least it drove him far enough away from the cliff edge for her to relax. She even managed to blend his noises with the cries of the gulls as she took out her camera and focused on an outcrop across the bay.

'What are you looking at?'

He was standing no more than ten feet away, a slight figure, with shifting eyes and features shielded by his tracksuit hood. 'Puffins,' Angie said. 'I want to photograph them.'

'Too far.'

'This has got a powerful zoom.'

'You're not sitting right.'

Angie stared at the boy. He looked away, stung by her eyes, shifting from foot to foot as though intending to set out in one direction then another. 'How should I be sitting?' she asked.

'Why? How? Don't know.'

She followed his eyes to the hollow in the grass where she'd sat the day before. A memory stirred. He reminded her of a young boy she'd worked with years before. 'I mean *where* should I be sitting?'

His frown cleared and he pointed at the nearby depression.

Angie moved. 'Am I sitting right now?'

He nodded and sat a little away from her, staring at a spot just in front of his feet.

She picked up her camera. 'Want to look?' She held it out. Within minutes he was using it as well, if not better, than her - exposure, zoom, all of it, absorbed as easily as changing TV channels. The roll would be finished very soon. 'Do you have a camera?' she asked.

Silence.

Angie smiled. He'd met his match. After so long with Paul she was master of the one-sided conversation. Paul. The temptation to call was almost irresistible but that was one of the appeals of the Lookout - no phone. She'd claw his trust back, Angie was sure of it, but the timing of this break was lousy. His cry for help couldn't have been clearer, and she'd ignored it. In his mind at least. 'Couldn't have been clearer,' Angie muttered. Maybe she was communicating in the wrong way. What were words to him? Mostly lies. The photographs were better but still not enough. They told nothing of Paul's inner world; his thoughts, his feelings. His drawings did that.

'Thank you, Tom…' she began. But he'd gone.

Angie made a mug of coffee, settled herself on the bench outside the Lookout and scanned the horizon. Morte Point was clear and she could even make out the coastline along to Ilfracombe. A gust of wind caught her hair. Maybe the sheltered track along the east of the island would be best tomorrow; see if she could get a glimpse of the deer amongst the rhododendrons.

A movement away to her right distracted her. Minutes later she was resting her arms on the stone wall, her camera poised to capture the ponies grazing their way towards the cottage. But before she could press the shutter a land-rover cut across her shot.

'Evening,' the warden called. 'Enjoying your stay?'

'It's taken a while, but... yes, I am, thanks.'

'Don't mind being up here all on your own then?' he said.

'Mind? Oh no. It's why I come, the peace and quiet. Well, mostly quiet. I've been spending time on the other side of the island, on the cliffs. There's this boy...'

The warden grimaced. 'That'll be Tom, Jackie's son. He's, well, different. At a special school on the mainland most of the time. Just here for a week I think.'

'He took some photographs with my camera. I'd like to get them developed. Any way I can do that?'

'Not over here. You could try offering Mike a pint to take it to one of the places on Bideford quay. He crews on the Oldenburg. You'll find him in the Marisco lunchtime.'

Three days later Angie was leaning over a pitched pine table at the Marisco Tavern, the island's pub. It was a low granite building, crouching in the lee of the Eastern slope, the first stop for most visitors when the weather was less than welcoming. But as the clouds cleared, the pub emptied. She'd follow them - just as soon as she'd unrolled the brown package in front of her.

Angie could feel Mike's eyes on her. He'd been happy to help. Even persuaded the developer to turn the prints round to fit in with the Oldenburg's schedule. She smoothed out the enlargement. It was stunning. Tom had done something with the exposure that gave his close up of a Puffin a shimmering, almost luminescent quality. Having an exceptional talent wasn't uncommon with children like Tom, but this was breathtaking.

'Never knew he could do anything like that,' Mike said, twisting his head to get a better view.

'I don't think he's taken any photographs before.'

'He's a bright kid, if you can get past the weird behaviour. Has a hard time of it here though.'

Angie looked up. 'Why?'

'Visitors don't like having their picture postcard idyll marred by kids running wild.'

'He's not out to cause trouble.'

Mike smiled. 'Shame they can't all be so understanding. Same again?' He was on the way to the bar before she had a chance to respond.

It was only her second time in the Marisco. She liked to keep to herself normally. Antisocial some might say; she preferred therapeutic. Not having to focus on anyone or anything other than her photography - now that was a holiday. But with the gentle background hum of quiet conversation, and Mike's easy company, this time felt different.

She unrolled a second enlargement. Tom had actually caught a Puffin emerging from its burrow, with the grass tussocks providing a natural frame for a perfectly focused picture. There had to be a market for his work. 'Mike,' Angie said as he placed the drinks on the table, 'is there a gallery on the island? I'm sure Tom could sell these.'

'Could try the shop. I'll mention it to Clive if you like.'

'Maybe I should ask Tom first.'

Mike smiled. 'Have you tried talking to him?'

'Okay, so it would be a one-sided conversation. But it's still his work.'

'But your camera I'm guessing,' Mike said, his eyes resting easily on her. 'You're different aren't you? Most people run a mile from Tom. It's really something, helping him like this.'

Angie shrugged. 'I'm envious of someone who can produce work like this so effortlessly. Takes me ages to compose a shot only to find my subject has got bored and wandered off.'

'I don't believe that.'

Angie smiled. 'Maybe there's a few good ones, but Tom's a natural.'

They lapsed into silence. It was time to move on. Angie rolled up the enlargements and drained her glass 'Thanks, for getting these done.'

'Pleasure. Will there be any more?'

'Probably not this time.'

'I'll have to find another excuse to invite you for a drink then,' he said, searching her face.

She set out along the now familiar coastal path. He was there, at the cliff edge.

'Hi, Tom.'

Silence.

'I've something to show you.' He swivelled on the rock, removing her from his line of sight. Angie hesitated, then settled into her spot. She pulled out his photographs. 'These are your pictures, Tom. They're good. You're good.'

'No,' he shouted. 'Weirdo. Should be locked up.'

'Who says?'

'Them,' he nodded towards the village.

'Well they're wrong. They don't understand,' she called. 'They don't understand how you see things.'

'I see colours.'

'I know. No-one sees Puffins like you.'

Silence.

'You have to take more, Tom.'

'Can't.'

'I'll help.'

'You'll help?' he repeated.

'Yes.'

He moved closer. Waiting. Angie placed the pictures on the grass. He hesitated, picked them up and was gone.

Angie was wrapped in her dressing gown clasping a mug of hot chocolate when the knock came. She could ignore it. Then again…

'I think these are yours.' A middle-aged woman thrust Tom's pictures at her.

'No, they're…'

'Come here.' The woman pulled Tom into view. 'Say it.'

Tom fixed his eyes on a point somewhere over Angie's shoulder. 'Sorry.'

'Did he take them?' the woman said. 'He does that you see. Just takes anything he wants. Doesn't get it that other people's things aren't his to take.' She turned to Tom. 'How many times have I told you not to take what isn't yours?' He stared at the ground. 'Oh… go home.' She turned to Angie 'See what I mean? He'll be the…'

'Please,' Angie interrupted. 'The pictures are Tom's. He used my camera and I got them developed for him. I gave them to him.'

'So he didn't take them?'

'No.'

'Well,' the woman flustered, 'maybe not this time but there'll be others. He's away, at school, most of the time. I'd have him home but, well, you can see he's… different.'

'Yes. And I think Tom can too.'

'Tom? No. He's in a world of his own. Can't see half of what the rest of us have to cope with. Goes over his head. You're not the first to be taken in, nor the last I shouldn't think.' The woman looked briefly at Angie, nodded as if to reinforce her prediction and turned.

Taken in. Had she been? If so, what into? An unreal world or simply a different reality? Something to ponder on the trip home. She checked her watch.

A couple of hours later Angie dropped her bag on the path outside the Lookout and closed the door. 'See you soon,' she said, addressing the building as an old friend. Perhaps it was the quirky fire that took a degree in aerobic combustion to encourage it into life; the technique needed to master the sequence of events in the tiny shower or the intimacy of a night spent alone with its creaking panels and mysterious sighs. It was an enduring relationship; she'd be back.

Angie settled on a rock at the back of the pebble beach and watched the day trippers gather to board the Oldenburg. Some fidgeted their way as close to the sea's edge as possible, keen to be first into the small boats ferrying them across the bay. But she wanted, needed, to hold onto her peace until the last possible moment. She leant against her rucksack, listening to the reassuring swish of the sea. You wouldn't catch a wave suddenly having a crisis over whether or not it was safe to break, fighting to claim part of the beach to break on, or tearing itself away to break alone. But fighting had become second nature to Paul. If he continued to repel all boarders he was heading for a very lonely life.

Chapter Sixteen

'Ready?' Bill said, holding his office door open.

Angie held back. 'Not quite. Can I have a word?'

'What about?'

'I need more time with Paul.'

'Angie, we've been round this loop. You've worked well with him, he's had more one to one than anyone else.'

'But not well enough. This situation with Paul started before I went - with that mental health emergency. We need dedicated teams handling those calls. What's the point in taking children into care, raising expectations, and then abandoning them while we react to the next crisis?'

Bill moved towards the door. 'Getting on your soap box isn't a great use of this time.'

'I'd like your support to get Paul back with the Clarke's.'

Bill shook his head. 'Paul's best interests will be met in the children's home.'

'Not long term. He was doing okay until this last incident. All he needs is another chance with the right support.'

'And he'll get it, from the staff in the home.'

'Even better with more hours from me. Ring-fenced.' Her eyes pleaded with him.

Bill half turned. 'You know it's not that simple. I don't have the budget for that kind of work.'

'I didn't say it was. But Paul needs a chance. And you can give it to him.'

'I can, can I?' His voice was heavy with sarcasm. 'Do you know how many cases I've got piling up on my desk? Other kids just like Paul who deserve a chance. What do you suggest I do with them?'

Angie sighed. Bill was backed into a corner as much as she was. She followed him in to the conference room. Kate and Steve sat silently in a corner. Angie went over to them. 'I was so sorry to hear what happened.'

'You can't be always be there. We know that.'

'But Paul doesn't.'

Two hours later, Angie returned to her desk and picked up the dictaphone. 'Case conference on Paul Wells. Present: Bill Stevens, Senior Social Worker; Angie Turner, Case Worker; Adrian Walker, Ellison Road; Jim Brooker, Whiddon School; Mark Jones, Police Liaison Officer; Kate and Steve Clarke, foster parents.'

That was the easy part. Keeping the notes impartial was the challenge now. She continued. 'Angie Turner summarised events since the last meeting. Individual life story work had been progressing and a successful weekend stay raised hopes that he might be placed back with the foster parents.

'However, things went rapidly downhill. Paul had to be physically restrained after kicking, spitting and swearing at a member of staff at Ellison Road. He subsequently had his pocket money stopped. A quantity of petty cash then went missing, later discovered under Paul's bed. He was aggressively uncooperative when interviewed by PC Jones but in view of his age, could not be charged or cautioned.

'Angie Turner considered Paul's behaviour was not malicious but a reflection of his frustration and distress at being abandoned by his mother. Through her work with him, Paul was developing an understanding of his past and the difficult feelings this generated. He was making progress on developing appropriate ways of managing his anger but more time and consistency was needed.' Angie sighed. She'd tried so hard to get the meeting to back her, but hers was a lone voice.

'After a relatively positive period at school, particularly with his art, Paul's behaviour reached crisis point. Jim Brooker recommended permanent exclusion and referral to a special unit for disruptive pupils. Adrian suggested the home could contain Paul's behaviour but considered it too great a challenge for his foster parents. Mr and Mrs Clarke reluctantly agreed.'

Angie's heart had gone out to Kate and Steve. They'd tried so hard but Kate had reached a brick wall. No questioning her commitment, but emotionally she was spent.

'Angie Turner recommended ongoing contact with the Clarke's and his sister with a view to placement in the future. This was not considered appropriate in the short term.

'PC Jones concluded the meeting by stating that Sonya Wells was now the chief suspect in the ongoing investigation into the death of Baby J.

'Actions: Placement at Ellison Road to continue for the foreseeable future. Paul to be excluded from Whiddon School and admitted to a Pupil Referral Unit. Psychological assessment to be followed up as matter of urgency.'

'Hi, Paul,' Angie said when she finally arrived at Ellison Road. He swivelled on the back of the sofa in the small sitting room and stared out the window. 'How's it going?'

Silence.

'Adrian tells me you haven't done anything with your life story book for a while.'

Silence.

'It's always there when you want it, Paul. You know that don't you?'

Paul fiddled with his watch, pulling the elastic strap tighter until it marked his wrist.

'Is that the watch Kate and Steve gave you?'

Silence.

'They loved having you visit.'

'Oh, yeah!' he shouted, his voice uncomfortably ironic. 'They told him,' he pointed a thumb in Adrian's direction, 'they don't want me no more.'

'It's not like that, Paul.'

'Yeah, it is. Like you. Said all sorts of stuff and didn't come.' He leapt down from the chair and ran through the door, slamming it behind him.

Angie followed him to his bedroom. He was lying face down on his bed. She sat on the floor, leaning against the wall. 'You're right. I made a promise I couldn't keep. I should have been here with you and I wasn't. Life sucks sometimes.'

Silence.

'You're smart, Paul. Do you get what you want by kicking off all the time? Or do you get grounded, have your money stopped, get sent to another school?'

Silence.

'It's your choice. Carry on like this and get sent to a special unit away from your mates or listen to people - and get to do the things you want to do.'

'It ain't fair.'

'It's how things are. Do you like Adrian?'

Paul shrugged. 'He's all right.'

'Then listen to him. Play the game.' Angie threw a ball into a miniature basketball net hung from the ceiling. 'We had a meeting, Paul - everyone who knows you.'

Silence.

'Adrian was there and your head of year, Kate and Steve, the policeman who interviewed you about the money…'

'He don't know me,' Paul snapped.

'But because you took the money he's involved. That's how it works. That's why you need to get smart.'

Paul rocked back and forth on the bed, his chin resting on his knees. 'I am smart. You tell them that.'

'I told them you know loads of stuff now. But when all they hear about is you hitting people, swearing and stealing money they'll make decisions you don't like.'

He rocked some more.

'You're the only person who can make things different, Paul. With our help.'

He leapt off the bed and stood inches away from Angie. 'I

don't need no help,' he shouted into her face. 'I got my mum. She's coming back. For me and Amy.'

'Paul,' Angie hesitated. 'I'm worried about what's happened to your mum. Just like you…' he ran back to the bed and stuffed a pillow over his head. 'But wherever she is, she'll want to know that you and Amy are okay. For Amy that means having a mum and dad there all the time. Kate and Steve are going to do that. They're adopting her.' Angie levered herself off the floor and sat on the end of the bed. 'You could have them too, if you wanted. You liked going out in the boat with Steve didn't you?'

Silence.

'And down the skateboard park with him?'

Silence.

'It's okay to have fun with other people. Mum would love you to do that. She won't be angry. If you play ball here, Adrian will help you make those smart choices and work out what comes next.'

Paul rolled off his bed and began tipping toys out of a box.

Angie picked up a drawing from Paul's bedside table. Colourful monsters were cavorting across a series of boxes, devouring stick people. It reminded Angie of an animator's storyboard where each box led you irresistibly on to the next. 'This is good, Paul. Tell more of your story like this.'

Silence.

She replaced the drawing. 'I know things are tough for you.' She paused. 'We've done some good stuff together though.'

He began pulling a Lego car apart. 'Don't care.'

'I do.'

Silence.

'We'll keep trying to find your mum, Paul, but it may take time.'

'My mum'll find me.'

'But if she can't, how good will she feel to know you're okay?'

Silence.

'Make smart choices, Paul. No more hitting or swearing at

129

teachers or stealing. Do okay… for mum.'

Silence.

Angie picked up the scattered Lego pieces and began fixing them together. 'There are a lot of bits here that made a car once. They got all broken up. But they can make something else, something good. Just different.' She put the Lego house on the floor.

'Bye, Paul.'

Silence.

Angie closed the door behind her.

Chapter Seventeen

'You had to be there, Ange,' Christine said, her voice breathless over the phone. 'It was awesome. I got within fifteen feet of Kevin Costner and blagged my way into a press conference with Anthony Hopkins and Jodie Foster.'

'So you said,' Angie cut in, having gone round this particular loop three times already.

'You have to come up. I'll show you the photos.'

'I don't think so.'

'What do you mean?'

'Exactly what I said. I don't think so.'

'Not still in a huff about the note are you? I said I'm sorry... I'll make it up to you. There's a great new restaurant opened up round the corner. It'll be my treat.'

'You know I can't get away just like that.'

'Don't be a wet blanket, Ange, it doesn't suit you. Time you got your spark back. See what you can do. Yes?'

Angie sighed. How did Christine do it? No matter what had gone before, nothing lingered. Just the warm embrace of her voice, dismantling any defences. 'Okay, I'll see...'

'Brilliant. Got to go.' The phone went dead.

The boom of the starting gun reverberated from the yacht club as a flotilla of small yachts raced across the estuary. Angie opened the patio door and leant on the balcony rail. It was the regatta and the front was packed with spectators. None of them with her grandstand view though.

'Hi, it's Angie isn't it?' The voice came from below.

Angie searched the crowd lining the yacht club drive. 'Mike?'

He waved. 'Great to see you. How's things?'

'Good, thanks.'

'Are you busy? Fancy a drink?' He nodded at the bar a few yards further along. Customers were spilling along the roadside, plastic glasses in hand.

'It's heaving. Why don't you come up here?' Curious, she thought as he disappeared to find her door. She wasn't usually quite so spontaneous.

'Doesn't get much better than this,' he said, nodding at the view, wine glass in hand. 'Are you coming along for the gig racing later?'

'Not sure. How about you?'

'Oh, I kind of need to be there. I'm rowing in the Lundy boat. Haven't a chance in hell, we have trouble scraping up a crew but, as they say, it's the taking part that counts.'

'So you live on Lundy? I thought the boat crew were over here.'

'I use a mate's floor when I'm stuck this side but I'm only occasional on the Oldenburg. My day job is monitoring the marine nature reserve off Lundy.'

'I didn't know there was one.'

'It's early days. Only been there for five years as a statutory protected area. Voluntary before that.'

'What's so special about it?'

Mike turned towards her. 'Eight species of coral in those waters - pink sea fans, dead man's fingers, several species of cup corals. Lundy's the only place in the UK where you get them all together. It'd only take a few more years of unregulated fishing to decimate the sea bed. It's the trawl nets. Imagine a cheese grater being hauled along underwater. The coral gets knocked about…'

Angie watched as he became more and more animated. He had a way about him that drew her in, invited a connection. He was so at ease with himself, knew what he believed in, was passionate about. His work seemed as much of a vocation to him as social work was to her. That's if it was - her vocation. She was seriously beginning to doubt it. Maybe Christine was right, maybe she'd abandoned her true passion. Even Bill had suggested a rethink. The reality of the job couldn't be further from her college ideals. More like rushing round with a box of sticking plasters covering over the cracks in people's lives.

'How about you?' Mike finished.

'Sorry?' Angie flushed.

'Ever see yourself on Lundy? Long time since I've seen anyone so at home there.'

'I'll be back in the spring.'

'I meant permanently.'

'Permanently?' She let the word sink in. 'Not sure how I'd do that. I mean, it's all owned by the Trust isn't it? Let for holiday accommodation.'

'They keep a couple of places back if they think they can get year-round rent. Helps the cash flow.'

'Not much call for social workers though.'

'I guess not. You'd need to be in the tourist game really. Anyway,' he looked across to where teams were moving boats down to the water. 'Better shift. Fancy coming to watch?'

The beach was filling with long, narrow gigs carried across from the multi-tiered racks lining the local car park. Angie found a sheltered spot against a wall and shaded her eyes. The gigs were beautifully painted and proudly named - *Socoa* and *Buller* in bold gold lettering on pale blue; *Good Intent,* a white flash on green; *Teazer* and *Dasher*, unmissable in Cornish black on white.

'Who's your money on then?' Mike slipped down beside her, his gentle touch on her arm so natural.

'Haven't a clue. Didn't even know there was such a thing as gig racing. Has it been around long?'

'Not really,' he paused. 'Only a couple of hundred years.'

She studied him. 'You're kidding.'

He shook his head. 'Serious stuff in the early days. Neighbouring boats used to race get their pilot aboard the ships plying along the coast to get the trade for their village.'

'They went out into the open sea in those?' Angie pointed at the overgrown rowing boats in front of her.

'Built for speed. But surprising what they can cope with.'

'The boats maybe, but what about the rowers?'

'Made of stern stuff in those days. I've a strong suspicion our club secretary is a direct descendant. "Nothing but a bit of a swell," is his way of describing ten foot breaking waves!'

A Cornish team assembled in front of them, three on either side. They lifted their gig in one fluid movement and carried it down to the water. Others were doing the same further along the beach. 'Do you need to go?' Angie prompted.

'Nope. These are the A teams. We know our place.'

They lapsed into an easy silence as they followed the progress of the gigs. At least, Mike did. Angie felt her eyes closing in the warm sun as she lay on the sand. If she changed jobs it would have to be here. No going back to London. But dropping her salary wasn't appealing. Maybe something would turn up.

'Angie... Angie.' She felt Mike's hand on her shoulder. 'Got to go,' he said. It took a moment to come round, to take in his face, close to hers. 'Won't be long though. How about something to eat afterwards? If you're free.'

Her response flowed easily. 'Yes, let's do that.'

He squeezed her arm. 'Great. See you later.'

Angie watched him weave across the beach. She wasn't surprised he was into rowing. He looked fit. Muscular but not heavy, ideal for the boat crew.

Half way towards the Lundy gig something distracted him. Seconds later he was beckoning to her. 'Someone over there you might like to see,' he called, pointing at a group of young people spilling out of a mini-bus.

The bus was from a local special school. 'Of course,' she said, recognising a familiar face. She walked across the sand. 'Hi, Tom. Good to see you. How's things?'

'How's things? Lots of things here. Boats, oars, cars...'

'Yes. Lots of things to photograph.'

'Yes, lots of things to photograph - after ice cream.'

'Hi, can I help?' The driver was polite but cautionary.

'Sorry, I shouldn't have gone up to Tom like that. My name's Angie, Angie Turner. I met Tom on Lundy a few weeks back and…'

'The photographer? You're the photographer?'

'Well, yes, I guess so.'

'He's talked about nothing else. So proud of the pictures you did for him. We got them framed. They're in the entrance hall now. Can't tell you what it's done for his self esteem. I'm Graham, Tom's housemaster.' He held out his hand.

'Photographs after ice cream,' Tom repeated.

'Just a sec, Angie. The promise of ice cream the instant their feet touched the sand was the only way I could get everyone on board. Jamie,' he called to a younger man on the other side of the group. 'Petty cash is in the glove box. Can you take them over the shop?' He turned back to Angie. 'So do you do much photography?'

'Day job doesn't leave much time but I fit it in when I can.'

'What is the day job?'

'Social worker. In the Bideford team.'

'I should have guessed. Not many people know how to get through to Tom.' He was unpacking some folding chairs from the bus as he spoke. 'Here, have a seat.'

'Has he been with you long?'

'Since he was eleven, when he was diagnosed. Can't see him going anywhere else now. Not till he's eighteen anyway.'

Angie took the offered seat. 'What happens then?'

'God knows. There's a few in that bunch I know exactly where they'll end up - Dartmoor probably. A prison cell has a bizarre security to it.'

'Not Tom, surely?'

'Depends. The hormones are flowing. All he's got to do is follow his urges in a public place once too often.'

'But it would kill him. He needs this,' she swept her arm across the horizon.

'You're in the business. You know how it is. There won't

be much sympathy for Tom. We've got him for a few years yet though. Listen,' he paused, 'Tom got me thinking. The photography did so much for him that I'd like to get a group going. I know it's putting you on the spot - but I don't suppose you'd be interested?'

'In what, exactly?'

'Running a photography group at the school. It needn't be too often. Once a month maybe?'

'I don't...'

'We couldn't pay much but any expenses, film, developing, that kind of stuff would be covered.'

She'd enjoyed seeing Tom's creativity blossom, but to take on a group... 'Could I think about it?'

'Sure, it's mean to pounce on you when you just came for a day out to watch the racing.'

'Oh my God, the race!' She scanned the water, straining to match what she could see of the gigs on the far side of the estuary with the commentary crackling from the loudspeakers.

Chapter Eighteen
Six months later

Angie gathered up Paul's file and excused herself from the meeting. The summer had passed well enough; very well in fact. She and Mike had been spending more and more time together and, until today at least, she'd managed to leave work behind more often than not. But one case conference was all it took for the frustration to come flooding back. After six months, Paul had been labelled beyond the pale. Not that she could put it that bluntly in the case notes. She sank into her chair and switched on the dictaphone.

'October 18th 1989. Case review on Paul Wells, age 9, placed at Ellison Road Children's Home since April. Present: Bill Stevens, Angie Turner, Adrian Walker, PC Jones and Lyn Jones, Tutor, Pupil Referral Unit. Apologies, Kate and Steve Clarke, previous foster parents.'

Angie paused. At first she hoped they'd got caught in traffic, or delayed dropping Amy off. But then Bill read their letter - *Kate and Steve Clarke regret they will not be attending Paul's review as they are not in a position to contribute to his care at this time.* Her heart sank. Paul's one chance of ever having anything like a normal life... gone. She turned back to her notes.

'Paul has been allocated a permanent place at Ellison Road following the breakdown of his fostering placement. Ongoing contact was attempted but discontinued given Paul's continuing antagonism to Kate Clarke.

'PC Jones supported a permanent placement for Paul given that the investigation in to the death of Baby J had concluded there was sufficient evidence to charge Sonya Wells with murder.

'Adrian Walker reported Paul was defiant, aggressive and unresponsive to staff at the home. The past six months had been a holding operation, keeping Paul safe but achieving little else. He frequently absconded and was well known to the police in Plymouth.

'Lyn Jones stated Paul was uncooperative, showed little interest or motivation and was considered unmanageable in the group. The only discipline that worked was depriving him of art materials. There was no question of a return to mainstream education and she recommended Paul be referred to a specialist residential facility.'

It had been a relentless bombardment with everyone damning Paul with each breath. Hers was a lone voice. 'Angie Turner discontinued intensive work with Paul due to caseload pressures. Her monthly visits were tolerated but unproductive. However, she considered a specialist residential placement was not appropriate and that extensive efforts should be made to reinstate contact with the Clarke's.'

That was as strongly as Angie dare record her passionate pitch for ongoing contact with Kate and Steve. The dysfunctional world of residential care became so bizarrely normal that workers genuinely believed children like Paul were better off there. 'What crap!' Angie exclaimed, glad the office was empty. But it was her job to record the majority decision.

'The meeting agreed Paul should remain at Ellison Road with the option of referral to a specialist residential unit if his behaviour failed to improve. Current Social Services resources did not allow for the reinstatement of one to one work.'

Angie gathered up the files, locked her desk and left the office, the damp, grey evening reflecting her mood. She flung her briefcase into the car, sank into the driver's seat and switched the radio on. *The Communist leader of East Germany, Erich Honecker, has been forced to step down. The official reason for his departure is said to be "ill health" but failure to deal with the tide of discontentment sweeping the country is thought to be the real reason.*

Angie gasped. Could it really be happening? The wave of protests across Europe was one thing but East Germany! She turned up the volume. *The recent visit of Soviet leader Mikhail Gorbachev is being seen as a contributing factor to the downfall of Mr Honecker. The Soviet leader was highly critical of the East German leadership saying there was a need for people to feel involved with their country and to have their opinions taken seriously.*

Gorbachev again. Since he'd publicly renounced the use of force, places like Latvia and Estonia had found the courage to agitate for independence but East Germany! Angie checked her watch and started the car. As she manoeuvred through the Bideford traffic, the discussion moved from Honecker's resignation to speculation surrounding the fall of communism. Six months ago they'd have been laughed out of the studio but now… Could John Le Carre's world of spies and double dealing really be crumbling?

Angie sat in the car outside Ellison Road listening to the end of the report. What was it about this year? Were the stars in some kind of mystical alignment creating this upsurge of people power? Everyone was talking about it, at work, the drama group, even during breathers on the trail. All speculating about the end of the cold war. There was such a feeling of hope in the air. She looked at the children's home. If only it could cross the threshold here. She took a breath and opened the door.

'No!' Paul threw the cushion across the room knocking a calendar off its hook.

Angie retrieved it, glad of the chance to turn away. The fury in his eyes had buried the boy she knew. 'I'm sorry, but everyone decided…'

'I wan't there.'

'But the people responsible for making the best decision for you were. And they think this is where you need to be.'

'I ain't staying. You can't keep me here.'

'What happened to the smart choices we talked about in the spring, Paul? If you keep fighting them, people will keep making decisions you don't like.'

'Fuck them!' He threw the cushion at her this time.

'This isn't the way, Paul.'

'Fuck off!' He leapt off the chair and picked up a table lamp. It was still plugged into the wall or Angie wouldn't have got there in time. She managed to wrap her arms around him forcing him to drop the lamp. 'Get off me, bitch. Get off!'

He was stronger than the last time she'd restrained him. He was a frightened child then. But now? Fuelled by anger that had been brewing for months he was almost unrecognisable. Paul worked an arm free and yanked her hair. The pain brought tears to her eyes but for him to get the better of her, to know he was uncontrollable, would do untold damage. He was a nine year old child driven by fear. She had to remember that. She grabbed her coat and wrapped it around him, pinning his arms inside.

'Paul, Paul, listen to me…'

'You're all bastards. I'll get you, all of you.'

Angie managed to hold on despite the pains shooting down her arms. The only alternative was to press the emergency button and let Adrian and his staff take over. What hope then of a future for Paul? No. She had to get through to him. 'I know you're angry, Paul but this isn't the way.'

Silence.

'Talk to me. We can sort it, together.' It would have to be in her own time but was there really any other choice?

Paul went limp. A ploy to make her let go? Or genuine? Either way, the temptation to relax was too much. She loosened her grip. 'We can finish your story, Paul.'

Silence.

'Your tutor tells me your art is amazing,' Angie leant back. 'Use that talent to get people to listen to you.'

Silence.

'We can see about you spending some time with… with

Steve. Out on the boat maybe?'

'He don't care. He don't come no more.' Paul's voice was cold, detached. Beyond anger.

'He does care, Paul. It's just that things have got... complicated. But I can talk to him. He's very fond of you. And so is Kate.' Angie rubbed her forehead. A nagging pain around her temples was making her sweat.

'I don't want nothin' from her!' Paul pulled away and in an instant had grabbed the table lamp and hurled it at Angie. This time he hit the mark. She struggled to stay conscious as she reached for the emergency button.

'You sure you're okay?' Mike helped her to the sofa and pulled a rug over her.

'Absolutely. It was shock that made me pass out. Nothing to do with Paul.'

'How can you say that?' He knelt down and stroked her hair away from the dressing on her forehead.

'Apart from a pounding head I'm okay, honestly. But it's good to have you here tonight. How come?'

'Sailing was cancelled.' Mike poured a couple of glasses of wine and handed her one. It was part of their evening routine when the Oldenburg was in Bideford. A drink here and there had led to a spontaneous offer of her spare room instead of his mate's floor when he needed to stay over. He was easy company and nights on call were more bearable when he was there. Whatever time she made it home he'd be waiting with a cup of tea and a listening ear. Sometimes she wished he wasn't so available; it made her acutely aware that she was the one holding back. It would be so easy to sink into his arms and let him blot out everything the day had thrown at her. Literally! But she'd regret it tomorrow. Wouldn't she? But it had been a hell of a day. Her eyes began to close.

Mike eased himself onto the sofa until she was resting against him. 'Do you want to watch a film or something?' He stroked her hair.

'No' she murmured. 'I'd like to stay just like this.' Regret it or not, the comfort of his arms around her was exactly what she needed. Being close to him, feeling his care, his love, was so seductive it would have taken a saint not to respond.

The bed was empty when Angie woke. An early sailing. She took her cereals into the living room to look for the boat but it was long gone. The tide was already falling, exposing the sand banks along the quayside. A phalanx of turnstones was scouring the foreshore in search of a fresh harvest of shrimps. She opened the patio doors and stepped onto the balcony. The last of the yachts were being lifted out of the water and mothballed in the yard for the winter. Cyclists passed beneath her on their way to work; motorists stopped at the shop for their morning paper and a coffee. It was just a normal day. Too normal. Shouldn't she be feeling... different? Maybe she'd lived too long in a world of exaggerated emotions to appreciate simple, uncomplicated love. Maybe this was contentment.

Angie's commute to work took longer than normal, an accident at the Westleigh junction, but she was still there before the rest of the team. She had to manage the fall-out before Paul was buried without trace in the care system.

'You're meant to be on sick leave.' Bill picked up Paul's file.

'Just want to write up yesterday. Has Adrian asked for Paul to be moved?'

'Not yet but I'm expecting it. A couple of years older and he'd be facing an assault charge.'

'Rubbish. It was only a graze. Hardly see it this morning.'

'He knocked you out.'

'I passed out. Not the same thing. I know we haven't seen eye to eye on Paul but if we write him off now that's it. He'll be in a Borstal in a couple of years and God knows where after that.' She held out her hand for Paul's file. 'Don't let them move him. Not yet.'

The phone rang. Angie picked it up. 'Okay, thanks. Interview room one please. Yes. Thanks.'

'Who's that?'

'The Clarke's. I asked them to come in.'

Angie squeezed into the interview room. It doubled as a store for the walking frames and miscellaneous aids Sarah and the other therapists insisted of putting anywhere other than their own office. She'd complained but at least it was providing a diversion for Amy who was happily playing park-keeper with an extending grip. Steve and Kate looked less comfortable.

'Has Rosemary offered you a coffee?' Angie asked.

'Yes, but we're fine thanks.' Steve answered.

'Thanks for coming. I wouldn't have asked but there have been developments, with Paul.'

'Is he okay?' Kate looked anxious.

'Physically, yes. But…' She looked at them. 'I won't beat about the bush. I understand why you haven't seen Paul lately and why you didn't come to the review but I needed to know if there's any chance you might…'

'I can't have him back,' Kate interrupted, on the verge of tears. 'We go along fine but as soon as he walks through the door this shadow descends. All the joy we have with Amy, everything, becomes… I don't know… tainted.'

'It's the chip on his shoulder,' Steve said.

'Chip!' Kate exclaimed.

'Okay, so that's an understatement. He's a good lad at heart but with everything that's happened, there's been too much damage. Maybe if there was more support.'

'For you?' Angie asked.

'Us, Paul. Amy too. Don't get me wrong. You've been great, but since Paul went back to the children's home they don't seem to want us around. Like it's too much trouble.'

'It's sitting in that room with him,' Kate said. 'Trying to talk. All of us trapped together. He hates it. Hates us.'

'And he always kicks off after we've gone,' Steve said. 'Picking fights with the staff and the other kids. So we decided to stop going, for everyone's sake. They didn't argue.'

Angie watched Kate pick phantom bits of fluff off her jacket. 'I'm sorry the visiting hasn't worked out. And I didn't ask you here to pressure you into taking Paul back.'

'So what is this about?' Steve said.

'Honestly? I'm not sure. Paul has been getting more and more uncontrollable and yesterday he crossed a line. It feels important to do everything I can to pull him back now, before it's too late. You know him better than anyone. I suppose I thought talking with you might help.'

'What did he do?' Kate asked.

'He lost it when I told him the review board had decided he was staying at Ellison Road, threw a lamp at me. There was no reasoning with him.'

'So that explains the dressing?' Steve said.

'It's not serious.'

'But it could have been,' Kate interrupted.

Angie looked at her. All her gut instincts told her honesty was vital but what was the honest answer?

'I mean,' Kate continued, 'he's so angry, all the time. It's like treading on eggshells never knowing when he'll blow.'

'Not all the time,' Steve said. 'You remember when I took him out on the boat? For a good couple of hours he was just a normal kid having a great time. He was a hundred per cent focused on the conditions and what to do. He listened to me. Did what I said,' Kate's expression said it all. 'I know... but he did.' Steve looked at Angie. 'If I had any advice it would be to find an activity, sailing, anything that he needs to totally concentrate on. The children's home is too claustrophobic. He needs space, the chance to pit himself against the elements, or in a competition of some sort. I'd lash out stuck in that place.'

'You know what would work,' Kate said, suddenly animated. 'Speed racing. Get him on one of those bikes round the dirt track at Exeter. Noise, mud, physically really challenging.' She paused. 'I guess he's a bit young for it though. Maybe football?'

'The way things are he'll need more than just the occasional trip but the home don't have the staff for regular one-to-one

144

outings,' Angie said. 'And I'm fighting a losing battle over my time with Paul, but I'll think of something.'

'What happens if you can't?' Steve asked.

Angie hesitated. 'They're talking about a secure unit.'

'Secure... but wouldn't that mean even more restrictions?' Kate looked at Steve. 'He'd hate it. There's no knowing what he'd...' her voice broke. Steve took her hand.

'I'm sorry. I didn't want to upset you,' Angie said. 'We'll leave it there. But thanks so much for coming in.'

Angie leant against the wall, gasping for breath. The run to Fremington Quay and back was a favourite after work but it had taken more out of her than usual. Too much good living now that Mike was around. She was on her way to the shower when the phone rang.

'Ange?' The voice was unsteady.

'Christine?'

'I wondered if you could come up for a few days. I'm a bit under the weather. It would be really good to see you.'

'Oh, Christine. How many times do I have to...?'

'Well, when I say under the weather, it's a bit more serious.'

'How serious?' Her mouth suddenly felt dry.

'I... I can't talk about it over the phone. Be so much easier if you could be here. I could get the deli to drop us some goodies round so we can hunker down. I need a friend, Angie. You will come won't you?'

Angie swallowed. 'Of course I'll come. It'll take me a day or two, but I'll be with you, soon.'

'Thanks, Angie, can't tell you how much I... I mean... you've always been there...'

'It's okay,' Angie interrupted. 'Do you need anything?'

'Just you.'

'Anybody home?' Mike shook off his boots in the porch and walked through to the sitting room. He slid his arm round

Angie's shoulder and kissed her. 'Sorry I couldn't get here at the weekend. Busiest half term they've had for a while. Not often they put on another sailing from Ilfracombe.'

'It's okay. Kettle's just boiled.' Angie was on the sofa with a half-finished report balanced on one knee and Garfield spread-eagled on the other.

'Prefer this.' He produced a bottle of Rioja. 'Join me?'

'Not tonight. I need to finish this,' she waved the report at him, 'then I'm off out.'

'Didn't you get my message, that I'm just here for tonight?' His disappointment was tangible.

'Sorry, but I can't change all my arrangements to fit in with your shifts.' There was an uncomfortable edge to her voice.

Mike ousted Garfield and sat next to Angie. 'What's up?'

'Nothing.'

He took her hand. 'I've missed you this week.'

'We've talked.'

'I know, but it's not the same as being here, waking with you beside me…'

Angie pulled her hand away. 'I need to get this done, Mike.' She stared at the sheet in front of her.

'Suit yourself,' he said eventually. 'Sure about the wine? He searched the dresser for an opener.

She hesitated. 'Maybe just half a glass.'

'How are things at work with what's his name?'

'Paul? The same. At least Adrian's agreed to keep him.'

Mike filled his glass, picked up the paper, flicked through a few pages, dropped it onto the sofa, walked to the window then turned back to Angie. 'What's happened?'

'Nothing's happened.'

'Then why are you being so… offhand?'

'I need to get this done.' She checked the clock. 'Too late now though.' She drained her glass and busied herself collecting art materials. 'We'll talk later, I promise. Got to go.'

'What is it tonight?'

'Photography club. I've persuaded the art gallery to give the school some wall space for an exhibition at Christmas.'

'Tom's stuff?'

'Mostly, but the others are coming on. Graham's done a great job keeping them interested.' She gathered up a black portfolio, kissed him briefly and headed for the door. She flinched at the cold. The autumn had been so mild she'd got used to going without her coat, but not tonight.

'Sorry I'm late,' Angie said, finally stepping inside Christine's immaculate apartment. 'Bomb scare on the underground shut the circle line and everyone and his dog was waiting for a taxi.'

Christine laughed. 'I'd forgotten what living in the back of beyond does to a girl. 'Everyone and his dog! You're in need of some serious city time.' A waft of Chanel preceded her as she leant to kiss Angie. 'Come on in. I'll get us a drink.'

'So, how are you?'

'Plenty of time for that. The bathroom's over there. You get yourself titivated and then we're going to town.'

'But on the phone...'

'Indulge me, Ange, please. I promised you *Miss Saigon* and that's exactly what we're going to do.'

Christine was always difficult to resist but now, when she was making light of God knows what, Angie had no chance. She found herself wafted into the bathroom, a warm scented bath run for her and the softest white towels laid ready, scattered with rose petals. It was wonderful to feel so nurtured. And with Christine perched on the end of the bath they could talk.

'Did I tell you about Cannes?' Christine began. 'You should have been there. I tell you it was...'

Angie didn't need to listen. There was nothing new in the words, but something was different. Her mind wandered, tracking random thoughts that led nowhere. And lying there, warm, cosseted and a world away from social services, that felt absolutely fine. Nowhere. What was nowhere? Was it one of those magic lands at the top of Enid Blyton's Magic Faraway Tree? What did it look like? She traced the word in the steam on the mirror tiles. *Nowhere.* 'Wow!' She traced it again underneath. *Now here.* You could go from nowhere to somewhere just by adding some space. 'That's amazing.'

'What's amazing?' Christine said, pausing mid flow.

'Oh, just some semantics.' She pointed at the fading words.

'You haven't been listening to a word I've said, Angie Turner!' She put her hands into the water and flicked some bubbles towards Angie.

'Guilty as charged but totally unrepentant,' Angie laughed, gathering a mound of bubbles and launching them at Christine.

Christine smiled. 'Now that's the Ange I know. You're ready to hit the town. Come on.' She held out a towel.

It was later, much later, that Angie realised what was different. They'd shouted their encores at the show, danced themselves ragged clubbing and sat curled up together on the white leather sofa talking and talking - was it any surprise if Christine's voice was a bit rough? But this was different. Through the blur of too many cocktails it was suddenly crystal clear. It wasn't her words, but something about her voice she'd sensed earlier. Christine's wonderful, engaging, delectable burr was missing. Angie finally summoned up the courage to ask. 'The problem... is it your voice?'

Christine rolled away. 'What shall we do tomorrow? How about lunch at Casa Viera? They've got a new chef. He's rather cute.'

'Chrissy, please.' Angie felt strangely sober. 'It's why you called. Why I'm here. Please, tell me.'

'Oh, it's probably nothing. I felt this tiny little lump... no bigger than a pea really but BUPA comes with the deal so I thought, why not? Just get them to tell me it was nothing worth worrying about and I'm out of there.'

'But that's not what they said.'

'Hey,' she refilled their glasses. 'What do those jumped up doctors know anyway?'

'What did they say?' Angie took both Christine's hands in hers. 'Tell me.'

The sound of a river boat passing filled the space as everything inside the room became eerily still. 'Apparently... apparently there's a fifty-fifty chance I've got throat cancer.'

Angie wrapped her arms around Christine. 'I'm so, so...' The tears were too close.

'My throat. Of all places.'

'How...when will you know?'

'I've a biopsy tomorrow.' She looked at the clock. 'Today.'

'If it is, you know, can they operate?' Angie stroked Christine's hair as if trying to wipe the rogue cells away.

'The miraculous world of modern medicine can do anything. But they said I needed to know there was a substantial risk of permanent damage to the vocal chords. Substantial risk!' Christine pulled away. 'Just words to them. They don't care it's the end of everything. Everything.' She sank back, her head in her hands.

'But if it removed the cancer... there'll be other things...'

'I don't want other things! I want my life... this life...' The words dried up as the tears finally came, smearing her make-up, stripping her of the last remnants of a face so carefully presented to the world.

Angie had never seen Chrissy so vulnerable. 'Come here.' The impulse to hold her close, to will the pain away, or at least to carry it for her, was irresistible. 'It's okay, I'm here. I'll help you through this.'

'Promise?' Christine sobbed, holding on to her.

'I promise. Let's start by getting you to bed. Come on.' She led her to the bedroom. It was like laying a rag doll down; limp, submissive, defeated. Angie helped her out of her dress and covered her with the duvet.

Christine's hand reached for hers. 'Don't leave me, Ange. Don't leave me.'

'Ssshhh. I won't.' She quickly undressed and slid in beside her. Christine pulled her close until their bodies melded into one. Angie felt consumed by the presence that was Chrissy:

Chrissy who needed her right now. No-one else. Just her.

'Hey sleepy head. Time to rise and shine.'

The words came from somewhere above her. Angie felt Christine stroking the hair from her face. The sensation somehow managed to register over the protest raging inside her head. 'Oh, God,' she groaned. 'I'm dying.'

Christine dumped a coffee cup on the bedside table. 'Great choice of words.'

Angie pulled herself up and reached for her arm. 'Chrissy. I'm sorry. I didn't think. It's this hangover. How can you drink like that and still,' she looked at her, 'still look fantastic the morning after?'

'Years of practice, darling. You've got forty minutes.'

'Forty minutes?'

'You are coming with me aren't you? There's no way I can face this on my own.'

'Yes, of course.' Of course she was. If she could just be sure she wasn't going to throw up as soon as she moved.

It was another world, private health care. No heaving waiting areas with a sign announcing a fifty minute delay. No unsmiling staff, remarkable by their absence. No six week wait for the information you're desperate not to hear. 'They'll call you today?' Angie had exclaimed as they walked out.

And now Christine was taking the call. 'Yes.' She spoke with difficulty. The investigation had bruised her throat, giving her a taste of what was to come. 'My date of birth? Why…? I see. January first, fifty-six. Yes… Yes…

Angie strained to hear the consultant's voice. Christine had wandered into the bedroom. She should follow, be there for her when the news came. Christine needed her. She knew that now, after last night. She was half way across the living room when the strangulated shriek came. Angie rushed in, her heart pounding. Christine was lying on the bed, her face in her hands.

Angie couldn't bear it any longer. 'What did they say?'

Christine looked up, her eyes bright again, the old Chrissy safely back. 'Storm in a tea cup, thank God. Apparently my little pea is benign. How good is that?'

'Oh, Christine, that's fantastic.' Angie rushed to embrace her, her cheeks wet with tears of relief.

Christine gave her a squeeze then slipped out of her arms. 'Give me five will you? Want to get my face on.'

Angie sat on the bed, her heart racing. Everything was going to be okay - no, not just okay, better! All this... it had brought them closer than they'd ever been. She felt complete, as a child might with her family around her.

The bathroom door snapped open. 'I'm ravenous. Let's get some breakfast... Angie?'

'Sorry, miles away,' Angie replied.

'I guess you'll need to be soon, miles away that is. Duty calls and all that.' Christine dodged round Angie and blotted her lipstick in the mirror. 'Unless I can tempt you to another night on the town?'

'Maybe. It's about time I...' Christine's phone interrupted.

'Frances, put your glad-rags on, girl and meet me at the Phoenix at seven... Why? Because it's the only place to be tonight. Tell you later.' She replaced the receiver and turned back to the mirror. 'What were you saying, Angie?' she called over her shoulder.

'Hi.' Angie dropped her case on the living room floor.

'Hi.' Mike led her to the sofa. 'You look exhausted. How did it go? How's your friend?'

'She's, umm, she's going to be fine. Is fine.'

'That's great. I bet you're relieved.'

'Yes.' It should have been the truth, was the truth; but the complete truth? That was something she'd spent the long journey home trying to disentangle. It felt important to know; know why she felt such an aching void inside. It had been a close call. She should be over the moon it wasn't cancer. And she was. But after last night... why had Christine been so pleased to hear from Frances? When she was there with her, for her, waiting beside her to support or celebrate. Why? Why had she suddenly felt so... redundant? Why hadn't Christine protested when Angie said she should get back, as long as everything was okay? She'd almost looked relieved. But of course she'd looked relieved, she'd just escaped cancer.

'What's up?' Mike asked.

'Oh, just the strain of everything I guess. I'll be fine after a good night's sleep.'

'You need a nice, long soak. I'll run the bath for you...'

'No! No. I think I'll just watch TV for a while.'

'Okay. I'll get a bottle. White or red?'

'Whatever you fancy.' Just a few short hours ago she'd felt so alive but now? Had it all been a mirage, her and Christine? A re-run of all those years ago when a college crush had ended their friendship.

Mike handed her a glass. 'Budge up.' He settled himself next to her. 'Let's see what's on.' He landed on a few minutes of *Casualty* before the picture cut to the BBC newsroom. *We interrupt this programme to bring a news flash from Berlin. At a press conference just before 7pm this evening, GDR central committee spokesman Guenter Schabowski was asked when a new law permitting GDR citizens more freedom of travel would go into effect. He told the journalist: "As far as I know, that goes into effect now, immediately." Hundreds of GDR citizens who watched that broadcast are now streaming to the border separating East and West Berlin.'*

'You can do without this tonight. There must be something lighter.' Mike reached for the remote.

'No, leave it... please.' Whatever else had happened, this was real, life-changing. They watched as the camera zoomed in on Checkpoint Charlie. Crowds were pushing forward, dangerously close to the guards. The commentator continued. *There seems to be confusion amongst the border guards, probably unaware of the press conference. I can see several on phones, probably looking to their superiors for guidance.* Angie gripped Mike's hand. *A large crowd has gathered on the Western side; there's an enormous sense of expectation that something momentous is about to happen.'*

Much later, Angie switched off the lights and went to bed, though not to sleep. The images swirling round her mind were too vivid. It was just before midnight that the unthinkable happened and East Germany's Communist rulers gave the order to open the gates. Hundreds of people surged through, cheering and shouting, to be met by jubilant West Berliners on the other side. She'd gasped as hoards actually clambered on top of the Wall and began to hack at the concrete. Something that had been a symbol of fear and oppression, that had claimed so many lives, was being dismantled by the very people it had imprisoned.

Mike stirred as she lifted the duvet. 'Are you okay?'

'It's down, the Berlin Wall is down. People are streaming across. You need to see it.'

'I will, tomorrow. Just now, you need some sleep.'

Angie leant on her elbow, running a finger down his tanned back; strong, supportive and there for her. She leant across and kissed his shoulder. 'Thank you, Mike,' she whispered.

He turned and wrapped his arms around her. 'What for?'

'For caring.'

Chapter Nineteen
Spring 1990

'Are you coming in?' Steve held the car door for Kate.

'This is a mistake. I shouldn't have come. You know how he is. I don't want him taking off as soon as he sees me.'

Steve leant against the car. 'We don't have to do this at all. You heard Adrian. Paul wasn't exactly busting to come out with us either.'

'We can't back out, not now. It wouldn't be fair.'

'Better now than later.'

'No, I meant what I said. We can't abandon him.' She smiled at him. 'Just you though. No point in stacking the odds against us right from the start.'

'If you're sure.'

'I'm sure. Now get out of here!'

Kate watched as Steve walked down the concrete path to the door of Ellison Road. It was almost nine months since their last visit. Time they'd spent becoming a real family with Amy. Time without the constant emotional battering from Paul reducing her to tears more often than she wanted to remember.

If only he'd got on okay, if only Angie hadn't called, if only she hadn't painted such a graphic picture of the future that lay ahead for him, then life could have gone on in its comfortable groove. But now she knew, what choice did they have?

The front door burst open and Paul raced through. 'One step out of line and you're grounded, you hear me?' Adrian called after him. He shook Steve's hand. 'Good luck.'

'Thanks,' Steve said. 'Don't go too far from the phone!'

'What's she doing here?' Paul pointed at the car. 'I ain't going nowhere with her.' He started walking down the street.

'Hey, Paul,' Steve called. 'Wait up.' Paul kept walking. 'Fine. Do what you want. But I've got the tickets.'

Paul made a show of kicking a can along the kerb, first away, then back towards them.

'Steve,' Kate handed him the keys. 'You two go. I'll get the bus back.'

'We can't let him win.'

'It's okay. We knew it'd be tough. I should have thought it through and let you get on with it. This way I get to make the decision.'

Steve took her hand. 'I won't let him drive us apart.'

'I know.' Kate kissed him. 'Go on, before he puts that can through someone's window.' She walked towards the bus stop, passing within hailing distance of Paul. 'Right, I've got things to do. Enjoy the match.' She kept walking, resisting the temptation to look back. It had always been her intention to go, her choice. That was the message. And if he hadn't spotted her hands trembling as they gripped her bag she might have got away with it.

'Sorry to call so late but I was out and couldn't get to a phone.' Angie waited, senses acutely tuned to Kate's voice. 'How did it go?'

'You should be putting your feet up at this time of night not thinking about work,' Kate said.' Anyway, relax. Steve got him to the match and back without any major incidents.'

'How about minor ones?'

'Had to pull him up on his language a few times but mostly it gave Paul the chance to shout, swear and leap up and down without it being anything out of the way.'

Angie had to ask. 'You said Steve?'

Kate hesitated. 'Paul wasn't exactly over the moon to see me so I left them to it.'

'I guess that was always on the cards. How do you feel about it?'

'Too soon to say, Angie.'

'Of course it is, sorry. Getting ahead of myself. Has Steve arranged anything else?'

'Couple more football games, speed racing at the Exeter track and a promise to take him out in the boat as soon as we get it in the water.'

'Bit of male bonding then.'

'Seemed best. No point fighting a losing battle.'

'He'll get there with you, Kate,' Angie said, though the words sounded hollow, even to her.

'I'm not sure he will, but it's different this time. I guess I expected too much before. I'm happy to back off and let Steve do what he can.'

'Happy?'

'Yes, honestly.'

'So Shelley is doing okay at the minute. Anything else?' Bill pushed the file across the desk. He'd squeezed an extra supervision in before Angie went on leave.

'Nothing I can predict. Sean is covering my on-call. The only situation that might blow up you know all too well.'

'Paul.'

'Last reports are he's calming down a bit, thanks to the Clarke's. Still rocky with Kate but Steve's been brilliant.'

'Early days though. They've blown hot and cold before. How's Kate coping?'

'Much better. Bit of a seed change there. Probably because things are going so well with Amy she's not so sensitive to Paul. She lets Steve get on with it and does the practical stuff like lifts and lunches.'

'Any news on the mother?'

'Not yet. Given the arrest warrant, though, can't see it'll be long.'

'And school?'

'Could be an issue. He's still volatile with the other kids. His street cred leapt when he got that art prize though.'

'What art prize?'

'A national ran a competition to find a new cartoon strip. He came third, even up against adults. They ran his storyline for a week. Did more for him than any amount of therapy.' Angie gathered up the files. 'If anything does blow can you try and stop Adrian over-reacting. Paul's been on his case ever since the bubble wrap incident.'

Angie drew back the sitting room curtains. Waves were already crashing over the Bar and it wasn't even high tide. Inevitable really at this time of year. March winds and all that. She stuffed a couple more jumpers in her case and locked the door behind her.

'Morning, Angie.' The Oldenburg's skipper greeted her when she reached the quay.

'Hi, Adam. Bit of a swell running.'

'Better than any fairground ride.'

Angie climbed the steps to the top deck. She'd be okay for the twenty minutes or so it took to reach the mouth of the estuary. Then she'd fix her eyes on the horizon and pray her breakfast stayed down. Lundy was her refuge but this rite of passage was cruel. There was one brief respite as they neared the lee of the island. A shout from the port side had her crossing the deck just in time to spot some dolphins shadowing the boat, riding its bow wave. For a few blissful minutes she followed them as they arched through the waves, flashes of symmetry overlaying the churning sea.

Half an hour after landing she was still feeling queasy. 'Here, drink this.' Mike handed her a mug.

'What is it?'

'Ginger tea. Works every time.'

She was perched on a wooden chair at the end of Mike's bed in the cabin-like room he rented. With its corrugated exterior and plain walls it felt more like a converted shipping container than a home. A small stove in the corner radiated heat but the sound of the wind probing and piercing the fragile building made her shiver. 'Where's your roommate?'

'Doesn't come over until till next week. All ours until then.' He scanned the room with fresh eyes. 'Sorry, not exactly the Ritz. I tried to get the Lookout but it was booked up months ago.'

She kissed him. 'Thanks for trying.'

She'd had better nights. Sharing a single bed was novel, risqué even, when you're eighteen and escaping home for the first time. But now, cupped together after their lovemaking, feeling the heaviness of his limbs, his breath on her neck, the heat of his body she felt… what? Loved? Desired? But something else too. As the night wore on, his touch, at first comforting, arousing, became almost suffocating. In her king-size bed at home she could quickly slip out of his embrace and claim her space. It was early morning before Mike gave her a final kiss and dressed. He'd scheduled a survey of the sea bed off the North Eastern tip of the island. Perfect conditions apparently.

When she finally woke, Angie dressed, layered on her waterproofs and set off across the moorland covering the centre of the island. If she headed for the coast path just beyond the Lookout she might see Mike's boat. But she was barely half way there when the weather closed in. Within seconds the swirling cloud made a mockery of her senses. Looking back there was no sign of the old lighthouse or the cluster of buildings surrounding the Marisco tavern. But was she was even looking in the right direction? She scoured the ground. Plenty of tracks crossing each other but impossible to pick out a path. She chose a direction at random and set off in a straight line. She'd to come to the cliff sooner or later.

The boggy hinterland eventually gave way to the shorter, springy turf that fringed the coastal strip to the west. Angie could feel the faint trace of a breeze against her cheek. It was southerly when she started out, so walking into it should take her back. Dark shapes loomed out of the mist, rocks marking the cliff edge; reassurance she was on the right track but a warning to tread carefully. She wouldn't be the first to stray too close. Suddenly a shape lunged towards her. She dropped to the ground, convinced she was falling towards the cliff.

'Not right to be walking here. Dangerous.'

The voice was familiar. 'Tom? Is that you?'

He stepped closer, becoming real. 'Should go back.'

'I am, or thought I was.'

'That way.' He pointed at right angles to the direction she was taking, as if seeing the path with the X ray vision of one of Paul's characters.

'My lucky day, you being here.'

'Lucky day, yes.'

'Of course, it's Easter. You're with your mum.'

'No.' He recoiled as if scalded. 'This way.' He took off into the mist.

'Wait, Tom.' Angie hurried after him. She'd thought nothing about Tom could still surprise her, but he twisted and turned through the undergrowth with a certainty that was unnerving. She could barely see her feet, yet he was striding out as if it was the clearest spring day.

He eventually stopped outside the bunkhouse. 'You knew I was here?' Angie asked, careful to focus on scraping the mud off her boots, anything to avoid his eyes.

'Came on the Oldenburg yesterday, staying with Mike, here till Friday. Taking pictures.'

'Hope so. If this mist clears.'

'Clear tomorrow. No puffins yet. Just guillemots and razorbills. Can show you where to go. Where to get the best shots. Can show you mine.'

'You've been taking photographs?'

He shuffled from foot to foot, looking over his shoulder as if he needed to be somewhere else.

Angie tried again. 'I mean, yes please, I'd like to see your pictures.'

He started walking away, then stopped. Perfectly still,

waiting. Angie followed. He led her past the shop, down the track and turned into a field on the right. There were two tents pitched in the lee of the wall, the most sheltered spot. He disappeared into the smaller tent and emerged with a large black folder. Angie recognised it from their sessions at school. But all recognition ended the moment he opened it. She glimpsed guillemots, razorbills, kittiwakes, many of them caught in flight, spectacular compositions against stormy skies. And grazing deer against a backdrop of a flaming sunset. 'Tom, these are... spectacular.' She looked at him. For a second, maybe two, he looked back. 'So much better than anything we've done in the group. Astonishing.'

He shifted from foot to foot then disappeared into the tent. Angie waited, unsure what was expected of her. The tent flap moved. Tom was holding it open. She crept through. He'd laid the photographs out on his sleeping bag. 'This one,' he began, 'taken at 6am with a 300mm telephoto lens. Had to use a tripod, slow shutter speed.'

'How did you get them developed?'

'Mike. This one,' he pointed at a print of two kittiwakes mirroring each other as they spiralled down towards a blue-green sea, 'shutter open, against the light.'

Angie let the words wash over her as Tom pointed at each print, recounting minute details with a clinical accuracy completely at odds with the breathtaking artistry of the shots. He'd captured a deer's head tilted towards her, the eye so perfectly focused she'd swear he was gazing straight at her. She could hear the cacophony of nesting guillemots, their black heads stark against the grey-white guano spattered across the cliffs. His close-up of a kittiwake in flight drew her eye to its wing tips, looking as though they'd been dipped in ink. And all the time, Tom spoke with a fluency she'd thought impossible.

It took Angie a while to hear the silence after the last photo. He'd shifted away from her, straining at the fabric of the tent. Angie understood. Back in this moment she was an intruder. 'Thank you, Tom. These are so good. Exceptional.' She didn't wait for a response.

The Marisco was busy. Mike waited patiently at the bar, giving Angie a reassuring grin each time their eyes met.

'I saw Tom today,' she said when he finally returned. 'He showed me his prints.'

'Amazing, aren't they.'

'He said you got them developed.'

'He takes a bit of keeping up with, but I drop the negatives in whenever I go over. Good job he's only here holiday time. Have me bankrupt.'

'It's kind of you.' Angie heard the warmth in her voice.

'Don't sound so surprised. I do have the odd philanthropic urge.' He leant across and kissed her. 'Love the way you've got your hair. Fancied a change?'

She brushed her fringe back. 'What's with the tent, though? I'm surprised Graham let Tom camp. He doesn't have a clue how to look after himself.'

Mike leant back and picked up his glass. 'Maybe he's never had the chance to learn.'

'I still can't see Graham agreeing.'

'He didn't. That's to say, he doesn't know. Tom's meant to be with his mum but she chucked him out. He'd only been there a day, poor kid. I passed him sitting on the bench outside the Marisco. Still there two hours later, in the pouring rain.'

'Poor Tom!'

'We took him in and dried him off. Tried to take him home but she wasn't having any of it. So I dug out my tent for him.' He smiled at Angie. 'You're right, though. Not a clue what to wear, when to eat, sleep, that kind of thing. But we're looking out for him.'

Angie frowned. 'Wish I hadn't asked. I ought to call Graham.'

'And ruin the kid's only chance of some freedom? He won't come to any harm.'

'You don't know that,' she snapped. 'He's vulnerable. I've a duty of care.'

'Give the kid a break. Okay, so he might forget to eat until we take him something. Or stay up all night and sleep all day.

161

Does it *really* matter?'

It was the kind of impassioned plea Angie could hear herself making. Did it matter? What was the greatest risk? Maybe physical injury if he wandered at night. But he'd just rescued her from the cliff edge and been far more sure-footed in the mist than she was. 'Will his mother take him back?'

'In a day or two. She usually comes round. Anyway,' he leant towards her, his face eager, excited. 'Stop thinking about the kids. I've something to show you tomorrow.'

'Assuming I can see anything.'

'Mist will be gone by then. But it's only across the green.'

'What?'

'The Trust is looking…' he paused. 'No, I'll save it for the morning. I'm off until lunch. We can look together.'

'Look at what? You can't stop now.'

He moved his head from side to side, considering.

'Mike!'

'Okay, okay. There's a loft over the information centre used for storage. They've started clearing it out. Apparently they're considering letting it as some kind of visitor attraction.' He looked expectantly at her.

'And…?'

'Don't you see, it's the perfect opportunity.'

'For what?'

'A photography studio, for you.'

'Me!' Angie exclaimed.

'You've always said it's what you want. To have your own studio. Imagine it. Waking every day to the sounds of Lundy. Your commute to work a stroll along the coast path. Days spent walking the cliffs taking photographs.'

'It's a lovely dream…' Angie paused. Mike had a way of making all things seem possible. She'd put the thought out there long ago, but he was the one who'd taken the baton and run with it.

'It could be more than a dream. You've real talent, Angie. And you love it here.'

The next morning there was no mist, nothing to stop her seeing things clearly. Why was she making life so complicated? For the first time in ages she felt... what? Excitement? Optimism? It was as though she was waking from a dream and realising this life had been there, waiting for her, all the time. The loft needed vision to see it as a studio, but Mike was right, it had potential.

'What do you think?' he asked as they stood in the doorway.

'Honestly?' Angie burst into a smile and hugged him. 'It's perfect.' She picked her way through the upturned furniture and boxes to the triangular window that framed the view. 'Display of originals here, trays of prints for customers to browse along there,' she described a space along one wall with her arms. 'Counter back here,' she climbed over a collection of tools, 'then a partition to create a work space over there.'

'Come here, you,' Mike wrapped his arms around her. 'So good to see you happy. Not just happy, free. It's like you've shed this weight that's been keeping the real Angie prisoner.'

Angie turned and kissed him. A long, tender kiss that came from somewhere deep inside, from her whole self. She could feel his body respond, not just with passion, but relief that an unseen but all-too-present barrier had dissolved. It was time to move on.

Chapter Twenty
Autumn 1990

'How's it going, Kate?' Angie asked wrapping her hands around a mug of coffee to keep the touchline chill at bay. 'Paul must have been, what, a dozen times now?'

'Yes, with some other bits and pieces in between.'

'What's the verdict?'

'Go on, Paul...Yes!' Kate cheered as Paul scored. 'Well, your suggestion to give him some rope has worked. Neither of us is making a big deal about being around each other.' Kate nodded at the pitch where Paul was running wide to take a pass. 'This was inspirational. He's not hemmed in so he doesn't feel the need to take off. Besides, he's getting all the running he needs out there.'

'Something's changed though. Did you see the way he looked round just then, after he scored? Your approval is starting to matter. I'm so glad you didn't give up on him.'

Kate winced. 'It came close didn't it? You remember when you tried explaining about Paul pushing buttons? Well it started all over again on that first visit when he refused to get in the car with me. It was like the months apart hadn't happened. He was on my case instantly. But, like I told you, this time it didn't work. I just decided I wasn't going to let it matter. And it didn't. I guess you'd say 'simple'.'

'But not easy.'

'I don't know. Once I stopped taking everything so personally it was almost easy. He got on with Steve, so all the contact was boy stuff. Out in the boat, constantly pitting himself against the elements. Football matches where he could shout and holler and not have to face any 'meaningful' conversations. Big lesson that. Then he started supporting Tottenham - stuck in front of the TV for every game was perfect bonding with Steve.'

'Every game? So how often have you been in touch?'

'Lately, I guess every week about something or other. He asked to go to Plymouth last month.'

'Plymouth!'

Kate smiled. 'I know. Adrian almost put his foot down but Steve thought we should go with the flow. Said he'd chain Paul to his wrist if necessary. I hardly slept the night before but Steve... he's been amazing, Angie. When I think how I almost drove him away.'

Angie touched her arm. 'Hey, that was a long time ago. A lot's changed. So what happened?'

'Sorry?'

'Plymouth.'

'Oh, nothing. Suddenly, everything was spookily normal. No fight to get him in the car, no arguments on the way, no sulks, no scrapping. It was like he'd decided to... I don't know, toe the line I suppose.'

'Where did he go?'

'That was easy. The Barbican. We thought he'd want the shops, or to see a film, but no. We walked the Barbican from end to end. Have you seen the mural down there? It fills the entire wall of this house. He stood looking at it for ages.'

'That's where he was the time he absconded overnight. Do you remember?'

'What kind of a question is that!'

Angie smiled. 'How's it going with Amy?'

'That's the weird thing. She absolutely adores him. Soon as she sees him she rushes up and grabs his hand. I panicked the first time, physical contact is such an issue, I was afraid he'd lash out.'

'But he didn't?'

'No. You won't believe this, but he let her kiss him.'

'So the time you're spending with Paul, it hasn't rocked the boat with Amy?'

'Just the opposite. It's like seeing him has filled a gap she didn't realise was there. Nothing she could explain, it's an instinctive thing.'

Out on the pitch the whistle blew. 'I'm off,' Angie said. 'You don't want the evil witch sabotaging things.'

Kate put a hand on her arm. 'You're okay. He takes at least ten minutes in the locker room. And there's something I want to ask.' They walked towards the cars. 'I know it's only been a few months, and there's a long way to go but... we wondered about having Paul stay over the odd weekend. Just to see how it goes.'

Angie stopped mid stride. 'Stay over?'

'You think I'm mad.'

'No, of course not. I'm sorry, I didn't mean to react like that. It's great that things have been going so well, really. I just didn't see it coming.'

'It was Paul who asked. When Steve saw him last week. He didn't come right out with it, of course. In true Paul style he went on about how the football would look much better on a wide screen, like the one we've got. And how we could leave earlier to get to Plymouth next time if we didn't have to start out from different places.'

'It would be great, but are you sure? His relationship with you is getting there, but all this talk of Plymouth, it's only about one thing, you do know that don't you?'

Behind Kate a stream of boys erupted from the club house. 'I don't care, Angie. Not anymore. If my only relevance to Paul is as someone who keeps him fed, clothed and on the road every spare minute he has searching for his mother, then that's okay. I've seen what it does to them in that so-called home.' She waved at Paul. 'I gave up on him once. I'm not going to make the same mistake again.'

Angie watched as the Oldenburg manoeuvred into place alongside the quay. It had become a ritual to meet Mike off the boat. Work still interfered with their relationship more often than he was comfortable with but she was getting better at saying 'no' when yet another colleague called in sick, better at delegating, better at helping clients find their own solutions. It had given them time together; easy, intimate, companionable time. So easy that Mike's lingering frustration at the twenty or so watery miles that separated them seemed to be fading. And, for Angie at least, their frequent partings and reunions added a certain frisson.

'I called in the estate office yesterday,' Mike began as they stood side by side in the kitchen, clearing up after their evening meal. 'About the loft on Lundy. Looks like they're letting it soon.' He put his arm around her waist. 'You've got to go for it, Angie. I've been watching the visitors pour over all summer. We get a hundred on the boat in the season. Two hundred and fifty peak weeks.'

'Oh, Mike. It sounded so... so doable back in the spring but how could I survive without my income? Pay the rent on this place?'

He drew her closer. 'We could get something together, on Lundy. You love it there. You know you do.'

'For a week every now and then, but permanently? I don't know.' She pulled away. 'I mean, being cut off in the winter, not able to catch up with friends when I want to.'

'Friends? Like Christine you mean? The so-called friend who hasn't been in touch since she realised she didn't need you after all?'

'You don't understand...'

'Maybe I don't,' Mike turned her to face him. 'But I can see. See when someone I love is being taken advantage of and selling herself short. You're worth more than that.'

'Please, don't...'

'Don't what?' He was suddenly very still, gripping her arm. 'It's time to stop playing games, Angie. Time to decide who you are, what you want. This is a fantastic opportunity, for

167

both of us. Can't you see that?'

One thing Angie could see was that she was running out of time. He'd been so patient, tolerating her blowing hot and cold. And even when he blew a fuse, coming back. Always coming back.

'Yes, I can.' She walked onto the balcony. Down-river, Lundy was clear. 'Lundy high, sign of dry,' she whispered. It was her dream wasn't it? Hers… and Christine's. It had always been Christine who'd seen her talent, believed in her creativity, mocked her for settling for less. She missed her. She'd waited and waited for her to call but life, Christine, had moved on. Maybe it was time for her to do the same.

'So?' Mike said. It sounded like an ultimatum.

It took a while for the words to surface. 'Let's do it.'

'You mean it?'

'Yes.' Angie realised with surprise that she did.

Mike threw his arms around her. 'You're absolutely sure?'

'Yes.' She turned to face him. 'Next spring though. I'll need time to build up some stock.' It felt unreal, but the spark of hope she'd felt the first time she stepped inside the loft was back. 'And there's a few things at work I need to see through.'

'I knew it,' he pulled away.

'What?'

He gestured her to stay away from him. 'There's always some crisis that'll be okay in just a few weeks time. If this move depends on you sorting things at work it'll never happen. I know it.'

'No, Mike. This is different. It's Paul. He has a chance… with the Clarke's. I just need to be around for a little longer.'

'Define a little longer.'

'Give me four months, six at most. That's all, I promise.'

'Oh yes we do!' The theatre shook with the combined cry of a hundred or more children. The pantomime Dame feigned surprise for the third time in a row, waved her hands and turned back to Jack. His hands encircling the beanstalk.

'Thank you, children,' he said. 'See mother, they all want me to go.'

'Oh no they don't...' She glared in the direction of the auditorium. 'But I can see your mind is set. Boo hoo.' She peered over her apron at the audience as Jack began to climb. 'Boo hoo,' She wailed again. 'Does no-one have sympathy for a poor mother who fears for her child?'

'No,' the audience shouted back, all except one. Angie looked along the row. Paul was slumped in his seat biting the quicks of his nails.

'It's amazing you've got him here, Kate,' Angie said.

'I know. It was touch and go but he loves anything like this, anything larger than life. An extension of his characters I guess.'

'Is he still drawing?'

'All the time. I worry about it a bit. It's like he inhabits this separate universe where everything is on a knife edge until his superheroes save the day.'

'Do they? Save the day?'

Kate thought. 'I guess they do.'

'Time to worry is when they don't. Meanwhile, sounds like he's doing okay. Only two callouts in the last three months. Either you're doing all the crisis management or things are getting easier.'

Kate grasped the wooden arm of her seat. 'Touch wood. There's nothing we haven't told you.'

'I'm so pleased for you, Kate.'

'Don't get me wrong. By any normal standards he's still completely unmanageable, but given how things were, yes, he's definitely improving.'

'See you soon boys and girls.' The interval curtain came down on Dame Trot at the same time as the ice creams appeared in the aisles. Standing in the queue, Angie looked back at Steve, Kate, Amy, Paul, a family like any other, enjoying an afternoon out. So, Paul held himself apart, but his frequent glances towards Kate and Steve left her in no doubt where he wanted to be. The gap might still be too wide for him to make the move but he wasn't resisting it anymore.

'Two chocolate, a vanilla and a strawberry.' Angie handed the ice creams along the row.

'Say thank you, Paul.' Kate said. Paul turned away.

'Don't worry,' Angie said, putting a hand on Kate's arm. Better he resents me than you. I'll be fading into the background. Hopefully you won't.'

'No, in fact, this might not be the right time or place but there was something we wanted to say.' She looked at Steve then nodded at Paul. He took the hint.

'There's a transformers exhibition in the foyer,' he said to Paul. 'Come and take a look.' Steve walked by with Amy. She reached down for Paul's hand. He took it, unfolded himself from the seat and allowed her to lead him out.

'What would you think if we…' a cheer went up as a Mexican wave swept across the balcony. Kate tried again. 'If we applied to adopt Paul.'

Angie was convinced she'd misheard. 'Did you say…?'

'Yes. We want to adopt Paul.'

'It would be amazing. But are you sure? It's not been long.'

'I know. But our biggest fear was for Amy, and you can see how he is. Whatever goes on between us, he always responds to her. It's kind of weird and always one-sided, with Amy taking the lead. But he never rejects her.'

'I guess she's family.'

'That's why we want to do this. I can't bear the thought of him ending up alone.'

'We'll have to go through the consent issues again and you realise it would mean all support from the department would stop? Financially and from me. Not that I've been able to offer much recently and…'

'And what?'

'Like you said, this might not be the right time, but I'm thinking of moving on myself.'

'Is this where I get to ask about the engagement ring?' Kate said.

Angie found herself leaving the flat earlier and earlier with the lighter mornings. Best time to get things done at work, before the phone started. Her self-imposed deadline had brought a surprising clarity. In six months she'd closed more cases than in the previous year. The last one had been the catalyst for the letter she'd slipped into her briefcase before she left. It was time to deliver on her commitment to Mike. With outstanding leave, she'd be gone in two weeks, just in time for Easter, the beginning of the season on Lundy.

'I gather congratulations are in order,' Bill stopped Angie in the corridor. 'Getting an adoption through with Paul's history is an achievement. God only knows how they'll get on but it's one less the department will have to worry about.'

'Have you got a minute, Bill?'

He looked at his watch. 'Case conference in fifteen minutes. But I need to see you too. Come in.' He ushered her into his office.

'About Paul, I'll stay in touch, just for a bit. It's not fair to leave them completely unsupported.'

'No remit for that. They're his parents now. End of story.'

'But…'

'See this?' Bill pointed at a pile of folders on his desk. Seven new cases. Three of you in the team. One off sick. You do the maths.' He paused. 'Come on, Angie. I don't want to be on your back all the time, especially as you've done so well with this one, but you've got to let go. It's the only way we survive.'

'You know what, Bill, you're right.' She searched her case for the envelope.

The door opened behind her. 'Bit of a scene in the duty room. Can you come, Bill?' her colleague said.

'Back in a minute, Angie. Take a look at that file will you? Urgent one, came in this morning.'

Angie turned the folder to face her. She wouldn't be taking it of course. But she could look. She pulled out the yellow referral sheet. 'Tom!' she exclaimed. His mother was refusing to have him home for Easter, only a couple of weeks away. It would be impossible to find suitable foster parents. You had to know him. As she did. Angie shivered as she pictured Tom at Ellison Road. He'd never survive.

'Sorry about that, panic over.' Bill nodded at Tom's file. 'Graham, the housemaster, said you knew this lad, thinks you're the one to take him on. The photography was inspired, completely transformed Tom's opinion of himself apparently. And you've done a good job clearing dead wood out of your caseload lately so you've got capacity.'

'I don't know…'

'From where I'm sitting you're the one to handle it. Can you get out there today?'

'I mean I don't know if I can take it. I wanted to see you…'

He looked at his watch. 'Christ, the conference. What did you want - in a sentence?'

She hesitated, then closed her briefcase. 'It doesn't matter.'

Mike must have been watching for her. The champagne cork popped the instant she walked through the door. He handed her a glass. 'Here's to us, to a bright new future and most of all… to Angie Turner. Photographer in Residence. How does it sound?'

What could she say? Sounds great, but not yet. 'It's wonderful but…'

'What is it? What?' His face fell. 'Oh no, don't tell me you changed your mind.'

'I saw Bill, had the envelope in my hand, but there was this file on his desk.'

Mike threw his hands up in the air. 'I don't believe this. Months you've stalled on me. First this case, then that - always someone who needs the amazing, the incredible, the indispensable, Angie Turner.'

His sarcasm was so out of character. 'Please, Mike, you don't understand.'

'No, Angie. You're the one who doesn't get it. Doesn't get that I need you too. Well maybe you're not so indispensable after all, to me.' He grabbed his coat.

Angie reached for his arm. 'Mike, please, listen.'

'That's all I ever do, Angie. Trouble is, it's not enough is it? God knows what you do want but don't worry, I've got the message. Actions speak louder than words - and yours have been shouting at me for months. I was just too deaf to hear.' He shook her arm away and headed for the door.

'It's Tom. The file was about Tom.' He paused just long enough for her to draw breath. 'His mother's refusing to have him home at Easter. They're talking about Ellison Road. I can't let them send him there. It'll crucify him. You know how he is, Mike. He needs someone to fight his corner. Someone who understands him.' He still hadn't moved. 'Please, just another few weeks. We can give him that can't we?'

'I'm really sorry about Tom,' he said softly. 'No kid deserves to be left in the lurch. But you have to decide where your heart lies. With these kids or with me.' He turned round, 'and believe me, Angie, I'll understand if that's how it is. Understand and admire it. But from a distance.'

'Is that an ultimatum?'

He shook his head. 'No. It's a lot simpler than that. I want to be with you. If we don't take up this lease now we'll lose it and there won't be another opportunity for us, on Lundy.'

'But there might. Or maybe there'll be something over here, when I've got Tom settled somewhere.'

'You just don't get it do you! I've had enough.' The door slammed behind him.

Angie slumped on the sofa and stared at the open champagne bottle. Why wouldn't he understand? He was an adult, an intelligent, mature adult. Tom was a vulnerable boy whose future lay in the balance. Surely it was obvious who needed her more? She could make a difference. Why was he making this so hard for her?

She slid the patio door open. It was a clear night and the moon was casting a silver pathway across the water, out over the Bar towards Lundy. If she'd been superstitious she'd have said it was a sign. But she wasn't. She was quite capable of making her own decisions. Wasn't she?

173

A burst of laughter from the pub distracted her. There was a party of sorts going on. Christine would be in her element. Christine. She could do with a friend right now. Was she still a friend? The impulse to find out was irresistible.

Her hand gripped the phone as she waited. 'Christine?'

'Ange? Hi. How are you doing?'

It was always a fresh start with Christine. No inconvenient memories polluting the conversation. Nothing even remotely on the radar. 'Good, thanks. Mostly.'

'And the rest?'

'Oh, the same. Vulnerable kids verses, well, life I guess.'

'And the winner is…?' Christine's burr was back. Warm, familiar, relaxing.

Angie slid down on the sofa. 'Depends who you ask.'

'Who's on the short list?'

'Me, my boss, Mike.'

'Mike? Tell all. No. Wait.' The phone went silent. 'Okay, glass of Chablis in hand, go for it.'

'Not a lot to say really. We're sort of engaged.'

'Sort of? What does that mean?'

'Long story, and maybe history now, but his answer to your question would be, the kids have won. Mike's just walked out.'

'Must have known that was part of the package with you.'

'It's a bit more complicated. I said I'd resign. He's found this studio on Lundy. It's a chance for me to do what you've always badgered me to do… set up on my own, get creative.'

'Hang on a sec, sweetie.' Angie could just make out a muffled conversation in the background. 'Got to go soon. Give me the edited version. What's on offer and why aren't you biting his hand off?'

'You know why. The kids… and, well, after the time we spent together, I thought that maybe we… I don't know, might end up sharing again sometime.'

'We as in you and me? I'm sorry, Ange but you've got the wrong end of the stick there, girl. If you've got a chance of something don't hang about. I didn't. Frances and I are having a ball. Like living in technicolour instead of black and white.'

'You and Frances...'

'So, tell me about the studio,' Christine said.

'It'd,' Angie struggled to keep her voice even. 'It'd mean living on Lundy.'

'Okay, that would be the end of it for me but you love it... so what's the problem?'

Angie took the words at face value. 'What if it doesn't work out? With Mike? He's a nice guy but, well, we might be talking sepia not technicolour.'

'Wake up, girl. He's offering you the chance of your own studio! The old creative Ange, that you've buried under all that social services crap, wouldn't have hesitated.'

'It is a great space. Right over the information centre. And the boat brings over hundreds of tourists. Captive audience really. And I've been building up stock over the winter. A few large signature pieces but mostly unframed prints, perfect for carrying home in a suitcase.'

'Listen. Did you hear that?'

'What?'

'You. Talking with energy, excitement. You... only alive. Send me your best print and all the details. Got some great contacts for business cards. You could sell on the mainland too. Exeter should be a doddle for that kind of thing.'

Her excitement was catching. 'Do you really think I could make a go of it?' Silence. 'Christine?'

'No question... whoops, getting the evil eye. Got to go, we're off to a premiere. Bye.'

The phone went dead. Angie's hand trembled as she replaced the receiver. Sometimes you had to say the words out loud. *After the time we spent together, I thought that maybe we...* 'We what?' Angie whispered. She shook her head. Christine would never change. Unreliable, self-centred, narcissistic, absolutely impossible... what kind of friend would be there for her one moment yet shrug her off so lightly the next?

Angie caught her reflection in the mirror. The short dark hair, the hesitant gaze, they were the same. But the worry lines etched into her brow had deepened. Was she really passing up such an amazing opportunity for more of the same? She wasn't indispensible. Other social workers would take on her children... her children! She shook her head. For all her faults, Christine was right. A tear blurred the image of the open bottle and glasses, discarded on the coffee table. Mike had been there, waiting, wanting to celebrate a life together. She grabbed her coat. Maybe it wasn't too late.

Angie closed the door on her colleagues. Bill's speech had been touching, generous even given his reaction when she'd finally handed her notice in. 'Oh, God, the last thing I need is another vacancy to fill.' But she hadn't wavered, not this time. Paul was okay. And there'd be other ways she could help Tom. But there was only one chance, this chance, to give Mike and herself a future.

She picked up the last two manila folders from her desk. Just these to file, her diary to hand in and her career as a social worker was over. She'd struggled so much but it hadn't been that hard in the end. No-one was indispensable. Here at least.

Her phone rang. 'Angie, police on the line for you. Can you take it or are you officially gone?' Rosemary asked.

'It's okay. I need to let them know I'm leaving.' She waited while the call was transferred. 'Hello...? Yes, Angie Turner here... about whom...? He's not actually... yes... yes... it is something we needed to know... thank you... thank...' Her voice faded away.

It was a few seconds before she replaced the receiver. This wasn't happening, couldn't be happening. Not now. She steadied her hand then picked the phone up again.

'Hello?'

'Kate, it's Angie.'

'I'm so glad you called. Wanted to wish you all the best and to say thanks again for everything you've...'

'Kate,' Angie interrupted. 'We need to talk.'

'What is it? What's wrong?'

'It's Paul.'

'What's happened? Please, don't tell me something's happened.'

'It's his mother… they've found her, they've found Sonya.'

Chapter Twenty-One

Exeter, England, 2005
Fourteen Years Later

'Shut the door, Charlie and we'll get going. Everyone got a drink?' The MD of Ark Animation surveyed the group of employees gathered in the board room. Seven years ago it had been plenty big enough to hold the entire company but now, the fifty plus employees were spilling out into the corridor. It had been a gamble going it alone in the wake of Aardman's success, but one that was beginning to pay off - largely due to the even bigger gamble he'd taken employing one person in particular. 'Where's the man of the moment?'

Paul was pushed to the front.

'Come here, Paul.' He pointed to a space by his side then turned to the group. 'When Paul Wells arrived at Ark no more than five years ago I think many of you wondered what we'd done. There's no doubting his talent, but even the most generous would have to admit tact isn't his strong point.' A knowing murmur rippled across the room. 'But his determination to succeed has paid off time after time. Just in case you've forgotten, Best Newcomer at the St Laurence Animation awards, Best Feature at the Cardiff Animation Festival and now, Best Short Animation in the European Awards. An impressive record for anyone, but to achieve all this before his twenty-fifth birthday is going some.

'And that's not all. As most of you will know, Paul recently created a pilot for the BBC. Earlier today I had a call.' He turned to Paul. 'They've commissioned six, ten minute episodes.' A fluttering of applause. 'So I'd like you all to forget the handsome pay rise he'll be getting, and raise your glasses. To Paul. Congratulations.'

Paul nodded briefly in the direction of his colleagues. 'Thanks, but,' Paul looked at his boss, 'let's wait till we have it in writing.'

'It's on its way.'

'In that case, I'd better get to work.' He exchanged a few words with the Ark Animation directors clustered around him, downed the champagne in one, and pressed through the crowd, briefly acknowledging the occasional, 'well done'. Outside the boardroom, he crossed the rough wooden floor of the converted warehouse, a cavernous space built to store cargo unloaded on the quay outside. It was abandoned when the railway reached Exeter but resisted the elements too well to oblige developers looking to replace it with a sixties monstrosity.

Paul strode past a row of iron pillars to a far corner sectioned off by two display boards. The official line was that open plan enhanced creativity. He'd proved otherwise. This was his space, where characters spilled out of his imagination onto the drawing board and then materialised as the six inch high plasticine figures that filled the deep set windowsill behind him. The world was constantly brought to the edge of destruction then saved by his hand as it moved swiftly over the pristine paper, creating storyboards that sold for outrageous amounts of money amongst 'Time Bubble Man' fans.

'How did it go?' Gemma yawned and slipped into her new breakfast routine. Thin slice of toast with a scraping of low fat spread and marmite. Not exactly a diet but the pounds were creeping back. Everyone said she looked fine but what kind of a word was that? Fine. Polite speak for 'not looking great but not bad enough to risk upsetting her by saying exactly what I think.' And what did they think? Probably that her upper arms were starting to look squidgy and as for her thighs... Maybe she should get back to the gym this week, soon anyway.

'Are you actually going to give me that?' Paul said.

'Sorry.' She handed him a coffee. 'So how did it go?'

'Okay.'

'Okay! Is that it! Aren't you excited? I mean it's the BBC.'

'Of course I am.'

'You don't look it.' Gemma bit her lip. After two years, the pattern was all too familiar. She put another slice of bread in the toaster.

'I'm excited, all right?' Paul snapped. 'I've hardly spent five years working on something I'm not excited about.'

'How do you manage to turn something we should be celebrating into an opportunity to have a go at me? I'm sick to death of it.' She spread her toast with butter and honey and propped the paper between them on the breakfast table.

'I've a lot on my mind, sorry,' he mumbled.

'Tell me something I don't know. You're hardly ever here and when you are you're miles away or stuck up there,' she nodded towards the attic, 'where I hardly dare step over the threshold.'

'I've said sorry, haven't I? Don't go on.' He picked up the paper and folded it around one article.

'I'd love the chance. Oh, what's the point? You're not listening. You never do.'

'Have you seen this?' He thrust a headline in front of her. 'New Adoption Act leads to flood of enquiries. The 2002 Act, to be implemented on 30th December 2005, represents the most radical overhaul of adoption law for twenty six years. The Act gives adopted adults the legal right to request an intermediary service if they want to make contact.'

'So? You got your birth certificate when you were eighteen.'

'Just a piece of paper. It wasn't any help finding her. This means the local authority has to do something.' He read on, '...passing on or requesting information which may lead to indirect or direct contact.'

'It's been so long. How do you know she'll want contact?'

'Why wouldn't she?'

'Mr Wells?' A woman appeared in the doorway of the social services waiting area. She held out her hand and guided him to a small interview room. 'Morning. I'm Carol Morrison. Take a seat.' She shut the door and edged round the desktop until a slim manila folder was within reach. 'I'm glad you could come. I know we've talked on the phone but some things are much better discussed in person. Can I get you a drink?'

'No, thanks.'

'Have you read the leaflet I sent, about this process?'

'Yes, but all I want is contact details. Why this interview?'

'Getting in touch after so long can be traumatic for everyone so...'

'Does that mean you've found her?' Paul interrupted.

Carol hesitated. Clients usually found their way to her after years of indecision. But there was no uncertainty in the man sitting opposite. 'It took a while, but yes, I've found Sonya.'

He leant forward. Years he'd been asking. Always the same answer. 'Are you sure? Where?'

'I understand your impatience but there are a few steps we need to go through first.'

'Why? Where is she?'

'Please, Mr Wells, this won't take long.' This was never an easy process. Some cancelled appointment after appointment, one minute adamant they wanted to know, the next convinced they didn't. She was experienced in offering reassurance, helping clients take things a step at a time, but Paul Wells was different. Impatience was understandable but this pent up aggression was troubling. Especially given the information the manila folder contained. She pulled it closer. 'The legislation requires that we provide a pre-counselling service to adoptees seeking to make contact with their birth family. It can be an unsettling time for everyone. We act as an intermediary to ensure the process is as successful as possible but you should be aware that not all birth families want contact.'

'Mine will.'

His knee-jerk response flashed a warning. She continued. 'It depends on their circumstances. The parent may have another family who has no knowledge of any previous children. You can imagine how that might cause problems.'

'Does my mother have another family?'

'Let's take it a step at a time. In your application you said you believed your mother went to Plymouth but you'd not seen her since 1989 when you were…'

'Nine. That's right.'

'And no contact of any kind since?'

'No.'

'After your mother disappeared, you spent,' she checked her notes, 'two years in care, before Mr and Mrs Clarke adopted you?'

'Something like that.'

'And mostly at Ellison Road. How did you get on there?'

'What's this got to do with my application?'

Carol was aware of the tension creeping into the pit of her stomach. 'I wondered if anyone took the time to make sense of what was happening for you.'

'What the hell does that mean?'

'Did you understand what was happening and why?'

'Not at first. But there was a social worker, Angie someone, she did my life story, took me back to places, and people.'

'Your gran?'

'We saw her, took a photograph. But she didn't talk much. Probably cussed a bit, then told Angie to leave.'

'Who else?'

'Amy, my sister.'

'And Justin?'

'Justin? How could I? He went with mum.'

'So you didn't talk about Justin with Angie?'

'No.'

'Or with your adoptive parents?'

'No.'

Carol paused. There were things she had to know, but it didn't take much for him clam up. She persevered. 'How about your mother? Has anyone given you any information about her since she left?'

182

'No.'

'Do you have any idea what might have happened?'

He shrugged. 'Maybe she had an accident, lost her memory. Only thing that explains it.'

'What are your last memories of her?'

Paul looked out the window. He remembered her hand shivering as she shook his shoulder to wake him. She only had one hand free because she was holding Justin in her other arm. He could still hear her voice, so quiet, so close.

'Paul, Paul. Tell me about last night.'

'What?'

'Did your gran... was she okay?'

'Dunno.'

'What does that mean?'

'Just dunno. Didn't see her.'

'But she... didn't she put you to bed?'

'Nah. I went to bed on my own. I didn't tell no-one. I kept your secret mum, 'cause the neighbours would tell and we'd be thrown out. Nobody knows you went out, only me and Amy and we won't tell.'

'It's okay, Paul. Your Gran came later. You weren't on your own. You're a good boy, Paul.'

He looked at Carol. 'I remember her coming in that morning. She asked a few things, then she said, "You're a good boy, Paul". I'll always remember that. And her holding me tight. I could hardly breathe, but it didn't matter.'

Carol leant forward. 'Did she hold you often?'

He shrugged. 'She had a lot on, with Justin and everything. There wasn't always time for Amy and me.'

'How did you feel about being left out?'

'I wasn't,' he snapped. 'What's it got to do with this?'

Sometimes the defences were too strong and the support needed to tackle them well beyond the scope of this interview. But the feeling of treading on eggshells was a valuable pointer she was on the right track. 'It helps if you're aware of how you felt about your mother before you meet. If there's a lot of anger around it can make things difficult.'

'I loved her,' he said, leaving no room for contradiction.

'What happened next? The last time you saw her.'

'She said, "I'll just be a minute." Paul paused.

'And...?'

'She left.'

Carol softened her voice. 'Did she make contact after that?'

'No.'

'No letters, birthday cards?'

'No.'

'And you've no idea what happened to her?'

'I've said so haven't I?' He glared at her. 'If you've found her you already know.'

'Sometimes parents make contact but swear their child to secrecy because they don't want to be found.'

'I'm hardly a child.'

'No.'

'So where is she?' Paul said.

Carol hesitated. Having the authority to withhold information when it was in the best interests of both parties was one thing, but exercising that authority was quite another. 'When she left you she went to Plymouth...'

'I knew it,' Paul interrupted. 'I went there, loads of times, looking. Where in Plymouth?'

'She shared a house on the Estover estate.'

'Not the Barbican?'

'No. Did you think she was there?'

Paul shook his head. 'It doesn't matter. You said she shared a house. Who with?'

'A man called Stuart.'

'She left us for a man? Never! She wouldn't leave us to go off with some man. She brought them back to the caravan but she wouldn't... there was no reason for her to.'

'It wasn't quite that straightforward.'

Paul leant across the table. 'He didn't like kids, was that it? He made her choose, him or us - was that it?'

'No, I'm told he's very fond of children. They...' she paused. Breaking the news about the trauma locked in a child's past was never easy but this was off the scale. And there was something about the man in front of her - his eyes sweeping the room, his body about to burst out of the chair - that urged caution. Some things could wait.

'They what?'

'You said your mum took Justin with her but Justin... never left Exeter. On the day your mum disappeared she took him to the hospital.'

Paul was suddenly still. 'Hospital? Why?'

'Was he ill a lot of the time?'

'He coughed a lot. And cried. Got on mum's nerves.'

'Something happened that day. I'm sorry, Paul, but your mum took Justin to hospital because he'd died during the night.'

'What!' Paul stared at Carol.

She was suddenly aware of noises outside the room; a child crying, footsteps, conversation, life continuing as normal on the other side of the partition wall but suspended in here, the calm before the storm.

He leant towards her, his voice low, controlled. 'No. You're wrong. He couldn't have. I told you, she was holding him.'

Carol forced herself to look him in the face, now uncomfortably close. This wasn't a six foot three adult bullying her into submission but a nine year old child, a very frightened child facing up to his own personal nightmare. She resisted the temptation to cower. 'Was Justin crying?'

Paul stared at her, the memory playing in his mind. 'No. No, he was quiet.' He sank back into the chair.

'There was nothing the hospital could do. It was too late.'

'How did he die?'

'It's difficult to say.'

Paul wasn't in the mood to be fobbed off. 'The death certificate must say.'

'Asphyxia was given.'

'Asphyxia? How? What happened?' he pressed.

'No-one really knows.'

'There must have been a post mortem.'

'There was.'

'And…?'

Carol paused. She'd allowed him to take control, become the interrogator. It would be a challenge to rein him in if he insisted on meeting his mother. She consciously slowed her response. 'They couldn't say for sure. The general conclusion was that he'd suffocated on something, possibly a pillow.'

'So she was rushing to take him to hospital.' He gripped the chair. 'There wasn't time to… I mean, if she'd found him like that, it'd… anyone would…'

Carol half rose 'I'll get you a drink.'

'What? No.' He took out his keys and began rhythmically slapping the key fob against the back of his hand. 'So what happened? I mean, something must have stopped her coming back. Why didn't she come back?'

'There were concerns at the hospital.'

'Concerns? What do you mean, concerns?' he snapped.

'About how Justin died. There's no easy way to say this, Paul. The consultant came to the conclusion that Justin's death wasn't an accident.'

He shook his head. 'I don't understand.'

'Justin… was killed.'

'No, that's crazy. There was only us there, and gran and mum. No-one could've have got in. The door was locked. I checked… Why? Why would anyone…?' He slumped back, holding his head in his hands.

'I'm so sorry, Paul.'

He stared at her. 'All this time… everyone knew this… except me?'

'Yes.'

'Social workers, Ellison Road, my adoptive parents?'

'Yes.'

'And no-one thought I had a right to know that my own brother was murdered?'

Decisions taken at case conferences echoed further across the years than anyone could realise. 'You were young, your mother's disappearance was enough for you to cope with. It was information that could wait.'

He raised his voice. 'How long? How long would I have waited if I hadn't come to you?'

'When you left care it became your adoptive parent's decision.'

'That figures. So what else haven't they told me?' He pushed his chair back and leant over desk.

She hesitated. 'Is there anyone I can call to be here with you? When the information is as difficult as this…'

'God, there *is* more. What?'

Carol held his stare. 'I understand how you're feeling but if you don't sit down I'll have to bring this interview to a close.'

'If you think…' There were times when Paul was able to control his outbursts, when it was the only way to get what he wanted. He sat. 'Go on.'

It was a judgement call, her call. She moved her hand away from the red button under the desk. 'Are you sure? You don't have to hear more, not now anyway. Maybe you'd like to take some time. Talk it over with your partner or your sister.'

'I want to know.'

Carol took a breath. 'Immediately after Justin's death your mother disappeared. They couldn't tell you at the children's home where she was because they didn't know. No-one did. Then she slipped up - a visit to a dentist. The police found her. She'd been living in Plymouth under an assumed name.'

'That doesn't make sense.' He shook his head. 'Why change her name? Why were the police after her?'

'To question her about Justin's death.'

'To question her? You mean… they thought she… No!' He leapt to his feet. 'It's all a pack of lies. You should check your facts before you dish up this kind of garbage.' He jabbed a finger at Carol.

Carol hesitated. 'I'm afraid it isn't. They had enough evidence to charge her.'

'No, you've got it wrong.' All pretence of adulthood was stripped away. It was the nine year old boy who was now pacing the room, torn between his dreams and an unpalatable reality. 'They couldn't make something like that stick.'

She was walking a tightrope but instinct told Carol there was only one way she could go. 'I'm so sorry, Paul. She was convicted.'

'No, no.' He fell into the chair, his head in his hands. 'No, this is crazy. You've got it all wrong.'

'I wish I had. They gave her fourteen years. That's where I found her, in Holloway.'

Last autumn's leaves still covered the grass on either side of the path from the cottage. Steve Clarke wasn't the type to brush them into neat piles; senseless when westerlies roaring in from the sea sent them spiralling all over the garden again. But today he'd cleared the path so there was no danger of Kate slipping. She was too frail to withstand another hospital stay. He steadied her with a hand on either elbow. 'Turn right... two steps down... straight ahead.'

'Why are we going outside?'

'Infinite patience brings immediate results.'

'Is that so?'

'Definitely. Well, that's what my 'Quote for the Day' calendar says.' He guided her past the bins round to the front of the house. 'Okay, open your eyes.'

It took a second for her to focus on the boat in the driveway. 'Oh my God!' she exclaimed. 'Is it ours?'

'Yep.'

'How? I mean, can we afford it?'

'Bit of wheeling and dealing and... yes, we can.'

Kate ran her hand along the gunnels of the Wanderer sailing dinghy. 'It's in beautiful condition.'

'Bought it off an old guy who had a stroke three weeks after he took delivery. He hung on to it hoping he'd be able to go out again but it was never going to happen.'

'That's so sad.' She looked at him. 'It's not... I mean, I'd hate the same thing...'

Steve wrapped his arms round her. 'Don't go there. This

boat will bring us nothing but pleasure. Your reward, for getting through the last few weeks.'

Kate squeezed his arm. 'Thanks, Steve. I don't know what I'd do without you.'

A driving school car swung wide as it pulled into the drive and kangarooed to a stop a few feet from the house. Kate smiled. 'At least she's back in one piece.'

'Got it then, dad,' Amy said, waving her instructor away.

'You knew about this?' Kate exclaimed.

'Yep.' She looped her arms around her mother and gave her a kiss.

'How did it go?' Kate nodded at the disappearing car.

'Said I did really well for a first timer. "Natural coordination and ability" were his exact words. I'd rather be in this though,' Amy said, perching on the edge of the dinghy. 'When can we try it, dad?'

'I was planning to take your mother out this afternoon.'

Amy paused. 'Sounds great. If you make it back without sinking I'll come next time.'

Kate linked her arm through Amy's. 'How did I get to deserve such a considerate daughter?' She looked at Steve. 'But it would be fun - all of us. Besides,' Kate continued, 'we've so much catching up to do.'

'It's only been two terms. You've visited and emailed.'

'Not the same as sharing a cuppa over the kitchen table though. And I've only got you for two weeks so we'd better start right now. Any boyfriends?'

'Mum! Anyway, it might be longer.'

Kate stopped. 'How come?'

'I might want to be around, that's all.'

Kate paused. 'Listen, Amy. I don't want you changing your plans because of me. Is that clear?'

'Perfectly. Only you're forgetting one thing.'

'What's that?'

'I've got used to making my own decisions.'

It was dusk when they finally pulled the boat onto the driveway. 'You go in, Kate,' Steve said. 'Amy and I can stow the boat.'

'Go on, mum.'

'Thanks, I do feel tired...'

'Paul!' Amy interrupted, running across to a figure waiting under the trees. 'How did you know I was back?'

'Back?'

'From Uni. I bet mum told you.'

Kate hesitated. She should be the one to welcome him. But she was so tired. He'd have come to see Amy anyway. She pushed the front door open and went inside.

'When would you have told me?'

Kate opened her eyes. 'Paul, it's good to see you.'

He strode across to where she was lying, his pent up anger filling the room. 'I want to know. I mean you must have considered it when I was eighteen, key to the door and all that stuff. Or maybe you were more traditional and decided on twenty-one? Only that came and went too.'

Kate shrank from him. Years of fostering had taught her the importance of never letting these kids know they were getting to you. Ever. Even when they appeared to be adults. But she hadn't the strength. 'I don't know what you're...'

'You must have had a reason for keeping it from me. What was it? Amnesia? Some warped sense of what was right? I know it will have been you.' He was standing over her now.

'I... I don't know what you're talking about.' She was trembling.

'No?' He leant forward, his face close, too close. 'How was it when the phone call came? "Mrs Clarke, we've found Paul and Amy's mother." Bet you wanted to put the phone down didn't you. Didn't you!'

Kate flinched. It took everything she had to control her voice. 'I won't be bullied by you, Paul. You'll show me some respect in my own home, in your home. Sit down.' For a moment they were a tableau frozen in time, a scene from a Victorian melodrama, the villain towering over the cowering heroine relishing his power. It was something Kate had pictured countless times when imagining the adult Paul would become if abandoned to a life in care. But they hadn't abandoned him. However much he rejected her, however hard it had been, they'd gone on loving.

Paul hesitated, then backed away and half sat on a chair opposite her. 'Well?'

Kate realised she'd been holding her breath. 'Yes, I wanted to put the phone down. It took years to build this family, with you fighting me every step of the way.'

'I never…'

'Do you want to know?' She forced herself to look at him. 'Then for once in your life come out of wherever you are in your head and listen. Listen to how others see it. Others who, God knows why, really care. Who love you.'

'So ignoring me when I turned up - that's loving me is it?'

'Ignoring you?'

'Soon as you saw me you couldn't wait to get inside.'

'It wasn't like that.'

'So how was it?'

'That's… I'll come to that.' Kate said. He was on his feet again, pacing in front of the window, watching Steve and Amy wrestling with the tarpaulin. 'You saw most things anyone did as an attempt to get you one way or another. Put yourself in my place for once. I was worn out with trying.'

'I never asked you to.'

'I know. But you were a child. An angry, unhappy child who'd lost the only family he had and I was determined you wouldn't miss out on being loved.'

'I had a mother to do that,' he snapped.

'Yes you had a mother. Still have. But from the age of nine she wasn't there for you. Worse.' Kate pulled herself up on the sofa. 'Look at it from my side for once. Hours we spent on the road, taking you wherever you wanted to go, helping you look for her. What was I meant to do? Tell you the mother you idolised was in prison, convicted of killing your brother!'

'They got it wrong.'

Kate watched as he paced, a caged animal looking for a way through the bars but frustrated at every turn. 'I couldn't do that to you. You needed a mother's love. I wanted to give it.'

He stared at her. 'You weren't my mother. You never will be.'

It was too much. She fought back the tears. 'And you wonder why I couldn't cope anymore? At least when you were younger I could put it down to immaturity and a run of tough breaks. But you're not a child now.' She stared back. 'It's time to move on,' she said, her voice clipped, raw. 'I'd hoped we'd given you enough to do that.'

Amy burst into the room. 'You've got to come with us tomorrow, Paul. It's so much better than anything we've sailed in before.'

Chapter Twenty-Two

Paul gazed at the identically dressed women filtering through the door. He stared at each face in turn, waiting for the look, the mannerism, the feature that would unlock the past. He remembered deep brown eyes, tumbling hair, a raucous laugh and slender fingers... leaving their trace. He shivered. Sometimes his mind played tricks on him.

There were no physical characteristics to link him with any of them that he could see. Carol gestured towards a slight figure with closely cropped hair, eyes cast down, walking towards them. He hung his jacket over the back of the chair, tweaking the folds until it hung freely - anything to fill the space created by sixteen years of not knowing. Finally, he snatched a glance at the woman sitting opposite him - his mother.

Carol nodded. 'Hi, Sonya. This is Paul.'

She glanced at him, her pinched eyes recoiling as if from a bright light. 'You're taller than I thought.'

'I can't believe it's you,' he said. 'I'd have come... years ago. But they didn't tell me. The bastards all knew but no-one told me.'

She looked again. Longer this time. 'What good would it have done?'

'Good? I'd have told them it wasn't you, couldn't have been you...'

'I'm not having this conversation.' She half rose.

'Paul knows that.' Carol shot him a warning glance. 'You agreed to meet to fill in the gaps, talk about before you had to leave. He agreed to stick to that. Paul?'

He shrugged. 'Questions have been in here so long...' he tapped his forehead.

Her face gave nothing away. Her eyes blank, emotionless. 'So what do you want to know?' she said.

The words welled up. 'What was it like? What was I like? I remember a caravan. Is that where we lived?'

'For a bit.'

'What did we do? What sort of a kid was I?'

'Christ, I don't know. It was years ago!'

'I don't think Paul's looking for anything specific, Sonya,' Carol mediated. 'Just something to help fill in the gaps.'

She rubbed at an imaginary mark on the back of her hand. 'You used to go off round the site. You was always running off.'

'Why? I loved being with you. We were good, weren't we?'

Silence.

'I remember we used to do stuff. Go to town.'

Sonya picked at a chipped fingernail. He let the silence hang.

'Yea, we used to go to town,' she said eventually.

'All of us?'

'Mostly.'

'But sometimes just you and me, yeah?'

'Maybe, when you needed something, like trainers. You was always getting through trainers.'

'What did we eat? What was my favourite?'

She pressed her fingers against her forehead. 'I don't know. Fish and chips maybe. Burger on our way back from town.'

He'd tried, really tried. But he had to know. 'Why did you say it was you?'

She looked at him now, for a fraction of a second, before she pushed her chair back. 'Just a minute.'

'You're innocent... I'll prove it,' Paul called, fighting the impulse to run after her, to wait by the door, to make sure this minute didn't last another lifetime.

Carol broke the silence. 'How are you doing?'

He shrugged.

'It took some courage to come.'

'Guess I must be as crazy as she is.'

'Do you think she is? Crazy?'

'If she did it, maybe. I mean… she loved me. I know she did.' He looked at her. 'Now you think I'm crazy. I was a nine year old kid. What could I know?'

'At gut level, maybe a lot.'

'What if I imagined it? What if she didn't give a toss?'

'You obviously cared about her - to spend all these years looking for her.'

'Maybe I shouldn't have.'

'I don't think you had a choice.'

He stared at the table. 'Looking for her became normal. I was a character from my cartoons - 'abandoned boy' searching for his mother. That's who I was. All I was. Pathetic.'

'Who are you now?' she asked.

He shrugged.

'That's why counselling is compulsory before contacting natural parents. It rocks the boat.'

He stared at the door. 'Is she all right?'

Paul watched as Carol approached a warder. Maybe his mother had disappeared again. Part of him hoped she had.

'Paul,' Carol was standing beside him. 'We need to call it a day, for now at least.'

'What's happened?'

'Sonya's not feeling too good.'

He could read between the lines. It was something he'd learnt in care. No-one ever meant what they said. You had to be smart to get at the truth.

'How did it go?'

Paul dropped his coat on a chair and joined Gemma. 'It didn't.' He poured some coffee.

'Was she anything like you remembered?'

'No.'

Gemma looked up from washing a bowl of salad. 'I'm sorry, Paul. But she's been inside a long time. It would change anyone. And...'

'And what? She is a murderess after all!'

'You said it.'

'No I didn't. The courts did. But they don't always get it right do they?'

Gemma's shoulders sagged. 'I knew this would happen.'

'You never wanted me to see her, did you?'

'For your sake.' She put her arm around him. 'What good is it, dragging up the past? Honestly, what was better - your memories of her or this awful truth?'

He shrugged her away. 'Maybe it isn't the truth.'

'She was convicted, Paul. You can't argue with the jury.'

'I'm going up to work.'

'But supper...'

He picked up a bottle of wine and a glass and headed upstairs, to the studio he'd created in the attic; his take on Lenkiewicz's warehouse. It was a vast space open to the rafters with his art work covering the walls. Crazy that all this was his but if the tossers out there wanted to pay over the odds for his work he wasn't going to argue.

He selected a box file from the tailor-made storage running the length of one wall and lifted out a blue folder. It was all here: his first request for information under the Adoption Act; confirmation of his searches through the counselling for adoptees programme; the official letter confirming Carol's findings; the first note stating that Sonya Wells was refusing contact and then finally...

The sound of paws clattering up the wooden stairs interrupted his thoughts. He opened the door.

'Hey, boy,' Paul leant down and scooped the dog up in his arms. 'How've you been, Spider? Did she shut you out all day again?' He put the mongrel down, opened a drawer and held out a biscuit. 'Sit.' The dog sat. 'Spin.' The dog chased his tail in a circle twice, caught the biscuit and snaffled it in one gulp.

Paul laughed. 'Good boy. Basket.' He pointed down by his desk, then turned back to the folder.

The court transcript felt like an intruder in this space dedicated to fun and fantasy. He poured a glass of red wine and pulled out the prosecution summing up.

MR HAWKINS

Members of the Jury. You cannot expect to resolve every aspect of this case. There are bound to be occasions when you are unable to decide on something but that does not make your task of reaching a proper verdict impossible.

Although it would be much more satisfactory for you to say with certainty exactly when and how the defendant suffocated Baby J, we do not suggest you will be able to be that precise. But, members of the jury, you do not have to be. All you have to be sure about is that she killed him. Once you reject the alternatives - that it was a cot death, an accident or that another party was to blame - we simply ask, what is left?

The defendant claims she was frozen to inaction by panic and fear and is unable to recollect the detail surrounding the death of Baby J. Let us look then, at her behaviour.

Does she ring for an ambulance? No, she does not.

Does she go to a neighbour for help? No, she does not.

Does she seek out her mother? No, she does not.

Paul leant back. Why? Why wouldn't she go for help? It didn't make sense. He poured another glass and read on.

She conceals her dead child inside a blanket and, leaving her other two young children completely alone, walks out of the caravan park. Are these the actions of a distraught mother? No, they are not. They are the calculated actions of a woman who resented being burdened by a child with his own needs when she wished to pursue her own selfish pleasures.

You will recall the defendant claimed that Baby J was alive when she left at 7.45pm. We submitted evidence proving beyond doubt that Baby J died between 7.30pm and 9.00pm, giving not only means and motive but crucially, opportunity.

The defendant claimed it was a cot death. I refer you to the testimony of Dr Marcus Wilson, the expert witness, conclusively eliminating this possibility. Another lie.

She then implied someone could have broken into the caravan. Police testimony confirmed there was no evidence whatsoever of a forced entry. Another lie.

So we arrive at the conclusion that the murder could only have been committed by someone either inside or with a key to the caravan. I put it to you that the most likely scenario is that Baby J died before the defendant left that night.

Your task was made easier here by evidence submitted by prosecution witnesses and the defendant's own admission that she found life challenging with her disabled child. She was on the brink of a new future with the man who colluded with her to evade the consequences of her actions. His was a passionate plea for cot death. Was this part of the plan? The plan for a future free of an extremely demanding child?

Then we have her unequivocal admission of guilt. When finally forced to take the body of her child to the hospital does this grief stricken mother wait to quiz the medical staff about what happened to her baby? No, she does not.

Does she ask for her baby's body to be returned to her so she can arrange a funeral? No, she does not.

Does she return to her precious living children to clasp them in her arms? No, she does not.

Sonya Wells seizes her opportunity and disappears. She becomes a woman on the run, changing her name, her appearance - doing everything she can to evade detection. Does she do this because she is innocent? No, she does not.

Members of the Jury, we may never be able to prove precisely what happened that night but we suggest you have not heard the truth from the defendants. Remember Dr Wilson's words. "So called cot death is an extremely rare phenomena and I can find no evidence that supports it as a diagnosis in this case. In my experience young babies die at the hands of their parents, not their cot."

The door burst open. 'Pick up will you. Amy's on the phone,' Gemma said abruptly.

'No need to get shirty. I didn't hear you.'

'If you didn't shut yourself away up here I wouldn't have to stop what I'm doing and run up three flights of stairs every time the phone goes.' The door banged behind her.

'How did it go?' his sister asked.

'Dunno.'

'Why's that?'

'I wasn't there long. She went to the loo, never came back.'

'Did she say anything?'

'Not much.'

'Well she must have said something.'

'Just some bits about when I was young.'

'Like what?'

'I don't know.'

'You're hopeless.'

'Well you'll just have to come next time then you can interrogate her yourself!'

'I... I don't know. It's...'

'It's what? She's our mother.'

'*Your* mother, maybe. Kate's been more of a mother to me than that woman ever was - and to you too if you weren't too stubborn to admit it.'

'It's nothing to do with being stubborn.'

'Whatever.' The silence grew. Amy sighed. 'Come up tomorrow. We'll have all day. We can talk. Please, Paul.'

'Will she be there?'

'No, Kate's... she'll be out from about ten.'

'Okay.'

It felt wrong, stepping out of his car and striding towards the house a man in his own right. He had to fight the impulse to run down the garden path into the woods.

'Paul.' Amy flung her arms around him in welcome. He pulled away but it made no difference. Amy linked her arm in

199

his and ushered him through to the kitchen. 'Don't worry, mum's gone.'

'Don't call her that, especially now.'

'Now more than ever. Can't be comfortable for her, having a rival for our affections appear on the scene.' She paused. 'But I guess it's always been that way with you and her. Drink?'

He threw his coat down. 'How can you stay here after what she did? She's known where our mother was all this time!'

'Maybe we were better off not knowing.' Amy opened the cupboard.

He wouldn't have taken it from anyone else, but there was something about Amy that overcame his natural resistance to people contradicting him. It was the way her words spilled out without any hidden agenda. There was no side to Amy. But she'd been too young, couldn't remember their mum as he did. The coffee grinder swamped Amy's words. 'What?' he said.

'Did it feel weird? Seeing her there. Well, seeing her anywhere would have been weird I guess, but in prison. I've never even been in one.'

'I guess it did.'

'What does she look like?'

He considered. 'Kind of haunted. Her eyes were all over the place, like she was distracted by things in the room.'

'Or avoiding you? She refused to see you for ages.'

'She changed her mind.'

'Why?'

'What kind of a question is that?' he snapped.

'A reasonable one I'd have thought. Is it because she's coming up for parole and got nowhere to go? Is that it? She needs us now.'

Paul ignored her. 'Look at this.' He laid a pile of closely typed sheets on the table.

'What is it?'

'The trial transcript.'

Amy glanced at the pages. 'Why are you reading this? Isn't it painful enough - knowing what she did?'

'That's just it. How do we know she did it?'

200

'Doh… stupid - because the jury said so.'

'Not all of them. It was a majority verdict. Here,' he pulled out a sheet marked in red. 'Read this.'

THE CLERK OF THE COURT

Will the Foreman please stand. Mr Foreman, please confine yourself to answering my question with a simple yes or no. Members of the Jury, have you reached verdicts on all counts, in respect of both defendants, upon which you are all agreed?

THE FOREMAN

No.

MR JUSTICE SIMPKINS

Ladies and gentlemen, the time has now come when I will accept a verdict one way or the other upon which at least ten of you are agreed. In other words, ten to two or eleven to one.

(Jury retire)

(Jury return)

THE CLERK OF THE COURT

Will the Foreman please stand? Members of the Jury, have you reached verdicts on all counts in respect of both Defendants upon which at least ten of you are agreed?

THE FOREMAN

Yes.

THE CLERK OF THE COURT

Members of the Jury, do you find the Defendant, Sonya Wells, guilty or not guilty of infanticide?

THE FOREMAN

Guilty.

THE CLERK OF THE COURT

Is that the verdict of you all, or by majority?

THE FOREMAN

By majority.

THE CLERK OF THE COURT

How many of you agreed and how many dissented?

THE FOREMAN

Ten agreed, two dissented.

Amy looked up. 'So two jurors said she wasn't guilty.'

'Precisely,' Paul said. 'Two people who sat through all the evidence thought she didn't kill Justin. What did they see that the others didn't? And if it wasn't her, who was it?'

'Hi, Paul.' Kate hovered in the kitchen doorway.

Silence.

'Mum,' Amy exclaimed. 'How did it go?'

Kate shot her a warning glance. 'Oh, you know, okay.'

'You look tired. Go and sit down. I'll do dinner.'

'That'd be great, Amy. Thanks.'

Amy turned to Paul. 'Say you'll stay. There's loads more I want to talk about. When's your new animation on TV?'

'I can't.'

'Why not? There's plenty of food, mum won't mind.'

'But I might! Just leave it, Amy.'

Later that evening Paul climbed the stairs to his studio, lifted down the box file and extracted the blue folder again. There had to be something.

MR JUSTICE SIMPKINS

Stand up, Wells. Sonya Wells, you betrayed that most sacred of human responsibilities, that of caring for a defenceless child. You are the one person who knows how Baby J died and you are the one person who knows why. This court might have looked more sympathetically on your case had it been mitigated by your behaviour subsequent to the death of Baby J. However, it is plain to me that you made a cold and calculated decision to escape the consequences of your actions. After failing to alert the emergency services, you used another person's tragedy to escape from the hospital. You then executed a carefully planned change of identity to evade detection for a further two years.

This sequence of events involved abandoning your three year old daughter and nine year old son without making any plans for their care. However, it is not a culpable case of child neglect that brings you before me today. There are few worse crimes than the murder of a child. The sentence I pass upon you today is one to which I am impelled by law. On count one, you will go to prison for fourteen years.

I now turn to you, Stuart Saunders. The gravity of your offence must reflect the gravity of the offence for which you were an accessory. You had plenty of opportunity to refuse to persist in a course of lying and deception. You chose not to. If you had had the slightest true regard for Baby J you would have refused to aid and abet the defendant's flight and brought it to a swift and just conclusion by telling the truth at the first opportunity.

Instead of this, your selfish concern for yourself and for Sonya Wells led you all too readily to lie. However, I have chosen to take into account your evident compassion, good character, the child for which you care and the time spent awaiting trial. The least sentence I can pass consistent with my duty is one of three years imprisonment, suspended. You will remain on licence for five years. That is all I have to say.

Paul picked up the phone. 'Amy?... I know it's late... but you need to hear this. She's innocent... Well to start with she stuck to a 'not guilty' plea... I know, but it's more than that. Don't ask me how, I can't explain it... But one thing bugged me. Why did she run? If she wasn't guilty why did she abandon us? Hang on... it's obvious isn't it? This Stuart had some hold over her... think about it. She'd have been in a real mess, finding Justin like that... what mother wouldn't be? Maybe she was in shock and he persuaded her to run... or... or what if she was protecting him? Amy that's it! What if it was him? If we can get the evidence, launch an appeal... I don't know... how do you expect me to... no I don't remember anything... how many times do I have to say it... Amy? Amy?' He replaced the receiver.

Chapter Twenty-Three

'So how did it really go yesterday?' Amy placed a mug of tea on the bedside table.

Kate winced as Amy adjusted her pillows. 'Your dad had to stop three times on the way back. I was sick as a dog by the side of the road.' She attempted a smile.

'How long will it last?'

'Should feel better in about four days - so that gives me two whole days before it starts all over again with the next chemo.'

'I hate to see you so ill.'

Kate lifted Amy's hand. 'Hey, I'll be okay.'

'But why you?'

'Listen. Tell me about Paul,' Kate said. What did he want last night?' Amy looked away. 'I hope you're not thinking any rubbish about protecting me. What's going on?'

Amy hesitated. 'He went to see Sonya.'

'He's found her then.'

'Yes.'

'Where?'

'In Holloway,' Amy said. 'You knew... didn't you?'

'Yes,' Kate whispered.

'Why didn't you tell us? I mean, I think I know, and I wouldn't have wanted it any other way. You're my mum and that's all I need to know, but...'

'It's okay.' Kate stroked a wayward strand of hair back from Amy's face. 'You had every right to know, both of you, but when I first found out, Paul was finally starting to think of this as his home. Do you remember how it was?'

'Not really. What was I? Five? Six?'

Kate thought. 'You must have been six by then.'

'But I'd been here for years. Why didn't Paul come too?'

'He did, for a while. But it didn't work out.'

'Oh?'

Kate smiled. It was the nearest Amy would get to pressing her. 'You know how he felt about his mum - how he still feels about her. He couldn't accept anyone taking her place.'

'So what happened?'

'He'd keep running away and each time Angie…'

'Angie?'

'His social worker. Each time she brought him back he'd be a bit angrier and more determined not to let us help. We tried but,' she looked at Amy, 'we were adopting you and his behaviour was making things difficult. I couldn't risk anything happening to…' her voice drifted away. 'You brought us so much joy.'

'Oh, mum.' Amy wrapped her arms around Kate.

Kate reached for a tissue. 'But Angie encouraged us to keep in touch after he went back to the children's home. And he did change, slowly. Your dad did it really. Took Paul out in the old boat. You could see how much he loved it, the rush of the water, the speed. Scared me half to death with the risks he took but it was like… like he was in his element, suspended over the boat, daring the sea to take him.'

'Yep, that's Paul,' Amy said.

'He wasn't alive unless he was challenging someone or something.'

'But something must have changed. You adopted him.'

'He's smart, your brother.' She paused. 'Don't take this the wrong way, but as he got older he realised where he was well off. He stopped fighting us quite so much and we ended up with a kind of truce.'

'He was okay with me.'

'Yes,' Kate said hastily. 'He was. And he was a joy to have around at times. Don't get me wrong, despite everything, I love him and I'd put my life on the line for him. He didn't ask

205

to be how he is.'

'So when did you find out about Sonya?'

'Right after the adoption, just as life was returning to something like normal. They said it was our decision what we told you both.' Kate's voice trembled.

Amy squeezed her hand. 'You don't have to tell me.'

'It's okay.' Kate wiped her nose. 'I know she gave birth to you, but when I found out what she'd done. How could any mother...?' She shook her head. 'All I could think was that it might have been you,' her voice shook. 'And for Paul to find out that the woman he idolised was a child killer, how could I inflict that on him?'

'You couldn't, mum, of course you couldn't.' Amy gripped her hand.

'I was tempted... I'm not proud of this, Amy, but I thought if I told him it might change everything. That if he knew what she was really like, all that passion, all that devotion might come to me, that he'd see I really loved him and...' she closed her eyes. 'But I couldn't do it.'

'You need to rest.' Amy kissed her mother on the cheek.

'He's every right, you've both every right to be in touch with your... your mother.'

'She's not my mother,' Amy interrupted, 'and I don't want to see her.'

'If you're sure.'

'Definitely.'

Kate leant back on her pillows. 'But Paul won't let it go. I know he won't.'

Paul checked the scrap of newspaper in his hand. It was a long shot - but all he had. He rang the bell. Cars streaming along the main road into Plymouth made it impossible to hear any movement inside the flat. He shaded his eyes and peered through the heavy net curtain. Nothing. He looked over the edge of the concrete balcony running the length of the block. The area immediately below was a car park but weeds had smothered any formal parking bays. A few boys were playing football at one end, using an old BMW and a green bin as goalposts. A lone teenage girl watched, but other than that - nothing. It was a desolate part of the city. As many flats boarded up as lived in.

A bus paused briefly at the stop opposite, barely giving enough time for an elderly passenger to step off. He stumbled and fell against a double row of wires suspended between the concrete posts fringing the path. He recovered, shuffled along the pavement then hesitated, retraced his steps and covered the same ground again - his shoulders hunched, head down.

Paul turned back towards the door, searched his pockets for a pen and paper then paused. What the hell could he write? I suspect you of murdering my brother and letting my mother take the blame. Please call me. Hardly.

'Excuse me.'

Paul looked up. It was the drunk from the bus. He wasn't elderly at all - maybe somewhere between forty and fifty. Paul stepped back to allow him to pass. But he didn't. He took out a key and fumbled for the lock on the door.

'Here,' Paul took the key. 'I'll do that.' It had to be him. 'Are you Stuart Saunders?'

The man squinted at him. 'Who wants to know?'

'My name's Paul Wells.'

'Do I know you?'

'That's what I want to find out.'

'Paul…' The man stared at him. 'Oh yes, Paul.' He walked into the hallway, leaving the door open. 'You'd better come in.'

Paul followed him along the narrow corridor into a small but tidy sitting room. Photographs covered a bureau set against one wall. He lifted one. A young boy, ten or eleven Paul guessed, returned his gaze.

'What do you want?' The man removed his coat and sat in an easy chair by the window.

'So are you? Stuart Saunders?'

'Yes.'

'You knew my mother.'

207

The man swivelled in his seat, opened a drawer in the bureau and pulled out a pair of glasses. He put them on. 'Yes. Sonya and I were together for a while.'

'Two years.'

Stuart took his time to respond. 'If you say so.'

'Well that's how long you were on the run wasn't it?'

'I wouldn't put it quite like that.'

'So how would you put it?'

'I understand you're angry…'

'That's not the point.'

'Isn't it?'

'No.'

Stuart took his time. 'Why are you here?'

'I want to know what sort of man you are - to let a woman you say you loved rot in jail for a crime she didn't commit.'

Stuart looked out the window. 'If there'd been anything I could have done, I would have.' His voice wavered. 'But… the jury had made up their mind before we even stepped into the courtroom. There'd been lots of tragedies… children killed by their parents. And Sonya didn't always care for Justin, or you, so well.' He looked at Paul. 'I guess you'll remember that.'

'My mother loved me.'

'No doubt. But there were plenty of people happy to testify how often they heard her screaming at you or the times you went begging for food…'

'It wasn't like that.'

'If you say so,' he sighed. 'It wasn't easy, bringing three kids up on her own. It got her down.'

Paul sat on a hard dining chair set against the wall. 'What happened that night?'

'I don't…'

'I have a right to know,' he snapped.

'Right!' Stuart retorted. Then sighed. 'I guess you do.' He paused. 'We'd been seeing each other for a while. Mostly on a Friday night when her mother could babysit….' He stopped. 'I'd like to see some ID.'

'What?'

208

'To prove you're who you say you are.'

'I'm the one that wants answers.'

'Suit yourself.' He turned away.

Paul opened his wallet and pulled out a driving licence. 'That good enough for you?'

Stuart scanned it and handed it back. 'Sonya wanted to see this film, Shirley Valentine it was. Only we missed it first time around. I'd arranged to pick her up outside the site.'

'What time?'

'I don't remember exactly…'

'You must remember. If it'd been me, every last detail would be tattooed here,' he jabbed a finger at his forehead.

Stuart gripped the arm of the chair. 'It was about seven forty-five, maybe just after, it was a long time ago.'

'So you keep saying. What then?'

'It was getting late. Her mother hadn't turned up to babysit. Sonya went to find her.'

'So when my mother arrived, how was she?'

'What do you mean?'

'Was she her usual self or upset, worried?'

Stuart thought. 'A bit wound up maybe.' He stood. 'I need a drink.'

'I bet you do.'

'A cup of tea.' He walked through to the kitchen. Paul followed. 'Do you want one?'

'What was she wound up about?'

'Being late, letting me down, that kind of thing.'

'What then?'

'We drove to Bideford and watched the film.'

'And you stayed there the whole time?'

'Not the whole time, no. Sonya didn't feel too good. She went out, said she felt sick, needed some air.' Water filling the teapot resonated in the silence. 'We stood outside for a bit then drove to a pub.' Stuart poured his tea and added two teaspoons of sugar. His hand was trembling.

'Do you think she did it?' Paul said.

Silence.

'Because I know different.' Paul moved closer to him.

Stuart edged sideways. 'She was young and doing her best but when Justin came along, well, he was…'

'He was what?'

'Justin was sick.'

'So? We all got sick.'

'But Justin was never going to get better,' Stuart said.

'What the hell are you talking about?'

'He had cystic fibrosis. You remember his coughing?'

Paul stared out the window. Did he remember?

Don't you think I've got enough to put up with without you bringing me more trouble? Get in there and clean up that mess.'

'She made it.'

'Just do as I tell you.'

Another weird bout of gurgling filled the caravan. 'See what's happened now. Every time I leave him for five seconds…' His mother turned away. 'He'll choke one of these days, and maybe I won't be sorry.'

'Your mum got impatient sometimes,' Stuart said, 'anyone would, but they used things she'd said in court.' Stuart carried his tea back to the sitting room and sank into the chair.

Paul leant over him. 'Do you sleep well at nights?'

'Not particularly.'

'Well at least there's some justice.'

Stuart stared back at Paul. 'I think you should go.'

'Not until you've told me all of it.'

'You can bully me all you like but you won't get any more.' He pushed past Paul into the hall, nudged a skateboard to one side and opened the front door.

'I can see through your bullshit,' Paul spat at him, his face close as he passed. 'My mother's going to appeal, and she will win, my Brief will see to that. He never loses. Neither do I.'

Stuart watched as the young man strode across the car park to a silver convertible sports car. Lucky it was still there. A mongrel leapt out and wrapped itself around his legs. 'At least somebody loves him,' Stuart said, then shook his head. No, no need for the bitterness to be catching, however tempting.

His gaze moved from the car as it sped away to the boy getting off a bus. He waved and waited for the footsteps to reach their walkway.

'Hi, dad,' the teenager called, still unselfconscious enough to accept a hug.

'How'd it go?' Stuart asked, picking up the rucksack and shoes shed along the hall.

Ian disappeared into his room, school shirt already off. 'Okay.'

'Just okay?'

'Yep.'

'So did you make it?'

Ian appeared at the door in jeans, sweatshirt and trainers. He smiled. 'First team from September.'

'Brilliant.'

'Yeah. Mr Jennings put me on the wing. I was faster than the others. What's for tea?'

'Haven't started yet. I had… I'm a bit behind.'

'No probs. Just going to tell Sam,' Ian said, the front door swinging behind him.

'Half an hour,' Stuart called, glad of the breathing space.

It had taken years to adjust to life as a single father. It wasn't how he'd planned it. Not at all. But somehow they'd got by. A bit hit and miss, but Ian was incredible. Tears at first, but he was only a baby when they took Sonya. The nursery warmed to a child whose mother had walked out on them - how else to explain why she wasn't around? Tell them she was in prison convicted of killing her other son? You couldn't of course. He couldn't. But Sonya would never be guilty to Ian. Better not to know at all. Better to say she'd left. That's what they'd agreed, until it was over.

But Paul's visit was a brutal reminder that time was running out. Sonya's parole was close. In the sitting room Stuart paused by the photos on the bureau. Ian on his first day at school, Ian in the nativity play, Ian at prize-giving, Ian and him at Butlins,

Ian as goalie on a freezing winter's day. Hours he'd stood on touchlines across the County in all weathers, determined to be all the parent a child could want.

Stuart lifted a photo from the back and adjusted his glasses - an old pair, not so sharp any more. It showed an older couple posed in front of a stately home. His parents had been so proud to be invited to tea by their MP. Recognition of their charitable works, they'd said. He'd returned the next letter marked, 'Gone away. No forwarding address.' That was soon after he and Sonya left a dead baby at the hospital, the day they went on the run.

'On the run,' he muttered. Ludicrous! He was a simple law-abiding man, a plumber by day and darts player by night. But that was before Sonya. He put the frame back, walked through to the kitchen and opened the fridge door. Sausages tonight. Traditional after a game. Sonya was so proud of Ian. She might be dead to him but he was very much alive to her. Every visit she wanted more. What's he wearing? Who are his friends? What has he done this month? Not that he, Stuart, could always go. Visiting Holloway was difficult without Ian, or anyone else, knowing.

But he'd been true to his word. He'd stood by her. It had almost been easy while she was inside. But now? He stared into space. What now? Stuart shook his head and sighed. He looked at the envelope on the cork pin board on the wall. His visiting pass. He hadn't booked the train yet… maybe leaving it one more month wouldn't hurt. And things might be clearer then, about after.

But then there was Paul. He unpinned the pass, filled it in and placed it ready.

He bent for a frying pan. Sausages and chips followed by a washing machine full of dirty kit and the usual tussle over bedtime before he turned off the light and wished Ian 'good night, sleep tight'. He always left the door ajar in case Ian called out. He would always be there for his son. Whatever happened.

Chapter Twenty-Four

Paul hovered in the lobby of Television Centre. It was a heady atmosphere. The building was like a multiple Tardis where each door led to an alternative reality, one that millions tuned into every day to escape the life waiting for them outside their front door. And why not? Why not choose your own reality? Paul had turned his into a healthy bank balance. Not the joint account he held with Gemma - but a new account, opened with one purpose in mind

He studied the contract in his hand. It had cost him three weeks working night and day to meet their deadline but it had paid off. Wouldn't have happened without the hours spent with Lenkiewicz though. Watching, learning - no, not learning, discovering what was already inside him and how to let it spill across the canvas. He tucked the signed contract into his inside pocket and joined the crowd funnelling into White City underground.

Thirty minutes later the train was only just pulling into Notting Hill Gate. He checked his watch. One more hold up like that and he'd be too late. It had taken a month to get this pass. He couldn't miss out now. He leant forward, straining to read each sign as the train slowed: Lancaster Gate, Marble Arch, Oxford Circus, Tottenham Court Road... he pushed through the commuters until he was wedged by the door... Holborn. Seconds later he was hurrying towards the Piccadilly Line. He looked back and forth between the clock and the empty tunnel. An occasional rush of air moved him closer to the platform edge but it was seven long minutes before he was on his way again.

It was raining when he emerged at Caledonian Road. He waited for the bus for the prison, checking and re-checking the time on his visiting card.

'Doesn't take long, luv.' A woman leant two bulging plastic carrier bags on the rail.

'Are you talking to me?'

'No need to bite me head off. Just offering some friendly advice that's all.'

'Well maybe I don't need it.'

'Suit yourself. It's here anyway.' She nodded at the bus and pushed past him.

Camden Road was streaming with traffic, forcing him to use the pedestrian crossing to get to the queue building outside the gate lock. When it finally opened, he filed through. They called the grey space beyond the gate the visitors holding room. Even the benches were screwed to the floor. What the fuck did they think he was going to do with them!

People were shuffling over to a small hatch in the wall. He watched. Carol had told him not to bring anything but it felt wrong. He gripped the box of chocolates.

The woman in front delivered her parcel and turned. 'Warders are gonna love you.'

'What?'

'You can't take them in.'

'Why not?'

'Ask her, not me.' She nodded in the direction of the hatch.

'They'll be put in a locker. You can collect them on your way out.' The warder said, holding out her hand.

He was called through eventually, but not until he'd turned his pockets out, been subjected to a metal detector scan and stood against the wall while a drugs dog walked past. It made his skin creep. They loved it, the warders. Revelled in it. You could see it in their eyes. So much power. He stared at the last one. Put his face far too close. Most people would have looked away, shuffled backwards, embarrassed. But not her.

He sat at the coffee table allocated to him. Without Carol maybe it'd be different. Yes, that was it. She couldn't talk in front of Carol. She'd been worried about saying something - because of her parole. Today would be different. The door at the end of the room opened, disgorging thirty or more inmates. This time he recognised her.

She sat opposite, her eyes fixed on the table. 'Why've you come back?' she muttered. 'There's nothing I can tell you.'

'You're going to be out there soon,' he nodded beyond the walls. 'We can meet whenever we like without these bastards calling the shots. I want that. Don't you?'

Silence.

'You can tell me...'

'I told you, I don't want to talk about it.'

The inmate at the next table laughed hysterically. 'You got to be joking,' she said. 'I couldn't hold down a ferret!'

Sonya called over. 'You tell him, girl.'

'I guess you didn't have a choice,' Paul said.

There was no sign she'd heard him at first. Something else had caught her attention. Two warders making their presence felt. 'What about?' She eventually said.

'At the hospital. When you took Justin. I know what happened, from the court transcript.' It was too abrupt, even he knew it, but it was out now.

She shuffled in her chair. 'Yea, well, those bastards twisted everything.'

'And from Stuart.'

She leant forward and looked him full in the eyes. It was mesmerising. 'What gives you the right to go sticking your nose in where it's not wanted?'

'Right! You're my mother. Most of my life I haven't known whether you were alive or dead. I was nine years old for Christ's sake.' He was suddenly aware of a presence behind him. The warder paused then moved on. He lowered his voice. 'I have to know.'

'What's to know? I'm a convicted killer. End of story.'

215

'But you stuck to your "not guilty" plea.'

She shrugged. 'I got bad advice.'

'I don't believe that.'

'Do you think I give a toss what you believe?' She leant back, a show of indifference.

Her words opened a chasm inside. He searched her face. He knew she cared. Even after everything.

She picked at her sleeve. 'You've done all right without me.'

'Is that what you think?'

'Maybe I have to.'

The silence that followed overflowed with all the vindication he needed. She'd thought about him, hadn't wanted to leave him, she cared. 'Yeah,' he said. 'I've done all right but it's all... I mean... I never stopped looking.' He watched as she scratched at the table with her fingernail. 'Did you ever try to see me?'

Silence.

'I mean, I know you couldn't just turn up or anything but did you ever stand outside the school or something?'

Silence.

'I guess you couldn't risk it.'

She shrugged.

He leant forward. 'Is there anything I can... I mean, do you want anything?'

'Hah!' She threw her head back. 'What could I possibly want? I have an en-suite bedroom decorated in a subtle shade of green with a background perfume of, what is it now?... urine, that's right. As to interior furnishings, black is all the rage of course. And then there's the view. Lovely view of a red brick wall, and more wall, oh... and more wall. What could I possibly want? She pushed her chair back and turned away, as if wanting, needing, to distance herself from him.

'I'd have come sooner only they never told me. I'd have taken care of stuff for you.'

'I don't need taking care of,' she said over her shoulder.

'Maybe not taking care of, but there is something.'

She turned. 'What?'

'An appeal.' Nothing; not a frown, not a word, not even the flicker of an eye-lid. She was perfectly, eerily still. 'I know you didn't do it. I can't get our time back but I can make damn sure you can start again - away from all this.' He nodded at the bars on the windows.

Sonya stood.

'Listen,' he grabbed her arm. 'I can do this. I've got the money.' A warder appeared and forced his arm away.

'Leave it. I've got parole coming up,' she hissed.

'Parole! What good's that? You could be free. Not on licence, not having to move on every other month when people find out they've got a child-killer living next door.'

'You've got a mouth on you. Try shutting it and listening.' She jabbed her finger at him. 'I don't want your money. I don't want no appeal.'

'You don't mean that. I'll get it out of him.'

'Him?' Sonya stopped.

'I know you're protecting Stuart.'

'You leave him alone.'

'Don't you want justice?'

Sonya reached over the table. 'Leave Stuart alone,' she said, her eyes fixing his, triggering a familiar sensation in the pit of his stomach.

Sonya turned as the warder locked the cell door behind her. 'He don't get no more visiting rights.'

'If you say so. Bit hard on the boy though isn't it? Just found you and now you kick him in the teeth.'

'You don't know nothing about it.'

'Whatever.' The warder turned to Sonya's cellmate. 'Parole board in a month. Keep a lid on it until then.'

'Piss off.' Ali stared at Sonya. 'So? Did you tell him?'

Sonya flung herself onto her bunk. 'No.'

'He doesn't have a clue does he? About you?'

'And that's how it's gonna stay. I've done the time. It's over,' she said to the springs above her head.

'It'll never be over. You don't know what it's like out there for ex-cons, especially with your record.'

'Stuart'll take care of me.'

'For how long? Face facts, girl.'

'Leave it, Ali. It'll be okay. He said so.'

'And what he says is gospel, right?'

Sonya pummelled her pillow and hugged it to her. 'Right.'

'So how come he didn't take up his last pass - right after they set your parole board date? And you still think he'll be there when you get out?'

'He'll be there,' Sonya whispered.

Ali swung her legs over the bunk and dropped down. 'Listen. I can get you a passport. Come to Spain. We can work the bars, have a good time.'

'I'm tired, Ali. I want my home… and my boy.'

'Wake up, Babe. You're a convicted child killer. They ain't gonna let you in the same street let alone the same house.'

Sonya stared at her. So that's what Stuart had meant. Only he'd called it 'complications'. Didn't spell it out. She'd never thought… fourteen years… she'd made it. Her decision. But no-one had told her. She sat up. 'But they've got to.'

'How old is he? Fourteen, fifteen? I bet that's why your Stuart missed. He don't know how to choose.'

'Choose?'

'For Christ sake,' Ali pushed Sonya's legs out of the way and sat down. 'Stuart is Ian's dad, yeah? Been the only parent that boy has known. He's hardly going to abandon him.'

'But we was going to be together, the three of us, after.'

'Get your magic wand out then, 'cause it'll take a bloody miracle.'

Sonya curled up on her bed, facing the wall. Fourteen years hadn't seemed such an impossible price to pay but if Ali was right… She couldn't be. Stuart would be here, soon, and it'd be just as they'd planned. He'd take her back to the house on the Barbican with the brilliant red door - so many times she'd walked through that door - and Ian would be there and she'd hug him and never let him go, ever.

Chapter Twenty-Five

Angie pulled across the Exeter traffic into the filling station and manoeuvred awkwardly alongside a pump. The hire car was a beast, but it was the only way to get her larger pieces to the gallery. It had been worth the effort; they'd taken twenty. The commission was criminal but the footfall in the city centre was something she could only dream of on Lundy. The gallery had worked brilliantly. Within two years she was breaking even and every year her turnover grew. But, and it was a big but, it was seasonal. They could get through the winter on Mike's income, just, but being on an island, the essentials weren't cheap. Then she'd woken one morning with Christine's words ringing in her ears. Sell in mainland galleries for year round trade. It had taken an age for Barnstaple to shift the few they took, but Plymouth was selling well and now the Exeter gallery was on board things were definitely looking up.

She opened the door and went to the pump. 'Damn.' Wrong side. It took a few seconds to re-position the car, just long enough for a silver convertible to pull in front. A tall young man leapt out and began to fill up. 'Some people!' Angie exclaimed. Well, there was no way she was hauling this beast about any more. She turned on the radio.

Only a few more hours and she could leave it all behind. The noise, everyone rushing like there wasn't a minute to spare, rude drivers. She watched as the man restlessly flicked his car keys back and forth on the ring, the leather fob rhythmically slapping the back of his hand. He was heading for a heart attack before he was forty. Exactly the future she'd been looking at years ago. Thank God she'd seen sense. Ironic really that it was all down to Christine. Intriguing, charismatic and yes, infuriating Christine. Without that last phone call would she have ever made the move? Angie doubted it.

The roads were quiet on the way back to North Devon. Not that she was in any rush. The Oldenburg wasn't sailing until the morning. Time for a nostalgic overnight in Instow. The Commodore was a massive indulgence but she missed her view over the estuary; and the views didn't get any better than from there. The tide was in when she settled herself by the picture windows lining the front of the hotel. It was early in the season but the boats were already appearing, lifted into the water by a massive crane on the quay. In high summer they filled the estuary, though few moved further than the extent of their anchor as they swung back and forth with the tide.

'Angie?' It was a familiar voice.

'Bill… good to see you.' They kissed. 'Got time to join me?'

'Your ears must be burning. Left a message for you with Mike only yesterday.' He removed his coat and draped it over an empty chair. 'What brings you over here?'

'Just trying to flog a few photographs to keep body and soul together.'

'The way Tom tells it, things are going pretty well.'

'Tom may have laid it on a bit thick. Did he mention dealing with the fickle British public?'

'But it's worked, the move?'

Angie paused. 'Mostly. Even the endless gales and stubborn fogs are bearable when you get such spectacular sunsets.'

'And Tom?' Bill asked.

'Ah, Tom.' Angie murmured. It all started a few years back when Tom was officially discharged from care. It was like falling off a precipice. After years of institutionalised living he was out there, on his own. Bill fought his corner, pleading with Tom's mother to give him a chance. Maybe it was guilt, maybe compassion, maybe just a case of the memory fading, who knows, but she relented. Not for long though. After the honeymoon period, Bill turned up on Angie's doorstep.

'I need a favour,' he'd said. Tom's mother wanted him out of her hair during the day or out of her house completely. Social services could offer occasional respite breaks but it wasn't enough. Angie was getting busier and needed an assistant. With Tom's special abilities, would she consider him? It was lunacy to even think of it. But maybe it was time to make amends - for leaving his file sitting on Bill's desk, for sacrificing his future for her own. Tom would be a public relations disaster in the gallery, no denying it, but he was a brilliant photographer. Angie could build up stock without leaving her studio.

'Can't believe I'm saying this, Bill, but it's going well. Some of his work is amazing. I wish I had his eye.'

'You took a massive gamble, going over there. Not many of us have the guts. I didn't. Fancied getting into business myself years ago.' He shook his head. 'Too late now though.'

'Not true.'

'That was pure Tom!'

Angie smiled. 'Once you get inside his head, a lot of the things he says make sense. Certainly cuts through the bullshit.'

Bill looked at his watch. 'Got to go. Good to catch up. And Tom will keep me posted.'

'I'm sure.' Bill was almost out of the door when she remembered. 'And the message?'

'Oh yes. Tom's not the only one doing all right for himself. Remember Paul, Paul Wells?'

'Paul…?' A few seconds was all it took for Angie to be back at Ellison Road, trying to be the calm amid the storm of Paul's emotions. 'Yes, of course.'

'Turned up at the office last week. Wouldn't recognise him now. Designer suit, flash car.'

'What did he want?'

'Used the new Adoption Act to track down his mother. He was looking for any information we had, about what happened, what we knew at the time.'

Angie struggled to take it in. Paul knew. After all this time, he knew. What would that have done to him? With a few years under his belt, a bit of maturity, maybe he'd understand, but somehow she doubted it.

'He wanted to see the records. Told him that was out of the question but he's as persistent as ever. Compromised by asking for your phone number. He wants to talk.'

'Did you give it to him?'

'Of course not. But I said I'd give you his. Mike's got it.'

'How did it go?' Mike took her case and helped her into the Land Rover. There was never any doubt he'd be there. Over the years, Angie had relaxed into his predictable ways, wrapping them around her like a duvet, redolent of home comforts.

She sank thankfully into the seat. The two hour sail to Lundy had been mercifully calm but her stomach still objected. 'Great. Plymouth took thirty and Exeter twenty.'

'Double celebration then.'

'Double?'

'Results of the review on the no-take zone are in. Been a massive increase in lobsters. And there are more brown crabs. We're going to start tagging them. Get a feel for migration patterns.'

'How will you know?'

'We're hoping the fishermen will report catches of tagged lobsters.'

He looked so youthful. Angie couldn't believe he'd be forty in the summer. Couldn't believe she was still here to witness it. A sneaking contentment had crept up on her as she'd settled into island life but the summer before last everything began to unravel. It was probably something to do with her biological clock ticking. It hadn't mattered at first, not getting pregnant. She was so busy at the gallery there was hardly time for a child. But then everything changed. It was as though an emotional black pit opened up inside her. For months she hardly set foot inside the studio. Mike was his usual amazing self, supporting Tom, rustling up temporary help, being there for her when she could hardly bear to be with herself. But it was only when he finally agreed to adopt that she was able to face life again. She knew it might take time - the agency stressed so few babies were available it could be months, years even - but that had been okay. For a while. But almost two years had gone by, two years when the waiting had become like a deepening shadow, slowly prising them apart.

Mike broke into her thoughts. 'Bill called while you were away,' he said. 'Paul Wells wants you to get in touch. Number's on the pad.'

Angie scanned the stretch of water between Lundy and the mainland then turned her binoculars towards an outcrop of rock. Three seals were stretched out on the shoreline - their equivalent of a theatre's green room and stage all in one. In a matter of minutes they'd be performing like seasoned professionals for the day trippers.

'They here yet?' Tom said, pacing along the quay.

'They're in the middle of the channel. Look, you can see them.' She handed the binoculars to him.

He paused then handed the binoculars back. 'No. Can't see them.'

'But I can see the boat from here.'

'Can see the boat, yes. Can't see them.'

Angie sighed. After so long working with Tom, she could mostly let his quirks float over her head but sometimes, just sometimes…

She watched as the Oldenburg tied up at the new quay. It had transformed the experience for day trippers. No more jostling for position as boats ferried a handful of visitors at a time back and forth to the beach. Now they were striding up the cliff road within minutes of arriving.

A party of bird watchers spilled past her, equipped with the kind of lenses she could only dream of. Too early for the young puffins but they might get lucky with the adults. The vicar followed close behind. He shook the boatman's hand, collected his bag and nodded towards Angie as he waited for his ride up to the village. Behind him, a tall young man, thin enough to be described as brittle, leapt up the steps then ran back to hold out his hand to a young woman. Yet his fingers released hers as soon as their function was over. The recognition was instant. Angie walked over.

'Mr Wells?'

'Yes, but that feels odd. Call me Paul.'

'And I'm Amy.' the young woman said, beaming.

'Well, Paul, Amy, welcome to Lundy. It's been a long time.'

'I'll take it.' Tom lifted a rucksack from Amy.

'This is Tom. He's a photographer. Exhibits his work in my studio,' Angie said.

Paul nodded at him.

'What a fantastic place to be a photographer,' Amy said. 'Have you always lived here?'

'No, there.' Tom pointed to the brow of the hill.

'Sorry, I meant on the island, not here on the quay,' she responded, without a pause. 'You're so lucky.'

'Here comes your taxi,' Angie said as a Land Rover pulled up. 'We're hitching a ride with the vicar.'

'Glad you came?' Paul asked, joining Amy on a bench outside the studio.

'You bet. I'll pay you back.'

'Bugger that.'

'I went to France with mum and dad last year but this is way more adventurous. Can't take too much time off Uni though. Need to save it for when… when I need it.' She watched as Angie wrapped a canvas for a customer. 'What are you going to say?'

He shrugged. 'Just get her to talk about how it was I guess, with mum. When she found out, why she didn't tell us…'

'Try giving the accusations a rest,' Amy interrupted. 'Just encourage her to talk. You'll get your answers that way.'

'Like I got them from mum you mean?' He pulled a

cigarette from a packet and lit up.

'I don't know why you're surprised, about Sonya. She's been inside for years, a convicted child killer - how tough do you have to be to survive that? She might have been our mother the night before it all happened but God knows who she is now. And all these years later you expect her to welcome you with open arms!'

Paul moved away from the bench. 'It wasn't like that.'

'No?'

'Whatever she thinks of me, it doesn't make sense.' He turned to face her. 'Why is she so against an appeal?'

'Like she said, she's got parole coming up. She'll have been counting the days for the last couple of years. Maybe she doesn't want to risk that.'

'No,' he shook his head. 'She's hiding something. I'm not a kid any more. She can't keep me out of it.' Even as a boy he always went back for more, only ever felt truly loved and needed when he was fighting her corner. And there was never a clearer corner to fight.

'You can't force her to let you help.'

'So I do it without her.' He flicked the cigarette end to the floor and ground it with his heel.

'Why? Why do you have to dig it all up? I understand you need to talk to Angie, to find out what happened but...'

'Don't you want to know?'

'It's different. I'm me whatever happened, but with you, it's like you have to find all these scabs and pick away at them until they ooze with pus.'

'I thought you'd understand. Well I got that wrong didn't I?' He thrust his hands into his pockets and stared at the horizon.

'Sorry, I didn't mean anything... it's just... you've got this great job and Gemma and the house and it's still like everything's wrong when it should be right.'

'What if she's innocent? What if she could be our mother again?'

'It's quite something isn't it?' Angie said, joining them. 'Still can't believe I'm here.'

Paul stepped away. 'Why did you leave social work? I mean, why do all that training and give it up?'

'I usually work up to that after a couple of glasses of wine.'

'Don't mind Paul, he's a both feet first kind of guy,' Amy said.

Angie smiled. 'Yes, I remember.'

'What else do you remember?' he asked.

Angie sat on the bench. 'I remember a child prepared to take on all comers…' it was Amy's turn to smile, 'and who had a passion and a commitment to his truth.'

'What do you mean by that?' Paul said. 'My truth?'

'You saw things your way. And whatever we did or said there was no changing your mind.'

'For example?'

'Crikey, it's going back a bit. But I do remember you were convinced your mum was living on the Barbican in Plymouth. You'd bunk off there on a regular basis. Kept me awake more than once waiting for the police to call. Then I'd be off to prise you out of that artist's studio - again. What was the attraction?'

'Mum, and the painting.'

'If she was there why…?'

'Why didn't she show herself? Well that's obvious, now I finally know where she is.' His voice was terse.

'They didn't tell you?'

'No.'

'It's understandable.'

'It is, is it? Understandable that everyone knew where my mother was except me? Oh, and I was the one looking for her every day of my life.' He prodded his chest repeatedly. 'That's understandable is it?'

'Paul…' Amy pleaded.

'It's okay, Amy,' Angie said. 'I think I'd be angry too if I was in your shoes, Paul. But is anger going to get you what you want? You've spent your whole life being angry. It's become this familiar old coat. You recognise its shape, its smell, everything. But maybe it doesn't fit any more. Maybe it's time

226

to swop it for one that will bring you some happiness.' She was talking to his back. She shrugged. 'But what do I know? I'm not a social worker anymore.'

Paul turned. 'What else? What else do you remember?'

'So that's it?' Paul said an hour later.

Angie took their coffee cups. 'Yes. Everything from the minute I tapped on your caravan until you were settled with Kate and Steve - that I can remember anyway.'

'And you never met my mother?' Paul was concentrating on digging a pock hole in the grass with his heel.

'No. Sorry, I get the feeling I haven't been much help.'

'Oh you have,' Amy said. 'I didn't know half of it. About me being so quiet and how much mum wanted us.'

'She'd fostered before of course, and it had always been hard for her when the children went back, but it was different with you. There was no way she was going to be parted from you.' She looked over her shoulder. 'I need to get back. I'll ask Tom to cover over lunch. We can talk more then if you like.'

Paul watched as Angie shook the dregs from the mugs on the grass and pushed open the gallery door. 'Let's get away from here,' he said, striding off up the only track in sight.

It wasn't until they were almost at the old lighthouse that Amy spoke. 'You were lucky to have Angie. She knows you. I bet she was really good, when Sonya went and everything.'

'Maybe.'

'Mum said you called her the witch.'

'Race you to the top.' He disappeared through a heavy door into the granite corridor connecting the old lighthouse keeper's cottage with the tower itself. She turned to her left, following the sound of his footsteps. 'Paul?' He was already out of sight, leaping up the stone staircase that twisted and turned like a strand of DNA.

Amy paused half way to catch her breath.

'Are you coming?' He was leaning over the railing high above her.

'What's the rush?' she called, but he was away again. When she finally emerged into the glass dome, he was sitting in a solitary deck chair balanced on a ledge hardly wider than the splay of its legs. 'Be careful, Paul, that doesn't look too safe.'

'Take a look at that,' he waved his arm round the glass. 'You can see from Hartland Point to Mortehoe. I want this.'

'You've got a fantastic view from your study.'

'Nothing like this. Place like this, you can think.'

'Maybe that's why Angie came. It's somewhere everything comes in to focus.'

'Ran away more like. You heard her. She knew what I needed but she didn't do anything,' Paul was shifting uneasily in the deckchair, biting at the quicks of his nails.

'But she couldn't! You were just one child on her caseload. She had all the others to think about.'

He sprang out of the deckchair to peer through the glass. 'So no-one gets what they need. Great solution. She should have done something. And she knows it, I can tell.'

'I hate it when you're so bitter. She was doing her best.'

'Well it wasn't good enough was it?' He grabbed the hand rail and swung himself down the steps.

'Our mother's innocent. You know that,' Paul said. They'd joined Angie at a table in the Marisco tavern. It was quieter than usual. A fine day had enticed the day trippers out to explore the island.

'Sonya? No, I didn't know,' Angie said. 'Did she say that?'

'No,' Amy said. 'But Paul will badger her until she does.'

Angie looked at Paul. 'What makes you so sure? I mean, I know it's difficult, but she was convicted.'

'So everyone keeps telling me. And like I keep telling them, not everyone on the jury thought she was guilty. It was a majority verdict.'

'But if there was any doubt surely…'

'The Guildford Four, the Birmingham Six… the courts get it wrong. I'll prove it.'

'How?' Angie said.

He stared at her. 'You tell me.'

'Excuse me?'

'Everything gets written up, yeah?'

Angie folded her arms. 'In theory.'

'I want to see those notes. From the hospital, police, social services,' he counted each one on his fingers. 'Everything. There's got to be something in there, something that says exactly what happened that night.'

'They'd never let you see them. They're confidential.'

'I bet you still have contacts.'

Angie leant back. 'Oh no, there's no way…'

'It's my life we're talking about,' he said, his voice raised above the background hum. 'My life. Who has more right to know what's in those files?'

'Paul,' Amy said, looking over her shoulder. 'There's no need…'

He looked at her. 'There's every need,' he turned back to Angie. 'You went back to the caravan, found my clothes, looked after. She cared. There's no way she could do that to Justin, to any of us.' He leant closer to Angie. 'And you cared. I know you did.'

'Yes, I cared. But the so called 'care' system is so…'

'Up its own arse.'

Angie almost smiled but there was no humour in his voice. 'I was going to say inflexible. I tried to get Bill to reduce my caseload so I could give you the time you needed.'

'But not hard enough…'

'Paul!' Amy tried again. 'Angie's been good enough…'

'So you threw in the towel,' Paul interrupted.

'Yes. I threw in the towel. Satisfied? Is that what you want to hear?' Angie snapped. 'I'd had enough of sleepless nights, slogging my guts out getting nowhere, caring too much. I was worn out.'

'And what about us? All the kids abandoned in that Borstal of a children's home.'

'I'm sorry. I wish it could have been different.'

'Wishing didn't get me anywhere though did it?' He was master of the piercing eye contact now. 'Two years of shit you left me with.'

'Leave it, Paul.' Amy gripped his arm.

He shook her hand away. 'Two years it took me to get out of there. Best bit of acting I ever did. And what was the only alternative? Kate and Steve doing their cosy, "we'll take you, Paul, but here are the rules" act.'

'It was no act,' Amy said. 'They cared. You were just too up your own arse to see it.'

He smiled. 'That's one for the record. Little sister bites back.' He turned to Angie. 'How about you? Is there any spirit left in you for a fight?'

'Meaning?' Angie couldn't control the tremor in her voice.

'I don't think you like leaving a job half done. This case won't be closed until the damage is made good.'

Angie forced herself to meet his stare. 'And how exactly do I do that?'

Finally Paul smiled. 'By proving my mother innocent. She's hiding something. And it can't be guilt. I mean it's out isn't it? So why hide it? Why refuse to see me?'

'Could be shame. Can't face you because of what she did.'

'No. It's because I know.'

'Know what?'

'She's protecting someone.'

He spoke with such conviction Angie couldn't help being drawn into his world. 'Who?'

'There was a man there that night, the boyfriend. He had means, motive and opportunity.'

'But why would she take the blame? It doesn't make sense.'

'Not yet. But it will.'

'You're back then.' Gemma was standing in the kitchen, her coat on, a set of keys on the worktop in front of her.

'What's going on?' Paul said, shrugging off his jacket. 'What are they doing there?' He pointed at a row of cases in the hall.

'I'd have thought even someone as insensitive as you could work it out. Cases, keys, coat. Bit of a giveaway don't you think?' Her voice was clipped.

'Another scene for my benefit? What is it this time? Poor Gemma's feeling neglected, is that it?' Paul opened a cupboard and selected a bottle of whisky.

'You really are a cold bastard.' She stared at him, gripping the worktop.

'Cold definitely the way the wind whips across that island. God knows how anyone sticks it.'

'You know perfectly well what I mean!' She watched as he walked around the kitchen. 'Paul, this is important.'

'So, I'm listening.'

'But that's the problem isn't it? You don't listen. It's like I'm invisible.' She waited. 'I've wasted so many years... hoping you'll...' her voice cracked, 'you'll show some love, some genuine affection even. Yes, I'd have settled for affection.'

'That's big of you!'

'Don't, Paul. Why do you have to be so bloody hard? All I ever wanted was to feel close... but it's like there's this Berlin Wall around you. Like you have to repel everyone.' She fought to keep the tears back.

He scanned the dishwasher for a glass. 'It's always the same. One bad day and it's "let's pick Paul to pieces" time. Well no more. This is how I am. Get used to it.'

She'd tried so hard to seal herself off from his callousness but he always got to her. 'After everything we've shared,' she said between sobs, 'you can speak to me like that... without caring... how it hurts.'

'Give it a break. I've had a long day.' He poured a drink and picked up the paper.

She stared in disbelief. 'You're just going to ignore me?'

Silence.

'You bastard,' she exploded. 'You soak up everything I give but when it comes to needing you, needing your love, that's your cue to put the knife in,' she was crying uncontrollably.

'If I give you so little why are you still here?' he said,

231

scanning the headlines.

She looked at him. 'Because I love you.' She searched her pockets and pulled out a crumpled tissue.'

Silence.

'Aren't you going to say anything?'

'What do you want me to say?' He glanced at her briefly.

'That maybe that you didn't realise what you were doing and things will be different from now on?'

He shrugged.

She grabbed the newspaper. 'You really don't care do you? Do you!' She'd vowed she wouldn't let it happen again. She'd steeled herself to walk out the door leaving some barbed comment floating in her wake that would strike him to the core, make him want to wrap her in his arms and tell her he loved her. Who was she kidding! Any attempts at a meaningful conversation always ended with her being sucked into his distorted emotional world and left a wrung-out husk. She was no match for him. But something in her had never been able to let go... until now.

'Are we done?' He downed the whisky.

'You tell me.' Gemma blew her nose.

There was a noise outside the door. 'Here, Spider.' The dog skittered across the kitchen tiles and leapt on Paul, licking his face. Paul smiled and hugged him close. 'Hey boy, how are you? Had a good day. I guess you need a walk don't you?' He reached around Gemma to unhook a lead from the wall then hesitated, his face close to hers. 'You're better off without me,' he said, suddenly meeting her eyes.

Chapter Twenty-Six

The warder nodded in recognition as Stuart filed into the visiting room. He was late.

'Hello, Sonya.'

'Thought you were going to miss again.'

'Sorry about last time. Had to do something with Ian.'

She leant across the table, eager for news. 'How's he doing? Did he get in the team?'

'Yes. He's dead chuffed. You should see him...' Wrong words again. After all this time he still did it.

'But I will, soon, won't I? I'll be able to come and stand on the touch-line and cheer him on.'

'Sure.' It sounded hollow even to Stuart's ears.

'What? What is it?'

'Nothing. It'll be fine. Heard anything, about how it'll go?'

'No reason why I shouldn't get parole. Been keeping my head down. Why wouldn't they give it? Have they written to you? Only they write to find out where I'll be living, for the licence,' she was leaning forward, her eyes searching his.

'No.' He looked away.

'They've got your address, our address, haven't they? You've made sure they've got it?'

'Yes.'

'So it'll be there soon.'

'I expect so.'

She gripped his hand. 'Fourteen years, Stu. We done it! It'll all be over soon. Then it'll be just as we planned. Like this never happened.'

'If you say so.'

'Of course it will. Why shouldn't it be? You… you still love me don't you?'

He met her eyes. 'I'll always love you, whatever happens.'

'What do you mean?'

'Nothing. It'll be fine.'

'Tell me!'

He paused. 'We need to talk… about Paul.'

'I told him, I told him to leave you alone.'

'He's your boy, Sonya. Do you think he's going to do what anyone tells him? You should have heard him. Like a battering ram going on and on.'

'You didn't tell him?' She tightened her grip.

'No.'

'Only you can't. Not ever.'

'Sonya…'

'You agreed, you swore…' Her eyes drilled into his.

'He's not a kid any more. He's a grown man, a wealthy one too. Managed to get himself a barrister with a reputation for winning. Says he's got a case, a good one.'

'What case? There isn't one.'

'That won't stop him. He could destroy everything. It was so long ago, Sonya, how could it possibly hurt him now?'

'You don't know him like I do. He's sensitive.'

Stuart gave a sharp laugh, 'Could have fooled me.'

She snapped back. 'Leave him alone.'

If Stuart had been in any doubt before, he knew now. Knew what choice she would make. But maybe she hadn't thought it through. It wasn't a choice any mother should have to make, between her children. But Paul wasn't a child any more. 'Sonya, you do know that… that if they give you parole it doesn't mean… they may not…'

'What? They may not what?' Her eyes searched his.

'Let you come home.' The hardest words he'd ever had to say. What were they, words? You can't see them, touch them, but they'd just done more damage than any weapon.

'They've got to,' she curled up on the chair.

'Sonya, darling. It's best we know, isn't it? Maybe they'll let you visit, do stuff with all of us together, just till he's eighteen.'

'No!' she half screamed, half sobbed, crashing her arms down on the table. 'I'm coming home to my baby.' Two warders appeared, lifted her out of the chair and pulled her to the door. 'You tell them, tell the bastards...' Her protests bounced off the cold, uncompromising walls.

Sonya stared at the paper cuttings stuck to the board above her table with blobs of toothpaste. Fourteen years. Fourteen years since she'd stood in the dock behind the black railings in court one at the Old Bailey and heard the foreman say one word. 'Guilty'. It was such a short journey in the Black Maria, but with each mile her life slipped out of her grasp.

The gates at Holloway slid sideways with an irritating 'beep beep' then shut behind them with a thud. No sign from the two prison officers inside the van that they were being deleted off the face of the world. That was for her alone.

They led her to a door, mustard yellow it was - and not one door but two. All Sonya could see were the iron bars across the outside. The officer by her side pressed a bell and escorted her into a corridor. She flinched at the noise. Raised voices; caustic, demanding voices.

'Name?' This from the receiving officer.

'Sonya Wells.'

'Warrant?' This to the officer who'd 'escorted' her there. Escorted!

The receiving officer checked the warrant. Court. Conviction. Signed. 'Okay'. The escort handed over Sonya's bag and left. She was officially an inmate of Holloway prison.

'Spread your legs.'

Sonya flinched. It was so intrusive. She wanted to back away, tell her what to do with her rub down search. But this was her first taste of what 'powerless' really meant. Things were different on remand. 'Innocent until proven guilty' and all that. Now she was proven guilty - though what did they know - and of an unspeakable crime. This was only the beginning.

'Open your mouth.' The woman checked inside, her face too close. Sonya recoiled from her breath. 'Sit over there.' The officer pointed at a

strange wooden chair with a triangular seat. There was only one place she could balance properly. They gave her a card to hold and the light flashed. Seconds later the chair was turning, a rackety noise as it swung on a turntable. To the left, then to the right. Camera flashing.

'How does it feel then? Filling that seat. Ruth Ellis, Myra Hindley. They've all sat there. Just like you.'

How did she feel? No feeling left. At least she hoped not. The officer grabbed her fingers and rolled them over a brass block filled with black ink. Then onto the paper. All at once. Shouldn't it be one at a time? They gave her a tissue. She rubbed until it was in shreds but the patterns on her fingertips still leapt out where ink had lodged in the grooves.

The officer selected a form from the desk. 'Name? Address?' The questions went on and on. She just wanted it to end. Minutes later she was wishing it hadn't. They gave her a dressing gown and told her to remove all her clothes except her knickers. Then they'd taken her to a weird three sided room, like a cubicle with the front open, and snatched the dressing gown away. She'd covered herself but they hadn't finished. 'Raise your arms. Now drop your knickers and give us a twirl.'

It was all a joke, humiliating her. Paraded like some Belsen inmate. Nothing. Nobody.

They held her clothes out, and a dressing gown, sheets, towels, toothpaste, brush, soap and shampoo. 'This way.' The officer led her towards the noise. It was coming from a room down the corridor. The officer guided her past the door. 'Be grateful I'm not putting you in there.'

'Why?'

'Word gets round about child killers. You're expected.'

'I'm not…'

'Save the act for later. You'll need it.' They stopped outside a blue door. 'Take those off.' The officer pointed at her shoes and handed Sonya some shapeless pale green foam slippers. She carried them into the small room. The door shut behind her. She was alone. And for the next fourteen years, couldn't make her own cup of tea, walk down a street, see her children… 'No, no,' she wailed, rocking in the middle of the floor.

And now they were going to make her choose.

'So?' Sonya's cell mate slumped down on the end of her bed.

'What?' Sonya was in no mood to talk.

'Are you gonna let him appeal?'

'What's to say?'

'Listen, girl. You, me, all of us in here, we spend the time surviving. Right? You've had it worse, because of... well you know why. But I believe you.'

'Believe what?'

'You didn't do it.'

'You can't know that.'

'No, but you do. And you talk, girl. At night. I could've made a fortune if you'd done a bank.'

'That's crap.'

'Crap eh? You sitting comfortably? Then I'll begin. "I'll just be a minute," you said as you left the caravan. You cradled Justin so close, your trembling fingers sent shivers across the blanket that covered his still body.'

'Stop. Right now,' Sonya said.

'You followed the dirt track through the caravans, stepping through the mud in your bright red shoes, chosen for your hot date the night before. You'd waited all your life for last night (do you hear the violins? I swear I did when you got to this bit.) But suddenly everything's different. And now...? "Oh, God," you call out. 'What do I do now?"'

'Stop you bitch. Right now. Or...'

Ali leant towards her. 'Or what? I'll pin you down before you've lifted an arm. And you know it.' She sat back. 'Where was I? What should you do? Phone for an ambulance? But what can you say? "My baby is dead." And what would they say? "And where were you Mrs Wells?" Ali mimicked Sonya. "I was out." "Out!" they said. "You left three children under nine alone?" Am I on the right track here, Sonya?'

She was of course. So much so that, like an old-fashioned record player, she wanted to nudge the stylus to make her move on a track.

'You followed the road to town, on automatic pilot, clasping Justin to you.' Ali moved closer. 'Too much detail, Sonya? Your dreams are full of it, girl. There's only one thing missing. What happened the night before?'

Sonya turned and pulled her legs up to her chest. 'Why the hell should I tell you?'

'Because you want to.'

Sonya dropped her head onto her knees.

'Well?'

'Don't rush me!' she muttered.

'Christ, girl, we've shared this cell for six frigging years!'

Sonya lifted her head. 'One condition.'

'I don't do conditions.'

'Nothing doing then.'

'For Christ's sake, what is it?'

Sonya paused. Trust was an awkward concept in a prison cell. It was all about getting by, usually at someone else's expense. But Ali had stood by her. 'Paul never gets to know.'

'I don't get it. What's the big deal with protecting him?'

'Yes or no?'

'Yes. Though you're crazy to take the word of an ex-con.'

Did she really want to go there again? Not in her dreams but in the cold light of day. Making it real. But it was real already. Stuart had made sure of that. 'It was about half seven by the time I got the kids sorted. I needed to go or we'd miss the beginning of the film. But my bloody mother wasn't there was she? I went to get her. She was yacking as usual. I didn't have time for it. Told her Justin and Amy were in bed. Paul would go soon. She said she'd be there in five, invite her friend over. I knew… knew it was bullshit, that she'd take her time, but Stuart was waiting.'

'Where?'

'In his van. We went as soon as I got back. Didn't want to miss the film, Shirley Valentine it was, the last night. But I ended up missing it anyway. Felt sick so I went to the Ladies. Stu came to the door after a bit. Asked if I was okay, said he'd take me home.'

'So you went back to the caravan?'

'Not exactly.' Sonya smiled. 'I felt better out in the air so we sat in his van deciding what to do. I mean, we had a babysitter.

238

Didn't want to waste time by ourselves. Maybe that's why he said it then, I don't know.'

'Said what?'

'Will you marry me?'

'He proposed?' Ali exclaimed.

Sonya was beginning to regret this. 'Just said so didn't I? What's wrong with that? My life had been crap, like forever. Nine years with Fred and then soon as Justin arrived he buggered off.'

'So lover boy asked you to marry him. What then?'

'We had to celebrate didn't we? So we went to town, drank champagne. It was dead romantic.' She stopped. 'Never going to happen though was it? Might have known it was too good for the likes of me.'

'So when exactly did you get back to the caravan?'

'Elevenish. Mum and her friend were asleep in front of the TV. I sent them home.'

'Just you? Where was lover boy?'

'Gone.'

'Bollocks!' Ali protested. 'You'd just got engaged. Why didn't he stay the night? Not going to tell me you were saving yourself for the wedding!'

'Piss off!' Sonya hesitated. But she was waded in too far. 'I didn't want mum knowing,' she continued. 'Not till I was ready to tell her, my way, my time.'

Ali softened her voice. 'So what then?'

'Checked on Justin and fell into bed.'

'What exactly does "checked" mean?'

Sonya shrugged.

Ali tried again. 'Was he breathing?'

'I… I don't know. I'd drunk too much and was starting to feel sick again. I had to lie down. He looked fine. It wasn't till the next morning I realised…'

Ali stared at her. 'When did it happen?'

'Between half seven and nine they said. The night before.'

'And your mother was with her friend the whole time?'

'Yes.'

'So it had to be before she got there.'

'If you believe them.'

'So if not you, who?'

'I… I don't know.'

Ali shifted to the edge of the bunk. 'Not many people it could be is there? Like you or Stuart basically.'

Sonya jerked her head up. 'It's all black and white with you isn't it? Did you do it - yes or no? Well how about maybe? Maybe I was to blame. Maybe I'm guilty of saying things that were taken the wrong way,' her words piled on top of each other. 'Maybe someone wanted to please me so much that he took everything I said to heart, too much to heart. He wouldn't harm anyone, not on purpose. It was an accident. It had to be.' Sonya threw herself back on the bed and covered her head. 'Just leave it, Ali. Leave me alone.'

'Are you telling me you've been through fourteen years of hell to protect a man?!'

'He wasn't a man.'

'Damn right he wasn't.'

Chapter Twenty-Seven

The call had come late last night. 'How is she?' Amy asked as Steve emerged from the side room.

'Tired. You can go in, but don't make her talk. It's too much...' his voice drifted away.

Amy looked through the door. Kate's face was so pale it hardly stood out against the harsh hospital sheets. It was a week since the pain had got so bad they'd called the ambulance. 'It's only constipation, they'll sort it, don't worry,' she'd whispered to Amy as they waited. Only it wasn't. The cancer had spread. Inoperable they said.

'I'm here, mum.' Kate's eyes flickered. 'No, it's okay, don't move. I'll just sit...' It took a while to stem the tears. 'Um... everything's okay at home. I'm keeping dad in order, making sure he washes up. It'll be just fine when you come back. Perfect in fact. The thrift is out all along the cliffs. We'll go for a walk down there in a week or two, sit on our bench or go crab hunting in the rock pools. I've never told you, have I, how much I enjoyed doing that. My after-school treat. You'd pack my favourite peanut butter sandwiches so we could stay for ages. You must have got so bored sitting there while I hunted though every single pool on the shore. Did you mind? You never said.

'I called Aunt Tilly. Just to let her know why you weren't at home. She wanted to visit but dad said best to wait until you got back. Hope that's okay.' A trace of a smile crossed Kate's face. 'Only she can be a bit, well, exhausting, and if you're not feeling brilliant...' Kate's smile turned to a grimace. She arched her back and gripped Amy's hand. 'What is it? What's wrong, mum? Shall I get someone?' The spasm slowly eased and Kate relaxed. She opened her eyes.

'My beautiful girl. Thank you for being my beautiful girl.' Her eyes scanned Amy's face, taking in every nuance of pain reflected there. 'I'm so sorry to do this to you. I said I'd be there for you, always.'

'And you will. It's going to be okay.'

'I don't think so. But we've had the best time haven't we? Me, you and your dad.'

'And Paul.'

'Does he know?' she whispered.

'I left a message on his phone. He'll call. Soon.'

'Maybe.' She closed her eyes.

'Don't talk. You need to rest.' Amy smoothed the hair away from Kate's forehead. 'Dad's gone home for a bit but I'll be here if you need anything.'

'Didn't you get my message?' Amy finally got through to Paul.

'I've been busy.'

'Don't you understand? Mum's… she's dying.'

'So you said. I'm… I'm sorry.'

'If only you meant that.'

Silence.

'Why are you like this? After everything she's done for you.'

'What do you want me to do, Amy? Pretend? What good would that do?'

'You could at least be here for me, and dad. I need you, Paul. It's awful, watching her like this.'

His voice softened. 'She'll be okay. It's amazing what they can do.'

'I don't think they can do anything. Other than manage the pain, but they're not even doing that.'

'What did the consultant say?'

She could tell he was doing something at his desk. 'They've done all they can.'

'That's the NHS isn't it. You need private care.'

'You know dad can't afford it. Not on his pension.' Amy waited. This was the time for him to offer but the silence became unbearable. 'She's been asking for you. When can you come?'

'In a few days. Got something to follow up.'

'She might not have much longer.'

'I'll be there, okay?' His voice was suddenly animated. 'Listen, Amy, you've got to come with me, to see Stuart Saunders. If he was there that night, before they left for the cinema, he could have got in when mum went for gran. I remember now, the door was open…'

'I don't believe this,' Amy interrupted. 'Kate's lying there and all you can think about is hounding some poor guy…'

'He's not some poor guy. He's a murderer.'

'I can't leave now. Mum needs me.'

'Well I need you too. When are you back at Uni?'

'I don't know. I've a couple of lectures on Thursday but…'

'Okay. I'll pick you up afterwards and we'll go then.'

She hesitated. 'Only if I'm back for visiting time.'

This time the man walked steadily down the hall to the sitting room. 'So you're Amy,' he said. 'You're very like your mother.'

'Not anymore,' Paul interrupted. 'Prison's seen to that.'

The man turned to face him. His gaze steady, penetrating. 'And from what I hear, you've taken after your father.'

'What's that supposed to mean?' Paul said.

Amy put a cautioning hand on Paul's arm. 'He's not like that,' Amy said, 'not really. It's just, well, he's had it tough, had to fight for everything. He can come over as a bit edgy.'

Paul shook Amy's hand away and turned towards Stuart. 'Okay, I'm listening.'

'What do you want to know?'

'Did you kill Justin?'

'No.'

'That's it? No protestations, no explanations, just "no"!'

'What do you want me to say?'

Paul stood. 'If my mother's innocent - and I know she is - you're the only person who could've done it.'

'That's not...'

'Where did you meet my mother that night?' Paul flicked his car keys back and forth on the ring, the leather fob rhythmically slapping the back of his hand.

Stuart hesitated. 'Outside the site. I waited in my van.'

'Sure about that are you?' Paul moved closer. 'I mean it's been a while, the memory can get foggy.'

'Paul, this isn't the way...' Amy pulled at his arm. 'Please,' her eyes pleaded with him. He finally shrugged and backed away. 'Mr Saunders,' Amy said, 'do you have any idea what might have happened that night?'

'Believe me,' he said, his voice softer, 'I wish there was something I could tell you. But... but it happened exactly as they said in court.'

'Why did you persuade my mother to run?' Paul said. 'Only a guilty person would run.'

Stuart looked at him. 'Is that what you think?'

'So how was it?' Amy pulled a stool over beside his chair. 'Please, if you can, tell us.'

Stuart removed his glasses and rubbed his hands across his eyes. 'Sonya said she felt ill so we left the cinema early. By the time we got to my van she wasn't feeling so bad. We chatted for a bit...'

'Sitting in the cold?' Paul interrupted.

'There was something I wanted to say, something private. We went for a drink then I took her back to the caravan.'

'What time?'

'About eleven. We said goodnight. I drove home.'

'You didn't go in, check she was okay, see if there was anything you could do?' Paul sounded incredulous.

'No. Maybe if I had... but I didn't.'

'And you expect us to believe that.'

'Paul!' Amy glared at him.

'I don't expect anything of you,' Stuart said, looking at him.

244

'It's simply what happened.'

'And then?' Amy encouraged. 'What happened then?'

'I went home. It was the next day before I saw Sonya again. When I opened my door she was standing there, holding Justin in this blanket. I brought her in.'

'What do you mean, 'brought her'?' Paul said.

Stuart paused, reliving the scene. 'It was like she was in shock. I sat her in a chair and that's when the blanket fell away from his face and I saw... it was the colour, I guess. I asked what had happened and she looked at me in this weird way, like a puppet.'

'...*nothing's happened. Why should anything have happened?*'

'*Let me take Justin, Sonya.*'

'*No,*' *she clutched him to her.* '*He needs to stay with me. He gets upset with strangers. Not that you're a stranger, but he don't know you.*'

'*Maybe you shouldn't hold him so tight. He won't be able to breathe.*' *I knelt in front of her and eased the blanket away.*

'*He loves having his toes tickled. He makes this sound, like Paul's play train, all huffy like.*'

'*Sonya...*'

'*He eats anything - pizza, fish, even curry. And he'll grab chips off my plate and stuffs them in like there's no tomorrow.*'

'*Sonya, I'm going for the van.*' *I got up.*

'*Where are we going?*'

'*We've got to take Justin to the hospital.*'

'*But can't we wait till he wakes?*'

I held her hand against Justin's face. Her whole body recoiled. She began to shake. '*Sonya,*' *I said,* '*Justin isn't going to wake. He's not asleep... he's dead.*'

'*No. No!*'

'*I'm so sorry. My poor, poor, Sonya.*' *I lifted Justin from her, laid him on the settee and wrapped my arms around her.*

I got her into the van and was going to put Justin in the back, but she started to scream, made me give him to her to hold. I thought it would be okay. She seemed rational but on the way she started ranting...'

'…we're gonna be all right, Justin, you and me. Now we've got Stuart. We're gonna live in his new house in Plymouth. It's got a red door and inside there's this massive room, loads of space for you and Paul and Amy to have your toys all over the place. He won't mind that, Stuart won't. He's gonna love you. Can't wait to see you, he said. All of you. I'd have taken you sooner but I couldn't could I? Nobody could know about Stuart - not till I was sure.

'It was like I wasn't there.' Stuart paused.

'What happened at the hospital?' Amy asked.

'She seemed to come round again. This young nurse took down her details and asked what had happened. I told them Sonya had gone in and found the baby dead in his cot. They showed us into this room then took Justin away. At first they were really kind and understanding but then something changed. There were two of them, asking the same questions over and over. They didn't believe Sonya - kept asking how much she'd had to drink, whether she'd really checked on him, whether he was breathing. They kept on at her so much… she wasn't in any state…'

He looked at Paul. 'They wanted to know about the two of you - where were you, who was with you? Then something clicked. It was like the numbness suddenly wore off. Sonya became hysterical, sobbing and asking over and over what had happened to her baby. That's when they said it…'

'…perhaps you can tell us, Mrs Wells.'

'What do you mean?'

'We have… concerns about your baby's death.'

'What do you mean, concerns?'

'We simply need to establish what happened.'

'But I've told you.'

'It's possible your baby was suffocated.'

'Suffocated? What on? Was he sick? What?'

'What are you implying?' I said. 'Sonya loves her kids. She'd never harm them.'

'Not intentionally perhaps.'

'Then they left, all except the young nurse who stayed in the corridor. I couldn't get what they'd said out of my mind. They made Sonya's story sound so…'

'So what?' Paul snapped, pacing the worn carpet in front of the window.

'Implausible. They were the experts. If they were right she had to be lying. I didn't know what to think, especially about the ambulance.'

'She didn't call one.'

'Precisely. If you discovered your baby dead what would be the first thing you'd do?' Put yourself in my place. Why didn't she call? Could it have been because she did… did kill him? Not on purpose, it had to be some horrible accident. But she'd have been terrified someone would find out.'

'Is that how you did it?' Paul said.

'What?'

'Put the idea in her mind she was guilty.'

Stuart slumped in his chair. 'No. All I knew was I had to get her out of there. Whatever happened, she wasn't a criminal. But they were never going to see it that way. She was going to lose you anyway - just the suspicion would be enough for them to take you - and I couldn't let her end up in jail. The thought of what they do to baby killers…' He shuddered.

'A policeman appeared at the nurse's station further down the ward. It looked hopeless. But then this alarm sounded and everyone rushed off. We got out the fire escape. She wouldn't get in the van at first, screaming that she couldn't leave Justin, or you, but I had to make her, you must see that.' His eyes pleaded with them for understanding. 'I told her I'd take care of her, that we'd come back for both of you just as soon as we could. I told her, it wasn't her fault, none of it.' He was suddenly still. 'And that's when she said it.'

'But it is my fault. It's all my fault.'

Chapter Twenty-Eight

'Thanks. Hope you enjoy it.' Angie closed the studio door behind the couple from Birmingham. They'd taken an hour to decide between a seal and a puffin. But it had been a good day. Over two hundred and fifty arrived on the Oldenburg - almost at capacity.

She pulled the blinds to protect the prints in the window, wandered across the green by the Marisco and through the narrow path that led to Heavens House and the beach. From the brow of the hill she could just see the passengers queuing on the quay for the return trip. To Ilfracombe this time. She depended on the day trippers for her income but this was her time, when everyone other than the self-caterers had left and a blanket of peace descended on the island.

She called at the shop to pick up the post. The handwritten envelope was such a rarity she opened it first. 'Good grief.' Had so much time really slipped by? Bill Stevens. Retiring. It would cost to get there but the invitation to his retirement 'do' was hard to resist. She could combine it with things she needed to do in Bideford. Go to the dentist… do a bit of shopping… there had to be other good reasons for going. Reasons that didn't involve her walking a fine line with the law. But at this precise moment she couldn't think of any. There was only one thought in her mind. Paul.

What's going on?' Angie looked at the boxes piled up in what had been the duty room at Social Services. Hours she'd spent there, interviewing drunks who threw bricks through shop windows to exchange a freezing doorway for a warm cell, desperate mothers down to their last fiver and the rent money due or the mentally ill struggling to make sense of existence their way.

'Moving up to the hospital,' Bill Stevens replied. 'This place isn't fit for purpose anymore.'

'Was it ever? What's with all these?' She pointed the boxes.

'Closed case files. Anything over ten years is being archived.'

She scanned the labels. 'Do you believe in synchronicity?' she said over her shoulder.

'What's that? New type of clock mechanism?'

Angie smiled. To have wormed her way in using deception and subterfuge would have been a step too far. But to see the very box sitting there. She owed Paul, had done ever since the day she abandoned him, ever since she discovered where his mother was and allowed Bill to convince her Kate was right, it wasn't the time to tell him.

'Chaos isn't it,' Bill said. 'Seemed like a good time to slip quietly away.'

Angie took in the thirty or so well lubricated colleagues enjoying an early end to the day. 'So what's next?'

'Well, after your carefully timed advice...'

'What advice?'

'When I was being a wimp saying I'd missed the time to go into business, you told me it was never too late. Gave me the kick up the backside I needed. I'm taking over a care home. Purpose built place at Westward Ho! It's where the money's going to be.' He waved at a woman advancing across the floor. 'Listen, thanks for coming. Keep in touch.'

Angie scanned the room. Some familiar faces, most not. The turnover of staff was even higher now than in her day. None of them were concerned with what she was doing. She wedged her phone on her shoulder, a good enough reason to turn her back on the gathering and place her bag on the box.

Minutes later she was walking back to her B&B. She'd just

browse the file tonight. Look for anything that stood out. Anything at all. Not necessarily use it. Just be aware. That's all. Then time tomorrow to get the Oldenburg back to Lundy and a quiet life.

Angie stood at the window of the B&B looking out over the Bideford rooftops. She had fifteen minutes to get to the quay for the boat. Fifteen minutes to decide. It wasn't nearly enough. Was accessing confidential files a criminal offence? Just how serious could this get? But Paul had a right to know.

'Two wrongs don't make a right,' Angie muttered. Why did he have to stir things up? It had taken years to shed the layers of frustration and responsibility that had finally forced her out of the job. And with one meeting the familiar straightjacket was back. 'Shit!' She picked up her phone.

'Tom? It's Angie. I won't be back today. Can you write a sign to put on the shop door... I mean to stick to the window of the door with sellotape, saying we are closed... because I can't... on your own?... until Sunday... okay... okay.'

It was a risk. Tom had never run the shop on his own, apart from the odd lunch break. But he sounded confident. That was a leap in itself. She gathered up the typewritten sheets, re-packed her overnight bag, settled her bill and walked down to the quay. The Oldenburg was preparing to leave.

'Angie, get a move on,' Mike held the gangplank for her.

The urge to throw herself onto the boat before they pushed off was almost irresistible. But what good would that do? 'There's a few more things I need to do, Mike. Can't explain now. I'll be back tomorrow.'

'Okay, don't forget it's an early sailing.' He started to pull the gangplank on board then turned back. 'I meant to say, the adoption agency left a message. Don't get your hopes up,' he said quickly. 'They made a point of saying there was no news. Just want us to call.' He looked over this shoulder. 'Time to cast off. See you tomorrow.'

Thirty minutes later she was packed into a creaking two-carriage train on the Exeter line, the rush of disappointment at Mike's words finally subsiding. She closed her eyes. Back home, Tom would be walking up from the bunkhouse, pausing to look for the Oldenburg, calculating how much time he had before the visitors arrived. Then, at the studio, counting the float, straightening the pictures - three times - and buttoning and unbuttoning his coat - seven times - before unlocking the door. She crossed her fingers, just once.

'Exeter St David's, this is Exeter St David's. Change here for London Paddington...' She walked briskly away from the station, keen to leave the constant hum of traffic behind. But the closer she got to Exeter quay, the slower her steps became. Angie checked the address. It was just ahead of her, the old grain store reinvented as a trendy warehouse. The memory was visceral. Instantly she was standing on the banks of the Thames looking up at Christine's apartment. She still missed her calls, missed her. But they hadn't been in touch for ages, not since the Independent ran a feature under the header, 'New face at the BBC.' Her weekly media review grew into a ratings winner. Angie watched occasionally but it was time to move on.

She looked up. The sun reflected off the windows running the width of the floor occupied by Arc Animation, creating a shield of light. But Angie knew he'd be there, pacing the floor, searching the cobbled approach for her. Once spotted there'd be no breathing space. The questions would come thick and fast, along with demands for action. There was still time to turn around, say she'd changed her mind. In her dreams.

'Angie.' He was waiting as the lift doors opened. 'I've got us a room.' He was off without another word, leading her past the worn red bricks of the original structure into a modern addition at the rear. 'What have you got?' he said as the door shut behind her.

'This is confidential material, Paul...'

'We've done that, remember? Without me, none of this stuff would exist. Who has more right to see it?' He stood with his hand outstretched.

'It's not just about you.'

'Who else is in there?'

Angie sighed, opened her bag and drew out a thick manila folder. 'Most of this I knew about, but some documents have been added, from after they found your mum.' She removed a slim yellow folder and handed the rest of the file to him.

Paul leant over the table and began flipping through the pages. He stopped half way and lifted out the post mortem report. He read, silently. 'I never knew him,' he said, finally. 'Not really. I remember the coughing, going on and on. And mum always there, sorting him out. I'd do stuff instead. "Paul, get Amy her tea," she'd say. "Paul, get Justin's bottle ready. Paul, go and get your Nan…" Her best mate she called me.'

'Sounds like you took on a lot.'

'She didn't make me. We were a team.'

'Can't have been easy.'

'She didn't do it!' he snapped. 'You're trying to say she couldn't hack it. Three kids, one of them ill. All on her own.'

Angie took a breath. She couldn't let him bully her into silence. 'Sleep deprivation can do weird things to your mind. Finally things were coming right for Sonya. She'd had disaster after disaster with men, must have been thinking that it was never going to work out for her. Then Stuart appears. She's excited about seeing him but Justin starts to cry. He goes on and on. How can she leave? Her mother won't babysit with him screaming. But what will Stuart do if she doesn't turn up? She was insecure, maybe she thought he'd dump her, find someone else. Maybe her whole future was at risk? She had to stop Justin crying.'

'No! It wasn't like that. He was okay when she left.'

Angie stared. 'How do you know? Do you remember?'

Paul's eyes swept the room. 'He started crying later. He was alive when mum left.'

'I guess your gran sorted it.'

He shrugged.

'Although, according to this,' she nodded at the file in his hand, 'she wasn't there at the time.'

Paul picked up a sheet of bubble wrap from a box on the floor and began popping it. 'You said there was some new stuff.'

Angie pulled a sheet from the yellow folder headed: *Sonya Wells Suspected Infanticide.* Paul flinched. 'It's a police report sent to Social Services a few weeks after Sonya's arrest. There's a summary of the case against her, including other lines of enquiry and recommendations for action.'

Paul snatched the sheet, devouring every word, his intense concentration punctuated by expletives. 'This is crap! How can they say she was the only one with the opportunity?'

'You might be right. Look at this.' Angie handed him a typewritten sheet from another section.

'You wrote this?'

'It's from my early case notes.'

He read. '*Paul stayed in the room for ten minutes this week. No less aggressive but he's finally communicating - after a fashion.*' He looked up. 'What does that mean?'

'You were angry, unhappy, worried sick that your mum had abandoned you - but couldn't put any of it into words. I had to find another way. We used Lego mostly. Do you remember?'

'No... *It's difficult to sort reality from fantasy with Paul. First of all his mum had gone for burgers, then to their new house, then to sort out their holiday. Finally got him to act out his fear that his mum had abandoned him. Long time since I've seen a child so consumed by despair. Very, very vulnerable.* Bollocks! I held my own with those tossers at Ellison road.'

'When we're threatened we fight. Doesn't mean the pain is any less.'

He read on. '*The policewoman wasn't able to take a reliable statement but the fragments that have emerged from my sessions seem to confirm their version of events. The caravan door was locked by the mother when she finally left. The grandmother took some time to get there so they were on their own for a bit, at a rough estimate about forty minutes given East Enders had finished. One thing may warrant further investigation. Paul told his story through creating a Lego caravan and moving characters around. He consistently placed a man outside.* Stuart Saunders! I knew it! What did they do?'

'The police? Nothing. You were as unreliable a witness as it gets. You never actually said anything about a man.'

'But it's here in black and white.'

'My supposition. No more than that.'

He stepped closer to her. 'And you let it go? What's the use of your so-called "professional expertise" if you don't use it. You could see what I was saying. Why didn't you make them follow it up?'

'It was the word of a nine year of child! I didn't know then that there was a witness.'

'A witness?!'

Angie hesitated. 'It's confidential material. I can't show you, but they interviewed someone on the site.'

'You don't work there any more do you? Do you? So what can they do to you?' He grabbed the file. 'Where?'

The line was so far behind her now the only way was forward. 'His name was Martin Hawkins. He was waiting for a lift to take him to the night shift at AMP. He'd been smoking at the door of his caravan for a couple of minutes when a van appeared.'

'Whose van?

'Stuart Saunders.'

'Paul,' a colleague was standing at the door. 'I need a word.'

'Not now.'

'It's about the contract…'

'I said not…' Paul paused. He looked at Angie. 'Back in a minute.' He followed his colleague out of the room, the confidential file clutched in his hand.

Chapter Twenty-Nine

'So you've heard, about your parole?' Paul asked.

Sonya was wedged sideways on her chair as far from Paul as she could get. It was Ali who'd persuaded her to give him another pass. "Think about it," Ali had said. "The Board have made it clear you won't be going within a hare's breath of Ian until he's eighteen. You okay with that?" But to sacrifice one for the other? There had to be another way.

He tried again. 'What did they say?'

'I get out in three months.'

'On licence or what? Do they keep tabs on you, make sure you don't…?'

'What?'

'Nothing.' Paul leant across the table. 'You know you're innocent. That's why we have to appeal.' He waited for her to protest, had come prepared this time. Nothing. 'I've got this lawyer. He says we have a case. And the social worker, Angie Turner, she's working with me.'

'Why've you got a social worker?'

'She was there, back when… when I was on my own. She's going to help. And there's a witness who can testify Stuart was outside the caravan. Right time, right place.'

Sonya pushed the heels of her hands into her eyes. Part of her ached to be free, completely free, without the past stalking her. To be with Ian again. To at least see one of her children grow up. But… She shook her head. 'Not Stuart. If we appeal it can't be to blame him.'

Paul heard the 'if'. 'I know what he did. He made you think

you were guilty to protect himself. Can't you see that? He's let you rot in here while he's been looking after number one.'

'No! Stuart's a good man. He's been taking care of Ian.'

'Ian?'

Sonya sighed. 'Your step-brother.'

Paul replayed his visit to Stuart's flat. The skateboard in the hall, the photographs. 'How old?'

'Fourteen. Loves his rugby. Just got into the first team.'

'He comes here?'

'No. I haven't seen him since…' she shut her eyes. 'Stuart's been looking after him until we can be together again.'

'That man's a dipso, he's not fit to look after my dog.' It was a brutal retort. His mother, the mother who'd abandoned him, was desperate to be with this Ian. Not him, another child.

'No, no, he doesn't drink.'

'Bollocks. I saw him. Drunk as a skunk when he got off the bus, falling all over the place. I even had to put his key in the lock he was fumbling so much. He's not fit to be a parent.'

Sonya shook her head. 'No, he couldn't have been.'

'Still want to protect him? Do you?' He leant closer. 'We can do this. Here.' Paul pulled a form from his pocket. 'All I need is your signature, there,' he pointed to the second page 'and we're in business. I've got money, the best barrister…'

Sonya gazed at the piece of paper. She'd trusted Stuart, believed everything he'd said. But… but he could have said anything. In all these years, how well did she really know him? One visit a month, a few hours a year. It was nothing. And Paul was right. He had been there. When she'd got back from chasing her mother, he'd been there, outside the caravan, waiting. Could she be wrong? She looked across the table at Paul. Saw her beautiful boy. Her beautiful trusting Paul, who adored her, would do anything for her. Anything. She shivered.

Paul put the pen in her hand. 'You have to do this.'

Amy hurried over to Paul waiting outside the station. He was moving away before she had her seat belt fixed. 'He's there,' he said. 'I saw him put the rubbish out a couple of hours back.'

'Mum's in remission, just in case you were wondering. She's back home. Dad said she even managed to get to the beach.'

Paul stared at the road. 'Sorry, that's good.'

'How long have you been here?' she said. From his crumpled suit and stubble Amy guessed he'd been watching all night. 'This is wrong, Paul. It's harassment.'

'You think he should get away with it do you?' Ten minutes later he pulled into the desolate car park and led the way up the stairs. By the time Amy caught up he was outside the door on the third floor landing, his finger jammed against the bell. The net curtain moved a fraction then fell back.

'It's not convenient.' Amy caught a man's voice.

'I bet it's not,' Paul shouted back. 'Maybe you'd prefer to talk to the police.'

'Wait there.' They heard voices inside, some movement. The catch released and the door inched open. 'Move along the landing.'

'You're in no position to give orders.'

'Just do it! There's a child here.'

Paul hesitated. Amy caught his sleeve. He wrenched himself free but followed.

Ian ran out, football boots slung over his shoulder. 'Can I stay for tea?' he called back. The response was muffled. 'Great. Bye, dad.'

Paul's gasp made Amy turn. The resemblance was uncanny. The child standing there could have been the brother she'd spent her whole life defending, with one difference. This boy was smiling.

'Hi,' Ian said. 'You lost?'

'It's okay, thanks,' Amy said, 'just waiting for someone.'

Ian beamed and ran on.

'Wait,' Paul called.

Amy held her breath. This wasn't the time or place. Surely even Paul could see that.

'Your lace,' Paul said, 'it's loose. Don't want to go breaking anything before the game.'

Ian dropped on one knee, fixed the lace and ran on, taking the stairs two at a time. Paul looked over the concrete balustrade, following him as he crossed to the bus stop.

'Did you know?' Amy said.

'Not until this week.' There was a rawness to his voice, as though a piece of armour had worked its way lose exposing his flesh. 'Something else the bastards chose not to tell me.' He walked back to the flat.

'Maybe this will help.' Paul pulled the police report from his pocket. It made an intimidating tableau. Paul leaning over the slight middle-aged man brandishing the document like a Bill of Rights declaring that justice must and would be done.

'What do you want of me?' Stuart Saunders whispered.

'Want?! What do you think I want? More of the bullshit you've been feeding me?' He grabbed the man's collar. 'People like you make me sick,' he hissed.

'Paul, stop!' Amy pulled at his arm.

'You were there! You know you were. And it would be a big mistake to treat me like some wet behind the ears pathetic kid who has to take whatever bullshit you decide to dish out. Maybe that's how it used to be, but not now. You lied. You lied then and you're lying now, you bastard. Must have been very inconvenient for you. This guy standing there waiting for his lift. Looking out for cars. Looking closely in case it was his mate. So closely that he identified you within seconds. You were there!'

Stuart sighed. 'Yes, I was there. We'd arranged that I'd wait just outside the site but it was raining so I drove up to the caravan. I saw Sonya, running across the site towards her mother's. So I waited.'

'Outside, in your van?'

'I didn't go into the caravan if that's what you're getting at.'

Paul raised an arm. 'You lying bastard…'

Amy pushed between them. 'Paul,' she pleaded. 'Whatever the truth, this isn't the way. Leave it to the police. Please, Paul.'

'This isn't the end. Believe me.' Paul hissed at Stuart, his face too close.

'Sadly I do,' Stuart replied.

They sat in silence in the car, ignoring Spider's yelps of delight and attempted licks. The rhythmic sound of Paul flicking the key fob back and forwards against his palm began to grate.

'Please, stop.' Amy put her hand on his. He pulled away.

'She could be free, Amy. It could be like it was.'

'It'll never be like it was. Maybe there's a chance for a fresh start, appeal or no appeal, but you can't go back, we're not children anymore.'

'You were too young. You never knew what it was like to be with her. She... she...' His voice broke.

Amy was astonished. Paul...on the verge of tears? 'What?'

'Nothing.'

'Tell me, I want to know.'

He looked out the window. 'Sometimes, when it was just her and me, she'd let me brush her hair. She had such beautiful hair, before those bastards mutilated it.'

'Forget them. Tell me about you and her.'

He bit his lip. 'Like you say, that time's gone isn't it. Stolen.'

Amy sighed. 'I'd do anything for you but I can't...' Her phone rang. 'Yes... when... I'm coming.' She turned to Paul. 'It's mum, we've got to get to the hospital.'

'I'm due in work. I can put you on the train.'

'Tell them it's a family emergency. Do it. Now.'

Paul hesitated. Martin Hawkins lived in Westward Ho! He lifted his phone. 'Paul here. I need a couple of days... I know it's sudden but you don't get notice of an emergency do you... family business... yes... yes,' he looked at Amy, 'close family, my... step-mother. It's terminal.'

Paul pulled up outside the main hospital entrance.

Amy stared in disbelief. 'Aren't you coming in?'

'She won't want to see me. Not if things are as bad...' his voice tailed off.

'You'll regret it, Paul. You need to take this chance to... to say sorry.'

'Sorry! Why the hell should I say...'

'That's enough!' Amy cut him off. 'It's time for this to end. All this anger, bitterness, all the times you've thrown their love back in their face, have they ever blamed you? Can you think of a single time they haven't been there for you?'

'Whatever that means.'

'I'll tell you what it means. It means day after day, week after week sacrificing their happiness for yours - even though all they got in return was a bucket load of shit.'

'So I should be grateful for something I never wanted?'

'Stop it, stop it!' She hit his chest with her hands, sobbing. 'Listen to yourself. Every word reeking of this grudge or that. Grow up, Paul. You've got to let it go, you've got to, before you push us all away. Kate and Steve could have given up on you any time, but no matter what you did, however cruel you were, they didn't. They did more for you than Sonya ever did. She's the one you should be angry with, she went.'

'She didn't have a choice, I know she didn't.'

'You have to listen to me, Paul.' She placed her hands one on either cheek and turned his face towards her. 'Remember how I used to do this, when I was little and pestering you to do something with me. How you'd make this big fuss about not caring but in the end you'd always come round. Do you remember, Paul?'

There was a trace of a smile on his face. 'No option if I wanted some peace.'

'Those few seconds when you held my hand were so precious. I knew then that, despite everything I saw, deep down you loved me as much as I love you.'

'That was kid's stuff, Amy. You need to get real.'

'You're wrong. That was real. This you, the one that's always pushing people away, using them, this isn't my Paul. My Paul knew how to care, knew how to love. My Paul hadn't built this wall around him thinking it would keep him safe, when all it's doing is destroying him from the inside.'

His knuckle's grew white as he gripped the steering wheel. 'Even if you're right…'

'I am, you know I am.'

He shook his head 'It's too late. Too much has happened.'

Amy dropped her hands. 'If you carry on like this you'll end up a sad, lonely old man. Open your eyes, Paul. Let us in. It really is your choice.' She turned away. Time spent here was time lost inside the hospital. Her choice was clear.

The wind was getting up as Paul drove west towards Bideford. It greeted him head on as he dropped into Westward Ho! It was a long time since he'd seen, and heard, the rollers breaking along the beach. The memories were instant. Diving into the waves, making dugouts in the pebble ridge, trying to surf on the board his mates had rescued from the tip. All kinds of treasures piled up behind their caravan until his mother cleared them out, deaf to his protests. Just like she'd never let his gang come back. Master of the excuse he'd become, until they dropped him. Not pulling his weight they'd said.

No, that's not how it was. His mum made a special shelter for his treasures and all his mates came back for one of her amazing teas…

'No.' He pulled the car into a lay by. His mum loved him, that was definite. But sometimes… some of the things she did… He stared into the past.

Kipling Terrace towered over Westward Ho! A Victorian edifice divided into seven floors of flats. Paul pulled into the drive, checked the number and found the stairway. It had to be at the top. He paused to catch his breath and pressed the bell.

'Yes?' A man appeared in his pyjamas.

'Martin Hawkins?'

'Who wants to know?'

'Paul Wells. You don't know me but you were once

261

interviewed by the police about the family in the next caravan to you, along Beach Road.'

'Christ, it's years since I was there.' He started to close the door.

Paul wedged it with his foot. 'I lived in that caravan.'

'So?'

'Can I come in?'

'It's not convenient. I'm on nights. I was just getting up.'

'It's important. It won't take long.'

He looked Paul up and down then stood back and let him into the narrow hallway. 'Through there,' he pointed to a door immediately ahead. It led into an irregular sitting room, the light from the single bay window barely reaching all the walls. 'What do you want?'

'The police questioned you about an incident at our caravan. You gave them a statement.'

'If you say so.'

'You can't remember?'

'What do you think? You turn up out of the blue asking me about something I did or didn't do sixteen years ago. I can't remember what I did last week!'

'But it's not every day a baby gets murdered. They put my mother in prison for it. What happens now depends on what you can or can't remember.'

'Shit. Don't lay that at my door. You need to go.'

Paul lowered his voice. 'I can make it worth your while.'

'Meaning?'

'Call it a reward, for your lost memory. All I need is for you to confirm the statement you gave the police. That's all.'

'If it's so important why didn't I hear no more about it?'

'Very good question. Lazy coppers not doing their job. Never mind an innocent woman gets to spend the best years of her life behind bars.'

'You've got my statement?'

'Yes.'

'I won't ask how. What's in it?'

'Be good if you could have a stab at remembering.'

Hawkins walked to the window and lit a cigarette. 'It was something about the kids being left. You I guess, and the baby, Christ that baby could cry. Felt like doing it in myself. Nancy would bang on the door, telling her to shut it up. Useless though. That woman didn't care. Not about you neither. You were always round scavenging for food.'

'You're wrong,' he snapped. 'We did all right.'

'Do you want me to have a stab at this or not?' Paul nodded. 'I remember the police coming. Went round all the caravans. Nancy set them onto me, told them I might have seen something while I was waiting for my lift.' He paused. 'That was it. I was outside having a fag waiting for Terry. We was always on the same shift at AMP so we went in together.'

'What did you see?'

Hawkins stretched out on the leather sofa, the corner type that came in small sections, only way they could get it up here, Paul thought.

'They were asking when your mother came and went.' He looked at Paul. 'So the dead baby...'

'Was my brother.'

'Got her for it then? Can't say I'm surprised. Must have been plenty to say she'd given you all a good belting.'

Paul fought for control. 'Like I said, she's innocent. What did you see?'

'Give me a minute.' He lapsed into silence.

'So...?'

'Your mother left the caravan, I remember that. It's all the coppers went on about. When did she go? Was she alone? When did she come back? Like I had a stop watch on her! They'd have had me for stalking if I'd had the answers.'

'Then what?'

'Nothing. Not the first time. But they must have come back. Yes, after it was all done and dusted. Nancy went on at me. 'Had I told them about the plumber? Well, no, I hadn't.'

'Why not?'

'They didn't ask. Like I said, all they wanted to know about was your mother. A local bobby came. Said he'd report it but it was probably too late so not to worry.'

'How did you know he was a plumber?'

'Plastered all over his van. And his name. Couldn't tell you what it was now.'

'Stuart Saunders.'

'If you say so.'

'That's what you said at the time.'

'Well that'll be right then.' He looked at the clock. 'I've got to go.'

Paul moved towards the door. 'I'll be in touch. Come back with my lawyer, just to make it official.'

'Not too official. The reward?'

'Yours. Just want to take it all down. That you saw him by the caravan, that sort of thing.'

'Oh no, he never got out of his van.'

Paul froze. 'What!'

'She went back in, your mother, but not him. She was out in a jiffy and they went off.'

Paul opened the file. 'It doesn't say that. You've forgotten.'

'No I'm definite on that 'cause he gave me the creeps, sitting there looking at me.'

'No,' Paul walked back towards him. 'You've got it wrong. He went into the caravan.'

'What's with you?' Martin Hawkins stood. 'You turn up demanding answers then tell me I'm wrong. Get out of here.'

'No', Paul hissed, 'not until you've told me the truth.'

'You want the truth?' Hawkins backed Paul against the wall. 'Well, I'll tell you. That mother of yours didn't give a toss about you. Always leaving you on your own while she went out. And she had a temper on her. You never stood a chance. Now get out of my flat before I show you the emergency exit.' He glanced over his shoulder at the bay window.

Paul watched a curtain of rain sweep across the bay, blotting out his view of Lundy. He lit another cigarette. So close. But Martin Hawkins was useless. Couldn't remember a thing. All that stuff about his mother... His hands shook. He threw on his coat, locked the car and walked through the streets to Beach Road. The caravan park was still there. He wound his way through the pitches until, at the very back, he reached the green and beige row. He walked to the last caravan, their caravan, his polished brogues out of place on the muddy track that led to the door. He ran his hand across the green slime that covered it each winter. Tucker would come along before the summer and hose it off. They had great fun, running under the spray, playing chicken, daring each other to stand in the jet.

He peered through the large window. It was just as he remembered. The orange covered bench seats, chipped table, sliding cupboards so old they were coming back into fashion. And down the side, the small window to his bedroom. The three of them all crammed in. Night after night of Justin's coughing. Days shut in there because of some misdemeanour or other. 'No, that's not how it was.' His memory was playing tricks again. He walked round the end and looked into his mother's bedroom, the place where he sat close to her and brushed her hair while she talked and... and... There had to be other memories. Other times they'd spent together.

One memory was clear. Angie sitting in her car out the front, waiting to catch him, to take him away. He'd gone round the back, with Spider, that was right, and prised the window open. He'd been so sure his mother would be there, waiting for him.' Only she wasn't. She'd never be there again.

Kate and Steve could have given up on you, but no matter what you did, how cruel you were, they didn't. Sonya was the one who went. Amy's words filled his ears. He slumped against the caravan. 'Why?' The cry came from somewhere deep within him. 'Why did you leave me?'

Chapter Thirty

'Hi.' Sonya smiled at Stuart. She searched his face, trying to meet his eyes. 'You could look a bit happier to see me.'

'Sorry, of course I'm happy to see you. How are you?' His nervous smile wasn't reassuring.

'How do you think? You got the letter? About my parole?'

'Yes.'

'What are you going to do?'

'What can I do? It's horrible. I can't begin to… But what can we do?' He wiped his palms on his trousers.

'There's got to be something. They can't stop me coming home. I got to come home. You want that, don't you?'

'Of course I do but it's in the letter. You can't live with a minor. If you come home they'll take Ian into care. You can't… we can't do that to him.' His hands were trembling.

She leant back. 'So all we got left is Paul's appeal,' she said. 'Only problem is, he thinks it was you.'

Stuart nodded. 'I know.'

Sonya scratched at the table. 'Was it?'

'What!'

She looked up. 'Was it you? You were there, outside the caravan, before we went. You could have done it.'

Stuart's mouth fell open. 'You know I didn't!'

'Do I? How do I know?'

'All these years… you've never once said… I can't believe you're doing this. Look at me.' He grabbed her hands. 'Look at me, Sonya. I've stood by you haven't I? It's always been you and me.'

'And Ian.'

'How dare you remind me!' He'd found his voice 'I'm the one who's been there for him day after day. Gave up my job, everything, for him. He comes first, you know that.'

She pulled away. 'Being so pissed you couldn't get your key in the door, that's putting him first is it?'

Stuart frowned. 'What are you talking about?'

'The first time Paul came you fell off the bus, couldn't walk straight and were so drunk he had to let you in.'

'I wasn't...'

'Did he or didn't he?' She interrupted.

'Yes, but...'

'So maybe I should let him appeal, let him put you away. Maybe Ian would be better off with me.'

Stuart half rose. 'Stop it, Sonya, just stop. You've got it all wrong. It was my contact lens. I tripped getting off the bus and lost it so I walked up and down searching for it. But it wasn't any good. I couldn't get my key in the door because I couldn't see, not because I was drunk. I wouldn't do that.' Sonya closed her eyes. 'Please, Sonya, don't let him do this to us. I love you.' He wiped his cheek. 'Please, tell me we're okay.'

Sonya's face crumpled. 'He made it sound... I mean... what do I know... stuck in here.'

He reached a hand towards her. 'It's okay. We'll find a way. Trust me.'

Angie sank onto the sofa. What a day! The sun had brought the biggest crowd yet over on the Oldenburg. Be better if they'd stagger their buying through the day, but at least they were buying. She picked up the remote and flicked through the channels. A quick catch-up on the news then the next episode of Morse, perfect. The headlines were just finishing. '*Professor Marcus Wilson has been found guilty of professional misconduct after the verdicts in three cases of child infant death were found to be unsafe. Our reporter, Andrew Crane, reports from...*'

'Call for you, Angie,' Mike interrupted.

'Who is it?'

'Paul Wells.'

'Tell him I'm out.'

'Already done that, twice.'

She hauled herself off the sofa. 'Hello?'

'You were going to call.'

'I've been busy. There's so much to do with the season getting going. New stock to…'

'You said you'd help.'

'I know what I said. But this has gone far enough, Paul. I've already stepped over the line. I can't do any more.'

'So you were bullshitting me were you?'

'You know I wasn't. Only you've never been too keen on my definition of help.'

He paused. 'I want to talk. Please.'

It was still there, the internal radar picking up the signals and triggering all her professional instincts. Paul had just laid himself bare in his terms. 'I'm not sure I can help. I've told you how things were. You see things differently. From what I gather, your mum doesn't want to you pursue this and neither does Amy. I think you should try seeing things their way.'

His tone changed instantly. 'And I'm sure the authorities will see it my way when I show them the confidential police report you gave me.'

'I didn't give it…' Angie hesitated. 'What do you want?'

'Martin Hawkins says Saunders didn't get out of his van that night. Could he have got it wrong?'

'Hawkins… how… have you seen him?'

'I need to know if there are more reports because it's not in the one you gave me.'

'I'll support you anyway I can, Paul, but not with blackmail. I want that report back. Then I'll see what I can do.'

'Do you know how many people have said that to me? "I'll see what I can do". Staff at the care home, social workers, Kate. Steve was the only one who didn't bullshit me. Do you know that?'

'So why did you turn your back on him?' Silence. 'Paul?'

'I don't know. Satisfied!'

'Do you remember the times they took you to Plymouth, to look for Sonya? All on your say so. Week after week.'

Silence.

'Kate often took you on her own. All your relentless rejection of her yet she still gave up her weekends to take you to look for the one person you were pushing her aside for. The woman convicted of killing your brother. How easy would it have been for her to tell you, to shatter your image of your mother so you'd be free to love her?'

'But it wasn't my mum…'

'Whatever the truth, she had the power to shatter your illusions, a chance to take Sonya's place. But she didn't. And do you know why? Because despite everything she put you first. That's love, Paul, real love. You're an adult now. Open your eyes.'

'That's quite a speech.'

Silence.

'So what do you expect me to say?' He muttered.

Silence.

'So I'm the one that's screwed up am I, got it all wrong?'

'It's not about right or wrong, Paul. It's about seeing things differently. It's time to stop pushing people away because you're frightened they'll leave, like your mum did. You need to listen to those who care about you, and you know it. Why did Gemma leave?'

'It didn't work out.'

'Because?'

He thought. 'She always wanted more. Why do women do it? I gave her the house, money, we did things, but no it wasn't enough. Apparently I had to be more loving.'

Pau had done so well professionally, Angie had to remind herself he was still young, with all the emotional immaturity most twenty-five year olds displayed, even without the extra baggage. 'Loving is tough when you've taken so many knocks. Makes you push people away who are brave enough to try.'

'It was never going to work with Gemma.'

'Maybe not, but there's still time for Amy, Steve... Kate. Though maybe not so much time.'

'Not you as well. I've had an earful from Amy.'

'Who knows you better than anyone. If she's found the courage to say something then it's important. Don't throw it back in her face. Listen to her. It's no fun trying to tell you something you need to hear - believe me, I know.' For a moment all Angie could hear was the hum of background traffic and the sound of his breathing.

'So I'm a complete bastard am I?'

'Stubborn, bloody minded, blinkered - all of the above. But a bastard? No. You were the most engaging, gutsy, deep-down likeable child I ever worked with. And, despite the facade, I believe you still are. Somewhere in the pit of your stomach there'll be a feeling that recognizes what I'm saying, knows the real you is there, desperate to come up for air...'

'Amy said that,' Paul interrupted. 'The bit about the real me.' His voice was calmer, missing its usual edge.

'She only wants what's right for you. Listen to her, Paul... Please.' She paused. 'This is tough on the phone. I'm in London next week. I've got a forty minute wait between trains at Exeter on my way back. We could meet if you want to talk.'

'What can talking do?'

'Why don't we find out? I'll be in the café at St David's at about seven next Friday evening. It's your call.'

'Angie, please, don't go.' Mike stood in the doorway. 'Since Paul's turned up you've been all on edge. You're not sleeping and you've hardly had a civil word for me.'

'Sonya sent the pass. I can't ignore it.' It had arrived out of the blue a week ago. The last thing she expected. Her first impulse was to throw it away, things were complicated enough with Paul. But curiosity had won.

'You're very good at ignoring people when you want to.'

Surely there was something she could say? But he was right, about ignoring him. She was spending more and more time in the studio - the one place where she could lose herself in a world she chose to see through the lens of her camera.

'What's happened, Angie, to us?' Mike was studying her.

She hesitated. 'Nothing... it's nothing. Like you say, I've been a bit on edge about Paul.'

'I thought you'd left all that behind but here we are, back where we started.'

'That's not how it is. I just have to see this through. Paul's getting there. A bit more time with him and I can make a difference, I know I can.'

'He's a man now. Well able to take care of himself from what I've seen. And not too worried who he tramples in the process. Don't let him suck you in.'

'It's a bit more complicated. The man you see, it's not him, not the real Paul. But he's there, I know he is. I can reach him.'

'Listen to yourself!' Mike grabbed her arms. 'You stopped being a social worker years ago. He's not your concern.'

'You want me to walk away? I admit I was tempted when he started getting a bit... manipulative. But it's just a knee jerk reaction. He thinks it's the only way to keep people close. So if I walk away it confirms that doesn't it? But not if I stay. The chinks were there in that last call. I can help him take down the barricades, let people in.'

Mike sighed and released her. 'All very noble, but why does it have to be you?'

'I abandoned him as a child. I'm not going to do it again.'

Mike stood beside her, staring at the sea; white horses were beginning to show as the wind picked up. 'I've seen more passion from you in these last few moments for someone you barely know than you've shown for me in ages.'

His hand was so close to hers. It should be so easy to reach out and take it. So why couldn't she? Why did she turn from him in bed, get up before he woke? Why couldn't she give him the reassurance he wanted? He was a good man. He deserved to be loved. 'Mike, I...' The words wouldn't come. 'I'm staying at the B&B next Friday. The train gets back too late for the boat.'

271

'That's it?' He sighed. 'You're very like Paul you know. Only your barricades are never going to come down, are they.' He grabbed his coat and slammed the door.

Angie watched him go. He was right. She'd retreated further and further into herself. There was affection, gratitude for the way he was there for her, a sense of belonging even. But none of those filled the aching void inside.

A week later Angie waited on the island's quay to board the Oldenburg. Thankfully the white horses had gone and it was a calm voyage. By early evening she was waiting for her connection at Exeter. It was a gamble, throwing Paul the challenge to meet. But he thrived on conflict. He'd come tomorrow. Not at seven, that would smack too much of compliance. But soon after.

The Paddington train was on time. She settled herself into her reserved seat and tried to doze. But the questions wouldn't go away. What would she find at Holloway? More to the point, who would she find? She'd only seen Sonya through Paul's eyes or the police reports. And why did Sonya want to see her? What possible reason could she have?

A large envelope arrived just before she left. It was the trial transcript with a note from Paul simply saying, 'you have to read this'. She'd resisted, until now. Stations came and went but Angie was oblivious, immersed in a document that raised more questions than it answered. Sonya had stuck to her not-guilty plea throughout the trial but there were times when she wouldn't speak in her own defence. It didn't make sense. Was she protecting someone? Stuart? Did she think he was guilty? She put the transcript back in the envelope. No point dwelling on it. There were no answers there.

After the solitude and peace of Lundy it usually took Angie time to adjust to London. But this time she was a willing hostage to the buzz that swept her up the minute she stepped onto the platform at Paddington. It was a while since she'd felt so... so what? Excited? Alive?

She slept surprisingly well in the budget hotel close to Russell Square. The bottomless coffee pot at breakfast was welcome and the cosy reception perfect for browsing the morning papers. But she couldn't concentrate. She checked her watch. Four hours to visiting time. Suddenly she craved the noise of the London streets. She set off on foot, meandering past the familiar shops and terraces of Mornington Crescent into Camden High Street, until she found herself barely a few yards from their student pad, hers and Christine's. It was only one room up an endless flight of stairs with a cupboard for the kitchen and a bathroom shared with... how many others? But it couldn't have been more perfect. The beds were built into the eaves leaving space in the middle for life to unfold. Endless pasta meals on beanbags shared with friends, music played at antisocial decibels and a bit of studying squeezed in round the edges. It was a carefree time, her years with Christine.

At Camden Lock market she found herself surrounded by studded and zipped black leather, ethnic kaftans, pink Mohicans, tattoos, piercings... every variation of human expression. It was a different world. No - more like all the world crammed into one space. She couldn't remember the last time she'd seen dreadlocks, a black face or a spike of purple hair in Devon. She'd almost forgotten what multicultural meant. It gave the city such energy. They'd thrived on it, her and Christine. Any excuse and they'd be here. Late brunches grazing the street food stalls trying one unrecognisable delicacy after another. Evenings moving from one bar to the next, the live music pounding their bodies into a daze, melding the crowd into one pulsating beat. So what if Mike thought Christine self-centred. Time spent with her was always fun.

Angie took out her phone and scrolled through the contacts. It had been so long. Several times she'd almost deleted Christine's number but something had stopped her. It was there, but was she? There was only one way to find out. Her finger hovered over the call button. Then pressed.

Chapter Thirty-One

Allow thirty minutes for routine checks prior to visiting, the pass had instructed. Angie checked her watch. She had time to walk part of the way along the canal. Cutting it a bit fine but she might be grateful for an excuse to shorten her visit.

Holloway had always existed in the periphery of her mind but nothing prepared her for the reality. The imposing walls, cameras, warders; guilt washed over her just being here. Angie presented her passport, stood as directed for the rub down, put her personal belongings in the locker and waited quietly as the dog made its way along the diminishing queue. It stopped at the woman behind her. A warder pulled her out of the line.

Angie had never knowingly met a child killer, though she'd had dealings with the perverts who sexually abused children and come close to attacking them with her bare hands. The feeling in the pit of her stomach now wasn't so different.

'So you're Angie.' Sonya stared at her across the table.

Angie steeled herself to return the stare. 'I was surprised to get your pass. How did you know about me?'

'Paul. He said you've done things for him.'

'Years ago. I was his social worker when he was in care. I knew him well then. Not now though.'

'That's not what I hear.'

Angie stared at her. What had she expected? Whatever it was, the slight woman sitting opposite didn't fit the image. 'He came to see me, wanted to know what happened when you... left. Not much I could tell him though. I mean none of us knew did we?'

Sonya took a sheet of paper out of her pocket and pushed it across the table. 'You know the system,' she pointed at the letter. 'Is that right? Can they do that?'

Angie scanned the parole sheet. Sonya's finger rested at a paragraph headed *Conditions of Licence*. It specified address, reporting conditions and...' Angie looked up. 'This says release is conditional on you having no contact with a minor, specifically Ian Saunders. Who's that?'

Sonya drew deeply on her cigarette. 'My son.'

A son, with Stuart presumably. Of course they weren't going to allow her any contact with a child. She pushed the sheet back. 'They can impose any conditions they like. Ask your parole officer.'

'Paul says you're helping him.'

The sudden change of tack was obviously a family trait. 'I'm doing what I can. It's my patch, emotional stuff, coping with everything that comes with...'

'Comes with what? Being abandoned by his mother? Stuck in care? Is that it? Shit happens. He's done all right.'

'Financially, no doubt about it.'

'Got himself a big house, a woman...'

'That didn't work. She left.'

'Plenty more.'

'There's only one woman he's ever loved,' Angie said. Sonya lit another cigarette, her eyes darting around the room. 'And she knocked him back.'

'You don't know shit,' she clicked her fingers, 'about it.'

'I know he took the knocks every step of the way. Mother walks out on him when he's a kid. He spends years fighting to survive, rejecting the people who care. Why? Because he's spending every waking moment searching for his mother. Years later, he finds her, in prison, a child killer. The knocks don't come any tougher. But fight is the one thing he can do, the only thing maybe. He knows beyond a shadow of a doubt that the amazing, irreplaceable woman who is his mother could never have done it. He tells you he's in your corner, that he has the money to fight for you, to prove your innocence. I wish I had someone with that kind of belief in me. And what do you do? Stop his passes. Reject the man as you did the boy. That's what I know. So tell me, have I got that wrong?' Conversations from nearby tables filled the silence. 'Have I?' Sonya showed no sign of answering. 'I'm wasting my time.' Angie stood.

'We're not done.'

'You might not be.'

'Please.'

Angie hesitated. 'Why did you send the pass?'

'I don't want no appeal. He's hired a barrister, says he's got evidence it could have been Stuart. I can't have another hearing, people turning things over, finding out. He'll listen to you. You got to tell him to back off.'

Was Paul right? Was she protecting Stuart? Angie sat. 'Why should I?'

'Because you care about him.' Sonya looked Angie full in the eyes. The effect was mesmerising. 'He's been through enough. Agreed?'

'Agreed.'

'Then you have to stop him doing something that'll destroy everything... everything.'

'Who for? You? Stuart?'

'For Paul.'

Angie stared at Sonya. There was an intensity in her voice that smacked of sincerity, but deceit had become a way of life in here. After everything she'd done, refusing to see him, returning his letters, why the sudden concern? 'What can he possibly lose by finding out his mother is innocent? Unless you're not? Is that it? An appeal might reinforce the verdict. Crush his belief that you didn't do it?'

'No.'

'I'm not here to play games. Are you telling me you didn't do it?'

'I'm not telling you anything. I just want you to stop Paul.'

'I've already tried. He's not great at listening.'

Sonya grabbed her arm. 'Try again.' With each word her nails bit deeper into Angie's flesh.

Angie pulled away. 'Paul thinks you're protecting Stuart. Is he right? Only I'm stuck with different stories on all sides. Why should I believe a convicted murderer?'

Sonya banged the table. 'Stuff this. Just because you're on that side and I'm on this don't make you no better than me!'

'You listen to me,' Angie hissed. 'I came here for Paul. Thought that if I knew what happened and why I could help him. So, is he right? Are you protecting someone?' Angie watched as Sonya lit another cigarette. 'Let's suppose you're innocent but cared so much for someone else you put their happiness, their life above your own. That you, Sonya Wells, spent fourteen years in the harshest conditions imaginable to save someone else's skin. Who? Who would you do that for?'

Sonya picked at the table.

'There's only Stuart isn't there? Why would you do that? Out of love? For a man you must have thought killed your son?' Angie stared at Sonya. Her face gave nothing away. 'Things were tough with Justin. Did you... I mean it would be understandable if you'd gone along with it.'

'Shut up!' Sonya was on her feet. 'You're just like the rest.'

'Sit down and keep it down, Wells.' The warder pushed her back into the chair.

Angie instinctively drew back. What the hell was she doing here? This woman was never going to tell her the truth. And why did she want her to? Getting stuck with that kind of confidence was the last thing she needed. Just one more thing to say and she was out of there. 'Have it your way.' Angie realised she was trembling. 'But there's something I do know. If you don't want Paul to go ahead with this appeal because you think it was Stuart, you're wrong.'

'You think he didn't do it?'

'I know he didn't. There's a witness. Swears he never went into the caravan.'

Nothing. What did Angie expect? An outburst that would get her hauled off by the warders shouting and screaming? Surely at least a few bitter tears that she'd got it wrong, sacrificed her life for nothing? Not this resigned calm.

'I knew it. Only when Paul came, he got me confused. Maybe I even wanted to think…'

'Well, if we're done.' Angie half rose.

'No…' Sonya stubbed out her cigarette on the table. Her hand was shaking. 'I… I need your help. Paul needs your help.'

Angie sighed but sank back into her seat. 'We've been round this loop.'

This time Sonya's grip on her arm was altogether different. Still firm but somehow pleading. 'You're the only person I can tell this to, the only person who can help him.'

Angie realised she was holding her breath.

'You said about protecting someone,' Sonya whispered, 'someone I must love very much,' she drew her chair closer. 'You can't ever speak of this. He must never know. Swear it.'

'Not until I know what I'm swearing to.'

Sonya hesitated, biting at the quicks of her nails, her gaze darting around the room. 'I left the kids when I went to get mum. If I'd known I'd never have…' She turned away, pinched her eyes with her fingers.

Angie hunched over the table, suddenly desperate to block out the words, to resist the picture seeping into her mind.

'When I got back Paul was standing by Justin, smiling. "I've been a good boy, mum," he said. He'd done what I'd asked him to do, kept him quiet so the neighbours wouldn't kick off. I thought he'd just got Justin to sleep. You have to believe me.'

'Are you saying…?' Angie could barely speak.

'Justin,' she almost wailed, 'Justin was so still, so peaceful. That's when I knew. My beautiful Paul, my lovely boy, had… had killed him.'

It felt like an age before Angie could speak. 'Why me?'

'You understand him. You know what it would do to him to find out. Swear you'll never tell him. Swear it!'

'But he was minor, there won't be any action against him.'

'We both know that isn't the point.'

Angie stared at Sonya. 'He'll never hear it from me,' she said eventually.

'Do you see now, why there can't be no appeal? If it comes

out in court…'

'Yes.' Angie saw all too well. Paul's defences would be useless against the knowledge he'd killed his own brother. It would destroy him. 'And you've known this all along?'

'Not at first. Something in me couldn't accept…couldn't believe… not until the next morning. At least, I didn't let it. I think it was half way through the film really.'

'When you were so sick? Your body reacting.'

She nodded. 'But I went drinking with Stuart. What kind of a mother does that when her baby…?' She began to sob, her body shaking with grief.

'You were in shock. Probably were for days afterwards. Nothing you did would have made sense.' Strange how a few words can change everything. The mask had disintegrated revealing a woman who had paid the greatest price, all for one thing, the love of her son.

The lift down to the Piccadilly line at Caledonian Road felt unbearably claustrophobic. The platform at Euston even worse. Angie pushed her way to the end, breathing in the stale, dank air of the tunnel. It all made sense now. Unbearable, agonising sense. The neatly folded clothes, the careful darning. Sonya Wells had gone to prison for the one person she truly loved.

She arrived too soon at Paddington. Why had she called Christine? Now wasn't the time. But she needn't have worried. It was twenty minutes before she heard the familiar cry.

'Hi, Ange, move over, I need a chair for these.' Christine piled some bags onto the seat. 'Just get a latte. Back in a mo.'

Angie watched. There was quite a queue. The old Christine would have had the afternoon commuters begging her to take their place. But today she waited.

'How are you doing, darling. Looking a bit peaky if you don't mind me saying so.' Christine kissed both cheeks and slid into a vacant seat.

'I'm okay, thanks…'

'Should have met at Tottenham Court Road, I could have come on the Northern. The Circle's a nightmare.' She paused, suddenly still, as though the bustle of the station had faded and it was just the two of them sitting there. 'Good to see you, Ange. What brings you to town and why didn't I get more than four hours notice?'

'It was all a bit last minute, I didn't know if I'd have time. And it's so long since we've been in touch.'

'That's the great thing about old friends isn't it? Pick up like it was yesterday.' Christine reached for Angie's hand. 'So, what's happening? Still stuck in the middle of the channel?'

She was so easy to respond to. That familiar warmth, easy touch, open face. Showing the signs of too much Botox and an over-ambitious facelift but, to Angie's eyes at least, as charismatic as always. 'Still living on Lundy, yes.'

'And the gallery?'

'Doing amazingly well. Taking the photographs to Exeter and Plymouth was a stroke of genius.'

'My idea I seem to recall. What else have I insinuated into your mind? Belly dancing yet?'

'Oh, Chrissy, I have missed you. No-one else is quite so…'

'Sassy? Sexy? Surprising? Come on,' she squeezed her hand, 'I'm running out of adjectives.'

'All of those but I was thinking more of refreshing.'

'Makes me sound like an Alka Selzter.'

'You know what I mean. Lundy has been great but…'

'Hang on a minute. Is that the past tense I hear? Thinking about a move back to town?'

Angie stared at her. There was no one like Christine for dragging self deception, in others of course, into the open and giving it a thorough shaking. She couldn't have put it into words herself, but now Christine had said it. 'Perhaps I have had enough of being so isolated. The summer's fine, when the island's full of people. Never know who you'll get in the gallery. Only last week I had someone from Florence…' She stopped. 'But, we haven't got long. I want to hear your news. How's the programme going? When does the next series start?'

Christine made a show of blowing her coffee. 'Not going to be one. Not with me anyway. Their loss, darling. I'm thinking of going back to radio. Got a couple of irons in the fire. At least I can put the face lift on hold. Bit of sellotape will do fine for the publicity shots.'

'I'm sorry. There'll be something soon.'

'Of course.' She smiled at Angie. 'At least I was free today.'

'Sorry I couldn't come to your place instead of dragging you over here. Are you still by the river?'

'Moved a while back. Got a little place in Archway now. I'd invite you round but it's only one bedroom and the sofa bed is a beast. Came with the flat; I know why now.' She drained her cup. 'So, when are you coming back?'

'I don't know. Weekends are a bit tricky in the season.'

Christine shook her head gently. 'I mean permanently. You've done your penance, buried yourself for far too long. Time to open a gallery in London.'

'Oh, Chrissy. What with?! I'd never afford London prices.'

'Have I ever got it wrong with you?' Christine leant across and took her hand. 'Well, have I?'

'I suppose not.'

'No suppose about it. Have a think and stay... in... touch.' She emphasised each word with a squeeze of her hands. 'Anyway, got to be going.' Christine gathered her bags and kissed Angie on both cheeks. 'You didn't say what brought you to town. Not your mother?'

'No, things are just the same there. I'll go next time, conscience won't let me abandon her completely.' Angie paused. 'No, this was just a visit I had to make.'

Angie realised she hadn't thought of Sonya once in the last half hour. Being with Christine was like that. All or nothing. And somehow years of nothing fell away after just thirty minutes of being everything. She checked the departures board. Twenty minutes to wait. But now Christine had gone there was nothing to distract her from a commitment she hadn't the first idea how to fulfil, her promise to Sonya. In just two and a half hours she would face Paul.

Chapter Thirty-Two

Paul checked his phone was on silent. Five missed calls from work and endless texts. They could wait. He scanned the bed plan and identified the single room on the left just beyond the nurse's station. He paused outside the door. Through the glass he could see Steve and Amy flanking the bed.

'You can go in if you like.' A nurse was passing with a trolley. 'We don't enforce the two visitors rule in side rooms.'

'Thanks. How is she?'

'Are you family?'

He hesitated. 'Yes.'

'We're doing everything we can to keep her comfortable. But I'm afraid that's all we can do now.' The nurse smiled and walked on.

He'd been downstairs for an hour, half walked away so many times. Then something had made him come up, but to open the door and walk in… He'd got so used to seeing Steve as the strong fire fighter, ace sailor, bit of a hero really. Not the broken man sitting beside the motionless woman in the bed. The woman who was running out of time.

Inside, the room was silent apart from the regular 'beep' of the monitor. Steve Clarke sat close to the bed, holding his wife's hand. Amy wrapped her arms around his shoulders. 'Dad.' It was all she could say.

'Hope I didn't worry you with my call, only they were concerned… she lost consciousness. But she came back. We had a chat, well, just a few words really.'

They sat, hypnotised by the rise and fall of Kate's chest. 'Have you had anything to eat?' she asked.

Steve shook his head. 'I couldn't.'

'Me neither. I'll get us some sandwiches in a bit, then I'll stay if you want to get some rest. Were you up all night?'

'Mostly. I can't bear to…'

'I know. Time's precious,' Amy said.

'Amy?' Kate's voice was weak.

'Mum. I'm here.'

'Tell your dad he's to eat something. I bet he's been sitting there all night.'

Steve moved his chair so Kate could see him without straining. 'It's good to hear your voice.' He stroked her hair away from her forehead. 'Can I get you anything?'

'I'd love a drink.' Steve poured some squash from the bedside jug. 'I said a drink, as in a glass of Chardonnay. Been fantasising about that for hours.'

'Sorry, don't have it on tap. Maybe when we get you home.'

She grabbed his arm. 'Are they going to discharge me? Say they are, please. I so want to come home.'

'We'll have to see what the consultant says.'

'You know what he'll say. But it's all palliative. We could do the same couldn't we?'

'It's not so easy, mum,' Amy said. 'There are injections and drips.'

'The district nurses could do it.'

'We'll find a way, Kate. I promise you,' Steve said.

Her eyes closed.

'Is she sleeping?' Amy asked.

'That's how it goes. One minute she's here, the next…'

Amy sat next to him. 'Can we do it? Bring her home?'

'It's not that simple. She needs regular medical supervision and special equipment. They talked about a ripple bed to avoid bed sores but they're expensive. Money shouldn't matter but I've still got to find it from somewhere. I'm seeing the bank manager tomorrow. Which reminds me, can you…?'

Amy squeezed his arm. 'Of course I'll be here. Whenever you need me.'

'You mustn't miss anything important at Uni though. Your mum gets upset if she thinks you're taking too much time out.'

'Like she will if I don't feed you. I'll go and get those sandwiches.' Amy kissed his cheek. 'Won't be long.' She stepped into the corridor in time to catch sight of someone walking away. 'Paul?' she called, excusing her way through a group waiting anxiously by another door. 'Paul.' She hurried down the corridor and turned the corner as the lift doors swept shut.

Angie checked her watch. Twenty-five minutes before the Barnstaple train was due.

'Excuse me, anyone sitting here?'

Angie looked up. A woman was leaning awkwardly against the chair rubbing her foot.

'No, but I'm expecting someone any minute.'

'I'll move when they get here. A day in Exeter has killed my feet.' She eased her shoes off. 'Been shopping yourself?'

'No. Visiting London.'

'Never remember I'm on the train. Buying these was crazy,' she pointed at two large, flat parcels balanced against the table, 'but I couldn't resist.'

'What are they?'

'Prints of Lundy. Brilliant images.'

'May I see?' Angie asked.

The woman eased the frames out of their packaging. 'This one is…'

'The Lighthouse stairway,' Angie interrupted. 'Taken early morning when the sun catches the glass dome.'

'How do you know that?'

'It's one of mine. Well, my associates actually. I'm Angie Turner. I have the gallery on Lundy.'

'What a coincidence. I've got three more at home. The seals down by the quay, puffins of course and one of that building right up the island, with the sun setting behind it, I forget what it's called now.'

'The Lookout.'

'That's it. Do you live on Lundy?'

'Yes,' she paused. 'For now anyway.'

'Braver than me. I guess the summers are great but to be stuck there in the winter,' she shivered. 'Wouldn't suit me.'

'That's the person I'm expecting.' Angie waved at Paul, hovering in the doorway.

'Maybe I'll see you next time I'm over, though it might be a while…'

'Maybe,' Angie cut her off.

The woman gathered her parcels and moved to an empty table by the window.

'Hi, Paul. Drink?'

'No. So… I'm here. What now? Did you read the report?'

'Yes. What makes you so convinced she's innocent?'

He paused. That was more promising. The old Paul would have rushed in with a knee jerk reaction, deaf to anyone else's thoughts. Probably why he was so good at his job. Master of destinies, subject of none.

'I just know.'

'I doubt if that'll stand up in court.'

'You told me to listen to my gut. Well it's telling me she couldn't have done it. There's something I need to remember, something in here,' he pressed his finger against his forehead, 'that proves it. Sometimes I dream about that night…'

'Okay,' Angie interrupted, uneasy with his train of thought. 'I… I think you're right. Sonya is innocent.'

'Why? What do you know? And don't bullshit me.' Paul's raised voice attracted glances from nearby passengers.

The familiar feeling of walking on eggshells was back. But she'd been rehearsing this all the way from London. 'The transcript. Two people thought there was enough doubt to bring in a not-guilty verdict. And I agree with them. Too much is circumstantial. Maybe as a mother she wasn't all she could have been, but it doesn't make her a murderer. They saw that.'

'I told you it was a majority verdict.'

'It was reading it in black and white. And through everything, she stuck to her "not guilty" plea.'

'But you said she was guilty because she didn't defend herself.'

Angie sighed. 'Black and white for you, Paul isn't it? You'd have been brilliant in court. Able to switch sides, defence to prosecutor, grilling your witnesses.'

'Okay,' he leant forward. 'Let's play that game. Just answer the question. Why didn't she defend herself?'

'And say what? Put yourself in her place. She knows she didn't do it but isn't sure who did.'

'But her son was dead, she'd want his murderer caught.'

'Not if she suspected it was someone she loved just as much, maybe more.'

'So she was protecting Stuart.'

Angie hesitated. 'May have thought she was. But there are no more reports. Stuart never went into the caravan. He loved your mother. Any lies he told, he told for her, I see that now.'

He leant back and stared towards the platform. This was a public place for such a private struggle but he was oblivious to anyone else. 'So who?' This time the question was tentative.

'I don't know.' She looked at her watch. 'My train's due. Can you go back through the transcript?' It was a dangerous strategy, but challenging him head on to drop the appeal would be like a red rag to Paul. At least this way she could buy time.

'You mean it? You believe me?'

'Yes. More than that, I think she loved you as much as any mother could ever love her child.' It was a step too far, a knee jerk reaction of her own. She waited. But there was no cross examination, no challenge. He stared into space, thrown by the hole opening up inside him. Anger, struggle, fight had defined his life for so long, what was left?

Angie fixed her eyes on the horizon as the Oldenburg rose and fell with the swell surging across Bideford Bay.

'How are you doing?' Mike swayed into her eye line. 'Might take a bit longer with this sea running.'

'Thanks for that nugget.'

'You'll be fine as soon as you get home.'

'I need to get into the Gallery.'

'Might find you're not needed.'

'How come?'

'Well, you've been away so much Tom's kind of taken over. Handling things really well by all accounts.'

'But what about the customers?'

Mike smiled. 'You'll have to see for yourself.' He swayed back down the gangway, hesitated then walked back. 'I know this isn't the time but we need to talk. The agency called again.'

Angie held her breath

Mike leant on the rail beside her staring at the bow cutting through the swell. 'I'm sorry, Angie, but it's not good news. It's been so long, they don't…' His words were drowned out by a burst of laughter from a group of nearby passengers. 'We'll talk at home,' he said.

The walk up from the quay and a mug of ginger tea should have settled Angie's stomach but it was still churning as she waited for Mike to speak.

He knelt beside her. 'I'm so sorry, Angie, but the agency, they… they can't offer us a baby.'

She stared ahead, needing to blot out his words 'No! We just have to wait, that's all. It takes time, they said so.'

He shook his head. 'There just aren't the babies available. And we're getting older. It's only natural they'll look for younger parents.'

'They can't do that. We're fit, healthy. Look what we can offer,' she swept her arm around the room, encompassing the island, their life.

'There was something else.' He paused. 'They want to know if we'd be interested in an older child.'

Hope flickered in Angie's face. 'But that's it, Mike. I can't imagine why I didn't think… after all the years I spent with those kids, knowing how much they needed homes, needed families. Don't you see…' she was on her feet, searching his face. 'We could still have a child.'

He drew her closer. 'I know how tough it's been for you, and if there'd been a baby things could have been so different. But… I saw you, day after day, week after week, driving yourself into the ground trying to help those kids. I don't understand, Angie, how can you want to bring all that suffering into our lives, our home?'

'It doesn't have to be like that.'

'Really? All this with Paul again, it's brought it home to me. I'm truly sorry but…'

'No,' she interrupted, 'don't say it, please, don't say what I think you're going to say. We can talk.'

He shook his head. 'We haven't been able to talk in years, not properly. You used to love it here but now, it's like you resent Lundy, the studio, me. What's happened, Angie? To us? I hate to see you so upset but we've been good, haven't we? Just you and me. We've got so much here, and so much more ahead of us.'

It was as though she hadn't heard him. 'You were great with Tom, making sure he was okay when his mother threw him out, getting his photographs developed…'

'He's a good lad, but my world's out there,' he pointed at the sea. 'Crabs, lobsters, coral, that's what I understand. Not kids like Tom… or Paul. I know they've had it tough, that it's not their fault, but I've seen what they can do. We may not have much of a relationship now, but there'd be nothing left if we had a child like Paul in our lives.' He laughed, a hollow humourless sound. 'What am I talking about, we already do!'

'So that's it? Decision made. We'll never be a family?' Angie stared at him.

The phone broke the silence. Mike picked it up. 'It's for you, some solicitor.'

'Hello… my mother?… what?… when?…' She sat. 'I see… yes… yes. This week?' She looked at Mike. 'Yes, I'll call when I get there. Thank you.'

'What is it?' Mike asked.

'It's my mother.' She stared at him. 'A neighbour... found her this morning. She didn't answer the door so they looked through the window and saw her lying on the floor. They think she... she died sometime yesterday.'

'I'm so sorry, Angie. What was it?'

'Her heart.' She shook her head. 'I can't be a hypocrite. You know how it was. But it's still a shock, coming out of the blue like that.' She walked to the kitchen, filled a glass with water and slumped back against the sink. She felt numb, consumed by loss - of the family she had and the family she might have had. It was too much. The impulse to get away, from Mike, from Lundy, from herself, became irresistible. She stood in the doorway. 'I need to go back, to sort out the funeral and things.'

He put his arms around her. 'I'll come with you.'

'No. No, I'd rather go alone. Take some time.' She pulled away. 'It's not your fault, but... if that's how you really feel... about the adoption.' Her hand trembled as she put the glass down.

'Angie, please. Don't go, not like this.'

She looked at her case, lying unopened on the floor. 'What time's the boat?'

'Six,' he said automatically, 'it's a late tide.'

'Good, that's good. I'll get Adam to pick up my bag.'

'There's no need. I'll drop it down.'

'No, best we leave things here.' She grabbed her coat. 'I...' She shook her head and closed the door behind her.

'Ange, over here.' Christine flung her arms around her in the middle of the concourse at Paddington station. 'So sorry to hear about your mum. Not exactly the mother a girl would want but still the only one you had.'

The warmth of Christine's embrace was in danger of opening the floodgates. 'Thanks, Chrissy. Like you say, not the best mother and I can't say I'll miss her, she was never there for me to miss, but it's been a shock.' Angie had called from the train. It had all come flooding out - about her mum, the adoption agency, Mike.

Sympathy wasn't Christine's style but action was. 'You're staying at mine…' Angie made to protest. 'No argument. And when you're ready we'll talk about my idea for expanding your business. A gallery might be too pricey but a stall in one of the markets would be perfect. I've set it all up. You're meeting Mark at Camden on Monday, as long as you feel up to it of course. And now I'm going to treat you to my favourite restaurant. Fantastic food, indulgent surroundings, just the sort of pampering you need.'

Angie smiled. Being swept along in Christine's world could be maddening but right now it offered a welcome respite from the wreckage of her life. She felt cosseted, cared-for… mothered. But she'd regret giving Christine too much free rein. 'Hold on, Chrissy. I'm just here to explore things. Nothing's decided. Mike and I, we need some time.'

'Sounds to me like he made it pretty clear. Has to be all about what you want now, Ange.'

'Precisely. So I won't be railroaded by you either.'

'Railroaded? As if…' Christine smiled and tucked her arm into Angie's. 'Come on, let's get you home.'

So those are the terms and conditions, two copies, both need signing, one back to me, the other you keep, or your solicitor.'

Mark, it turned out, was a young man in his late twenties. Perfect for Camden's target customers but for her work? 'And if I want to go ahead you need these back when?' Angie asked.

'Couple of days. I've others interested.'

'What do you think?' Christine said as they left.

'I'm not convinced. I'm going to sleep on it.'

'But you heard Mark, you'll lose it.'

'Look around you.' Angie turned Christine to face the crowds jostling for space around the stalls. 'What do you see?'

'Buyers. Lots of them.'

'And?'

'A swish two bed flat in central London for you and me.'

'Be serious.'

Christine smiled at her. 'I am.'

Angie hesitated. 'We've hardly seen each other in ages and you're suggesting a flat share?'

'Why not? You'll need somewhere to live. Fancy paying a grand a month for a flat on your own?'

Angie shook her head. 'I haven't said I'm coming yet. There are things to consider.' Angie saw Mike standing in front of her, his eyes pleading with her to give him time. Time to explain, time to look forward.

'You always thought too much.'

'But I haven't even decided about the stall. Like I said, I'm not convinced about Camden.'

Christine studied her. 'Okay. I'm guessing not so trendy but busy, wider age range, open every day, classy.' She linked her arm in Angie's. 'Come on. We've a boat to catch.'

Angie pressed their number and waited for Mike to answer.

'Angie. How are you? Where are you?' Mike said.

'At the moment, on a boat on the Thames but I'm staying at Christine's.'

'Oh, I thought you'd go to your mum's.' There was an edge to his voice she couldn't quite place.

'Christine's been kind, taken my mind off… things.'

'How was the funeral?'

'Bleak.' She'd been a lone figure following the coffin into the crematorium and the few mourners who'd braved the rain briefly offered their condolences before hurrying away. 'It was an ending, maybe in more ways than one.' She swallowed. 'Christine's got an idea for the business.'

'Christine! This'll be good… sorry, go on.'

Angie hesitated. 'Plymouth and Exeter could be the tip of the iceberg. Imagine how much I could sell up here.'

'A gallery in London! It'd be way too expensive.'

'I know, but Christine suggested taking a stall at the markets. We've been to Camden. It's heaving every day and a stall doesn't cost anything like a permanent shop…'

'Are you seriously talking about having Christine as a business partner? She's the most unreliable, scatty… I can't believe you'd do something so…'

'So what?'

'Daft.'

Angie bristled. 'Well I'm not. I'll be the one on the stall.'

'You? As in leaving Lundy?'

'Splitting my time maybe. Lundy in the summer, London in the winter.' She paused, waiting. 'So what do you think?'

'Do I figure in these plans of yours?'

Angie hesitated. 'It might be what we need. Would give us time… to think about what we want. I mean, can you really say you're happy, with how things are?'

'Not as they are, of course not. But we can talk.'

'You've made it clear how you feel so what's the point in talking?'

Silence.

'I'm sorry, Mike,' Angie fought the tremble in her voice. 'Maybe in a while… but now, I can't see what there is to say.'

Two hours later Angie had signed for a trial stall at Greenwich. It wasn't a done deal; the Market Manager, a suited man in his fifties, had the final say. She'd be assessed for creative input and uniqueness before landing a permanent spot. 'What if I don't make the grade?' Angie said.

'You will,' Christine squeezed her hand. 'There's nothing like your work here.'

'Definitely more my kind of customer. I recognise them.'

'So that's that.'

'I guess so.'

The return trip along the Thames was so civilized compared to the Oldenburg, the perfect way to absorb London through her pores. The story of the city was laid out along these banks. No longer a novelty for Christine though. She'd nodded off. Afternoon nap, Angie thought, a giveaway for incipient middle-age. She studied Christine's face. Cosmetic surgery was losing the battle against too many years of hard living, tough when her looks were the safety blanket she'd clung to. Now Frances had gone and she'd been 'retired' from the BBC she was in need of a friend.

Angie shook her head. It would be far too easy to slip back into their old ways. She'd hung on to the illusion of happiness with Mike for too long. Surely she'd learnt enough not to exchange one illusion for another? But was it an illusion with Mike? They'd been good together. If there was even a glimmer of a future, of a way to heal the gulf between them, shouldn't she be looking for it?

She picked up a paper discarded on the seat next to her and scanned the headlines. 'Oh, my God, that's it!' she exclaimed leaping to her feet.

Christine stirred. 'What?'

'I've got to talk to Paul.' She'd had no intention of returning to Devon so soon, but this changed everything.

'What's so important?'

Angie gave Christine a hug. 'You're right, Chrissy, things do work out. It's all here.'

'What!'

'The grounds for our appeal.'

Chapter Thirty-Three

Paul was as good as his word, drawing up outside Barnstaple station as she emerged from the ticket office. 'I've gone back through the transcript,' he said. 'You're right, he was the expert witness.'

'I knew it!' Angie exclaimed. Paul did a U turn and headed for Bideford. 'You need to get a message to your barrister.'

'Already done.'

Angie smiled. 'Did you read the piece right through?' She pulled the paper out of her bag. 'A panel has been set up by the Attorney General,' she read, 'to review convictions for murder, manslaughter or infanticide involving Dr Marcus Wilson. Ministers wanted to ensure there were no other cases like it.' Angie turned to Paul, her face flushed with excitement. 'There have already been two cases where convictions have been ruled as unsafe and quashed. The Department of Health has been ordered to review the whole issue of cot death. We've got to be in with a chance.' Angie stopped. Paul was heading straight on at the roundabout at the end of the new bridge, away from Bideford. 'I thought we were going to the King's Arms?'

'Amy needs to know about this.'

'And she's at Abbotsham? Does that mean Kate's...'

'Going home. Today.'

Angie breathed a sigh of relief. If he was in contact with Amy, knew what was happening with Kate, it was good news. She looked back at the paper. 'Three appeal judges deliberated for just four minutes. Four minutes! It says their ruling has major implications for several women convicted of killing their children.' She looked at him. 'Your barrister has to be able to use that. The judges stated there were too many grey areas surrounding cot death for experts to exclude unknown causes.' She folded the paper, highlighting a paragraph near the bottom. 'Did you see this? These children were at high risk of cot death because their parents smoked. Sonya smokes. Did she then?'

'All the time,' he said.

Angie gripped the door as Paul took the turn into Abbotsham too fast, his knuckles white on the steering wheel.

'And Justin had problems with his breathing. Did they consider that?'

'No.' He accelerated down the narrow lane.

Angie braced herself against the dashboard. If anyone came the other way... 'Paul, slow down, please.'

He slammed on the brakes and veered into a gate opening. 'The bastard! Fourteen years all because some overblown ponce liked the sound of his own voice.' He pounded the steering wheel. 'Bastard!' The veins were standing out on his forehead creating channels for the beads of sweat beginning to drip from his temples. 'Just two sentences was all it took. Did you know that? "So called cot death is an extremely rare phenomena and I can find no evidence that supports it as a diagnosis in this case. In my experience young babies die at the hands of their parents, not their cot," he recited from memory. That's all it took to put my mother inside. Bastard, fucking bastard!'

'I'm so sorry...' It sounded pathetically inadequate.

Paul burst out of the car and paced the lane. Angie hesitated then sank back into the seat. She made herself breath steadily. Of course he was going to go off like a volcano. He'd spent years fighting to get someone, anyone, to listen to him. She should have anticipated his reaction, she'd been on the receiving end often enough. 'Please, please,' she whispered, 'don't let him go after this man.' Angie shivered.

The driver's door was suddenly wrenched open. Paul made

a half-hearted attempt to scrape some mud off his shoes before slumping back into the seat. He started the car and pulled off without a word.

Angie was thrown forward as Paul pulled into the driveway at Kate and Steve's, braked at the last minute and leapt out of the car. He was pushing the doorbell before she had her seat belt off.

'Paul. You're here,' Amy threw her arms around him. 'Angie, it's lovely to see you. Come in.'

She followed Paul down the hallway. He stopped at the door to the front room. 'Hi, Paul.' Steve was standing beside a medical nursing bed holding an instruction manual.

'Is it right?' Paul asked.

'More than right,' Steve replied. 'It's perfect, thanks.'

'And the nurses?'

'Coming with Kate. Be here in an hour or so.'

'Did you know?' Amy tucked her arm though Paul's.

'Of course he did,' Steve said. 'He made it possible.'

'Angie's got some news,' Paul interrupted, looking at Amy. 'You two talk in the kitchen. We need to get this done.'

Angie almost gasped. It was the first time she'd heard Paul say 'we' for years. 'I' or 'them', yes, but 'we' was reserved for him and Sonya, until now. She watched him standing side by side with Steve, the usual tension absent from their closeness.

'Coffee or tea?' Amy asked

'Coffee would be great.' Angie watched as Amy filled the kettle, so like the times she and Kate had sat here when Amy was a child. It had been a house full of laughter and roses, tears and tantrums, but most of all, love. Was it possible that just a fraction was finally breaching Paul's defences?

'Sugar?'

'No... yes. Damn the diet.'

'So what's this about?' Amy perched on the table.

'Have you caught up with the news lately?'

'No. I've hardly seen it, with mum so poorly.'

'Of course, I'm sorry, I should have asked. How's she doing?'

'They… they say…' her face crumpled.

Angie wrapped her arms around Amy. 'It's been tough for you,' Amy's shoulders began to shudder, 'trying to stay strong for Kate, and your dad.' She nodded, unable to speak. Angie held her tighter. 'It's okay. Let it go, all of it.' Amy's sobs took over. 'Here, sit down. I don't want you to stop but just breathe.' Angie held Amy's hands until her crying eased.

'I'm… sorry…' she gasped.

'You've held on to this for too long. Is there anyone supporting you? It's too much on your own.'

'One or two friends… but only Paul otherwise.' She looked at Angie. 'I know, you're going to say I won't get much comfort there. It's been one-sided for years but something's changed. He… he's not so edgy, doesn't snap so much. He even listens!'

'That I do need proof of,' Angie smiled at Amy and squeezed her hand. 'But it's good news. Like you, I know there's a loveable guy inside. To think he might be letting you in… it's just great.'

Amy pulled a tissue from her pocket and wiped her eyes. 'Anyway, what's this news?'

Angie pulled the newspaper from her bag and smoothed it out on the table. 'It's this man,' she pointed at a photograph. 'Dr Marcus Wilson. Ring any bells?'

'Vaguely, but I can't think why.'

'He was the expert witness at Sonya's trial, the one who said it couldn't possibly have been a cot death.'

'I remember now, from the transcript.' She scanned the article. 'It says he's been discredited, that convictions based on his evidence have been quashed.' She looked up. 'Is that right?'

'Yes. And Sonya's case may be next.'

'So Paul's been right all this time? Sonya's innocent?'

'Yes, she is.' Angie said.

'How can you be so sure? I mean, they're only suggesting this Dr Wilson was wrong.'

'I've other information, confidential information.' Angie looked away, avoiding Amy's questioning eyes. 'But even without that, her conviction is unsound.'

Amy gazed blankly at the article. 'Assuming… assuming they're right, what happens now?'

'Paul's been on to his solicitors. We'll know more when they get back to him but a successful appeal looks hopeful.'

'It'll mean everything to him.'

'There's something else,' Angie hesitated. With Kate's imminent arrival this really wasn't the time. But when would be? 'Do you know about Ian?'

'Yes. Paul took me to Stuart's. Ian was leaving as we got there.'

'Did Paul…?'

'Say anything? I was worried he would, but no.'

'Before all this,' Angie pointed at the article, 'Sonya was in a bad way. The parole board made it a condition of her release that she couldn't live with a minor.'

'But that's terrible!' Amy exclaimed. 'I mean, not being able to go home to her family after all this time.' She stared at the table. 'I know I haven't always been sympathetic, and Kate will always be my mum, but if they overturn Sonya's conviction they won't be able to stop her will they?'

'No. She'll be free, free to go back to both of them.'

The next half hour was all about preparing Kate's room. Which sheets to choose, flowers or no flowers, window open or closed? Angie offered to go, it was an emotional time, family time, to be shared between father, daughter… and son. But they'd asked her to stay. She waited in the kitchen, gazing down the path to the wooden gate and Paul's camp in the woods. Her skin prickled with the memory of the brambles that clawed at her as she fought her way to his den, her heart beating so fast, her mind frantically searching for the right words. She smiled. That much hadn't changed. Finding the right words would always be a challenge with Paul.

She jumped as the door opened and he strode into the garden, phone to his ear. He paced along the path, listening briefly, speaking animatedly. Seconds later he burst into the kitchen. 'Amy,' he called, 'Amy, come here.'

She appeared at the door. 'What is it?'

'Her case is already on the list. The Chancellor has ordered a complete review as a priority. All sorts of legal bullshit but the barrister's talking like it's a rubber stamp.'

'So it's going to happen?' Amy said. 'Sonya's coming out?'

'How long?' Angie asked.

'Could be days.'

'That's... that's great news,' Amy looked at Paul. 'Isn't it?'

'Great! Our mother's been in prison for fourteen years for a crime she never committed. Those bastards put her away, destroyed her...'

'Amy, Paul,' Steve rushed to the front door. 'Kate's here.'

Amy followed Steve but Paul remained rooted to the spot. 'The bastards,' he repeated. 'They'll pay for this.'

Angie was acutely aware of the disturbance as the ambulance crew negotiated the difficult turn into the front room, transferred their patient and left.

'Paul, you should see Kate's face,' Amy peered round the doorway. 'It means the world to her to be home.' She waited. 'She wants to see you. Paul...?'

He gazed blankly at her.

'Give us a few minutes,' Angie said. 'Can be a bit much, everything happening at once.' She turned to Paul. 'I know it's hard, the news about Sonya. The pressure to say how great it is when all you want is to make someone pay.'

'Too right. And they will,' he said, his jaw clenched.

'Don't let it eat away at you, Paul. All that anger, it can distort things.' Angie paused. Something was shifting within Paul, in his support of Amy, his softening with Kate, but right now he was on an emotional knife edge. She had to find the right words. 'Do you remember, years ago, I talked about making choices? Choices to get you what you wanted instead of leaving you in the shit?'

'I don't remember those exact words,' Paul said.

She smiled. 'Maybe not, but you get the gist.'

He shrugged.

'You're not a kid any more, but he's still there, inside, fighting for survival. Think about how you were with Stuart, the way you almost pushed Amy out of your life, the way you refused to listen to Sonya - the one person who's proved her love for you more than any other...'

'What do you mean?' Paul interrupted.

Angie's stomach lurched. Her promise!

'You're hiding something,' he said.

She steadied her voice. 'Sonya asked to see me.'

'You! Why?'

'She was afraid we were working together, on an appeal. You wouldn't listen. She thought I might.'

His face hardened. 'You scheming bitch... going behind my back...'

'That's exactly what I mean,' Angie snapped. 'Yes, I saw Sonya. No, I didn't tell you. Why? Because I knew you'd leap to conclusions, you always do.' It was her turn to hold his stare. 'Don't do this, Paul. The last few weeks, you've been there for Amy. She said something had shifted inside that let you... let you care. I've seen it, seen the person you really are, the person your mum knew and loved. Please, Paul, don't bury yourself under a mountain of bitterness. Not again. Don't push us away.' It was a poor defence, but all she had left. She rested her head on her hands and closed her eyes.

She heard the scraping of a chair. Sensed him sitting down opposite her. 'Do you know how I made my money?' he said. 'I created this character, Time Bubble Man he's called. He's got magic powers - searchlight vision that discovers people's secrets and a time cloak that catches their thoughts, spins them round and sends them back all mixed up. When I was a kid my searchlight eyes would reach all the way to my mother, see her missing me, feel her arms around me, so I'd know I was okay because...because she loved me.'

Genuine emotion, from Paul. Something Angie had despaired of ever hearing. She half reached across the table, hesitated, then laid her hand on his. He tensed but didn't snatch it away. 'You don't need to be with someone to feel their love,' she said.

'You said about my anger being like an old coat. I recognised its shape, its smell, everything, but maybe it didn't fit any more.'

'God, that sounds glib. Did I really say that?'

He looked at her. 'I know you and Amy think I don't listen. But I do, sometimes.' There was a trace of a smile in his voice. 'It's not that simple though is it?'

'So channel that anger. Use it to get the biggest compensation package for Sonya the bastards have ever known.'

Now there was no mistaking the smile.

'It's time for me to go.' Angie squeezed his hand, put her coffee mug in the sink, picked up her coat and walked towards the hallway. Gentle voices were coming from the front room.

'Paul, is that you?' Kate's voice was weak, but unmistakable.

He hesitated, looking at Angie.

'Go on, Paul,' she nodded towards the room. 'We're done.'

From the gateway Angie could just make out Paul taking Kate's hand. If only words could become a self-fulfilling prophecy. She'd poured every ounce of confidence she had into those two words, 'we're done'. But Paul was still walking an emotional knife edge. He had so little to fall back on… she paused. No, that wasn't true. She remembered the child, passionate about his mother, driven by love. Maybe he did have a chance. Maybe they all did.

She leant against the stile and let the sun play on her face. 'And what about you, Angie? Do you have a chance?' She looked towards the coast. Lundy was standing proud on the horizon. It had been her refuge for so long. But now? She checked her watch. The Oldenburg would be leaving in a couple of hours. Time to walk back along the coast, time to think, time to feel.

301

She sat outside the café on the quay watching the holidaymakers jostling for position as they waited to board.

'Hi, Angie.' Adam swung down the gangplank and joined her. 'Mike asked me to give you these if I saw you.' He handed her two envelopes, one with a distinctive scrawl on the front. *Ange, The Studio, Lundy, Devon.* Angie smiled. Trust Christine to launch something into the world with absolute confidence it would land where it needed to. The other was from Mike.

Adam pointed over his shoulder at the boat. 'There's room if you want to... you know. Pushing off in about an hour.'

'Thanks, Adam.' She picked up Christine's envelope and tore it open. A key on a heart-shaped fob fell into her hand. A key? She unfolded the letter. *Hi, Ange. Perfect flat came up. Knew you wouldn't want to miss it. See you very soon.* Angie smiled. Her message about not being steamrollered hadn't quite sunk in. But would it be so bad? A life with Christine made no sense, and Technicolor lives had a habit of fading, but not to have experienced one at all, wouldn't that be the biggest regret? She closed her eyes and imagined herself en route for London, looking forward not back. But there was no sense of an unmissable future propelling her out of her seat.

She picked up the second envelope, tracing Mike's familiar writing before pulling out the single sheet.

Dear Angie,

I've started this so many times, wasted so much paper, you'd hate that. Maybe as much as you hate me right now. I'm sorry for being clumsy, hurting you as I did. I truly believed it was for the best, for both of us, the only way for us to have a future. You have to believe me, Angie.

But something happened and now... I don't know. Tom got in a panic at the Studio, a surge of customers all wanting to buy late in the day. He needed you but he got me! I did my best to help him through. He hardly spoke, but it seemed enough, my being there. Anyway, the rush died down, he got back into his stride so I left.

Later, Tom appeared at my door. He stood for a minute, then threw his arms round me and squeezed - the nearest he'll ever get to a hug I guess. He didn't say anything, just turned and left, but something happened in those few seconds, Angie. I can't explain it and I don't have

the words for how I feel but I do know there's more to say, to discuss.
Please, come home. We can talk and maybe hope. All my love, Mike.

Angie read and re-read Mike's words, oblivious to the waitress asking if she'd like a refill, removing her mug, wiping the table. Finally, she folded the letter, paid the bill and wove her way through the growing crowd to stand beside the river. So many times she'd shared their anticipation and the intoxicating mix of relief and excitement at rounding the end of the island and stepping onto the pier. It was like entering another world, a moment when she became acutely aware of the cry of the seagulls, the smell from the lobster pots, and Mike, waiting as always, with his easy smile.

She fingered Christine's key, a red heart symbolizing more than a passing friendship? Possibly, but why was it beginning to weigh heavy in her hand, feeling more of a summons than an invitation? Angie closed her hand over the heart then lifted her phone. 'Christine? I've a proposition for you.'

'Been a while since I've been propositioned.'

Angie smiled. 'Something's come up. I can't get to Greenwich, at least, not yet. You'd be absolutely brilliant at persuading customers to put their hands in their pockets. Will you stand in for me? I know it's not the BBC...'

'You're right.' Christine interrupted. 'It would be much more fun.' Angie could hear the smile in her voice. 'I may be the most self-deluded, egotistical, impossible friend you have, but even I know when fate, destiny, call it what you will is staring me in the face. I'd be honoured to be your partner.'

'That's not quite what I...'

'Who was the first person to recognise your talent? Who encouraged you to open the studio on Lundy, to branch out on the mainland, to think about London?' Christine paused, waiting for Angie to say her line.

Angie laughed. 'You did.'

'Any perks? Healthcare, flash car, Oyster card?'

'Sorry. Sandwich allowance maybe?'

'That'll do.'

Angie uncurled her hand, raised her arm and flung the heart out into the river. It floated for a few seconds before the weight of the key dragged it under. She smiled and turned towards the Oldenburg, joining the few remaining passengers waiting to board. As she reached the deck, a young boy shrieked with excitement, pointing over the side at a stretch of river shaded by the quay. Angie watched as he tugged at his mother's hand until she was kneeling beside him, looking deep into the water. Freed from the glare of the sun, he'd seen flashes of silver from a shoal of fish twisting and turning around the keel of the boat - his first glimpse of a secret underwater world, a world revealed by a shadow.

Reader Reviews for *Seeds of Doubt*

"I finished Seeds of Doubt last night. It was a great book ... I loved the story, Ingrid's voyage and struggle, and the sense of Devon and history. The research struck me as particularly impressive ... thanks for the entertainment of a great book."

Simon Hall - Home Affairs correspondent for BBC South West, www.thetvdetective.com

"... thanks for a Great Book, can't stop reading it ..."

"... To build a conspiracy thriller on an event as well known as the Lynmouth flood disaster, and to make it both plausible and exciting, is no mean feat. The dialogue is well written and convincing and the plot is unpredictable with enough twists to keep any thriller reader happy."

"... I've just finished Seeds of Doubt; WONDERFUL. I loved it; it has all the right ingredients - drama, tension, intrigue, love, secrets, danger and truth. Looking through the references, why hasn't this made more of a splash (unintended pun) in the national and local press? It's huge. Thank you so much for a thought provoking and thoroughly edge of the seat read."

"... I couldn't put (it) down! It is an amazing story, vividly written... some of your insights and or descriptions are so 'word perfect' and then there are the subtle sub plots! The actual theoretical basis is very disturbing - terrifying? - and so it took some hours in the day to shake off from being inside the book. Remarkable. Brilliant! Thrilling. Enthralling…"

"…Just had to let you know that I REALLY enjoyed your book – it is well written & constructed, and a very good read."

"The main character of this intriguing story is a woman who experienced at first hand the disastrous flood at Lynmouth in 1952. Some thirty years later she still has difficulty in coming to terms with the events of that fateful night, particularly when, in the course of her job as a provincial journalist, she comes across material which suggests that the disaster may not have been an act of God but man-made. Her urge to find out the truth brings her into conflict with her boss and her husband, and attracts unwelcome attention from government agencies. She is forced to confront issues from her earlier life, and finds her own life in danger again.

With many unexpected twists to the story, this is a book which I found difficult to put down. With an appendix of references to official documents, one is left wondering whether the Lynmouth flood was really a freak of nature or something more sinister."

"I thoroughly enjoyed this book. The way that fiction was blended with fact was very well done, and the list of references to the official documentation really makes you think. Living in the local area, there has always been speculation about the cause of the flood. Have already bought this for friends!"

Seeds of Doubt
Chapter One

March 1982, Salisbury, England

'Rainmaking!' Nick Pearce pushed the café door open and threw his dripping coat over the first available chair. 'Are you seriously saying that...?'

'Not me,' Ingrid interrupted. 'Private Dean.'

'Who's he?'

'The old boy in the photo.'

'Oh, yeah.'

Ingrid's heart sank. Her boss's off-hand response wasn't exactly encouraging. She edged round the marble bistro table to the chair opposite. 'I interviewed him yesterday for the British Legion piece. Here,' she leant down and retrieved the black and white photograph from her bag, 'there's a cutting stuck to the back all about rainmaking. And before you ask, it's nothing to do with voodoo or ancient pagan rituals. He swore he'd seen planes make it rain when he was on manoeuvres on Salisbury Plain.'

Nick slid the photograph towards him, flipped it over and scanned the text on the yellowing piece of paper. 'So according to this, planes flew overhead, the clouds got heavier and blacker and about thirty minutes later it rained.'

'Bit more to it than that, but yes.'

He shook his head. 'I'll order. What do you want?'

'Tuna roll and a coffee. Thanks.'

Ingrid took in the lunchtime crowd. Half a dozen office workers were clustered at the food bar, probably tempted in by a leaflet campaign advertising the café's grand re-opening. Although a few balloons and a free cappuccino with every meal hardly qualified. But they seemed happy enough; unlike the regulars, who looked a lot less at home with the stark black and silver art deco theme - not a trace of cosy red gingham anywhere.

A young mother struggled to the entrance with a baby asleep in a buggy and a toddler tugging at her hand. Ingrid scraped her chair back and held the door open. As the girl turned, Ingrid couldn't help noticing the heavy bags under her eyes, the lines creasing her forehead, her dull, sallow complexion. 'Sit here,' she said, moving their coats across to the next table. 'There's more room for the buggy.'

'Thanks.' The mother pulled a high chair over for the toddler, gently removed his coat, lifted him in, tied his bib, wiped his hands, found his cup and placed a banana on the tray before sinking into a chair. Ingrid felt their closeness. It was a bond she could have known, once; but it was too late now. Work filled the gap. She'd been covering stories of triumph and tragedy at the Salisbury Post for more than twenty-five years - not bad for an agency typist who came for a week. The work suited her and, according to the previous editor, she suited the work. 'You've a nose for the domestic stuff,' he'd said. And she'd been happy enough to cover the hatches, matches and dispatches and everything in-between. Until now.

She turned back to her boss, stuck in the counter queue. He'd been at the paper for five years; semi-retired from one of the nationals. In a rare moment of confidence he'd shared his frustration at being sidelined as soon as he hit fifty. His clean sweep at the Post had been brutal, but she'd survived: more than survived recently in fact. He'd started involving her at briefings and running copy past her. Not exactly a promotion but she'd definitely been invited to step up a rung.

He was different too. His clothes, routines and, lately, his mood. Ingrid watched as his eyes drilled into the assistant, intensifying every second of waiting time as she slapped two slices of tomato, some wilted lettuce, two slices of cucumber, a ring of onion and a squirt of mayonnaise onto their rolls. It was going to take more than fancy art deco fittings to up-market the market café. Nick snatched up their plates and headed back, making a point of having to negotiate the buggy and highchair.

'Oh my dear Lord, what have they done to the weather?' Dimpled elbows pushed against the door as an overweight woman backed into the café. She thrust a pile of plastic shopping bags into an empty chair and shook her umbrella out in their direction.

'For goodness sake.' Nick spun round, his face soured with irritation.

'Sorry my love, didn't see you there. Still, no harm done, it's only a bit of rain,' she said with a smile as she pushed on towards the counter, dislodging a trail of chairs in her wake.

Nick grabbed a paper serviette and began stabbing at the offending drops on his sleeve. Ingrid looked out the window, finding sanctuary in the kaleidoscope of umbrellas outside. Hopefully it would stop raining before they left.

She turned back. 'I noticed the circulation figures are up this month,' she said.

'About time.'

'Getting behind the Hospice campaign was a good move.'

'I guess so.'

She bit into the granary roll; mayonnaise oozed over her fingers. She licked it off and tried another tack. 'Are you and Liz going away this year?'

'No. She's taking Ellie to Cornwall but I don't suppose I'll get any time with her.'

'With Liz?' Ingrid asked.

'No,' he said abruptly. 'With Ellie.'

So Alice had got it right for once. The paper's young receptionist had been spreading rumours about Nick's marriage for weeks. 'I'm sorry,' she said.

The silence lengthened. Taking a deep breath, Ingrid finally summoned up the courage to get to the point. 'What do you think of Private Dean's story?'

Nick was lost in his own thoughts. 'What?'

'Private Dean. What do you think?'

'I think it's an old boy winding you up.'

309

'He was pretty convincing,' she said.

'Yeah?' Nick muttered, swilling his free cappuccino around an over-sized cup.

'I'd like to follow it up.'

He looked up. 'Why?'

'Why not?'

'Because our readers want to know what happened last week, not thirty years ago.'

'I still think there could be something in it.'

The toddler threw his cup overboard. Ingrid retrieved it, winning a smile.

'Where would you start?' Nick asked.

'Ministry of Agriculture might be worth a try. Remember the droughts in '75 and '76 when people were queuing at standpipes? Imagine being able to make it rain to sort that lot out.'

'But according to this,' he pointed to the faded text on the back of the photograph, 'your Private Dean was talking about the early 1950's. Any experiments couldn't have been much good if we were stuck with a drought twenty years later.'

Ingrid shrugged. 'Maybe, but think of the spread we could run if it's true. Taxpayers money being spent on making it rain, in our climate!'

Nick pushed his empty plate away. 'I suppose Danny could take a look, but it'd be a waste of his time.'

'No!' She didn't mean to react so violently. Danny and Mat were two young career reporters at the paper. They wouldn't be staying twenty-five years; just long enough to get noticed by a national. Of course Nick was going to pass anything controversial onto them. But not this time. This story was hers - it had to be.

Seeds of Doubt is available on Kindle at £2.99 or £7.99 in paperback. For more information on Pamela Vass and her writing see www.boundstonebooks.co.uk

About the Author

Pamela Vass was drawn to Devon thirty years ago and only afterwards discovered a family tree firmly rooted in Devon soil. Since then it has provided much of the inspiration for her writing. *Seeds of Doubt* grew from suspicions that outside agencies played a part in the 1952 Lynmouth floods, suspicions that provide a gripping background for her novel.

Pamela's career includes several years as Director of *The Whodunnit Company* offering murder mystery events in this country and abroad. Prior to this she was a social worker with Barnardos and two Social Services Departments. This professional experience provides a strong foundation for *Shadow Child,* a gritty and realistic depiction of the challenges faced by a child abandoned by his mother. He never gives up searching for her, not as a child, not as an adult. But the past casts a long shadow and his quest for the truth threatens his very future.

An interest in historical research led to *The Power of Three*, an account of the nineteenth century Devon inventor, Thomas Fowler. Tragically Fowler's ground-breaking work on the principles later embodied in the modern computer was lost, but a combination of the research carried out by Pamela and the expertise of an international team has reinstated him as a significant figure in computing history.

Pamela continues to live and write in Devon, finding inspiration in the unique landscape and the stories it holds.

For more information on Pamela Vass and her writing see
www.boundstonebooks.co.uk